For Bre
Sh

[signature]

September 5, 2005

THE PERFECT SEASON

By
Robert C. Powers

A Novel of the High School Gridiron
And More Than That…
A Novel of Growing Up!

Powerful Publisher, LLC
Virginia Beach, Virginia

Copyright © 2005, Robert C. Powers

All rights reserved. No part of this publication may be reproduced, stored in a retrieval system or transmitted in any form or by any means electronic, mechanical, photocopying, recording or otherwise, without the prior written permission of the publisher.
This is a work of fiction. All characters and events in this novel are fictional, and any resemblance to real people or events is coincidental.

Published by:
Powerful **P**ublisher LLC
2317 Broad Bay Road, Suite 17
Virginia Beach, Virginia 23451

Web Site: www.powerfulpublisher.com

Library of Congress and Catalog Number: 2005904813

International Standard Book Number
ISBN 0-9769773-0-3

PRINTING HISTORY
Printed in the United States of America
First Edition, 1st Printing

Preface

This novel is based on the true story of the 1954 Churchland High School football team of Norfolk County, located in the suburbs of Portsmouth, Virginia. The Truckers were undefeated, untied and unscored upon; a perfect season. I played center and linebacker for that team. The story in this novel, the incidents and the characters are fictional. The schedule of games is as they occurred. The play by play action and plays called in each game are fictional, representing both memory and imagination.

In 1954, Portsmouth, Virginia had another championship football team; the downtown rival of Churchland, the Wilson High School Presidents whose record was 9-0-1 for the season. It was a friendly rivalry between Wilson, a "Group I (large school)" and Churchland, a "Group II (smaller school)". The scrimmage (unofficial game) described in this novel actually took place, but at the beginning of the season instead of at the end. The scrimmage score in the novel is accurate.

In 1954, Churchland was a small High School in Norfolk County in the rural suburbs of Portsmouth, Virginia. Portsmouth is the home of the Norfolk Naval Shipyard across the Elizabeth River from the Navy town of Norfolk, Virginia. The village of Churchland consisted of a Post Office, a General Store, a Baptist Church, a cluster of traditional homes and a brick, two story school house. It was surrounded by lush forests and farmer's fields filled with crops and livestock. The nickname "Truckers" came from the history of the Churchland area where people before World War II were mostly "Truck Farmers", or farmers who grew their crops to truck into Norfolk and Portsmouth for use there, or for transportation to Baltimore on Chesapeake Bay steamers.

The Perfect Season begins in the summer of 1954 as the new Churchland High School opens. It was a time of "iron man" football when eleven men played "both ways", offense and defense, without face masks. It was the year rock n' roll became big and new cars had fins.

You can read about the main characters in this story, Harry Quester and Allman Buddinger in my three novels that form the "Quester Trilogy"; Quester, The Mud Fox and Black Dragon. The Perfect Season is their prequel.

Robert C. Powers
Author
www.robertcpowers-author.com

Acknowledgements

Many thanks to the coaches, classmates, teammates and friends who contributed to the writing of this novel

Charles E. Brown
Slade W. Phillips
Zenas E. (Ellie) Fearing
Frank D. Beck

Churchland Football Teams
Past and Present

With special thanks to
Charles W. Hawks, Jr.
A Trucker
For his suggestions in the writing of this novel.

Dedication

Dedicated to the Churchland High School Football Team of 1954
And their Coaches

Coach Charles "Shotgun" Brown
Coach Slade Phillips
Coach Ellie Fearing

With Thanks to
The Cheerleaders
The Marching Band
The Fans

With Appreciation to
Principal Frank Beck
And
The Varsity Football Supporters on
The High School Faculty

With Appreciation to
A.W. Johnson, Jr.
The "Mayor" of Churchland

In Remembrance of
Team Members Departed
A Trucker Salute

Other Novels by Robert C. Powers

Quester
A Story of the River Warriors
Read about Harry Quester and Allman Buddinger in Vietnam!

The Mud Fox
Ghost of the Jungle
Sequel to Quester… Allman becomes the Mud Fox and hunts down the notorious Viet Cong Leader, Cobra de Mer!!

Black Dragon
An Adventure at Sea
Sequel to The Mud Fox… Harry finally leaves Vietnam, but the war keeps coming back… and so does the Mud Fox!

The Wara Wa
The Ultimate Campfire Story
That creepy camp legend comes true!

Old House on the Island
A Traditional Family With a Dark Secret
An erotic coming of age romance… a terrible monster… and the best in war time adventure at sea!

Chapter One
Try-outs I

It was August of 1954 when the perfect season started. No one knew how tumultuous a season it would be, or how it would change the lives of so many. The morning sun was low in the sky, already beginning to steam the green fields of the countryside. Harry Quester sat in the front passenger seat of the gray, 1947 Dodge as it rattled northward on Route 17 away from Portsmouth, Virginia and toward the village of Churchland.

"Thanks for picking us up, Bubba," said Harry.

"Sure… you guys got a treat waiting for you at try-outs," said Bubba with a chortle.

"What do you mean?" asked Harry guardedly.

"You'll meet the Hoods and the Farm Boys," chuckled Bubba. "They like to beat up on the Squares!"

Harry was a tall, compactly built junior in High School of sixteen with very blue eyes, a straight nose and a brown crew cut. Bubba Hawkins, Harry's cousin, was driving. Bubba had luxurious, curly brown hair, turned almost blond by the summer sun. He was bigger than Harry, slightly taller and much heavier. He had a round face and a happy-go lucky air that made him instantly likable. Bubba was a sophomore, one year behind Harry. Tony Zee sat in the back seat. He was a sophomore like Bubba.

"Who're the Squares?" asked Tony, wide eyed.

"That's what the Hoods call us… anyone that ain't cool, ya know!" exclaimed Bubba with a smile.

"How do they know who's cool?"

"The Hoods think they're cool guys," said Bubba "and no one else is… according to them!"

Tony was the son of Harry's father's best friend. He was as tall as Harry, rawboned and lanky with dark curly hair. He had a thin face and boundless energy dancing in his brown eyes. Harry and Tony had grown up together, almost as brothers, as their fathers had moved about the country in their naval careers.

"Why is this Coach… Shotgun… so tough?" asked Tony warily.

"Don' sweat it… you'll see!" exclaimed Bubba taking a bump in the road that rattled everything in the car.

The countryside rolled by them as the Dodge rumbled along. It was flat and topped with a forest of green trees, interrupted occasionally by a cornfield or a house set well back from the road. The radio was on, crackling with the sound of AM and vintage age as the *Four Aces* crooned:

*Three coins in a fountain,
Which one will the fountain bless?*

"Which one will the fountain bless... enough of that stuff!" crooned Bubba awkwardly, reaching abruptly for the radio. He fumbled with the dial as the radio squawked and whined, finally settling on a station that blared out the new rock 'n roll song, *Shboom* by the *Crew Cuts*. "Now that's more like it!" he said snapping his fingers and bobbing to the rhythm.

*Hey nonny ding dong, alang alang alang,
Boom ba-doh, ba-doo ba-doodle-ay,
Oh, life could be a dream, sh-boom,
If I could take you up in paradise up above, sh-boom...*

"Is that the new Disc Jockey I hear people talking about?" asked Harry.

"Yeah... Rocky Rawls, WNV 1150... he's the only one that plays rock and roll!"

"You like that stuff?" asked Harry

Bubba swayed with the fast beat of the music as he drove. "Yeah... I do!" he said. "Don't you?"

"It's pretty cool," said Tony.

"I like to dance... and it has a good beat!" said Harry.

"Yeah, you're a real jitterbug!" said Bubba. "And I know just the girl to dance with you!"

"Yeah?" asked Harry doubtfully.

"She plays clarinet in the band," said Bubba, "with a girl I take out, Alice Gibbs. I'll introduce you to Janet... if you make the team."

"What do you mean... if I make the team?" asked Harry testily.

"Come on, Harry!" exclaimed Bubba. "You know the girls all date you if you make the team!"

"And if you don't?" asked Harry.

"Well... the girls don't look at you so much," said Bubba with a grimace, "that's all... but you'll make it!"

"I hope so," said Harry mustering his confidence. "We'll all make it."

"Sure we will," said Bubba.

"This Janet... what's she like?" asked Harry.

"Aha!" exclaimed Bubba, "got your interest huh?"

"So... what's she like?" asked Harry impatiently.

"A little blonde," said Bubba, "fills out a sweater real good... you'll like her, Harry... she's like you... always has an opinion!"

"Oh great!" muttered Harry.

"She got a sister?" asked Tony.

"Naw," said Bubba, "but there's plenty around, Tony... if ya make the team!"

Harry knew he could play football. But, making it with a new team and a bunch of guys he didn't know worried him. He had heard a lot about how tough these Churchland guys were... a lot! He gritted his teeth... he had to make this team if he ever expected to play for Navy!

Sh-boom sh-boom... ya-da-da da-da-da da-da-da da, sh-boom!
Dee-oody-ooh, sh-boom, sh-boom SWEETHEART!

"Now here's that song you've been asking for," shouted Rocky Rawls in raucous tones on the radio, "... *Hearts of Stone* by the *Charms*... get a load of the sax in this one... it'll blow your mind!"

Hearts!... made of stone,
Doody wadda doody wadda,
Will never bre-ake...

"Sounds like jabber talk to me," said Tony lifting an eyebrow.

"Come on, Tony," laughed Bubba. "Don't be a square!"

"But you said we were Squares!"

"Naw... Tony, I said that's what the Hoods call us!"

"This'll be the first time I meet a lot of these guys," said Harry. "I knew some Wilson High School guys when we lived downtown in Park View... when my Father was stationed in Norfolk the last time... but I don't know these guys."

"You knew Linwood Honor and that bunch... right?" asked Bubba.

"Yeah, Linwood and Dennis Aimsley and a few others," said Harry.

"They're both big deals on the Wilson Team," said Bubba. "Wilson is supposed to be State Champions in Group I this year!"

"Yeah?" asked Harry. "What about Churchland?"

"We're supposed to have a good team."

"That's all?"

"Ain't that enough?" said Bubba. "Do ya know Willy Scooter?"

"I know him," said Harry, "but not very well."

"He's the quarterback at Wilson," said Bubba.

"Yeah?" asked Harry.

"Yeah," said Bubba. "And Linwood and Dennis are Team Co-Captains!"

****

Harry remembered back to 1948 when he was ten years old. He was wiry and slight for his age. It was his gutsy determination that kept him up with the larger boys in the neighborhood. It was Saturday, and as he did every Saturday in the fall, he strapped on his junior shoulder pads, put on his blue and white helmet, pulled on his cleated shoes and rode his blue and cream colored Schwinn Streamliner bicycle around the corner to the vacant lot behind the Drug Store. Linwood Honor, a boy a year older than Harry, waited for him. Harry pushed the button on the side of the Streamliner, honked its horn and waved. Linwood was also clad in football gear. He was a serious faced boy with blond hair and long legs. He waved back.

Bobby O'Briar, an older boy in the neighborhood, stood beside Linwood tossing a football into the air. Bobby was eighteen and played center for the football team at Woodrow Wilson High School. He had a friendly smile, big shoulders and big hands. He was always at the vacant lot, ready to scrimmage with whoever showed up, and ready to coach the kids in the neighborhood.

"Come on, Harry," shouted Bobby enthusiastically. "We're gonna have a scrimmage."

Harry rode up and got off his bicycle. He leaned it against a big sycamore tree next to the sidewalk and ran onto the vacant lot.

"Where are all the other guys?" asked Harry.

"We're the only ones here so far," said Linwood.

"You two guys line up in front of each other and let's see what y'all can do," said Bobby, fingering the silver colored whistle on a cord around his neck.

Harry and Linwood faced each other. Bobby always got a kick out of making Linwood and Harry face off. They got down into three point stances. Bobby came over and pushed Harry's butt down. "Get lower, Harry," he said.

Linwood glared at Harry. "You can't block me, Harry."

"I can try," said Harry, gritting his teeth.

Bobby blew the whistle and Linwood and Harry charged at each other. Harry grappled with Linwood until his energy sapped and the larger boy knocked him down. He sobbed in frustration, infuriated that his strength and energy always seemed to fade when contested with Linwood.

"Good job! Keep those legs moving all the time!" shouted Bobby.

Harry got up and faced Linwood, containing his frustration.

"See what I mean?" asked Linwood with a smile of superiority.

"I'll get ya the next time, Linwood!" said Harry determinedly.

****

Bubba, Harry and Tony rode on as *Hearts of Stone* came to an end.

"Who should we look out for at try-outs?" asked Tony cautiously.

Bubba laughed loudly. "Look out for Shotgun... Coach Braun!"

"What about him?" asked Harry, snapping out of his thoughts about Linwood.

"He's a wild man!" said Bubba. "And Churchland has never beaten Suffolk High School. He's gonna push us and beat on us until we do... and every other team too!"

"Well, that's what it's all about, isn't it?" asked Harry stretching his arms. "Winning the Championship?"

"Yeah... I guess it is!' said Bubba swerving to avoid a hound dog trotting alongside the road. "We got a chance... maybe."

"Who else should we look out for?" asked Tony holding on as the car swerved.

"Allman Buddinger, the quarterback," said Bubba. "He's a senior and one of the Co-Captains of the team. Allman is a real character... always screwing around!"

"Who's the other Co-Captain?" asked Harry.

"Karl Darby... a halfback," said Bubba. "He's a pretty easy going guy... you'll like him."

"Do they accept new guys pretty easily?" asked Tony.

"We haven't had many new guys for a few years," said Bubba. "These guys have been playing together since they were in grade school."

"Sounds tough," said Harry good naturedly. "Who's that fullback that's supposed to be so hot?"

"That's Jack Sanders," said Bubba. "... a big old farm boy from Jolliff. Look out for him! He'll knock your jock off!"

"You're going for tackle again?" asked Harry.

"Yeah... with any luck I'll play first string by next year."

"I don't fell so good," moaned Tony.

"Come on, Tony," said Harry, "we can do it!"

The car pulled into a road that led to the side of the new brick school building and stopped next to the gymnasium as Rocky Rawls spun up *Bill Haley and the Comets* .

One two three o'clock four o'clock ROCK!
Five six seven o'clock eight o'clock ROCK!
Nine ten eleven o'clock twelve o'clock ROCK!
We're gonna ROCK around the clock tonight!

"All out!" shouted Bubba with a grimace as he turned off the radio.

****

The morning sun beat down on Harry Quester as he ran laps around the practice field next to the new High School in full football gear. The field was surrounded on two sides by pine trees towering over smaller trees and brush. There was an irregular line of trees right next to the grass of the practice area. The other sides backed up against Route 17 and the new school. The field was covered with rough grass, mostly crabgrass. Behind the school he could see builders putting the final touches on the new stadium. It was the fifth quarter mile lap, with one more to go. His legs ached and he felt his shins stiffening. He wore a pair of old yellow football pants with a white practice jersey. The jersey was plain and had no markings on it. All the other players had jerseys with numbers, except for him, Tony and a few other try-outs. He felt conspicuous.

Sweat rolled from under Harry's black plastic helmet with the orange stripe, off his forehead and into his eyes, making them sting. He brushed at his eyes, trying to wipe away the sting and felt the beginnings of cramps in his stomach. His mouth was dry and his panting was turning into gasps. Thirty-nine boys had started the laps around the practice field. Thirty-four were still struggling along. The other five had fallen out and were strung out around the field in various stages of collapse.

In Northern Virginia, Harry played fullback for the High School Team. They played the single wing in which they ran most of the time. He made the first string as a sophomore. He knew that the Churchland Truckers played the "tee-formation" and worried about how he would fit in. Just a few months ago, Harry's father, Commander Isaac Quester, U.S. Navy, was transferred to Norfolk to command a destroyer. The family chose to live near Portsmouth across the river from Norfolk near the village of Churchland, where his mother Helen Carr Quester had grown up.

Churchland was a village between the suburbs of Portsmouth and the farm land beyond. It had never occurred to Harry that he would not be on the football team there. He loved football. His Father had played guard at Navy. He had played from sand lot days to High School. Secretly, he someday wanted to play for Navy. But it had never been like this! He was feeling light in the head, suddenly wondering if he could make it with this new team, this little country team known as the Churchland Truckers. Harry started as a hoarse voice shouted suddenly, close and behind him. He felt a slap on his helmet.

"Come on, ya bunch of Sissies," shouted Coach Braun loudly as he jogged beside Harry clad in flimsy white shorts, an orange shirt and a brown, crumpled pork pie hat. The hat was jammed jauntily on his head, sitting just above coarse eyebrows. His ears stuck out from under the hat like jug handles. The Coach was a bit shorter than Harry. Harry estimated that he was about the same weight… 175 pounds. Braun removed the crumpled hat revealing wavy brown hair and a square face with squinting eyes set on a thick neck. He took the whistle that hung on a cord around his neck and blew a rapid series of short, staccato blasts. "Pick up the pace… pick up the pace… you're running like a buncha flower girls! Ya been sitting around getting fat this summer? Huh? What about it?"

Harry ran on, sneaking a glance at the Coach out of the side of his eyes.

"What're you looking at?.... Yeah!... You!" screamed the Coach. "Watch where you're running… if that's what you call that… that hopping and prancing along… and don't you look at me! Run! Run 'til your guts hang out!"

Harry ran on in the middle of the group. Coach Braun ran to the head of the pack, shouting at players as he ran. Karl Darby, the player in the lead, picked up the pace. He was a short and compactly built boy who ran easily. Harry strained to lift his legs higher and faster, matching the new speed. His head began to spin and he fought for control. He did not want to join the deflated bodies lying around the track. That would be the ultimate disgrace to his well developed ego. He glanced back and saw Bubba methodically putting one foot in front of the other near the back of the pack. Bubba was having a hard time. Tony was at the back of the pack of runners, lagging behind.

"Hey, New Guy, your butt is dragging!" said a voice beside Harry.

Running beside him was a tall, thin boy with watery eyes. He wore the number twenty. Harry knew he was Arnie Eberly, the starting left end, the leader of the Hoods from across the river. He had a slack jaw face and watery blue eyes that seemed to be sleepy all the time.

"I'll make it," said Harry, gritting his teeth.

"You look like you're gonna die, New Guy," said Arnie with a sneer.

"You don't look so good yourself," said Harry defensively.

"You got a chip on your shoulder, New Guy?"

"Not really."

"I think I see a chip, Square," said Arnie with a shake of his head. "You ain't gonna last… Shotgun likes to see who's gonna gut it out and who's not."

"Don't worry about me," said Harry. "I'll make it!"

"Aw, you guys from Green Acres are soft!" exclaimed Arnie. "You'll never make it!"

Harry ran faster and pulled ahead of Arnie. He instinctively didn't like him, but this was no time to get into arguments with guys who were

7

already on the team. Harry glanced next to him and saw a boy about his own height and weight running easily next to him. He wore a white practice jersey with the black numbers zero zero on it. Bubba had pointed him out as Allman Buddinger, the quarterback and Team Co-Captain. Allman had a flat, square face, gray eyes and a short, snub nose. Harry knew that he lived in Green Acres, just down the street from where his family had moved in. Allman moved with the easy grace of a natural athlete. His big, toothy grin was infectious as he showed it off in spite of the stress of the run.

"How're you doing, New Guy?" asked Allman curiously.

"I'll do it," gasped Harry.

"You're Quester… right?"

"Right… Harry Quester."

"Save some for later… this is just the beginning."

"I got enough!"

"Maybe," said Allman. "Maybe you do!"

"Who're those guys watching over there?" asked Harry nodding at two boys standing beside the practice field in blue jeans and tee shirts. One of them was a big guy with long black hair, the other thinner and smaller. They both wore jeans and had a pack of cigarettes rolled up in the left sleeve of their tee shirt.

"Why? They worry you, Harry?" asked Allman.

"I just wondered," panted Harry.

"Guys from the team last year," said Allman, "The big guy is Johnny Calcione… the other one is Carson Quinn. They hang around with Eberly and the Hoods. Coach lets guys from past teams come out to watch practice during the summer."

"That's good," said Harry.

Allman reached into the pants of his practice uniform and took out a half of a lemon. He casually sucked on the lemon and stuck it back into his pants. Coach Braun ran up beside Harry and Allman, squinting at them, crouching menacingly and easily matching their pace. His expression was intense, his dark brown eyes boring into them like high speed drills.

"What're you doing there, Buddinger?" shouted Braun, his eyes intense, the veins standing out in his neck. "Having a little party? You'd better start running… you and that other guy! I'm watching for screw-offs! You wanna do more laps? Do ya… Do ya?"

"Sure, Coach," said Buddinger. "Let's do a few more laps!"

"Oh! A wise guy, huh?" shouted Coach Braun, his squinty eyes narrowing. And then in a louder voice, "Okay… okay! Buddinger here says he wants you guys to do a few more laps! So, take ten!"

A mixed cheer and groan went up from the pack of boys running and staggering around the field in the heat of the sun. The sun seemed to Harry to rise higher and become hotter with each passing minute. He wasn't sure he could make the ten laps. The humidity made the air so thick it hurt to breathe it.

"Thanks a lot, Allman," panted a hulking boy running beside Harry.

"Think nothing of it, Bart," said Allman merrily.

Harry glanced at Bart. He was shorter than Harry, but broad in the shoulders, carrying much more weight. He had a face that sprouted thick black whiskers beneath eyes that looked cruel.

"Remind me to whip your ass next chance I get," muttered Bart.

"Oh, you wouldn't do that to old Allman," laughed Allman, "your best Ol' Buddy!"

"Don't count on it," panted Bart with a menacing look.

The Coach fell back and Harry felt his mouth go dry as he watched Allman suck on the half lemon and lope easily along. They finished the sixth lap. Harry summoned another round of energy from his body and turned up the speed, moving to within three of the pack leader.

"Who's that guy, Allman?" asked Harry.

"That's Bart Whitely," said Allman seriously. "He replaced Johnny Calcione at tackle last year when Johnny… got hurt."

"He's pretty big," muttered Harry.

"Watch out for him," said Allman, a serious note in his voice, "He hangs around with the Hoods… Eberly and Calcione. He can be as mean as he is big… on and off the field."

"I'll remember that," panted Harry.

Harry saw Eddie Fearless, the Assistant Coach walking around tending to the boys who had fallen by the wayside. Eddie had on white shorts, an orange tee shirt and a black baseball cap. He was well built with a pleasant, open face that was wrinkled in concern as he looked at the boys sitting on the ground gasping in the sun. All but one of them was sitting up. Harry looked back and saw that one of the boys sitting beside the track was Tony Zee. He worried that Tony had fallen out. It wasn't like Tony, who was usually full of pep.

"What're you looking at, Boy?" shouted Coach Braun falling back and sticking his face into Harry's.

"Nothing… nothing," stuttered Harry, trying not to look at the Coach.

"You see something you like back there?" shouted Braun in a falsetto, whiny voice. "You wanna go over there and sit with the girls?"

"No Sir," gasped Harry.

"Who are you, anyway?" asked Coach Braun in a threatening tone.

"Harry... Harry Quester," panted Harry.

"Well, I've got my eye on you Kester," shouted Braun into his ear. "So don't you screw up... and watch where you're running!"

"Quester... Harry Quester... that's my name."

Coach Braun stared at Harry with a ferociously wrinkled brow as if Harry's response had somehow insulted him. "Well... whatever the... heck... your name is... keep your doggone eyes on the field ahead of you and run... run!"

"Okay Coach!" panted Harry, and he picked it up a pace, though he didn't know where he found the energy.

The Coach ran to the back of the running pack of boys shouting at each of them in turn. "What're you doing there, Bubba?" came the shout of the Coach from the back of the pack. "Ya look like you're hauling a tub of lard! You wanna be on the Team, ya better tighten up that gut and run... or you'll be carrying water again!!"

Poor Bubba, thought Harry. He was carrying a lot of weight. Could he take this grueling run?

"Okay...Harry... you'd better watch yourself with the Coach!" came the voice of Allman Buddinger behind him.

"I'm okay."

"If Shotgun finds someone he can beat on, then that guy's had it."

"I'll be okay."

Harry ran on, feeling his leg muscles beginning to tighten, falling behind Allman. His pores seemed like open faucets, pouring out sweat in the heat of the morning. He had never run to the point of his endurance, but by the ninth lap he felt he was nearing it. He was afraid that his leg muscles would at some point just tighten up and malfunction, and he would tumble head over heals into the ground and be trampled by the other runners. Or, the pains in his lungs, as he struggled to keep enough oxygen to his straining muscles, would overcome him and he would fall with cramps he couldn't control.

"What's the matter, Hot Shot?" The voice was a gruff one, coming from Bart Whitely panting along beside him. "You can't take it?"

"I'm okay," wheezed Harry.

"Someone told me you think you're a hot shot fullback," said Bart sarcastically, "a big shot fullback from Northern Virginia... is that it?"

"I played fullback," wheezed Harry, trying to conserve his energy. "It was single wing."

"You're pretty tender to be a Trucker," panted Bart, "you ain't gonna make it, Pretty Boy!"

"Just stand clear of me," gasped Harry as they neared the end of the tenth lap.

A tall man with blond hair that was almost white ran up beside Harry and Bart. Assistant Coach Slate Phelps was wearing white shorts and a gray tee-shirt, cleated shoes and a white baseball cap. He was in his early thirties, tall and well built with a handsome, open face.

"You boys doing okay?" asked Slate as he jogged easily alongside Harry and Bart.

"I'm ready to go, Coach," said Bart. "I don't know about this new guy!"

Coach Phelps looked inquisitively at Harry.

"You okay, Harry?" asked Phelps.

Harry was surprised that Coach Phelps knew his name. "I'm okay, Coach," panted Harry.

"Okay," said Phelps. "Save some breath... we're going to do face offs next!"

Coach Phelps jogged away and dropped back to join Coach Braun.

"Ol' Coach Phelps just can't break away," wheezed Bart.

"What do you mean?" panted Harry.

"Ya don't know?" asked Bart. "He was Coach here year before last... but now he's Assistant Principal over at Cradock Junior High."

"And he still comes here?"

"He and Shotgun are buddies," said Bart. "Coach Phelps comes over to help out."

"He looks like a good guy," muttered Harry as sweat poured down his face.

Bart laughed. "Hey, he can be pretty tough, too, New Guy... you'll see, 'cause you're gonna have to get by me... I got you for face offs!"

"What are face offs?" asked Harry between gasps.

"You'll soon find out!" said Bart with a wicked chortle. "Coach Phelps likes 'em... let's ya see what guys are made of, New Guy."

Harry heard a shout from the back of the pack of runners. "Keep running, Norwood!" screamed Coach Braun. "Don't ya quit on me! Your Paw told me you were a real tough guy! Well are ya... are ya?"

There was no answer. Harry turned his head and dared to glance back. Coach Braun was hopping and skipping along beside a tall, lean boy, delivering a kick to the boy's backside with every other skip. Coach Phelps was jogging behind him, a worried look on his face.

"What's going on back there?" panted Harry.

Bart laughed. "Shotgun's always giving Benny Norwood some encouragement, that's all."

"By kicking him in the butt?" wheezed Harry in an astounded voice.

"Benny screws off too much... always lagging around the back of the pack," said Bart, "and he was one of Shotgun's favorite targets last year… along with Buster."

"Buster?"

"Buster Stanley," said Bart. "Over there."

Harry glanced over his shoulder and saw a big, heavy set boy plodding along with dogged determination. He saw Coach Braun and Coach Phelps arguing about something. Braun threw his hat on the ground and said something to Phelps. Phelps picked up the hat and handed it to Braun, still talking to him.

"It … it's wrong!" muttered Harry. "I mean, wrong to kick him, to pick on the guy!"

"Shotgun can get real mean if he thinks you're not putting out, New Guy," said Bart, "so you'd better watch your ass or he'll be kicking you!"

****

Slate Phelps and Cliff Braun walked away from the practice field as the players ran wearily into the dressing room.

"Whatta ya think, Slate?" asked Cliff with a determined expression.

"They seem like a good bunch of kids," said Slate, nodding his head. "I think you'll have a good team."

"Yeah, maybe," said Cliff, "but they're outa shape… and need toughening up if we're gonna beat Suffolk this year!!"

"I'm sure you'll toughen 'em up, Cliff," said Slate. "Just be careful about how you … work with 'em."

"Yeah… yeah, Slate," said Cliff. "I know. They need to understand how to take a big hit… and give one… you know that!"

"Yeah, I know that," said Slate. "You might have a shot at the State Group Two Championship this year, you know."

"Maybe," growled Braun. "If I can keep Sanders healthy."

"You put on a real convincing show out there at try-outs!"

"A show?" asked Cliff vehemently. "Ya think all that was a show?"

"You know what I mean, Coach" laughed Slate.

"What're ya laughing at?" asked Cliff suspiciously.

"Nothing… nothing," said Slate quickly. "I was just remembering back to when we were kids… and how we started out."

"Yeah," said Cliff. "I remember… it started when we were running papers on that paper route… pretending like we was football players!"

****

The perfect season really started in 1936. That was when Slate Phelps and Cliff Braun solidified their friendship and started thinking about football. It was during the Great Depression and no one had any money to buy anything. Many didn't have jobs. Those in Portsmouth who had work in the Naval Shipyard or the Southern Railway were the lucky ones and clung to their jobs jealously.

It was a dark morning in November. An icy drizzle fell from the sky as Slate turned the crank on his 1926 Chevrolet. He was a tall, blond headed boy with curly hair and a body with strength beyond his fifteen years. He turned the crank easily. The Chevy was a black two-seater with goggle like headlamps sitting atop its front fenders and thin tires around spoked rims. Slate had carefully painted the spokes a dark gold color. It was pretty spiffy, he thought, even if you did have to crank the thing to get it started. And, for a car only ten years old, he had gotten it at a bargain using his paper route earnings from last year and a little help from his father. Slate's father was Minister of a small Christian Church in Prentiss Park that kept his family of eight reasonably secure, though poor. Slate was lucky to have the Chevy at age fifteen, and a paper route. It helped the family get along.

Slate cranked one last time and the Chevy exploded into action with a loud chugging sound and a cloud of black smoke. He was glad it started as it was a very cold morning in Prentiss Park. Prentiss Park was a nice neighborhood of working people in the middle of Portsmouth. The homes were mostly two story houses of wood and shingle siding with front porches painted white. Slate got into the Chevy. He had to get all the papers delivered before the sun came up or his customers wouldn't see them before they left for work. If they didn't see their paper, they would complain, and that wasn't good. His paper route last year covered 75 houses in Port Norfolk, a community on the Western Branch of the Elizabeth River a little over a mile from his house on Elm Avenue. Last year, he rode the distance each morning on his bicycle. This year, with the Chevy, it was different. He had taken on 75 more houses in Port Norfolk and gotten his best friend Cliff Braun to help him.

Slate steered the Chevy out of his driveway and onto Elm Avenue. He drove the few blocks to Cliff's house on Maple Avenue to pick him up. Cliff was standing in the doorway of a white duplex house. It was a two story structure with four windows across the front. The Brauns had the left side of the house. There was a sidewalk with several big cracks in the front. Cliff ran the short distance to the Chevy. He was a bit shorter than Slate and weighed a little less at 140 pounds. He had wavy brown hair and a square face with squinting eyes. He wore a two colored blue and orange jacket and a black ball cap pulled down over his jug handle ears. Slate didn't know what bound him to Cliff. They were such opposites. Cliff was always getting them into trouble. Slate was always finding ways to get them out. They had been best buddies since they met six years ago in a Prentiss Park Play Yard. A local bully by the name of Ennis Hathaway was picking on Slate, and Cliff joined Slate in facing the bigger boy down. Ennis was three years older than Slate and Cliff and twice as big as both of them, but he had backed away and left Slate alone. After that, Ennis always looked for a chance to catch either one of them alone, but they became inseparable. Slate shook his head, wondering at himself. Maybe he liked the adventure of being around Cliff. You never knew what the kid was going to do next! Cliff opened the door of the Chevy and climbed in.

"You're late!" exclaimed Cliff with impatience.

Cliff seemed to always have a concerned expression on his face which Slate had gotten used to. This morning he was only impatient.

"Only a few minutes," replied Slate.

"We'd better get our asses to the Mount Vernon Avenue pick-up or old Mr. Mays will be yelling his big puffy face at us!" grumbled Cliff.

"You worrying about Mr. Mays?" asked Slate, a picture of the pudgy, ill tempered, cigar chewing Circulation Manager popping into his head.

"Naw! I don't worry about that ass-hole," said Cliff with a snort, "I just worry about collecting fifteen cents a week from a hundred and fifty houses… that's what I worry about!"

"We'll keep on collecting," said Slate, pushing in the clutch and grinding the car into gear. "We need this route!"

"My Mom gives me the dickens about it all the time," said Cliff with a furrowed brow.

"What do you mean?" asked Slate.

"Just what I said!" exclaimed Cliff. "She beats up the Old Man about not earning enough money at the Railroad… and then she beats up on me about not giving her enough money from the paper route."

"She yells at you?" asked Slate thinking about his own mild mannered mother and his Christian father.

"Yell?" exclaimed Cliff rubbing his square chin. "I said she beats up on me… and the Old Man… and that's what I mean! She has a wicked right cross!"

Slate said nothing in response, trying to imagine Cliff's mother, a big woman with Cliff's square face and temperament, throwing a right cross.

"She hits you?" asked Slate.

"Hey," said Cliff. "I love my Mom… but she can get rough when she's excited, ya know… that's just the way she is!"

Slate pulled the Chevy into gear, let out the clutch and allowed the vehicle to jerk away and head toward the corner of High Street and Mount Vernon to pick up their papers. They bounced across the railroad tracks near the Lumber Yard. They came soon to the pick up and found three mounds of newspapers titled *The Virginian Pilot*, each tied tightly together with bristly twine. They got out of the Chevy and loaded the newspapers into the small trunk. Cliff cut the bristly twine so that the newspapers lay free in the trunk, ready to be placed inside the screen door of each house. They got back into the Chevy and started down Mount Vernon Avenue into Port Norfolk.

"Ennis is trying to get our paper route," said Slate worriedly. "He's going to give us some trouble, I think."

"Ennis Hathaway," said Cliff in disgust. "I hate that big fat sonofabitch!"

Slate laughed. "You hate him because he beat the piss out of you last month," he said.

"He's older..., I think he's seventeen, maybe eighteen," said Cliff. "But I ain't afraid of him!"

"You keep picking fights with him, Cliff," said Slate. "It seems you'd learn... once he beat you up!"

"He thinks he's such a big man," said Cliff, "living in that fancy house near his Old Man's Grocery Store."

"At least his family has some money," said Slate, "which is more than you can say for our families."

"Ahhh," said Cliff, "he's a big pussy!"

"Well," said Slate. "He's on the football team at Wilson."

"Big deal!" exclaimed Cliff in disgust. "He's a second or third string nobody! I can beat him! I hope we see him... I'll fight him again!"

"What do you think of playing football?" asked Slate. "I mean... not just on the spare lot... what about in High School?"

"I've thought a lot about it," said Cliff.

"We could play, I think," said Slate. "I can run fast. And you like to fight... except in football, you can't fight... you have to just hit the other guys hard!"

"What's the difference?" asked Cliff. "Fighting or hitting?"

"Well," said Slate philosophically, "I guess in fighting you're mad... and in football, it's a game."

"I think ya gotta be mad to play football," said Cliff thoughtfully, "I mean... if you're gonna hit 'em good... ya gotta make yourself be mad!"

"Then I guess you can play football, Cliff," smiled Slate.

Slate stopped at the corner of Mount Vernon Avenue and Woodrow Street. Slate looked serious and turned to Cliff.

"You know... Ennis said he was going to get Mr. Mays on us about stealing milk out of the morning milk boxes," said Slate.

"I only did that once or twice... from old Mr. Edwards' house... he gets four whole bottles every few days. He can spare it! We don't get much milk at home!"

"You left a note for the Milkman to deliver some chocolate milk," grinned Slate. "I know that… and then you drank it before Mr. Edwards got the milk in the morning!"

"So?" challenged Cliff. "It worked, didn't it?"

"I know," laughed Slate, "I took some too, but we'd better stop! Mr. Edwards… or someone, might catch us and Mr. Mays would fire me."

"That sloppy bastard won't fire us," said Cliff, his eyes squinting and a sadistic twist on his mouth. "He knows I'd beat the crap outa him!"

"No you wouldn't," said Slate calmly. "Remember, the paper route's in my name and my Father wouldn't like it much if you beat up Mr. Mays… and you'd probably end up in jail!"

"Yeah…. yeah," mumbled Cliff angrily. "We'd probably have to go pray… or something like that."

"I've been thinking about it," said Slate. "Ennis will probably do something like take the papers from behind the screen doors… so they'll get all wet, and make the customers bitch to Mr. Mays."

"Let's get started," said Cliff, climbing out of the car.

They had the routine down perfectly. Cliff jumped out and went to the trunk. He opened it, leaving it open and grabbed an arm full of papers. He ran at full speed to the first house on Mount Vernon Avenue, a large, white Victorian style house with a big porch that surrounded the front of the house. It was surrounded by legustrum hedges. He dodged around the hedges as though racing toward a touchdown. A big sycamore tree dominated the front yard. He gave it a fake, dodged around the menacing tree and ran up to the porch. Cliff glanced at the metal milk box that sat on the front steps. He started to look inside to see if the Milkman had come. But he stopped, remembering what Slate had said. Cliff pulled open the outer door of the house and threw a paper inside. He ran on to the next house, and then the next, repeating the process six times before he turned back to the street to get more papers. Slate followed him along the street in the Chevy, slowly passing the big sycamore and elm trees that lined the sidewalk. Cliff ran to the trunk of the car, grabbed six more papers and headed for the next set of houses. He ran pretending he was a football player, racing along dodging hedges and flower beds.

They came to the last several sets of houses on Mount Vernon Avenue, near Bayview Boulevard. Slate stopped the Chevy under a sycamore tree, turned the engine off and went to the trunk. He and Cliff both got out six papers and ran to houses on each side of the street. Slate delivered a paper to the Edwards house near Adriatic Street. He ran on, delivering papers until he came to Bayview Boulevard. Suddenly there was a shout from behind them.

"You boys!" shouted Elias Edwards, a raw boned man with a droopy moustache running toward them. "Stop! You been taking my milk again!"

Slate turned and saw Mr. Edwards panting along the dark street followed closely by Ennis Hathaway. Ennis was even bigger than Slate recalled him to be. His stomach bounced in front of him as he ran. He had a broad face covered with acne. His black hair was long and greasy. Edwards ran directly at Slate. Ennis disappeared behind the Chevy on the side of the street where Cliff was.

"You boys've took my milk for the last time," shouted Edwards as he puffed to a stop in front of Slate.

"We haven't taken your milk, Mr. Edwards," said Slate, concern in his voice and fear in his heart.

"Yeah?" shouted Edwards. "Well, let's have a look in that jalopy!"

Slate walked back to the Chevy with Mr. Edwards striding along beside him. Ennis stood beside the car, a smug look on his acne covered face as Cliff came running up.

"What's going on?" shouted Cliff angrily.

"Mr. Edwards thinks we took some milk," said Slate evenly, controlling his anger.

"We ain't got no milk," shouted Cliff, balling up his fists.

Ennis smiled and pushed up his sleeves, exposing arms as big as hams. "Come on, ya little punk," he said shaking his fist at Cliff.

Elias Edwards reached into the open trunk of the Chevy and rummaged around. "Then what's this?" he exclaimed triumphantly holding up a glass bottle of white milk in the drizzling rain.

"He took it," said Ennis pointing to Cliff. "I seen him!"

Cliff charged at Ennis his fists flailing. "You sloppy lying sonofabitch!" he shouted in uncontrolled anger.

Cliff tried to tackle the larger boy. Ennis was like a brick wall and stood there laughing while Cliff strained to bring him down. Then he clubbed Cliff in the back of the head with a big fist. Cliff fell to the ground and then scrambled away like a crab seeking refuge. He got to his feet, his face red and contorted with pain and anger.

"You boys stop the fighting," said Elias Edwards, looking around nervously, hoping the ruckus wouldn't awaken his neighbors.

"Ennis put that milk in my car," said Slate pulling at Edwards' coat. "He's trying to make us look bad with Mr. Mays... that's all."

Cliff ran at Ennis again. This time he launched himself at the bigger boy, hurtling through the air without regard for his body. He hit Ennis in the chest with his full momentum. His arms thrust forward pounding the fat boy in the solar plexus and under his throat. Cliff fell to the ground as Ennis staggered backward with ungainly steps and fell against the trunk of a big elm tree. He slid down the trunk of the elm tree and sat on the ground, a dazed look on his face. Cliff crawled across the ground and began to pound Ennis in the face, his fists flying furiously. Blood spurted from Ennis' nose, covering the front of his coat. He threw up his arms to protect himself. Cliff was snorting like a bull, beating Ennis' face to a pulp. Slowly Ennis recovered and stood to his full height, a full four inches taller than Cliff. He seized Cliff by the shoulders while Cliff's fists still flailed at Ennis' face. He turned and slammed Cliff into the trunk of the elm tree. All of the air was forced out of Cliff's lungs and he fell to the ground. Ennis raised his big fists to club Cliff, but Cliff tackled him around the legs and this time brought him crashing to the sidewalk. Cliff, his face contorted with pain and a ferocious anger pummeled Ennis in the face. Ennis, using his great weight, rolled Cliff over, sitting on top of him and pinning his arms to the sidewalk.

"I'm gonna kill you, Braun, you little shithead!" shouted Ennis, blood spurting from his nose. He began hitting Cliff in the face.

Elias Edwards ran to them and tried to pull Ennis off of Cliff.

"You boys stop!" shouted Elias. "You're gonna hurt each other bad!"

Ennis ignored Edwards and continued to pound Cliff. Well, here we go again, thought Slate. He braced himself and rushed at Ennis. He hit him with all the momentum and strength he could build. The blow knocked Ennis from atop Cliff. Slate fell to the ground and struggled to his feet. Cliff staggered to his feet, his square face a bloody mess. He kicked Ennis in the ribs and tried to jump on him. Slate grabbed Cliff and pulled him away.

"Come on, Cliff," shouted Slate in an urgent voice.

Slate dragged Cliff away. Cliff fought him every inch.

"We got the bastard now," sputtered Cliff. "I'm gonna break every bone in his fat ass body!"

"No you're not," said Slate, pulling Cliff away.

Slate broke into a run, pulling Cliff along.

"What about the Chevy?" wheezed Cliff.

"We'll come back for it," panted Slate. "It isn't going anywhere!"

Cliff ran beside Slate. "I'm going to kill that sonofabitch!" he muttered.

"That's what I'm afraid of," said Slate, "if he doesn't kill you!"

****

Chapter Two
Try-outs II

Assistant Coach Slate Phelps looked at the sweating, exhausted boys assembled around him. They were on one knee, their helmets off and resting on the thick green grass.

"Now listen up, guys!" shouted Coach Phelps. "You guys on the far side have got ten seconds to get by your face-off man and run beyond where I'm standing. If you get by him... and me, you go to your try out section... ends and backs over there by the goal posts with Coach Braun, lineman over there near where Coach Fearless is. If you don't get by your man, you go back again... until you do. Any questions?"

There was a silence as the boys used the time to catch their breath and recover from the ten laps. There were varying degrees of misery written on their young faces, combined with looks of aggressive determination.

"Okay, then," said the Coach. "Get over there to that white line."

Harry picked up his helmet, stood up and began to walk toward the white line.

"What's this!" screamed Coach Braun charging toward Harry, his face red. Beads of perspiration stood out on his forehead. "What in the heck is this? Don't you know how to run, Boy?"

Harry picked up his feet and began to trot toward Coach Phelps' white line. Coach Braun ran alongside him, his squinting eyes focused ferociously on Harry.

"I didn't say piddle along like a girl," sputtered the Coach, running alongside Harry in a crouch, his fists clenched tightly, the veins standing out in his thick neck. "When you're at practice... or in a game, you run! You run all the time! All the... cotton picking time! And put that... helmet on!"

Harry put the helmet on and broke into a run. Coach Braun matched his pace. Harry turned on the speed, but Braun ran right beside him.

"So you think you're a fast guy, huh?" shouted Braun. "Well, we'll see this afternoon at wind sprints. You'll be the first in line, Kester!"

Harry ran up to where Bart was waiting for him in a three point stance. Harry got down in front of him. Coach Braun moved on, shouting at the crouching boys.

"Okay, New Guy," said Bart in front of him, "let's see what ya got!"

"Okay Bart... my name is Harry."

"Oh? That's sweet!" said Bart with a snarl. "I'm gonna knock your butt back to Northern Virginia, Pretty Boy!"

Harry got down into a three point stance feeling anger rise in him like a black cloud. "Bart," he said with a new found snarl. "I'm going to enjoy creaming you!"

Bart chuckled. "Hold on to your ass, Pretty Boy!"

The smell of the fresh grass was overpowering. The dew from the morning was evaporating off the grass, making the field steamy hot. The whistle blew. Harry charged at Bart, trying to stiff arm him to the side as he had done as a single wing fullback in Northern Virginia. Bart launched himself at Harry and hit him so hard in the chest that it knocked the wind from him and he fell back onto the grass. He had never been hit so hard by anyone… or anything. He lay on his back stunned, staring up at the bright sun that seemed to whirl about in the sky.

"Don't just lay there, Pretty Boy… you ain't dead!" said Bart, glowering over him. "Don't let Coach see you down there… or you're gone for sure!"

Harry struggled to get up. He got to his feet and lowered himself painfully into a three point stance.

"I'm gonna hit you like that again," said Bart with a grin that turned into a snarl, "just like the first time! And I'm gonna love it!"

"You can try," gasped Harry, still struggling to regain his wind.

Bart laughed and rolled his round eyes. "Get down and get ready… I need some fresh meat to work on!"

Bart got down into a three point stance and they faced off again. This was a level of football Harry had not experienced. With his previous team, it was sufficient to block a man. Here, it seemed that nothing less than destroying the other guy was acceptable. Harry wondered if he could adjust to that. The whistle blew. This time Harry charged directly at Bart and stiff armed him against the shoulder pads. Bart was momentarily stopped. Then Harry brought his elbow and forearm forward violently and struck Bart in the chest, knocking him backward. Bart recovered and charged at Harry, coming at him from a running crouch. He came up under Harry and delivered another stunning blow to Harry's midsection which knocked him backward. Harry fell to one knee, holding his belly and feeling nauseous.

"What's the matter with you Kester-from-Northern-Virginia?" shouted Coach Braun standing over him, his face jutting forward like an attacking guard dog. "Didn't they teach you how to block up there in the nawth? Get up!"

"Yes Sir… they did … teach me how to block," wheezed Harry breathlessly as he struggled to his feet.

"No they didn't!" shouted the Coach, his eyes wide and furious. "And don't you contradict me, Kester! What are you… some kinda wise guy? If I say they didn't teach you how to block… then they didn't! Got that?"

Harry stared up at the square face with the squinting eyes. "Yes Sir, Coach," said Harry weakly. "I got it."

"When ya block, ya gotta get low and explode," shouted Braun, a fierce expression on his face, "and I mean explode at the other guy... ya gotta put a forearm shiver right in his solar plexus... hard... hard!... ya gotta hit him in the face and make him feel like he never wants to see ya again!"

"Yes Sir... I understand."

"No you don't!" said Braun disgustedly, spitting into the steamy grass.

Practice stopped and the whole team watched the Coach and Harry. Braun crouched in front of Harry, his bulldog face contorted into a fierce image, his arms up in a blocking position.

"Put your fists in front of your chest... and bend those legs... get low and get mean!"

Harry did as he was told. He strained to stay in a crouched position, his back straight, and his arms in front of his chest. He felt anger rising in him which he tried to control. It boiled inside him and fueled his determination.

"Lower! Much lower... and a lot meaner!" shouted Braun. "You look like you're gonna ask me for a date... not knock me on my butt!"

Harry crouched lower and tried to look meaner. The anger in him grew.

"Ya gotta think mean, Kester! Think real mean!" said Braun between clenched teeth, his eyes squinting intensely. "There ain't no nice guys when you're a Trucker playing ball!"

Harry tried to think mean. He conjured up all the people he didn't like and thought about whacking them in the chest. He thought about whacking the Coach in the chest as his anger took on new proportions.

"What are ya... some kinda lover boy?" snarled Coach Braun. "I said look mean! Real mean!"

Harry put the worst scowl he could come up with on his face.

"That's better!" shouted Shotgun. "Then do it like this!"

The Coach came up under Harry and hit him in the chest.

"SHBOOM!" shouted the Coach as he delivered the blow. It was a hard blow, and it surprised Harry. The Coach's forearm knocked the wind out of his lungs and bounced up into his face. He staggered back in pain, clutching his nose and trying to keep from falling.

"That's called leverage, Kester," shouted the Coach watching Harry with some concern. "Hit 'em low when they're off balance! Understand?"

"Yes Sir," muttered Harry regaining his balance. There was intense pain in the center of his face. Blood was running from his nose.

"Ain't that what the song says?" shouted the Coach. "Send 'em up to paradise up above? I want you to send 'em all to the devil down below!"

"Okay, Coach," muttered Harry in pain, still holding his nose.

"What's wrong with you, Kester?" shouted Braun.

"My nose is bleeding, Sir," said Harry. "That's all."

"My nose is bleeding, my nose is bleeding," whined Braun mockingly.

Harry took his hands away from his face. "It'll be okay," he said, starting toward the Coach, a determined scowl on his face.

"Where do ya think you're going?" shouted Braun.

Harry stopped in his tracks in front of the Coach, clenching his fists. "To try what you showed me, Coach," he said, his voice wavering, blood streaming down his face.

"Get away from me, Kester! Go over there and knock Bart on his can!" said Braun, backing away and motioning toward Bart.

"I'll try Coach!" said Harry, looking over to where Bart stood grinning.

"Try?" shouted Shotgun in amazement, a look of mock horror on his square face. "Is that all you can do… try?"

"I'll knock Bart on his can," wheezed Harry, wondering if he could.

"You'd better, Kester… old Bart there is a pushover," grunted Coach Braun. "Wait 'til ya meet the rest of 'em!"

Coach Braun glanced at Bart and grinned. The Coach looked like a bulldog grinning over a raw steak.

"Come and get me, New Guy!" growled Bart, rolling his eyes.

Harry went reluctantly to where Bart was getting into a three point stance. He got down in front of the big tackle. His nose felt numb.

"You alright, Pretty Boy?" asked Bart sarcastically. "Your nose ain't so pretty like it was!"

Harry's anger overcame his pain. "Just play ball, Bart!" he said gritting his teeth.

The whistle sounded. Bart and Harry charged at each other with all the energy they could muster. They locked arms and began to drive their feet, tearing up the grass beneath them, each seeking to topple the other. Harry dodged to the side and pushed Bart away. Bart staggered to keep his balance and Harry ran to where Coach Phelps stood with his whistle.

Coach Phelps walked up to Harry. "Okay! Good job! Let me see that nose."

Coach Phelps grabbed Harry's chin and looked at his nose, which was beginning to scab over.

"Better get it checked out," said Phelps. "It might be broken."

"No Sir," said Harry, wiping the blood from his face, "it's okay…

I've been hit in the nose before!"

"Okay… but be careful. What're you trying out for, Harry?"

"Fullback, Coach."

"Well, do your laps and get on over there with Coach Braun!"

Harry ran toward the track to begin his laps. Benny Norwood jogged up beside him. "Hi, I'm Benny."

"Hi," panted Harry, still feeling the effects of the blow to his chest and nose.

"The Coach is too rough… don't ya think?" asked Benny hesitatingly.

"I don't know, Benny," said Harry rubbing the side of his nose tenderly.

"Your nose okay?"

"Yeah. I think so."

"It don't look so good!"

"Don't worry about me, Benny," said Harry impatiently.

"Well, let me know if I can help," said Benny hopefully.

Harry jogged on ahead, thinking about Coach Braun kicking Benny in the butt during laps.

****

The locker room after morning practice smelled like hot, putrid sweat, aggravated by the heat of the room and steam coming from the showers. Harry ripped off his dirty practice uniform which was soaked through and smelled sour.

"This uniform really stinks," muttered Harry.

"Yeah," said Bubba slamming open the locker beside Harry. "Hang it in the locker and it might dry some before this afternoon's practice."

"You mean we don't get fresh ones?" asked Harry in astonishment.

Bubba looked at Harry and laughed. "Are you kidding? Wait'll you come back and try to climb into that thing. Then we'll find out what you're made of, Cuz."

Tony Zee came in and sat dejectedly on the bench in front of the lockers. Tony usually exuded energy and enthusiasm, but after the morning's practice, he was painfully subdued.

"I really screwed that up," said Tony.

"You'll be alright, Tony," said Harry. "It's not like you to not finish. What's wrong?"

"I was sick last night" said Tony miserably, "but that's no excuse. I just… gave out… around lap five."

"What was wrong?"

"I don't know… upset stomach and headache, and all that."

"You okay now?"

"I think so."

"It was tough," said Harry reluctantly. "I don't know how I did it… and I wasn't sick."

"Shotgun roughed you up some, I saw."

"He… was coaching me… I guess that's the way they do it here."

"It didn't look like coaching from where I was," said Tony. "He was really getting on you… and he hit you pretty hard! You'd better see a Doctor about the nose. It doesn't look too good."

"The nose will be fine," said Harry. "Don't you say anything to our parents about my nose. I don't want to be pulled out of practice because of a darn bloody nose!"

"Okay, Harry," said Tony. "Whatever you say."

"You guys don't worry about it," said Bubba pulling a towel from his locker. "That's just the way Shotgun coaches."

"Pretty strange way to coach," said Tony with a grimace.

"I'll fix the nose for ya, Harry," said Bubba reaching for Harry's nose.

"Oh no you don't!" exclaimed Harry lifting his forearm to protect his nose.

"Come on! I just love to fix noses!"

"Go to hell, Bubba!" said Harry irritably.

"Coach Fearless says I have to run the ten laps in full gear tomorrow morning… or I'm out," said Tony.

"Well… you can do it," said Harry reassuringly.

"Don't worry, Tony," grimaced Bubba, "I almost didn't make it either!"

Harry, Tony and Bubba walked into the shower room together.

"I think I can make it," said Tony. "I've gotta get my head and belly right… that's all!"

"How many of the others have to run again?" asked Bubba.

"Me and that tall kid… Benny Norwood," said Tony. "I guess I'm stupid enough to come back for more! Those other three guys just quit."

"I saw ya talking to Benny," said Bubba. "I wouldn't get too close to him if I were you."

"What's wrong with Benny?" asked Harry.

"He's a strange kid," said Bubba. "He flunks the run every year… but comes back, at least so far."

"Coach lets him come back?"

"Coach Phelps did. Shotgun almost canned him last year. Benny is a pretty good football player when he wants to be… but that's probably not often enough to suit Shotgun."

The shower room was filled with naked boys luxuriating under the ten showers, soaping themselves and grab-assing. Allman had a towel rolled up and was busy flicking unsuspecting guys on the tail with it.

"Hold on your ding dong!" sung Allman with a laugh. "Alang alang alang!"

The towel cracked expertly in his hands. He flicked it at the burly rear end of Bucky Allison, the right guard, where it popped loudly. Bucky flinched and tried to cover himself from the darting towel.

"Dammit, Buddinger, ain't you got nothin' better to do?" asked Bucky angrily.

Allman Buddinger ran up to Bucky Allison, grabbed Bucky's head and planted a big kiss on his cheek. Bucky recoiled in disgust.

"Ah, I'm sorry, Bucky Bucky Bucky," crooned Allman through a condescending grin.

"Buddinger... you're disgusting!" shouted Bucky with a smile, pushing Allman away.

Everyone in the shower laughed. Bucky turned back to his shower. Allman snuck up behind him and goosed Bucky in the ear with a soapy finger. Bucky flinched, turned and planted a big fist on Allman's chest, making a thud that echoed around the shower room. Allman limped away whimpering in mock pain.

"Bucky! I'm injured! I'm out for the year!"

"Oh shut up, Allman," laughed Bucky.

"That Allman guy seems to get away with anything," said Tony in awe.

"Seems like it" said Harry watching Allman and Bucky closely.

Harry turned on a shower and adjusted the valves to give him a hot stream of water. He soaped himself and rubbed his aching muscles, beginning to feel better. He flexed his arm muscles and the oversized muscles of his chest, seeking relief from the pain and stiffness. He heard the pop of a towel behind him.

"Ow!" shouted Benny Norwood. "Goddamit, Allman, stop that!"

"Come on, Benny," shouted Allman good naturedly, "A little pop on your skinny tail is gonna get you around the track in the morning... again!"

"Just stop it, Allman," said Benny in a wavering voice. "It ain't funny!"

Benny stalked out of the shower room amid a chorus of mock moans. Harry washed off the soap and turned the shower to the off position. There was a popping sound and a stinging on his left buttock. Anger rose in him like a dark animal he couldn't control. He turned to face Allman. He charged at him and grabbed the towel, wrestling it away from the surprised senior quarterback.

"What're ya doing, Harry?" shouted Allman, astounded that anyone would oppose him.

Harry stood there for a long moment, facing Allman, trying to control his anger. "I'm just borrowing this towel for awhile, Allman," he said, flipping the towel over his shoulder nonchalantly.

"Alright, you guys, stop the grab-assing and get your shower," shouted Coach Fearless standing in the shower door in his shorts and tee-shirt. "And be back here and in uniform ready to go for afternoon practice... on the field at four o'clock sharp. We got wind sprints to do... a lot of 'em!"

Harry walked slowly out of the shower room, the towel over his shoulder. The boys in the shower room stared after him.

****

A.P. Johns' General Store was in the middle of Churchland Village. It was a two story building with the grocery downstairs and A.P.'s home upstairs. There was a gas pump in front of the store in the middle of a cement apron. Inside the store there were two rows of goods, a drink cooler and a butcher counter. Behind the counter, A.P. patrolled shelves of goods from which he made up orders and delivered them to Churchland homes. A.P. was a short man in his mid thirties with an athletic build who played shortstop for the Churchland Truckers men's baseball team... that is, whenever he could muster enough men from the local farms and stores to play the downtown baseball teams. He used to referee at football games, but had stopped to keep up with his business. Allman, Bubba, Harry, and Tony, were in the store after morning practice. They all wore jeans and colorful jersey shirts except for Harry and Allman. Harry wore tan slacks and an open neck sport shirt. Allman always managed to be different. He wore jeans and a ribbed sleeveless undershirt that showed off his well developed arms and shoulders.

"Hand me a True Aid, Bubba," said Allman hoisting himself up to sit on one end of the drink cooler. "A grape one."

"Get it yourself, Allman," said Bubba with an apologetic smile.

"Ah, come on Bubba, be a good guy!" said Allman, rolling his eyes.

"They're in the cooler, Allman," said Bubba, lowering his eyes.

Allman got off of the drink cooler and walked menacingly toward Bubba. "Bubba, I'm gonna have to kick your chubby ass," said Allman with a big grin on his face.

Bubba reached into the cooler mumbling to himself and brought out a grape True Aid. He thrust it toward Allman and extracted an RC Cola for himself.

"I knew you were a good guy, Bubba," said Allman opening the soft drink with a "church key" he kept on a chain hanging from his belt. It made a popping sound.

A.P. came to where the boys lounged. "I hear you guys are supposed to win it all this year!"

"We're gonna do that!" exclaimed Allman. "For sure!"

"Well, I'll be there to see you," said A.P. "I wouldn't miss a game!"

"You didn't miss any last year, A.P.," said Bubba.

"Are you really the Mayor of Churchland, A.P.?" asked Tony.

A.P. laughed, wrinkling up his leathery face. "People call me that, Tony," he said, "but Churchland don't have a mayor… last time I checked!"

Allman got up and went to the butcher cabinet. "Everyone knows who the Mayor is, A.P.," shouted Allman, "Lemme have a coupla them pig's feet… the pickled ones."

A.P. went behind the butcher counter wiping his hands on the little white grocer's apron he always wore. "You sure you want pig's feet?" asked A.P. with a raised eyebrow, "with grape True Aid?"

"It sounds revolting," said Tony, making a face.

"He just eats them to gross us out," said Bubba with a wink of his eye.

A.P. wrapped two pink pickled pig's feet in brown paper and extended it to Allman. "Thirty cents," said A.P., "and count up on those drinks… they're ten cents each."

"Put it on my tab, A.P." said Allman jumping on top of the drink cooler and brandishing a pinkish pickled pig's foot.

"You don't have a tab, Allman," said A.P. rolling his eyes in frustration.

"I don't?" exclaimed Allman wide-eyed. "Well then put it on Bubba's… I know his old man has one!"

Allman put a look of exaggerated pleasure on his face and gnawed at the pig's foot. Bubba snatched the second pig foot from Allman's hand and gnawed at it with a ferocious grimace. He gagged and spit out the offending meat in a noisy spray.

"Gimme that damn foot!" shouted Allman in mock anger, lunging at Bubba.

Allman grabbed Bubba's arm and wrestled it to the top of the drink cooler, knocking over a stand filled with loaves of bread in the process. Bubba gave up the pig foot and, looking embarrassed, began picking up the loaves of bread.

"You guys git your drinks and git out of here," said A.P in an irritated but friendly voice. "Bubba, I'm gonna git your Old Man after you guys if ya don't clean up your act!"

"I'll get the bread up," said Bubba apologetically.

"Git on," said A.P., picking up the bread. "I'll do it! I don't know how I put up with you guys!"

"It's because ya love us, A.P.," said Allman jumping down from the drink cooler and hugging the little man around the neck.

"Yeah… yeah," said A.P., pushing Allman away. "When's the first game?"

"It's against Gloucester," said Bubba. "Two weeks after school starts."

"Good!" exclaimed A.P. "I'll be there. Now git on out of here!"

A.P. grabbed a broom from the corner of the store and began making sweeping motions at their feet.

"Git!" shouted A.P.

The boys went outside and lounged against Allman's red open top jeep, nicknamed "The Red Rooster". They drank their drinks.

"Your nose broke, Harry?" asked Allman casually.

"Don't worry about it," said Harry defensively.

"Okay," said Allman flippantly. "I won't!"

Bob Porter drove up in his 1950 Ford convertible with Buster Stanley riding shotgun and Matt Pittinger in the back seat. The car was yellow, almost chartreuse in color, with a propeller spinning on the front of the chrome rocket shape in the center of the grill… the "Yellow Peril", as he called it. The top was down and the radio had Perry Como crooning:

Papa loves mambo,
Mama loves mambo,
Look at 'em sway with it, gettin' so gay with it,
Shoutin' "olé" with it, wow! Ooh!

The Ford rolled to a stop near the store and the radio flipped off. Bob, Matt and Buster got out. Bob was of medium height with a smooth face and a crew cut. Buster had a big, square body and face. His face held an expression that seemed to hide some joke he had yet to tell. Matt was a wiry farm boy with albino-like hair. He had a permanent smile plastered on his thin face.

"So, Mr. America," shouted Allman, "are ya ready to play some center this year?"

Bob smiled and walked to where they sat. "I'm ready," he said with a determined grimace.

"You'll be the only 150 pound center in the state," said Buster. "We're gonna have to feed you up some!"

"One fifty-eight this year!" said Bob puffing up his chest.

"Soaking wet! Have a pig's foot!" Buddinger brandished the pickled pig's foot at Bob.

Bob made a face and waved the offering away, "How do you eat that stuff, Allman?" he asked.

"Just tryin' to put some weight on ya," said Allman jumping up and sticking the pig's foot in Porter's face. "Gotta protect this pretty face!"

Porter grabbed Allman's arm and hit him in the chest with a playful blow. Allman screamed in mock pain and began to chase Bob around the gas pump waving the pickled delicacy.

"Don't worry, Allman," shouted Bob with a grimace, "you'll get the ball... and no one'll touch your pretty face!"

"You're sure about that?" panted Allman as he ran after Bob.

"Yeah," panted Bob, "if I can recover from this morning!"

Bob escaped into the store to get a drink, nursing a set of tight leg muscles. Allman returned to where the others sat and flopped down beside Harry.

"That guy plays center?" asked Harry in astonishment.

"Don't let him fool you," said Matt. "He looks small but he comes at you big!"

"What's the Mr. America stuff?" asked Harry.

Allman laughed. "Porter is a real All American boy type... the King of the Squares."

"How'd he come to play center?" asked Tony curiously.

"Last year, he moved here," said Allman, gnawing at the pig foot. "His Pop is in the Navy, like yours.... he went out for halfback... but Shotgun said he was too slow and he needed a center. So... Bob was a center."

"Just like that?" asked Harry.

"Bob never gives it up, no matter how ya hit him," said Buster. "Shotgun likes that."

"We sure got a lotta fullbacks this year," said Matt, "Harry, Chip Gross and Jack Sanders."

"No one's gonna beat out Jack," said Bubba, taking a swig of his RC Cola.

Bob Porter came out of the store with three root beers. He gave one to Buster and Matt and flopped on the cement next to Harry. He looked at Harry inquisitively and extended his hand. "I'm Bob Porter," he said.

"Harry Quester," said Harry, taking the hand.

Porter's grip was firm and brief. "Your Dad's Navy?"

"Yep," said Harry.

"Good," said Bob.

"Ya know how to play fullback?" asked Buster curiously.

"Played it at my last school," said Harry. "What about you?"

Buster puffed up his chest. "I was gonna try for fullback," he said. "That's what my Old Man wants... but Shotgun shifted me to tackle."

"Why's that?" asked Harry.

"Aw, Shotgun is always pissed at me... for some damn reason," said Buster shaking his head, "... says I'm too slow!"

"Shotgun's pissed at him 'cause he looks big enough to kill anyone," said Allman, punching the air with his fist, "but he don't kill no one!"

Buster lunged at Allman with an evil grin. "Come here, Buddinger... and I'll kill you!"

Allman grabbed Buster by the arm with quick hands and delivered a Charlie horse punch to his arm. Then he jumped up and ran behind a gas pump. Buster swatted at him, but missed.

"Help! Buster's gonna kill me!"

They all laughed as Buster chased Allman around the gas pump.

"Take it easy on him, Buster," said Bubba. "He's the only quarterback we got!"

Buster grunted, returned to the group and resumed drinking his root beer. Allman came back and flopped down beside Buster.

Bob looked at Harry and appraised his solid build. "You know, you'll have to beat out the best guy we have to play fullback," he said.

"Yeah," said Matt, "a big, tough Farmer named Jack Sanders!"

"I've heard he's tough," said Harry.

"What about you, Tony?" asked Buster. "You gonna make those ten laps?"

"I'm gonna try!"

"Don't sweat it, Tony," said Harry. "I'll pace you through ten laps this evening... and get you ready for tomorrow morning."

"Okay, Harry," said Tony, already feeling the pain in his legs," if you say so."

"You can do it, Tony!" exclaimed Matt. "If I can do it, so can you!"

Bob got up and went to his car, followed by Buster and Matt. Buster leaped over the side into the passenger seat, making the Ford rock on its chassis. Matt vaulted into the back. Bob got in the conventional way and the yellow convertible pulled away with a short squeal of the rear wheels.

"See you guys this afternoon!" shouted Matt. "Don't be late... or it's more laps!"

Harry waved at Bob, Buster and Matt and finished off his drink. A 1939 dark green, chopped Chevy Coupe pulled into the store and stopped with a screech of tires. It had fender skirts on the rear tires that made the rear end look like it was almost touching the street. Arnie

Eberly climbed out of the driver seat. He had short blond hair with ducktails plastered on the sides with hair wax, a cigarette lodged above his left ear. Arnie and Bart Whitely got out of the green Chevy. Johnny Calcione followed in his 1950 Studebaker Champion Coupe. It was bright red with white wall tires and a futuristic looking bullet nose. Johnny and Carson Quinn got out. They all wore tight blue jeans with no belt and a tight white tee-shirt. The blue jeans were pegged at the cuffs. A pack of cigarettes was rolled up in their left sleeve, as though it was part of a uniform. They swaggered to where the other boys stood.

"Well well well," said Allman merrily. "The Hoods are here!"

"Up yours, Allman," said Calcione, lighting a cigarette with a flair.

"Cool it, Johnny," said Allman good naturedly, "and be a nice guy!"

"Ya hanging around with all these Squares, now, Allman?" asked Carson, a boy with a face that looked like a gangster movie.

"Yeah! What of it?"

"That ain't so cool!"

"Ever since he moved to Green Acres last year, he thinks he's a big deal," said Bart with a practiced look of superiority.

"Leave 'em alone, Carson," ordered Arnie. "Let's get some cigarettes."

"No smoking during season, Arnie," said Allman seriously.

"Sure, Allman," sneered Arnie. "I just use 'em to put behind my ear, ya know."

Carson and Johnny laughed. Bart Whitely lit a cigarette. The Hoods went into the store.

"Come on, Bubba," said Harry watching the Hoods with trepidation, "we gotta go get some lunch."

"Don't eat much," said Allman, getting up and stretching with a pronounced yawn. "We don't want you puking all over the field this afternoon!"

"Yeah," said Harry with an almost automatic retort, "and we don't want to see pickled pig's feet dribbling down your chin, Allman."

Allman glared at Harry. "You've got a lot to say… for a new guy!"

"See you on the field, Allman," said Harry with a confidence he didn't feel. "And I'll have my own lemon this time!"

"Okay, Harry Ol' Buddy," said Allman, "and don't forget… you owe me a towel!"

"On your butt, I owe you a towel!" said Harry, looking straight at Allman.

Allman glowered at him. "Ya gotta catch me first, Harry, Ol' Buddy!"

****

Slate Phelps and Cliff Braun walked past Harrel's Sporting Goods Store and Blumberg's Department Store on High Street looking for the newspaper Circulation Manager's office. They found a narrow set of stairs that led up to a dimly lit office. When they reached the top of the stairs, they went through a door with a glass window that was marked *The Virginian Pilot, Circulation Manager*. They knocked. There was no answer, so they went in cautiously. Mr. Alfonso Mays looked from pudgy eyes across a cluttered desk in his office and motioned for them to sit down. They sat in straight back wooden chairs in front of him. Cliff's face still had the bruises and cuts from his encounter with Ennis. Alfonso smoked the last of a thick Cuban cigar, spreading blue smoke around the small room. The cigar went out and he began to chew on the two inch long stub, shifting the delicacy from side to side in his mouth.

"Slate, you're in big trouble with Mr. Edwards, you know," said Alfonso in a voice that amounted to a low grumbling sound.

"I know, Sir," said Slate. "Don't worry… we'll make it up to him."

"He says that Cliff here took his milk," grumbled Mr. Mays. "Is that right?"

"I didn't take no milk," said Cliff, his eyes staring a hole in Mr. Mays. "That asshole Ennis Hathaway took the milk… and put it in Slate's Chevy."

"He says you been taking it a long time," said Mays, rubbing his bleary eyes.

"Listen, Mr. Mays," said Slate, "I took some milk a long time ago… in the summer when I was really thirsty… and I'll apologize to Mr. Edwards. I'll even pay him back. But what Cliff says is right… Ennis is trying to frame us!"

"Now why would he do that?" grumbled Mays.

"Mr. Mays," said Slate looking at him directly, "hasn't Ennis applied for our route?"

"Well, I don't know," said Mays looking out a grimy window at a gray Saturday morning sky. "I get a lot of applications, you know."

"Doesn't Ennis' father advertise in the paper?" asked Cliff angrily. "I see shit in the paper about Hathaway's Grocery Store all the time."

"There's no need to curse, Young Man," said Mays pulling out a fresh cigar and lighting it amid a plume of smelly smoke.

"Mr. Mays…did Mr. Hathaway ask you to give Ennis our route?" asked Slate.

Alfonso Mays looked uncomfortable and shifted his considerable weight in his chair which groaned under the strain. "Mr. Hathaway's business is of no concern to you two boys," he said. "What is of concern is that Mr. Edwards is going to file charges of stealing against young Cliff there… that is, if he stays on the route."

"He what?" shouted Cliff leaping up from his chair and leaning across the cluttered desk. His jaw was set and he looked like a young bulldog preparing to savor Alfonso's flesh.

"That is, of course, unless you fire Cliff from helping with your route," said Mr. Mays with a small smile on his pudgy face.

"I'd never be able to handle 150 papers alone!" said Slate, taken aback by it all.

"I'm sure other help can be arranged," said Mays getting up to signal that the interview was over, his massive stomach swaying above a straining belt.

"You ass-hole!" shouted Cliff, his face beet red. "I need that paper route!"

Mays turned abruptly and glared at Cliff. "Keep a civil tongue, young man! It's like this… you stop delivering papers or you go to jail," he said, backing away from the threatening and intense eyes of Cliff Braun.

Cliff jumped on top of the desk sending papers scattering everywhere. He stared down at Mays and shook his fist at him. "I'll rearrange your ugly face, you sonofabitch!" he shouted in a rage.

Slate grabbed Cliff by the legs and pulled him down from the desk. Cliff continued to shout and sputter expletives at Mays.

"Don't worry, Mr. Mays," said Slate in a polite voice while he tried to restrain Cliff and push him to the door. "I'll take care of it!"

"You do that!" said Mays, his face contorted with anger. "And you apologize to Mr. Edwards too!"

****

It was a dark morning with frost on the ground near Mount Vernon Avenue. Slate and Cliff got out of the Chevy at the newspaper drop-off.

"You drive this morning, Cliff," said Slate, "and if Mr. Mays shows up, keep your mouth shut!"

"Who are you to tell me to keep my mouth shut?" asked Cliff belligerently.

"Your buddy," said Slate, steam forming from his breath as he paused, "and remember to keep your mouth shut!"

Cliff grumbled to himself and began loading papers into the Chevy's trunk. "You really think he'll check up on us?" he asked.

"Maybe," said Slate. "He drives that black '33 Studebaker coupe… the real streamlined looking thing."

Cliff went to the front of the car and began to crank the starter. The

Chevy coughed into action with the usual cloud of black smoke. Cliff climbed in and jerked the car into gear. He pushed down on the throttle and the car leaped ahead, turning down Elm Avenue with a squeal from the tires as he shifted to second gear.

"Take it easy, Cliff," said Slate with concern, "I don't have the money for any repairs right now!"

"Okay, okay," muttered Cliff, shifting to high gear with a less violent motion.

They drove down High Street to the Mount Vernon pick up station. They stopped, loaded their papers into the Chevy and drove to Woodrow Avenue. They began their routine, but this time Slate ran all the papers to the door. It wasn't long before a big black Studebaker coupe made a turn onto Mount Vernon Avenue with its lights off and began following the Chevy. It parked quietly by the side of the road. Slate returned to the Chevy for a fresh batch of papers.

"Seen any sign of Mays?" asked Slate anxiously.

"Naw… I ain't seen him!" said Cliff stretching and yawning.

"Okay," said Slate. "Keep your eyes open."

"Let me run some papers," said Cliff starting to get out of the car. "Sitting here in the car is boring!"

"No," said Slate, pushing him back into the Chevy. "You drive! I'll run."

Slate ran on, delivering papers. He ran as if he were a halfback, dodging trees and bushes as though they were tacklers. He looked forward to some side lot football after school where he could really show off his stuff. Cliff followed him slowly, turning left on Bayview Boulevard and turning right onto Broad Street. He went halfway down the block toward Adriatic Street before Slate returned for more papers. Slate saw the Studebaker out of the corner of his eye as it crept toward the turn at Broad Street.

"Mays is behind us in that Studebaker," said Slate. "He hasn't made the turn yet."

"Get in," hissed Cliff. "I can lose the bastard!"

"No!" said Slate. "We can't run from Mays forever. Just stay here! Pretend like you don't see him."

"What?" exclaimed Cliff indignantly.

"Do what I say," said Slate under his breath.

Slate ran to the back of the car and took out some papers. He began running the papers to the doorsteps as if they hadn't seen the Studebaker. Suddenly the headlights of the Studebaker came on and it rolled quietly to a position blocking the Chevy. Mays rolled out of the Studebaker, one flabby lump after the other and stood erect, the tip of his cigar glowing in the frosty night. He walked slowly toward the Chevy peering into the cab where Cliff sat, exhaling smelly smoke. Slate turned from his paper deliveries and began running back to the car. The door of the Chevy burst open and Cliff stepped out, his fists balled up, his square face bristling with rage.

"Get your car out of the way, Mays," shouted Cliff, waving the smoke out of his face, "or I'll ram it and make it into junk!"

"You'll do nothing of the kind," said Alfonso Mays. "I see now that Phelps hasn't done what I asked and fired you Braun!"

Cliff stepped toward Mays, his fists cocked. "I don't have much money, Mr. Mays," he said, uncontrollable tears coming to his squinting eyes, "and I'll beat the crap out of you if you take away this paper route!"

Slate ran up to where Cliff confronted Mr. Mays, his square jaw jutting into the obese man's face. Mays backed away uneasily.

"I did do what you told me, Mr. Mays," panted Slate. "I fired Cliff! He isn't running papers anymore… he's just driving!"

Mays looked at the two of them, for the moment confused. "I see Braun standing right there!" he said in a huff. "I don't care what he's doing, he's here… which means you haven't fired him!"

"No Sir," said Slate as politely as he could. "I did fire him! He's not delivering papers… just like you asked!"

"I'm afraid I'll have to take the route from you, Slate," said Mays in a smug voice.

Cliff pushed Mays backward. Slate grabbed Cliff's arm and held it tightly.

"Let me kick in his face!" shouted Cliff, his whole being bristling with rage.

"You're not going to take away my route, Mr. Mays," said Slate in a tense voice.

"Oh?" asked Mays in an irritated voice. "And just why not?"

"Because if you do, I'll expose to the Editor of *The Virginian Pilot* the papers I have that show that Mr. Hathaway… the grocer who spends a lot of money advertising in your paper… bribed you to give the route to his son Ennis… that's why!"

Mays looked further confused. "You don't have any papers like that, Boy," he said worriedly.

"I do," said Slate, "and I have someone who saw Mr. Hathaway give you some money!"

"The hell you do!" exclaimed Mays. "Let me see these papers!"

"You'll see them after I give them to the Editor, Mr. Mays," said Slate his eyes fixed firmly on the big man.

Mays backed away from where the boys stood, wringing his hands.

Sweat stood out on his pudgy face even in the cool of the morning. "Don't do that, Slate," he said cautiously.

"Then I have the paper route?"

"I suppose so," said Mays continuing to wring his hands, "but remember… I'm watching ya!"

"Thank you, Mr. Mays," said Slate smugly.

"Now get on with delivering your papers," said Alfonso Mays in a gruff voice. "You're going to be late!"

"Yes Sir," said Slate eagerly. "We're on our way!"

Mr. Mays went back to his Studebaker coupe, folded himself into the seat, started the engine with a roar and pulled away, headed south on Mount Vernon.

"Get in the car, Cliff," said Slate. "We have a lotta papers left to deliver!"

"Do you really have all those papers and things… like you said?" asked Cliff, getting into the Chevy. "You really scared ol' Mays!"

"No," said Slate with a chortle as he climbed in the Chevy. "I don't really have any of that stuff… but I'll bet it all exists… somewhere!"

"How'd you figure out all that?" asked Cliff. "How'd you know what to say… what to do?"

"Easy," said Slate. "I heard it on that radio show…*Detective Story Hour*… there was a guy in there that did the same thing!"

"You mean the program where that guy… the Shadow… tells the story?" asked Cliff.

"That's the one," said Slate. "That Shadow guy is real neat... mysterious and all!"

"Maybe you're gonna be a detective some day," said Cliff.

"Maybe," said Slate. "But I doubt it."

"It was a neat idea," said Cliff enviously. "But it woulda been more fun to beat the crap outa ol' Mays!"

****

Chapter Three
Try-outs III

It was four fifteen on the practice field and the sun was hotter than ever. Coach Braun's face was so close to Harry's that he could see the red lines in the Coach's eyes and the veins sticking out in his thick neck.

"Alright, Kester!" shouted Braun into Harry's ear. "Let's see if you can run!"

Harry was lined up with all the halfbacks. He recognized Karl Darby. The other two he didn't know.

"A hundred yards!" shouted Braun backing away from Harry and squinting at the others. "As fast as you can go down to the goal posts!"

Harry was in a crouching two point stance as were the others. The soggy practice uniform hung on him like an odiferous weight. The smell of fresh cut grass irritated his nostrils. His nose still hurt from the blow the Coach had delivered showing him how to block. He knew it was broken, but he wasn't going to let that stop him from making the team! Beads of sweat rolled down Harry's face. He braced himself.

Coach Braun blew his whistle, his cheeks puffing out to produce a shrill blast. Harry propelled himself forward and began to run as fast as he could. He strained as he saw Karl Darby pull ahead. Then suddenly, he was at the back of the pack and the goal posts seemed far away. He reached down into his gut for more energy, found a small pool of reserve and ran faster. His lungs were burning and he felt the muscles in his thighs tightening. His eyes burned as sweat rolled into them. He charged past the goal posts with only one boy behind him. He was at least five yards behind Karl.

Karl Darby walked over to him, his hands on his hips, taking great gulps of air, "Harry Quester... right?" panted Karl.

"I'm Harry," panted Harry wanting to kneel to catch his wind but not daring to as he heard Braun's whistle sounding loudly behind him.

"Not bad," said Karl squinting one eye, a slight, knowing smile on his face. "Just hang in there!"

"Thanks," wheezed Harry.

"Alright... alright!" shouted Coach Braun hoarsely. "Don't stand around like a buncha ladies at a tea party! Get lined up! We're going back!"

Oh no, thought Harry. He wasn't sure he could make it back. He jogged toward the goal line, taking a half lemon from his trousers and sucking on it. It was sour and tasted like sweat, but it was liquid... and there was some sugar in it. He put the lemon back into his trousers and got down into the crouching two point stance of a halfback. He gazed down the field at the distant set of goal posts and willed himself to run the distance.

Shotgun's whistle sounded and they were off again. Harry was painfully aware of each leg as it surged forward, of each foot as it struck the ground. But he seemed to be floating above them, his will moving the legs without directions from his mind. He felt the sweat bursting out of his scalp and running down his face, but it didn't distract him from the two white goal posts ahead of him. His whole being seemed to be encapsulated between the two sets of goal posts; his whole life being expended through a rapid transit between them. He saw Karl surge ahead again. He threw back his head and ran with every ounce of strength and energy he had. They crossed the goal line and Harry stumbled to the goal post, hanging on to it. His head was whirling and he saw Shotgun run up to him and stick his face close to his.

"Not good enough, Kester!" shouted Coach Braun. "Let's see how you do with the fullbacks!"

"Okay, Coach," wheezed Harry.

"You holding that goal post up, Kester?" shouted Braun waving his arms in the air in exasperation.

"No Sir," panted Harry turning loose of the goal post as though it were a hot branding iron.

"Get down at that line then," shouted the Coach, "and stop pussy-footing around!"

Harry jogged painfully to the goal line, taking a quick suck at the lemon. Jack Sanders stood there, a look of disdain on his face. Jack was an impressive figure. He was six feet tall and easily weighed in at 190 pounds. Harry was slightly taller but lacked the massive shoulders and legs of Jack. Jack had a square, rough looking face and a broad nose that looked as though it had been broken before. Chip Gross, a tough looking but smaller boy who lived in Churchland Village near Bubba stood beside Jack, his hands on his hips.

"You think you can play fullback, New Guy?" asked Jack in a rough, deep voice that sounded fresh and not winded.

"I've played it before," wheezed Harry.

"Don't worry about the nose," said Jack, examining Harry's face. "He broke mine last year."

"It'll be okay."

"Let's see what you can do!" said Sanders getting down into a crouched two point stance, his massive arms resting easily on his thighs.

"Get ready," shouted Coach Braun. He blew the whistle loudly.

The three boys launched themselves forward. Harry felt his legs moving as though they were under automatic control. The pain in his thighs had become his normal condition now, and he accepted it. He adjusted his breathing to his pace, pushing air in and out of his lungs rapidly to move the oxygen as fast as possible into his blood stream. He passed midfield and was amazed to find Jack next to him almost shoulder to shoulder.

"Is that all ya got?" panted Jack, glancing at Harry.

"There's more!" panted Harry.

"Let's see it!" shouted Jack, picking up the pace and moving slightly ahead of Harry.

Harry's body had reached its limits. He reached down into his soul and found a few more drops of energy. He accelerated and crossed the goal line a pace behind Sanders. Jack walked up and down behind the goal posts, his hands on his hips. Harry leaned over and grasped his knees trying to catch his breath.

"Well, you can run, New Guy," panted Jack, "but can you hit?"

Harry started to answer but was interrupted by Coach Braun's whistle.

"You gonna let that Navy kid outrun you, Sanders?" asked Braun in a condescending voice.

"He ain't got it, Coach!" said Sanders with a growl.

"Okay, get down," shouted Shotgun. "We're going back… and we'll see what he's got!"

Harry walked numbly to the goal line and crouched painfully. His head was spinning again and he felt weak in the pit of his stomach. He was suddenly aware of the bright sun that sent its rays down to torment him. Jack lined up beside him. Chip lined up next to Jack, panting heavily.

"You don't look so good, New Guy," murmured Chip. "You sure you want to run?"

"Whatever it takes," said Harry weakly, his face white and covered with sweat.

Coach Braun's whistle blew loudly and Harry lurched forward. For a moment he felt as though he was falling, but he grabbed at air and regained his balance. Jack was already three paces ahead of him and running fast. Harry pushed forward, passing Chip and catching up to a pace behind Jack. He shifted his eyes to the forest that surrounded the practice field and imagined himself soaring above it like a hawk, his wings pushing the air gently downward, flying with the wind. As he soared, his legs functioned, though he wasn't fully aware of what they were doing. His head felt light and hot… very hot. He crossed the goal line several paces behind Jack, the field whirling around his head. He pulled up to a stop and tried to kneel. Instead he fell over on his side, the practice field whirling hotly around him. For a moment, the world was black. Harry's eyes snapped open to see Coach Phelps looking at him with concern. He took off Harry's helmet and rolled him onto his back. Slate Phelps grabbed a water bucket and threw some water on Harry's head. Harry sputtered and sat up, holding his aching head.

"What ya doing, Slate?" asked Shotgun, his eyes wide.

"This kid's gonna go into heat stroke if we're not careful," said Slate, alarm in his voice.

"Water is for sissies," muttered Braun. He turned his back on Harry and Slate and stalked away. He blew his whistle loudly, his cheeks puffing out with the effort. "Okay! All you guys... get over there on the bleachers!" He pointed to a small set of bleachers with five rows of seats sitting next to the practice field. Harry got to his feet and stood unsteadily and took some of the water Coach Phelps offered him into his mouth.

"Are you alright, Harry?" asked Slate, looking at Harry's white face. "You'd better sit down again until you feel better. "

"I'm okay, Sir," said Harry trying to sound as if it were so, spitting the water out in a spray.

"Are you sure?" asked Slate wrinkling his brow and lifting an eyebrow.

Harry started to jog toward the bleachers. "I'm hanging in there, Coach." His feet felt heavy as he ran. He made it to the bleachers in time to contain his whirling head.

"Now listen up!" said Coach Braun in a loud, raspy voice. "I've pushed you guys pretty hard today. There's a reason for that! The reason we win games is 'cause when the Truckers take the field, we're better prepared! We're in better shape! We're physically tougher! We're mentally tougher! When we go out there on that... darn field, we go out there to take the other guys apart... and score points!"

The Coach paused and glared at the players with intense eyes, removing the pork pie hat and wiping his brow with the back of his hand. He jammed the hat back onto his head. "Now I expect you guys to stay in shape... no smoking... no drinking... eat right... and stay away from too much a' them girlies! Stay away from that little den of in-iq-ui-ty over there in Simonsdale... that Teenage Place!"

There was a snicker from the players. Braun glared at them. "Think it's funny, huh? Y'all won't think it's so funny when I run ya 'roun the field 'til ya drop!"

"We'll be good, Coach!" said Allman with a mock serious expression on his flat face. "Don't worry!"

"The only darn time football is fun is when you win!" shouted the

Coach. "It ain't any fun at all… to lose. We won't lose! We have a tough schedule against nine good teams this year. We'll beat 'em all! All of 'em! I don't care how good they are… if you're in better shape… and you're meaner, a lot meaner… and you want it more… you'll win the game. All of 'em! Anyone who don't believe that… who don't want that… who ain't willing to go through the hurtin' to get tough… well, you just leave now and don't come back in the morning!"

Coach Braun blew his whistle and the Truckers clambered down from the bleachers and ran back to the gymnasium door as cicadas rattled in the trees and the sun sank to treetop level.

****

That night, Harry, Bubba and Tony came back to the stadium field.
"How'd you get the key, Bubba?" asked Tony.
"I bribed the team manager… Larry Kidwell… for fifty cents," said Bubba. "I've known the kid all his life… lives out there near me on the road to Suffolk… and he owes me."
Bubba unlocked the chain link fence and they walked in. The field was dark as they walked out to the nearest goal post. It was still sticky hot, even at ten o'clock. They all wore shorts, tee-shirts and tennis shoes. Harry had contrived a backpack that he strapped on Tony.
"How's the nose?" asked Bubba.
"It's okay," said Harry trying to dismiss the topic.
"Let me put in back in place for ya!" said Bubba with a grin.
"Naw… it's not broken."
"The heck it ain't," said Bubba. "Now hold still a minute!"
"Wait a minute!" exclaimed Harry. "You can't even see my nose out here!"
"Yeah I can!" exclaimed Bubba.
Bubba grabbed Harry's nose between two thick fingers.
"Wait a minute!" said Harry defensively.
"Damn it, hold still, Cuz!" Bubba jiggled the nose gently and with a quick motion, snapped it back into place.
"Ow!" shouted Harry, tears coming to his eyes. "That hurt!"
"Now you look cool for that date I'm gonna get ya with Janet!"
Harry felt his nose. It was in the center of his face and felt better. "Where'd you learn to do that?" he asked.
Bubba laughed heartily. "Remember, I've been the water boy, the manager and everything for this team… including the first aid guy," said Bubba. "I've put all of Shotgun's broken noses back in place… including Jack Sanders' nose… last year!"

"He broke Sanders nose?"

"Yeah," said Bubba, "and Calcione's arm… Bart took Calcione's job away while he bitched about his arm!"

"What about Sanders?"

"He just ignored his nose and played ball."

"I'll be damned," said Harry.

"Shotgun thought he broke Norwood's shoulder last year," said Bubba. "Showing him how to block… like he did you."

"Was it broken?" asked Harry.

"Naw," said Bubba, "just a big bruise… but ya should've heard Benny whine about it!"

"I already heard Benny whine," said Harry.

"What're ya gonna do about the nose?" asked Bubba.

"Ignore it and play ball," said Harry determinedly.

"That's what I figured," grinned Bubba.

"Tony… you still feel sick?" asked Harry.

"Naw, I'm okay," said Tony. "I think I sweated whatever it was outa me this morning!"

"Okay," said Harry. "Good!"

"This pack is heavy," moaned Tony.

"That's the idea, Little Brother" said Harry. "You gotta get used to hauling a heavy uniform and pads."

"You guys don't have to do this," said Tony. "I think I can make it tomorrow."

"Confidence is what you need, Tony," said Harry. "You gotta know that you're gonna make it."

"You pace him for five laps," said Bubba, "then I'll do it."

"You sure?" asked Harry.

"Yeah," said Bubba. "I had a hard time making it this morning… I need some of that confidence stuff myself!"

"Okay," said Harry. "Come on, Little Brother…. one lap at a time!"

The three boys jogged onto the track.

****

The next day, the sun was low in the morning sky but already hot for morning practice. The dew on the grass had begun to evaporate making the practice field into a steamy sauna. Coach Braun's whistle blew and the Truckers started the morning laps.

"Stick with me, Tony," said Harry as they started out.

"I will," said Tony. "I made it last night… I'll make it today!"

Harry and Tony ran together, each sucking on a lemon to keep moisture in their mouths and energy in their bodies. At the end of six laps, Harry was beginning to feel the effects of the hard practice from the day before and the laps with Tony the previous night. They began to lag toward the back of the pack.

"What's wrong with you, Kester?" shouted Coach Braun running up beside them. He took the crumpled hat from his head and beat it against his thigh. "Pick up the pace... pick up the pace! I wanna see you up front... not way back here! I know you can run! You're screwing off back here... aren't you? Huh? Huh?"

"I can run, Coach," said Harry, trying to catch a second wind.

Coach Braun beat the hat up again and it fell from his hand to the ground. Harry paused and scooped it up. He handed it back to the Coach.

"Don't beat your hat up on account of me, Coach," said Harry with a mischievous grin.

Shotgun grabbed the hat away from Harry. His face held a heavy scowl. "Think you're pretty cute, huh, Kester," shouted Shotgun viciously. "Get your butt up to the front of the pack... move it out!"

"Okay, Coach," gasped Harry. He signaled his sore legs to move faster, and surprisingly, they did. He waved at Tony who also increased speed but couldn't keep up with Harry. Harry ran on with Shotgun matching him pace for pace. With a final burst of speed, he caught up to Karl Darby and ran just behind him.

"Don't ya screw off no more, Kester!" shouted Braun. "I got my eye on ya! Ya hear?"

"I got it, Coach," said Harry softly.

"What?" screamed Coach Braun.

"I got it, Coach!" screamed Harry.

"That's better!" shouted the Coach. "And I better hear it the first time loud and clear! Ya understand?"

"Yes Sir!" screamed Harry, feeling like an idiot as all the players snickered.

"Don't let him get to ya, Harry," whispered Burt Noonan, running next to Harry. Burt was a farm boy with sleepy eyes and a quiet, easy going manner. He played guard on the second string.

"I won't," panted Harry.

"You're doing okay," said Burt. "The guys want ya to make the team."

Harry looked at Burt and nodded, encouraged to hear support. "Thanks, Burt!"

Shotgun fell back and began shouting at the boys in the back.

"Come on, Bubba!" shouted Shotgun from the rear of the pack.

"Move your big butt! Move it!"

"Don't wise-ass the Coach, Harry," panted Allman as he ran up beside Harry.

"There has to be a sense of humor buried in there somewhere," panted Harry.

"If there is, it doesn't come out much," said Karl turning his head and looking at Harry and Allman curiously.

"What's this?" shouted Shotgun running up beside them. "Some kind of a tea party? A debating society? A love fest? Run fast and think mean! Think mean!"

"I'm thinking mean, Coach," shouted Harry between gasps.

"Oh, you are?" said Shotgun, his brow wrinkled into a furrowed mass. "Maybe you'd like to run twelve laps today?"

"Oh... he'd like that Coach!" said Allman jubilantly.

"Okay, Truckers," screamed the Coach, "we got a new guy here who wants to run twelve laps... so twelve laps it is!"

There was a universal groan from the running, sweating pack of boys.

"Thanks a lot, Allman, you bastard," panted Harry.

"Think nothin' of it, Harry Ol' Buddy!"

They ran on. Harry looked back and was thankful to see both Tony and Bubba finishing the twelve laps at the back of the pack. Harry knelt and removed his helmet, exhausted in the hot sun.

****

Five players were lined up in front of Harry and Jack Sanders. One of them was Bob Porter. Another of them was the biggest guy Harry had ever seen. He knew the big guy was Jim Jensen... Big Jim... there was no other name for him. He was at least six feet four inches tall and weighed upwards of two hundred and twenty pounds without an ounce of fat. He had a long, thin face that seemed to never smile and unruly black hair. He was from a farm outside of Churchland in Jolliff where he was used to hefting fifty pound sacks of soy beans as if they were toys. Big Jim had a reputation for being a tough guy, a farmer no one wanted to confront. Harry and Jack Sanders stood side by side, each holding footballs, staring at Big Jim Jensen.

"Stay away from Big Jim if you can," muttered Jack under his breath. "He's a nice guy... but he'll put the hurt on ya!"

"Thanks, Jack," said Harry. If Jack was worried about Big Jim, then he was worth worrying about. "I'll try to pick the right hole."

"Run at Buster," said Jack. "He's big... but not as tough as Jim!"

Coach Braun came jogging up to where they stood. "We're gonna take turns running through that line up there," shouted Braun eagerly. "And I wanna see some real hitting!"

Harry glanced to the other end of the field and saw Coach Phelps running the same drill with the halfbacks. Coach Fearless was on the side of the field with Allman throwing wobbly passes to the ends. Allman had it made, thought Harry... all he did was hand off the ball and throw passes... pretty plush job.

"You first, Sanders," said the Coach. "I wanna see if ya still got it this year!"

"I'm ready, Coach."

"How much tape ya got on today?" asked Coach Braun with the hint of a smile.

"Just enough to hold me together, Coach," said Jack without a smile.

Jack held the ball firmly cradled in his right arm, paused, snorted... and charged full speed straight at the line. He lowered his shoulder and butted Buster Stanley head on, knocking him backward.

"Awwww Buster!" shouted Braun. "Ya missed the tackle!"

Buster fell down and the other three boys closed in on Jack. Jack dragged them for a few yards and then Big Jim hit them all. They fell into a pile about eight yards behind the initial line.

"Not a first down, Sanders!" shouted Coach Braun angrily. "You gotta be able to make a first down or a touchdown on every play... and I mean every... darn play!"

Jack came trotting back to where Harry stood waiting.

"Buster! What the heck!" shouted Braun. "When are ya gonna get that two hundred and a lot more pounds going? Huh?"

Buster shook his head and didn't say anything. Braun ran over to him and gave him a hard shove. Buster stumbled backward and sat heavily on the ground. A snicker came from the players.

"When a back comes at ya low like that," shouted Braun, "ya gotta get lower... stand him up with a shot to the pads and then bust him in the legs to knock him down!"

"Okay, Coach," mumbled Buster, getting to his feet, looking embarrassed.

Coach Braun kicked at the grass disgustedly. "Ya need to get a lot meaner this year, Buster... ya hear?"

"Okay Coach," said Buster looking at the ground.

Coach Braun kicked hard at the grass again. Everyone knew the grass was a surrogate for Buster's butt.

"Okay, Kester," said Braun, turning to Harry with a savage look on his face. "Let's see what ya can do!"

Harry thought about how to get mean. He glared at the line. He imagined them as people who had tried to mess with his girl friend, if he had one, which he didn't. He worked up his rage, tucked the ball under his right arm and charged. He lowered his shoulder, but Porter came in lower and hit Harry's thighs with a jarring blow. He wrapped his arms around Harry's legs and there was nowhere to go except down. Harry picked himself up and looked at Bob with new admiration. Bob shook his head as if to shake away the fuzz.

"Nice hit, Harry," said Bob, shaking his head. "You rung my bell!"

"Nice tackle," said Harry. "I wasn't planning to go down!"

"What's this?" shouted Shotgun. "Some kinda love fest? A mu-tu-al admiration so-ci-e-ty? Get your butt back here, Kester! You let Porter take you down like that? He ain't big enough to be in the... darn band... and you let him take you down like that?"

Coach Braun grabbed the football from Harry, twirled it and jammed it back into Harry's belly so hard Harry had to strain to get his breath back. "Now go at Big Jim there, Kester," shouted Braun in Harry's ear. The raspy voice seemed to echo inside his helmet.

Harry glanced at Big Jim Jensen. He stood there stoically glaring at Harry, his arms hanging loosely at his side. Harry put the ball under his arm and charged at Big Jim. Big Jim crouched, his arms extended in front of him. Harry ran low in a wide stance, lowered his shoulder and felt Jim's hands hit his shoulder pads. He pushed through and hit the big man in the belly. Big Jim staggered back a few yards and then grabbed Harry by the shoulders and lifted him off the ground. He slammed Harry to the ground and Harry saw stars. He felt all the wind leave his lungs and he laid there, momentarily stunned. Big Jim glared down at him. He nodded silently at Harry and extended a big hand. Harry took the hand and Big Jim yanked him to his feet.

"Thanks," mumbled Harry through his pain.

Big Jim snorted and nodded. Harry jogged painfully back to where Coach Braun and Jack Sanders stood.

"You looked like some kinda poet skipping though the daisies out there, Kester!" shouted Coach Braun. "You wanna recite some poetry for us... instead of playing football?"

Harry didn't say anything. He looked at Coach Braun and smiled.

"Don't you smile at me, Kester!" shouted Braun furrowing his brow.

Harry erased the smile. He replaced it with a determined scowl.

"Didn't I tell you to be tough... to be mean?" asked Braun. "How many times I gotta say that to ya? Ya thick between the ears or somethin'? Let's see ya run again!"

Harry picked up a ball and charged again at the line. He tried to run over Bucky Allison, but the lineman got a grip on his legs and brought him down.

"That's all for you, Poet!" said Bucky with a savage grin on his rugged face. "You can't run on me."

Harry got up and pulled Bucky up. "I'll find a way," he said, an edge in his voice, "and don't call me Poet!"

Harry jogged back to where Coach Braun was standing with his hands on his hips and a disgusted look on his face.

"That time you looked like a ... like a cotton pickin' lame horse pulling a milk and cream wagon!" shouted Shotgun. "You're not out there to make cream puffs! Ya gotta run at full speed all the time! Ya gotta get that momentum... that stuff that makes a guy's eye's open wide when ya hit 'em! You understand that Kester? Do Ya? Do Ya?"

"Yes Sir," said Harry painfully. He grimaced and fell in behind Jack.

"Go at it, Sanders," shouted Braun disgustedly.

Jack charged at the line, meeting Bob Porter head on. He bounced off of Bob before he could get his arms around him and plowed through the other boys in the line with ease.

"Touchdown!" shouted Sanders, throwing his arms into the air. He turned and ran back to the line.

"Karl! You and Terry get over here," shouted the Coach.

Karl Darby and Terry Moddy jogged over. Terry was the first string left halfback. He was a compactly built boy the same size as Darby, maybe 150 pounds. He was from a family in Jolliff, a farm boy.

"Get out there," said Braun, his face in a bulldog expression. "Let's see what you two can do against Sanders and Kester in the open field."

"Sir, it's Quester... Harry Quester," said Harry impatiently.

Coach Braun looked at Harry with an annoyed look on his face. "Okay, Kester... whatever the heck ya name is... let's see ya get by Darby and Moddy." He blew the whistle with extra ferocity.

Harry grasped a ball tightly and started running straight toward Terry Moddy. Harry ran as though he were going to run over Moddy. He saw Moddy backing down, looking for a way to hit Harry without hurting himself. Harry faked right and went left at the last moment. Moddy grasped for him and missed. Harry ran on. He looked back and saw Sanders running toward Darby.

Jack ran diagonally left and then right. Darby had fast feet and he adjusted to the move quickly. He avoided Jack's frontal momentum and tackled him from the side, wrapping his arms around the big boy's legs, bringing him crashing to the grass. Harry jogged back to position.

"Sanders!" shouted Coach Braun waving his hat in the hot, humid air. "You're running like a pig in a field a' gooshy crap! Lift them legs high... keep 'em movin' and don't let any back bring ya down like that!"

"Okay Coach," said Jack, embarrassed. "It won't happen again."

"And Moddy! Are you sick again?" shouted the Coach in a disgusted voice. 'That was a sick... a real sick attempt at a tackle!"

"Yeah Coach," said Terry with a little moan, "I been a little sick... but I'm okay now!"

Coach Braun shook his head in disgust. "Ya better get well in a hurry... ol' Hero there is chomping at the bit!"

The Coach pointed to Johnny Current, better known as "Hero" for his theatrics after any score or long run. Johnny, a short, compact halfback with dark hair and a swarthy complexion, smiled and puffed up his chest.

"I'm ready, Coach!" said Hero with a flourish, running in place and pumping his arms vigorously to demonstrate his readiness.

"Cool it, Hero," said Terry irritably. "There ain't no one in the stands to see the show... yet!"

Hero just smiled and strutted around pumping his arms.

"Come on this way, Quester," shouted Darby in a polite but threatening voice. "You won't sucker me like you did Terry!"

"Get on with it, Kester!" shouted the Coach.

Harry stared at Darby, assessing the best way to go at him. Karl was too fast and too quick to fall for the juke he had used on Terry. He ran at full speed toward Darby and then took a thirty degree angle to the left of the halfback's position. He shifted nimbly to the right, causing Karl to change direction and run at him at full speed. Harry saw the relative motion between himself and Darby clearly in his mind and at the last moment, he stopped and allowed Karl to fly by him grabbing at air. Then he jogged to the left, ran on and turned, raising the ball high in the air.

"Touchdown!" shouted Harry, feeling the energy flow back into him.

Harry jogged back toward the line feeling more confidence.

"I won't fall for that one again," said Karl with a wry smile as he jogged by.

"Good," said Harry good naturedly, "then I'll get to hit you, Karl... and you won't like that either!"

"You're a right cocky kinda guy, aren't you?" asked Karl, an inquisitive look on his face.

"No," said Harry with a tired smile, "I'm just trying to keep up with you guys, Karl... that's all."

"Get on back here, Kester," shouted the Coach. "Ya were lucky that time! I wanna see ya do that again!"

****

It was the last day of the first week of summer practice. Harry and Tony sat on the long wooden bench next to the lockers in the gymnasium locker room in their street clothes. They still felt flushed from practice, even after the hot shower. The Team Manager, Larry Kidwell, came to where they sat.

"These are for you guys," said Larry with a boyish grin.

Larry handed Harry and Tony each a fresh, new practice jersey, eyeing them enviously. Harry unfolded his. The black number thirty-two stared at him from the jersey.

"What number did you get?" asked Harry.

"I got thirty-nine," said Tony staring at the jersey. "I didn't think I could do it... but I did, thanks to you and Bubba."

"You're a tough guy, Tony...you did it on your own!" said Harry. "All we did was give you..."

"I know... that confidence stuff!" grinned Tony.

"You need these things too," said Larry handing them two black three ring binders. "They're the play books. Coach says to learn your assignments, 'cause we're gonna start scrimmaging soon."

Harry and Tony took the black binders and thumbed through them.

"And don't lose 'em," said Larry, "'cause I got you signed out for 'em! And don't take 'em home. Lock 'em in your locker. Shotgun'll blow his mind if he thinks anyone has seen these things except the team!"

"There's not a lotta plays," said Harry, thumbing through the book, "not like I had in Northern Virginia."

"I guess they do the job," observed Tony.

Bubba Hawkins came up to them wearing yellow football trousers and a dirty practice shirt bearing the number twenty-six. "Congratulations, guys," he said. "We all made it!"

"Thanks, Bubba," said Tony. "Thanks for helping me."

"I didn't do nothing," said Bubba. "You guys better get dressed or you'll be late for practice."

"You're right," said Harry, standing and pulling off his slacks.

Harry and Tony undressed and donned their football practice gear. They jogged out the door of the gymnasium and to the practice field. Harry felt a strange warmness in his crotch. He ignored it and joined the other boys lining up for calisthenics. Tony fell in to the right of him.

"Okay, guys," shouted Allman Buddinger who stood apart from the others. "Jumping jacks!"

Allman began to do jumping jacks and the others followed his lead.

"Harry," said Tony painfully. "Something's wrong... my balls are on fire!"

"I know," grimaced Harry, "me too."

"Sonofabitch!" exclaimed Tony. "I gotta get outa this jock strap!"

"Don't make a sound," muttered Harry, feeling his testicles burning intensely. "Someone put analgesic balm in our jocks!"

"Who would do that?" asked Tony out of the side of his mouth, tears of pain combining with the sweat rolling off his brow. "We should've smelled the stuff!"

"We'd never smell it over all that dried sweat," said Harry, gritting his teeth, "but we don't want 'em to have their laugh!"

"I'm not laughing," muttered Tony.

"Just cool it… jump hard and the sweat will clear it," said Harry.

"You hope!" said Tony jumping harder and faster.

Harry reached down the front of his football trousers and pulled the offending jock strap down to his legs and away from his genitals. It brought some relief but not much.

"What's the matter, Quester?" asked Arnie who was exercising to Harry's left. He laughed a sneering laugh. "Got your jock on too tight? Or maybe ya ain't got no balls… and don't need no jock!"

"He don't need one," said Bart with a grumbling voice.

Harry ignored Arnie. He didn't like the boy too much anyway… or the gang of guys he ran around with.

"Got a little itch, Quester?" asked Arnie with a sneer.

"Shut up, Arnie," said Harry irritably.

Arnie laughed, a hollow emotionless sound. "Eat me, Quester, ya square sonofabitch!!"

There was an explosion of laughter from the whole team as Benny Norwood burst suddenly from the ranks of the exercisers and ran in seeming panic toward the gymnasium.

"Come back here, Benny!" shouted Allman, restraining an explosion of laughter. He looked at Harry and winked.

The pain in Harry's groin was now of epic proportions. He laughed with the team as tears ran from his eyes. "Laugh, Tony… laugh!" he said.

"I'm laughing… I'm crying!" said Tony under his breath as he jumped and laughed.

"It's that damn Allman," said Harry between his teeth. "We'll get him back later. Just keep laughing!"

Harry saw Coach Fearless running after Benny Norwood. Coach Phelps looked at Harry and Tony curiously. They kept laughing.

"Okay!" shouted Allman. "Thirty push-ups… hit it!"

Allman fell to the ground and began doing the push-ups. Harry did the same, feeling uncomfortable with his jock down around his hips. He survived through the rest of the exercises and adjusted the jock to its proper position. They began the usual ten laps. Harry was beginning to feel better. He ran up beside Allman.

"It's gonna be tough, Allman," said Harry in an even voice.

"What do ya mean, Harry, Ol' Buddy?" asked Allman wrinkling his snub nose.

"It's gonna be tough waiting to see when I get you back for that, you clown!" said Harry, venom in his voice.

Allman gave Harry the usual big toothy grin. "Harry, Ol' Buddy, I don't know what ya mean!"

"Yeah you do," said Harry with his lopsided grin splitting his face. "And I'm not your Ol' Buddy!"

****

It was the first year for Slate Phelps and Cliff Braun at Wilson High School. They walked together onto the football practice field clad in yellow football trousers and white jerseys with full pads. They held brown leather football helmets in their hands. It was the first day of summer practice to try out for the Woodrow Wilson Presidents' football team. The sun was warm over their heads, even at seven forty-five in the morning.

"Look out there," said Slate with a grimace, "it's your friend Ennis Hathaway."

Cliff growled like a tiger. "That big fat sonofabitch ain't no friend a' mine!"

"You'd better find a way to get along," said Slate. "He's a senior… and is probably going to be first string tackle this year."

"He's too chicken-shit to be first string," said Cliff, his temper rising.

"Maybe," said Slate, "but he's big."

"Yeah?" said Cliff. "Well… I'm a lot bigger than I was last year."

"I know," said Slate, "all hundred and fifty pounds of you! Just take it easy, will ya?"

Cliff grumbled to himself. "You ain't no bigger."

"We may have to give up the paper route to play football, you know," said Slate.

"Not a good time to do that," said Cliff dejectedly. "My Old Man just got laid off at Southern Railway."

"You're kidding!" exclaimed Slate. "After all that time…"

"I'm not kidding," said Cliff, "and boy is the Old Lady pissed!"

"What's your Father going to do?" asked Slate.

Cliff paused and looked around.

"He's got a job protecting the Hathaway Grocery Store around the corner from my house," said Cliff, embarrassed. "People been breaking in and taking bread and rolls and stuff, but don't tell nobody that!"

"I'll be darn!" exclaimed Slate. "Folks say Ennis Hathaway Senior does more than run a store, ya know."

"I know," said Cliff.

"They say he runs bookies on the games... high school, college and professional."

"He probably does," said Cliff. "I know some guys who bet... but they won't say anything about Ol' Man Hathaway."

"I don't know if it's too good to work for Big Ennis."

"Yeah... yeah... I know... but ya gotta eat! Dad sits on the porch of the store with a shotgun," said Cliff. "Big Ennis calls him his 'Shotgun'."

"Has he caught anybody?" asked Slate.

"Naw, but he fired the shotgun a few times to scare people off," said Cliff. "Big Ennis Hathaway says he'll take care of him and let us run a free grocery bill at the store as long as the store don't get robbed."

"I'm sorry, Cliff," said Slate.

"It's okay, Slate," said Cliff, showing some of the emotion bottled up in him. "I can handle it. The Old Man can handle it. I just hope someone don't shoot him. That would really piss the Old Lady off!"

"He'll get another job," said Slate reassuringly.

"He says he will," said Cliff hopefully.

Slate looked at Cliff, not knowing what to say. They saw a big bear of a man with a determined face yelling at a bunch of boys ahead of them. His skull looked like a block of granite from which emitted a string of expletives and roars. He wore white shorts, a blue tee-shirt with the word "Coach" on the chest, and a beat up old orange ball cap.

"Who's that guy?" asked Cliff watching him closely.

"It's Archie Ismail," said Slate. "He's the Assistant Coach... they say he's mean as sin!"

"I can handle him," said Cliff determinedly. "I can handle him!"

"You know, we really need to make the team," said Slate. "If we're good, maybe we can get a scholarship to play football in college... that way we won't ever have to worry about money... or protecting stores for the likes of Big Ennis."

"I ain't never going to college," said Cliff. "You got the grades... not me. And I don't like school and all them fancy pants teachers trying to tell ya what to do."

"You two!" shouted Coach Archie Ismail in a hoarse, gruff voice. "Get over here!"

****

Chapter Four
Summer Practice I

The Saturday in August was unusually cool for the late afternoon. The white fourteen foot power boat with a red racing streak maneuvered slowly in the Western Branch of the Elizabeth River in front of Harry's house. The Quester home sat on a hill overlooking the river near a small inlet where herons and geese congregated. Commander Isaac Quester bought the boat only the week before. Harry sat in the bow seat in a dark blue bathing suit, his chest bare except for a few tufts of brown hair between his well developed pectoral muscles. He held the steering wheel of the boat tightly. He looked behind the boat as Tony lifted his water skis from the water and nodded his head. Harry goosed the throttle and felt the hull rise onto a plane and pull Tony up behind the boat. He looked back past where Bubba sat and saw Tony skipping across the placid water, waving and smiling, his black hair blowing in the breeze.

"Hey!" shouted Bubba. "This boat is real cool!"

They passed Chandler Point and started toward Stern's Creek. Harry looked at the tall pines rising above Chandler Point. Standing beneath the pines was a tall girl with a long brown pony tail. He stared at her. Her face was perfectly shaped and smooth with large brown eyes and full, red lips. She had on a skirt that fit her tightly, showing the shape of her rounded hips. She wore a short sleeve, pale green cashmere sweater befitting the cool afternoon. Their eyes met briefly. He stared at her as she turned away bashfully and walked up the shore toward the Chandler House.

"Watch it!" shouted Bubba grabbing the wheel and pulling the boat to port.

The boat jerked to port with a flash of spray. Harry snapped out of his trance and looked ahead and to the right.

"You almost ran over that crab pot!" shouted Bubba. "We'd have been out here for an hour changing the shear pin on the motor."

"Yeah... okay," shouted Harry over the roar of the engine. "Who was that?"

"Who?" shouted Bubba.

"That girl on the shore watching us!" shouted Harry.

"Where?"

"Over there," shouted Harry nodding at Chandler Point which was now behind them to starboard.

"I didn't see any girl," said Bubba.

"Come on, Bubba," shouted Harry. "You didn't see that girl standing over there? Who is she?"

"I hear some girl moved over here from Suffolk," said Bubba. "She's related to the Chandlers... must have been her."

"What's her name?"

"It's a funny name," shouted Bubba, "Paige... I think that's it. Paige Garnette!"

"She's good looking!" emoted Harry. "Know anything about her?"

"She's a senior," said Bubba. "And I've heard she goes with that hot shit halfback out at Suffolk... Duane Starr."

"Really?" asked Harry, disappointment in his voice.

"Yeah," said Bubba. "Forget it, Harry... people say she's real cold and snooty anyway... up in the rarified air for you and me!"

There was a shout from behind them and Harry felt the boat leap ahead in the water. They looked back and saw Tony's head surfacing in the wake, the tow rope skipping along behind them. Harry turned the boat to port and made a big loop to go back and retrieve Tony. He kept glancing at Chandler Point but the girl was nowhere to be seen. The boat pulled up beside Tony. Tony clambered over the side, his long, lean body glistening with the salty water. He shivered and Bubba handed him a towel.

"Hey! That was great!" exclaimed Tony. "Almost makes you forget the aching muscles from summer practice."

"Okay... my turn," said Bubba.

Bubba jumped from the boat causing it to rock violently. He folded into cannonball position, entering the water with a giant splash that sprayed Harry and Tony in the boat.

"Thanks for that!" shouted Harry as Bubba surfaced in the green water.

"Think nothing of it," said Bubba with a mock polite smile.

"I'm not sure this motor will pull all that flesh out of the water, Bubba," shouted Harry with a chuckle.

"Sure it can!" shouted Bubba swimming until he found the skis and the tow rope. Bubba's head disappeared under water while he pulled on the skis. Harry moved the boat forward until the tow line was straightened out. He looked back at Bubba who gave him a thumbs up signal. Harry goosed the throttle all the way forward. The boat leaped ahead and then paused as if suddenly sensing the weight of Bubba behind it, pushing up fountains of white water with his two skis. The engine groaned and strained, the boat's bow high in the air.

"Come up here in the bow, Tony," shouted Harry as he leaned as far forward as he could.

Tony climbed over the midships seat and joined Harry in the bow seat. The bow came down and the boat leaped ahead, settling out on plane.

"Yeehah!" came the scream from behind them. They turned to see Bubba plowing along through the water, throwing up his own wake.

Harry cruised by Chandler Point again. He stared through the pine trees hoping to catch another glimpse of the mysterious girl whose name was Paige Garnette. She wasn't there.

****

The blocking sled sat like a wheeless chariot on the hot grass of the practice field. It was silver colored with big metal arms extending to support two foot long plates upon which were lashed pads covered with canvas. The backs and ends were grouped around the sled, helmets in hand. Coach Braun mounted the sled like a warrior preparing himself for battle, his porkpie hat set firmly on his head.

"Alright, you guys!" shouted Coach Braun. "Today we're gonna knock the heck outa this sled... and no pussyfooting around!"

Coach Braun looked at the panting boys as the hot sun rose in the sky. It was always hot on practice days, thought Harry remembering the pleasantly cool Saturday and the water skiing experience. He thought about the mysterious girl on the Point. What was it about her that had captured his imagination? Was it the graceful way she walked... or was it the long brown pony tail that seemed to float jauntily behind her? Or was it the rounded hips he thought guiltily?

"What're you day-dreaming about, Kester?" shouted Braun. "Ya thinking about some sweet little thing ya wanna hug and kiss?" The Coach made little kissing sounds with his mouth. "Or are ya thinking about knocking the heck out of this sled? What is it... what is it? Huh? Huh?"

The Coach's growl snapped Harry's mind back to the sled. "I'm gonna kill the sled Coach!" he said.

"Oh ya are, are ya?" crooned Coach Braun in a mock sweet voice, his lips mimicking a kiss.

"Yes Sir," said Harry, trying to look mean. "I'm gonna kill it!"

"Okay, Kester," said the Coach with a leer. "Step up here and show us all how you're gonna kill it!"

Harry stepped forward out of the group and put his helmet on, adjusting the strap. He lined up in front of the center of the two blocking pads. He hoped the Coach would order another player to help him, but he was alone. Coach Braun braced himself on top of the sled.

"Okay, Kester," shouted Coach Braun, "I wanna have a big ride! And I mean a big one!"

Coach Braun blew his whistle shrilly and Harry charged into the left blocking pad, his feet churning in the thick, green grass. The sled moved slightly and Harry kept his feet churning until he was able to move the sled about five feet. Then his legs turned to jelly and he fell to one knee.

"Is that it Kester?" screamed Braun. "Is that all ya got? What are ya... some kinda cream-puff?"

"I can go again," mumbled Harry getting stiffly to his feet.

"Oh ya can, can ya," shouted Braun climbing down from the sled. "Lemme show you something!"

Coach Braun lined up in front of the right blocking pad, the whistle still in his mouth. He blew the whistle shrilly and charged at the blocking pad. He hit it and raised his arms, delivering a mighty blow that lifted the front of the sled from the ground and established momentum. Braun pushed the empty sled a full twenty feet, his feet digging up divots of grass until the air was filled with falling sod. He stopped, turned around and glared at Harry.

"You've got to hit the darn thing... not run up and kiss it! And I mean really hit it... not just run into it, Kester!" he shouted, sticking his face into Harry's. "Ya got it!?"

"Yes Sir," shouted Harry. "I got it!"

Braun climbed back onto the sled. "Then let's see it!"

Harry lined up again in front of the left blocking pad. The whistle sounded. He ran low at the blocking pad and combined the force of a forearm shiver with the momentum of his body. The blow lifted the front of the sled about an inch, decreasing the friction with the ground and establishing momentum. Harry's legs churned, exerting all of his strength, his shoulders heaving into the pad. He pushed it for about ten feet before his energy was expended and the sled stopped.

"Alright," shouted Coach Braun. "You other girls get a try now! Buddinger, Dickson... line it up!"

Coach Phelps ran over to the sled and got aboard it with Coach Braun as the boys lined up. Allman and Renny Dickson strapped on their helmets and got down into a three point stance in front of the blocking sled. Renny was a quiet boy who drove a school bus to make extra money for his family. He played guard next to Bob Porter.

The whistle sounded. The boys charged at the sled, lifting the front end several inches off the grass, getting the sled sliding smoothly. Their legs churned. Finally, exhausted, the legs stopped and the sled resumed its position as a waiting chariot of summer torture.

"That's the way to do it!' shouted Coach Phelps jumping off the sled and running to the waiting group of boys. "You gotta work together more to keep it moving!"

The boys at the sled got up and turned back to the waiting group. A slimy brown liquid ran from under Allman's helmet and down his face. A subdued laughter arose from the waiting boys. Allman's snub nosed face broke out into a big silly grin as he walked back to the group. He didn't remove the helmet. He didn't wipe away the stain on his face.

"Hey Allman, you look a little shit faced!" shouted Terry Moddy.

Renny looked curiously at Allman and snickered.

"You'll get yours, Terry," said Allman in a mock threatening tone.

Allman took off the helmet revealing a runny brown, half congealed substance on his head. It ran down his face in little brown driblets.

"That stuff really stinks, Allman," said Karl Darby with an amused grin.

Allman wiped his face with the tail of his practice jersey, glaring at Harry.

"What's this? What is this?" shouted Braun. "All of ya... put those darn helmets on and get ready to kill this cotton picking sled!"

They all put their helmets on, including Allman. Small brown driblets ran again down his face. Allman nodded at Harry and winked his eye. Harry looked back and smiled.

****

It was the last day of practice before school started. It had been unusually hot the day before, and on this day it was even hotter, even at eight o'clock in the morning. The Churchland Truckers ran out on the field and did the usual calisthenics. Coach Phelps and Coach Fearless watched them. Coach Braun was not on the field.

"You still worrying about that pony tail gal?" asked Bubba as they did jumping jacks.

"I'm not worrying about any girl," said Harry avoiding Bubba's eyes.

"Okay, Harry," laughed Bubba, "if you say so!"

"I say so," said Harry.

"She says she wants to meet you," said Bubba. "But I got ya a date with Janet."

"Okay... I'd like to meet Janet."

They finished the calisthenics.

"You guys take three laps," shouted Coach Fearless.

The team began the laps, now running easily after the grueling try-outs.

"Only three?" asked Tony as he ran along easily.

"It's scrimmage day," said Bubba. "They want us to save some energy for the scrimmage."

"You got all the plays memorized, Harry?" asked Tony.

"Sure," said Harry as they ran along together. "Fullback is number three, left halfback is number two, right halfback is number four... quarterback is one. Holes on the line are numbered odd to the right and even to the left. It's not a hard system."

"Yeah, I guess not," said Tony, "so a thirty-eight means you're coming around left end... right?"

"You got it," said Harry.

As they finished the last lap, they saw Coach Braun coming out of the gymnasium holding a clipboard. They ran to the Coach and stopped in front of him.

Coach Braun read from a paper on the clipboard, his voice hoarse in the early morning air. "Alright!" he shouted. "I want the first string to line up on offense like this... center; Bob Porter; left guard; Bucky Allison, right guard; Renny Dickson, left tackle; Jim Jensen, right tackle; Bart Whitely; right end; Bud Darby, left end; Arnie Eberly, quarterback; Allman Buddinger; right halfback; Karl Darby, left halfback; Terry Moddy and fullback... Jack Sanders."

Harry knew it was coming, but his heart fell anyway. He had not beat out Jack Sanders... and probably wouldn't. He had to find another way to get on the field!

"The guys whose name I read will be second string and line up on defense," shouted Coach Braun. "On the line...Tony Zee, Bubba Hawkins, Burt Noonan, Hal Newton, Bryan Muller, Buster Stanley, Benny Norwood... In the backfield Harry Quester at fullback, halfbacks Matt Pittinger and Johnny Current, and quarterback, Rob Sonda."

"We'll normally play a six-two-two-one defense with the fullback and center at Linebacker," said Coach Braun loudly. "We play Gloucester in two weeks. From now until then we're going to run plays over and over... and over again... until you guys are in automatic. Then we're going to run them against the second stringers on defense over and over with full contact... and then do it all over again."

"Line it up at midfield!" shouted Coach Fearless.

"We'll run through the playbook," shouted Coach Phelps. "At first, no hitting. Move to your assigned block and set it up... that's all."

The defense lined up. Bob Porter signaled the huddle. "Huddle up!" he barked, holding his hands in the air. The first team assembled around him.

"Stop... stop!" shouted Coach Braun in frustration. "I've told you guys a billion darn times... a zillion times... that we run everywhere. We always hustle! When Porter says huddle up, it means you run your butts to the huddle and take your place. You don't amble over there like some girls prancing to a tea party! Now do it again!"

The boys ran away from the huddle and looked expectantly back at Bob.

"Huddle up!" barked Porter, holding his hands in the air. The first team ran to where he stood at full speed and assembled around him.

In the huddle, Allman called the play in a voice filled with confidence and authority. "Now listen up," he said. "This is the way Coach wants it... I call the play... Porter gets it and the hike number... he leaves and goes to the line and sets up. I call the play and number again, I call 'break' and we all hustle up to the line together. The play is twenty-two on two."

Porter left the huddle and ran to where the ball waited on the line. He got down over it, his hands clutching the ball.

"Twenty-two on two," hissed Allman looking at the eyes of the guys in the huddle to make sure everyone had the play. "Okay... break!"

The players broke out of the huddle quickly, slapping their hands simultaneously, and ran to their positions. Allman crouched behind center and surveyed the defense in front of him with his usual flair.

"Get down!" shouted Allman in a sing-song voice. "Get ready!... Hut one!... Hut two!"

Harry, crouched in the right defensive linebacker position, threw up his hands in front of him as the ball popped into Allman's hands. Allman moved back and jammed the ball into Moddy's belly as Terry ran to the two hole. Porter was out of the line in a fraction of a second, running straight at Harry and pushing him outward. Terry burst through the line at full speed. The whistle sounded. Porter ran hurriedly back to his position behind the line of scrimmage.

"Huddle up!" shouted Porter.

****

It was four o'clock in the afternoon. The Truckers were still running plays without contact, as they had all morning. The heat had mounted to over ninety degrees, and the sweat poured off of the players. Harry felt like he was in a sauna. His mouth was dry, his sweat stinging his eyes. He pulled his lemon out of his belt and sucked on it. The sour moisture provided little relief.

"Checked your helmet today, Harry?" asked Allman as they lined up for another play.

Harry squinted at Allman. "No... what about it?"

Allman laughed. "Just wondering what might be in it."

They ran the play. It was a slant off left tackle by Terry. Everybody tagged their block and jogged back to position. Harry took off his helmet and looked inside. There was a folded piece of paper jammed up under the supports. He pulled it out and read it.

The note read: "Keep your helmet on, dummy!"

"What the heck ya doing, Kester?" shouted the Coach. "Ya taking a holiday out here? Ya think it's too hot for ya or somethin'?"

Harry looked at the Coach in surprise.

"Put that helmet on, Kester… and keep it on!" shouted Coach Braun. "Ya didn't get it the first time I tol' ya to keep your helmet on at practice?"

"Come on, Harry!" shouted Allman containing a chortle. "Get your cotton pickin' helmet on so we can run a play!"

Harry jammed the helmet back on his head and snapped the strap in place. He nodded at Allman knowingly and gave him a thumbs up.

"Okay, Allman," muttered Harry. "Ya got me!"

Allman called the signals and they ran another walk-through play.

"Come on, Coach," pleaded Allman to Coach Phelps. "Why're we running these plays so many times? Let's play some real football!"

"Have you run them enough that you're not going to make any mistakes, Allman?" asked Coach Phelps.

"Yes Sir, I sure have," said Allman confidently.

"You know it's different when it's full action," said Coach Phelps. "You've done it before… some of these guys haven't."

"Yeah, yeah, Coach," said Allman in frustration. "But this is boring!"

"You'll get your time, Allman," said Coach Phelps. "Just concentrate on the plays."

The next play was an eighty-nine end around. The ball was snapped and Arnie pulled from his left end position and ran to the right past the quarterback to the nine hole around the opposite end. Allman slammed the ball into his belly and it popped free, landing on the ground.

Coach Phelps blew his whistle. "Okay! Let's see that one again… and Allman… you better get the ends to be as familiar with your hand-offs as the halfbacks are… got it!"

"Yeah," said Allman with a grin that looked a bit foolish, "I got it, Coach!"

At five o'clock, Coach Braun blew his whistle. "Next play is full contact," he said with a certain amount of glee. "I want to see some real hitting and blocking! You got no friends on the other side of the ball!"

The sweat ran down Harry' face in racing driblets. He knew what was coming. Allman would assuredly run Sanders first and probably right up the middle. He guessed it would be a thirty-two, which meant that Porter would be coming out of the line to block him. Harry had memorized what he was supposed to do on each play, but he had also trained himself to understand how the play was supposed to work and what the blocking assignments of the whole team were. He remembered things easily and had a knack for seeing the whole picture. He edged over to the two hole between the center and the left guard. He figured that he could charge the hole, knock the guard off his block and be right in the hole where Porter couldn't get him. Blocking was all a question of angles, balance and leverage. He understood that, just as he understood the angles of billiards, a game he played with his Father. Once past the guard, he'd have to deal with Sanders. He watched Allman's eyes as he came to the line. He almost always called the first play on two. Would he this time?

"Get down!" shouted Allman. "Get ready! Hut one... Hut two!"

A fraction of a second after the second "hut", Harry launched himself at the two hole. The ball was snapped and Harry crashed into the guard knocking him away from the defensive guard. He felt Porter shoving at him from the side, but he was already in the hole. Sanders took the ball from Buddinger and came running, his knees high, straight at Harry. Harry braced himself for the shock he knew was coming. He launched himself at Sanders and hit him in the thighs. Jack's forearm caught him in the face and his head rung like a bell. He felt a knee crash into his chest, but he managed to wrap his arms around Jack's legs. The two boys fell down, Jack's momentum carrying him through the line and on top of Harry. Several more boys fell on top of them. The whistle sounded.

"No gain, Sanders," shouted Coach Phelps

"Kester!" shouted Coach Braun running toward Harry. "You cheated out of your linebacker position!"

"Coach, I figured Jack was gonna get the ball," said Harry defensively, "so I just moved to get leverage on the blockers."

"Oh ya did, did ya? And what if the play had gone through the six hole?" shouted Braun. "Where would ya be?"

"I guess I'd have been in the two hole, Coach," said Harry rubbing his lip where Jack's forearm had clobbered him. "But I can mostly figure out what's coming!"

"You're thinking too much, Kester!" shouted Braun, his face stuck close to Harry's. "On defense we play the position... not what you 'think' is gonna happen!"

"Okay, Coach," said Harry, backing away.

Coach Braun glared at Harry strangely and ran back to the offensive side of the line. Harry jogged back to his position. The first string ran up to the line of scrimmage.

"Okay, New Guy... what's the play this time, Smart Ass?" asked

Arnie as he took his position at left end.

Harry ignored him.

"I thought ya knew everything, Mister New Guy!" sneered Arnie, getting down into a three point stance.

Harry ignored Arnie again. He had the sense that it was Karl's turn. They wanted all the backs to run. Karl would probably run off right tackle on his side of the ball, or near there. Harry edged a little to his left. The ball was snapped and Allman handed off to Karl. Karl sprinted toward the right end. Arnie came out of the line and tried to block Harry. Harry stiff armed him and ran nimbly down the line, matching Karl's speed. Bud Darby threw a block on Tony and Karl ran behind Bud. Harry grabbed Karl by the jersey as he rounded the end. He spun Karl around and tackled him. They fell to the ground and kicked up a cloud of hot dust.

"How'd you get over here, Harry?" asked Karl good-naturedly, sweat and dirt covering his face. "Ya thinking too much again?"

Harry grinned. "No thinking, Karl... just chasing!"

"Well, whatever it is... keep it up," said Karl with a sly wink.

"What kinda block was that, Arnie?" shouted Coach Fearless. "Ya let your man get away!"

"I'll get him next time, Coach," said Arnie, an angry scowl on his face.

"Yeah, Arnie," said Fearless in a disgusted drawl. "But next time don't count in a game!"

Harry and Karl untangled themselves and started to get up.

"Okay, Darby... Kester! What're you waiting for? Ya gonna lie there on the ground and take a nap?" shouted Coach Braun. "We'll be here 'til after dark if you don't get some good plays off! And I mean that!"

****

It was hot on the Wilson practice field. Slate and Cliff ran to where a group of boys were standing, waiting in their football gear. They couldn't help seeing Ennis Hathaway, all two hundred and fifty pounds of him. He was at least six feet two inches tall now, a full four inches taller than Cliff and two inches taller than Slate. His face was scarred from acne, but less chubby now than Slate remembered him. The face was covered with a stubble of dark black beard. His hair was cut short and was black and greasy. He had a large gut that hung out over the belt of his football trousers and he was perspiring profusely.

"Well, looky here," said Ennis elbowing his way to where Slate and Cliff stood. "I wouldn't believe it 'less I saw it with my own eyes! It's the

Two Mouseketeers!"

"Hello Ennis," said Slate trying to stand between Cliff and Ennis.

"What's a Mouseketeer?" asked Cliff suspiciously.

"It's a Mickey Mouse thing on television," said Slate.

"We ain't got no television," muttered Cliff.

"You Mouseketeers think ya can play football?" asked Ennis derisively. "Better turn in them helmets and get your mouse ears on!"

"We hope you'll give us some advice on making the team," said Slate.

"Hah!" said Ennis viciously. It sounded like an explosive expletive, accentuated with spittle. "You guys will get some help from me alright! I'll knock the crap outa ya until ya quit and go home to your Mommy!"

"Listen Fatso," said Cliff in a voice filled with hostility. "You just come on... I'll roll up that big gut of yours and cram it down your throat."

"Well, I'll be damned," exclaimed Hathaway in mock surprise, "if it ain't Shotgun Braun! The kid I love to hate!"

Cliff surged forward, his fists balled up. "What did ya call me?"

"Get the kid a shotgun," laughed Ennis, "that's all he can do, too... guard the damn store!"

Cliff's face was red and filled with anger. He wound up to take a swing at Ennis.

Slate restrained him. "Cut it out, Cliff... we can't fight here... we need to make the team!"

"Don't you call me Shotgun, Fatso!" shouted Cliff, struggling with Slate as the other players stared at them.

"I'll call ya what I wanna call ya," said Ennis. "And if you call me Fatso again, I'll knock ya lousy head off!"

A short, thin man walked out to where the boys waited. His face was handsome with pleasant eyes and dark eyebrows. He had a full head of hair which was carefully combed. With him was another, younger man who wore a snappy hat with a feather in the hatband. He had a prominent nose, a gold tooth and held a pad of paper in his hand with a long yellow pencil. His eyes darted among the players.

"It's Coach Wilder," whispered Cliff. "Eddie Wilder!"

"Who's the other guy?" asked Slate.

"That's Al Gollen," said Ennis. "He's a sportswriter from the *Virginian Pilot*. I was in his column once. But don't worry... he ain't never gonna be writing about you two!"

"Good morning, players," said Coach Wilder in a deep voice. "Some of you are players. Some of you are going to be players. Some of you are going home. We'll start finding out who's who this morning. Good luck! Now take ten laps!"

Slate and Cliff took the laps with the other players. At first, their legs tightened up, but as the laps continued, it became easier. All that running on the paper route had kept them in good shape. They teased Ennis with their easy speed as the big boy lumbered along.

"When I catch ya again, Braun," wheezed Ennis, "I'm gonna make mincemeat of ya!"

"You'll never catch us Ennis," laughed Slate with a burst of speed.

"I'll fight ya any time you're ready, ya big windbag," said Cliff.

"What is this?" shouted Coach Ismail running up beside them, his face red and the veins sticking out of his thick neck. "Some kind of bridge club? What are the ladies bidding there, Hathaway?"

"Nothing, Coach," mumbled Ennis.

"Four hearts, I'll bet," said Ismail in a mock whine. "Four big sweet hearts!"

"No Sir," panted Ennis.

"You boys run! Run until ya can't go no more!" shouted Coach Ismail. "If ya got breath for chattering, ya ain't running hard enough! Got it? Got it?"

"Yes Sir," wheezed Slate. "We got it!"

"You two… Phelps and Braun… report to me after the laps are over," shouted the Coach. "I'm gonna find out today about you two!"

The Coach ran off toward a set of white goal posts.

"What did he mean by that?" asked Cliff worriedly.

"I guess he means he's gonna find out if we can make the team," said Slate.

"But he said… today," said Cliff.

"I know."

They finished the laps and reported to Coach Ismail who was standing near a set of goal posts on the practice field. Other members of the team were lining up in front of him.

"Okay…okay," shouted Ismail hoarsely, "we'll have us a little scrimmage today to see what you guys have! You, Phelps… you claim to be a halfback?"

"Yes Sir," said Slate stepping forward.

"Get over there and line up as halfback," said Ismail. "No plays… I just want you to pick a hole and run at it. You lineman… block straight ahead and drive your man as far back as you can!"

"Okay, Coach," said Slate with a grin, "I can do that!"

"And you… Braun," said the Coach looking at Cliff with a glare. "What's your position?"

Cliff paused for a moment. "I dunno," he said, "just put me somewhere where I can hit people!"

Ismail looked Cliff up and down with a critical eye. "Okay, Braun, line up at defensive end there," he said, pointing to the position.

Cliff ran to the end of the line and fell in with the other players.

Coach Ismail went to Cliff and grabbed him by the shoulder pads. "So you like to hit do you, Braun?"

"Yeah, I do, Coach" said Cliff, his face filled with his usual anger.

"Get down there in front of Ennis and let's see what you can do," said Ismail.

Cliff looked at Ennis, who made gestures with his thick fingers for Cliff to come at him. "Come on, Shotgun, ya little bastard... let's see it!"

Rage boiled in Cliff's mind. He lined up in front of Ennis, his face set in a livid mask.

"On my whistle," said Ismail with an anticipatory grin, "Braun, let's see you get by Ennis."

Cliff got into a three point stance in front of Ennis, whose bulk made Cliff look like a marionette. Coach Ismail blew the whistle. Cliff exploded into Ennis' protruding belly. Ennis absorbed the blow and threw Cliff to the ground. He lay on top of him and gave him a rabbit punch in the kidneys where Coach Ismail couldn't see it.

"Come on, Shotgun," teased Ennis, "is that all ya got?"

Cliff struggled to turn over. He hit Ennis in the gut with his fist, but it was like punching a big bowl of Jell-O. Ennis just laughed at him.

"That wasn't a hit, Braun!" shouted Ismail. "You looked like you was patting him on the belly... not hitting 'im!"

"I know how to hit," said Cliff determinedly, getting to his feet.

"Get down there on the line, Braun," said Ismail with a snort. "I'll show ya how to hit!"

Cliff got down and Ismail lined up in front of him. "Okay, Braun," said Ismail, "I'm a lineman who's gonna block you... what're ya gonna do about it?"

"I'm gonna..." began Cliff.

Ismail came up under Cliff with both arms, rocked him backward and sent pain shooting up through his body. He fell to the ground and lay there trying to find his breath.

"I thought you could hit!" shouted Ismail standing over Cliff.

Cliff got up painfully and went back to his position in the line. "I got a better way than that, Coach," said Cliff defensively, feeling anger at Ennis and Ismail building up inside him.

"Oh you do?" shouted Ismail turning red in the face. "Line up here again!"

Cliff lined up in front of Coach Ismail. The Coach got down in front of Cliff in a three point stance, a fierce expression on his face.

"Come on, Braun!" shouted Ismail. "Give me a hit... anytime you're ready!"

Cliff hesitated and then charged into the big Coach. Ismail hit him in the face with a forearm and Cliff fell to the ground, pain shooting through his bleeding nose. He got groggily to his feet.

"Do ya know how to hit now, Braun?" shouted Coach Ismail. "Do ya know what the other guy oughta feel like?"

Cliff felt anger sweep through him. He walked toward the Coach. "I know how to hit," he said determinedly. "Let's go again, Coach!"

Coach Ismail turned to Ennis Hathaway. "Come here, Ennis! Line up in front of Braun here again."

"With pleasure, Coach," said Ennis lumbering over to take position in front of Cliff.

Coach Ismail stood behind Cliff. He blew the whistle, and at the same time he lifted Cliff by the shoulder pads and hip pads and threw him at Ennis. Cliff crashed into Ennis with a crunching of pads. He felt Ennis's arm smack him in the face and he tasted blood. Both boys fell into a heap on the ground. Cliff jumped to his feet, his nose and lip bleeding.

"Now you do it the way I showed you, Braun," said Ismail. "Get up under Ennis here and rock him back... don't let him push you down again!"

Ismail turned to the rest of the players. "Okay, Phelps, you take the ball. When I blow the whistle, block and run!"

Ismail lateraled a ball to Slate. Slate caught it and tucked it under his right arm tightly. The Coach blew the whistle. Slate ran right behind Ennis Hathaway looking for a hole. Cliff delivered a forearm shiver to Ennis' chest that stood him up. Then he dodged around Ennis and brought Slate down with a jarring tackle.

"Hey, good tackle, Cliff," said Slate as he lay on the ground waiting for the tingling sensation in his thighs where Cliff had hit him to stop.

"I thought I told you to come up under Ennis and push him back," shouted Ismail in an irritated voice.

Cliff got quickly to his feet, glaring at the hulk of Ennis on the ground. "I said I had a better way," muttered Cliff. "I can get aroun' big slow guys... like Ennis!"

"What was that you said?" shouted Ismail, his eyes squinting, his face turning red.

"He said he had a better way than what you told him, Coach," said Ennis, holding his chest where Cliff had hit him. He tried to haul his fat body up off the ground.

"Is that what you said, Braun?" shouted Ismail, the veins in his neck about to pop.

"Yep, I said that," said Cliff pushing Ennis back to the ground.

"Who do ya think ya are… saying ya have a better way than what I tol' ya?" shouted Ismail in a rage. "Get out of here!"

"What do ya mean?" asked Cliff suddenly worried.

"Just what I said, wise guy," shouted Ismail. "And turn in that uniform!"

Cliff started to walk dejectedly off the field. Ismail ran up behind him and gave him a boot in the rear. Cliff turned to face him, his face contorted with surprise and anger, his fists clenched.

"Why're ya kicking me?" exclaimed Cliff.

"Get outa here, Braun!" shouted Ismail, "'fore I kick ya again!"

"Coach, he didn't mean it," interrupted Slate running to where Ismail and Cliff stood facing each other. "He was just trying out something… and he did make a good tackle!"

Ismail turned to Slate with a growl. "Shut up, Phelps," he roared, "and get over there… you got one more chance to show me you can carry the cotton pickin' ball!"

****

The next day Cliff and Slate sat together in the old Chevy parked near the school. It was after school and Slate was getting ready to go to football practice.

"Well, I guess I had a great football career at dear old Wilson High!" exclaimed Cliff.

"Cliff, you're your own worse enemy," said Slate.

"What do ya mean?"

"You have a big mouth and a temper to match it!" said Slate. "That's what I mean!"

"I can't help it… besides… he kicked me in the butt!"

"I know… he shouldn't have done that… but he's the boss."

"The heck with him!"

"You gotta learn to keep your mouth shut and your temper down, Cliff… that's all."

"That's all, huh?"

"Yeah!"

"How'd you do after I left?" asked Cliff.

"Well, he didn't throw me off the team," said Slate.

"I guess that's good," said Cliff. "Say, if you're gonna play football, is it okay if I keep the paper route going?"

"Sure," said Slate, "I'll help on the weekends."

"Okay," said Cliff, "… and, thanks, Slate."

Slate got out of the car. "I gotta get on over there to practice," he said.

"I know," said Cliff glumly. "Give Ennis a shot in the head for me, will ya?"

"Okay," said Slate with a forced smile.

Slate walked away from the car toward the gymnasium. A loud voice hailed him.

"Hey! Phelps!" came the roar from behind him.

Slate turned and saw the granite head of Archie Ismail coming toward him atop a bear-like body. He stopped.

"Sir?"

"Where's your buddy… the ugly one who looks pissed off all the time?" roared the Coach.

"Cliff?... Cliff Braun?"

"Yeah… yeah… that's the one."

"He's… over there in the car," said Slate pointing toward the Chevy where he saw Cliff watching them.

Ismail turned and roared at the car. "Braun! Get your young butt over here! We got some more hitting to do today!"

Cliff got out of the car and ran toward them, a befuddled look on his face. "I'm ready, Coach!"

****

It was Halloween night, 1941. Slate and Cliff were seniors and starters for Wilson High; Slate at left halfback, Cliff at left end. They had been elected Co-Captains for the year. The two of them sat in the dressing room at Portsmouth Stadium pulling on their blue football trousers. The trousers were unique, with a broad orange stripe edged with white running down the back of each leg

"Well, Captain Phelps," said Cliff pulling on the blue trousers and reaching for the orange shirt with the blue number fifty-one. The shirt had blue pad outlines on each shoulder and triple blue stripes on each arm. "We're 3-2-1 so far… can we beat the 5-4 last year?"

"I hope so, Captain Braun!" said Slate, pulling on the jersey with number fifty-five. "Coach Wilder wants to beat Maury real bad."

"Yeah," said Cliff, "I think he does… but he don't seem too excited."

"That's just the way he is," said Cliff.

"I'm gonna knock their jocks off!" promised Cliff.

They finished putting their trousers and jerseys on and pulled the long white socks with horizontal blue stripes over their feet. They put on their cleated shoes and picked up their leather helmets.

"Just hit 'em tonight, Cliff," said Slate. "We can't afford any of those fighting penalties."

"Yeah, yeah," mumbled Cliff.

The new backs coach, Jimmy Johnstone walked up to them. He bent half over and clenched his fists in front of them. "You guys ready tonight?"

"We sure are, Coach" said Cliff enthusiastically. "I'm looking for blood."

"I feel good, Coach," said Slate. "We're going to win!"

"You guys are the spirit of this team," said Coach Johnstone. "You gotta not just play well, but get the other guys wanting it as much as you do!"

"I understand that, Coach," said Slate.

"I'll kick 'em all in the butt if they don't move it out!" said Cliff, his jug ears turning red.

"Then get out there and do it!" said the Coach slapping then both on the rump.

They went to the center of the dressing room where the team was assembling around Coach Wilder. "Okay Team," said the Coach in a steady, even voice, "we haven't beaten the Commodores for ten years… tonight we're going to do it!"

There was a chorus of cheers from the team.

"We're gonna crush these guys from Norfolk tonight," said the Coach with contained enthusiasm. "Ace Parks led the 1931 team to a twenty to nothing win… Slate is going to do it tonight!"

Cliff punched Slate in the ribs. "You're gonna be a hero," he said in mock envy.

"Shut up and listen!" said Slate emotionally.

"Okay, Gang," shouted Archie Ismail. "You heard the Coach! Sock 'em and rock 'em! Be out for blood!"

"We need a really good defense tonight," said Coach Wilder with an annoyed glance at Coach Ismail. "Shotgun… I'm counting on you to get to that quarterback of theirs in a hurry. He's got a good pass!"

"He's a dead man, Coach," said Cliff, his eyes squinting and his face becoming even angrier than normal.

"Let's go get 'em!" said Coach Wilder in even tones.

The team clattered toward the hall that led to the stadium. Portsmouth Stadium was brand new, built as a Depression Work Project in the past few years. It was concrete with wooden benches. Outside, the boys could hear the cheers of over eight thousand fans. They ran down the corridor and into the stadium where bright lights on tall poles momentarily blinded them. Across from them, they could see the Maury High School team running onto the field in their white trousers and blue jerseys.

"Look at those stupid helmets," laughed Cliff, "They got a white 'X' on top of 'em... 'X' marks the target!"

Slate lined up to receive the kickoff. He glanced up into the stands where Halloween merrymakers looked back behind skeleton and ghost masks. Jack-o-lanterns burned with terrible smiles on sticks at each end of the field. The ball was kicked and came high in the air toward Slate. He grabbed it and started running. He saw Cliff launch himself at a Commodore in front of him and knock the player flat. He cut to the outside and ran at full speed. He thought he saw a clear way to the goal line, but suddenly he was cut down from the side at the Maury forty-six.

In the huddle, Clay Coggle, the quarterback, called Slate's number. "Okay, Slate, Coach wants to test the guy at their right tackle... so run off our left tackle... Shotgun, get the end and the halfback both if you can. Twenty-six on two. Break!"

They charged up to the line. The ball was handed off to Slate and he plunged off left tackle. Cliff knocked the end out of the play and moved ahead of Slate as they ran down the field. Cliff slammed into the halfback who staggered backward as Slate flashed by. The Maury safety saved the day for the Commodores and Slate was tackled at the twenty-nine.

Back in the huddle, Clay was enthusiastic. "We can run on these guys," he said. He called the number of the other halfback, Billy McLow. McLow ran off right tackle and took the ball to the Commodore eleven. On the next play, Clay called Slate's number.

"Take it in, Slate," said Cliff. "I'm gonna kill that big tackle over there."

"What about the end?" asked Slate.

"Aw, I got him already," said Cliff. "He's backing up every play."

"Okay guys, twenty-four... on one," said Clay. "Break!"

The ball thudded into Slate's belly and he ran to the left. Ahead of him, Cliff charged at the Maury tackle and hit him from the side so hard that the big player in the blue shirt staggered backward. Cliff charged after him delivering stunning forearms to the player's chest and head. Another Maury player ran into Cliff and hit him in the head. Slate flashed past Cliff to the Maury six and was tackled. His heart fell as he saw a yellow flag float to the field as the whistle sounded.

"Unnecessary roughness!" shouted the referee in the striped white shirt. "Number fifty-one, Wilson!"

Cliff was lying flat on his back near the Maury goal line. Slate ran to him. "Cliff! Are you okay?"

Cliff's eyes snapped open and he tried to get up. "I'm okay... okay," he muttered, "... just dizzy."

"The ball goes back to the twenty-six!" shouted the referee.

"What?" shouted Slate. "That Maury guy hit our guy!"

The referee ignored Slate. Slate started toward him when he saw an extraordinary sight. Margaret Braun stepped over a three foot high barricade between the stands and the field and came running toward them, her stocky frame moving faster than seemingly possible. She ran to where Slate stood over the fallen Shotgun.

"Clifton!" shouted Margaret Braun, fright in her voice. "You get up! Don't just lie there like that!"

Cliff looked up at his Mother's square face through foggy eyes, the field still spinning around him. "Mother! You can't come out here!"

"I'm out here, aren't I?" said Margaret belligerently. "Now are you gonna get up or are you really hurt?"

The referee's whistle sounded and the man in the striped shirt came toward them, followed by Coach Ismail. Shotgun got up and hugged his Mother. "I'm okay, Mother," he said, "now please go on back to the stands."

The Referee took Mrs. Braun by the arm. "Come on, lady," he said gruffly.

Mrs. Braun turned and swatted the Referee in the face with a solid right cross. "Get your hands off me, young fella," she said, venom in her voice.

The Referee turned her loose as the crowd roared. He stepped back, surprise written on his face.

"Come on with me, Mrs. Braun," said Coach Ismail as gently as he could, which wasn't very gentle. "We'll take care of him."

"Alright, Clifton," said Mrs. Braun, "But don't you let those boys hit you like that!"

"Okay, Mother," said Cliff. "I won't... I promise!"

Mrs. Braun followed Coach Ismail to the sidelines. Cliff watched his mother as flash bulbs popped.

"I can't believe they called that penalty on me," muttered Cliff as he and Slate went back to the huddle.

"I can't believe your Mother was out here."

"She's like that," said Cliff nonchalantly. "But I made a good hit on that guy!"

"Yeah," said Slate, "I know you're always innocent, Cliff."

"Delay of the game!" shouted the referee. "The ball goes back to the thirty-one."

"Now that really pisses me off," muttered Cliff. "They're penalizing my Mom!"

They ran back to their positions. Cliff looked around at the team. They were just standing around looking dejected.

"Hey, you guys!" shouted Cliff. "Don't just stand there! Get it going! Get it going!"

"You guys are doing great!" said Slate in an even voice. "Keep it going! We're gonna run over these guys right here!"

Maury held on for the next several runs, allowing the Presidents only small gains. Clay gave the ball to the fullback, Les Caprio, on fourth down, but he was stopped. Maury took over at their own twenty-five.

"Dammit, Cliff," said Slate as they lined up in defensive positions, "did ya have to hit that guy so hard? It woulda been a touchdown!"

"Don't worry," said Cliff between clenched teeth, "these guys are afraid of us now! We'll have 'em for lunch!"

On the next play, the Maury quarterback tried to pass and was crashed to the ground by Cliff Braun.

"Don't you try that pass," whispered Cliff in the Maury quarterback's ear as they lay on the ground. "Cause next time, I'll really hit ya!"

Cliff got up and walked back to his side of the ball with an evil grin on his face. He did a little hotfoot dance with his feet, raised his arms and shouted. "We got 'em now, Gang! We got the bastards!"

The referee looked at Cliff strangely, but said nothing.

"Way to go out there, Shotgun!" shouted Coach Johnstone.

When it was all over, it was Wilson sixteen, Maury six. Slate scored a touchdown, McLow scored and Cliff got a safety in the fourth quarter. Maury scored a lone touchdown and missed the extra point.

"See?" said Cliff as they jogged off the field to the cheers of the fans. "I told ya we had 'em!"

"Yeah," said Slate. "We did. By the way, is your Mom always like that?"

"Yeah… mostly," said Cliff. "She ain't as mad all the time now that my Father has a job doing construction work."

"Good game, Shotgun," said Slate enthusiastically. "We might get those scholarships yet!"

****

Chapter Five
Summer Practice II

It was the Saturday evening before school started and the sun was setting brilliantly as Harry walked up to the big brick house near the river where Janet Williams lived. Bubba Hawkins and his date, Alice Gibbs, sat in Bubba's beat up 1947 Dodge waiting for him. Alice was a pert brunette with a slim figure that looked emaciated standing next to Bubba. Teresa Brewer was singing on Bubba's old radio.

Till I waltz again with you,
Let no other hold your charms,
If my dreams should all come true,
You'll be waiting for my arms.

Bubba liked the romantic songs when he took Alice out... "puts her in the mood", he said. In Northern Virginia, Harry danced with girls at the school dances, and flirted with them in the halls. But he had never really dated a girl, just the two of them together. He wondered how it would be with Janet. Apprehension filled him as he approached the door. Harry knocked on the door, feeling real fear as to what was on the other side. The door opened and a burly man with penetrating eyes stared at him.

"Hello, Mr. Williams... I'm... I'm Harry Quester," stuttered Harry, "to see Janet."

"Come in," said Mr. Williams in a voice meant to be friendly but containing a degree of mistrust that was easily detectable. "She'll be here in a minute."

"Thank you, Sir," said Harry in a practiced voice.

Harry went inside and sat nervously on a sofa that swallowed him up. Mr. Williams went into the kitchen where Harry heard him talking in low tones to someone. What were they saying? Something about him? Where was Janet? There was an old, porcelain wind up clock with naked little angels reclining along its top that ticked loudly from a table across from the sofa. The tick tock seemed to go on forever before the kitchen door opened and a large lady in an apron walked in, followed by Mr. Williams.

"Hello, Harry," said the large lady, "I'm Janet's mother."

Harry jumped to his feet. "Hello, Mrs. Williams," said Harry hoping he was doing this all right.

"I'm pleased to meet you, Harry," said Mrs. Williams. "I hope you children enjoy a good movie tonight."

"Yes Maam, we're going to the Commodore Theater to see the new Alfred Hitchcock film."

"Oh," exclaimed Mrs. Williams, "I've heard that it's very violent… what's the name of it?"

"It's called *Dial M for Murder*, Maam," said Harry cautiously. "I think it'll be okay."

"Just get her back home before twelve o'clock, Young Man," said Mr. Williams worriedly in a deep voice. "And… behave yourselves!"

"Yes sir," said Harry obediently.

Janet walked into the room. She wore a pink pleated skirt with a tight white blouse under a pink cardigan sweater. She wore the sweater open in the front. The skirt stood out from her waist with the aid of something fluffy underneath. She carried a small pink pocketbook. Her waist was narrow, cinched up with a pink belt. On her feet were brown and white saddle shoes with white bobby socks. Her hair was sandy blonde, cut short with gentle curls. Her eyes were a sparkling blue and her lips were colored a light pink. She broke out into a smile when she saw Harry.

"Hello Harry," said Janet in a slightly impish voice.

"Hello, Janet," said Harry cautiously, his eyes absorbing her freshness and beauty. "It's great to see you!"

"Thanks, Harry," said Janet. "We'll see you later, Mom… Dad."

"Be careful, Darling," said Mrs. Williams worriedly, looking at Harry's broad shoulders and handsome face with concern.

Harry and Janet went out the door and walked down the driveway. Bubba and Alice, sitting in the front seat, broke an embrace and waved at them. Harry and Janet walked to the car and climbed into the musty smelling back seat.

"Bubba Hawkins," snapped Janet in a spitfire voice, "you stop necking in front of my house! What would happen if my Father saw you?"

Bubba blushed. "Aw come on, Janet… it was just a little kiss for old Bubba!"

"Well, save it for later," said Janet, adjusting her skirt in the seat.

"Let's get going, Bubba," said Harry sitting stiffly beside Janet. "Or we'll be late for the movie."

They drove down Route 17 across the Churchland Bridge and on to High Street. They passed Woodrow Wilson High School on the left.

"Allman was going to come along…with Georgia," said Bubba. "But something came up!"

"Who's Georgia?" asked Harry.

"Georgia Blake," said Janet. "She's the head Cheerleader, and she's been going with Allman forever."

"The brunette with…" began Harry.

"Yeah!" interrupted Janet. "The real pretty one with the big you-know-whats!"

Harry blushed. "I've seen her."

"It would have been crowded in here with six of us," said Alice uncomfortably.

"Makes it real cozy," smiled Bubba.

"I wouldn't go anywhere with Allman and Georgia," said Janet haughtily.

"Whatsa matter with them?" asked Bubba.

"You know what I mean, Bubba," said Janet sounding embarrassed, "you big dummy!"

"Yeah... yeah," said Bubba. "They do kinda... get with it, don't they?"

They rode on in an embarrassed silence.

"You know, Harry," said Bubba, changing the subject. "Shotgun has been pressing Coach Sacker at Wilson to play us at the end of the season."

"Would they let a Group II school play a Group I?" asked Harry.

"I don't know," said Bubba, "but Shotgun's hot on it."

"Wilson is supposed to have a good team this year, aren't they?" asked Harry.

"Yeah," said Bubba. "Dennis Aimsley is a real good halfback."

They continued down High Street toward the Commodore Theater, near the waterfront.

"So how's football practice going?" asked Janet moving closer to Harry in the back seat.

"Okay, I guess," said Harry, conscious of Janet's closeness.

"He's doing great," said Bubba, "... giving Jack Sanders a run for the money, I'd say."

"Really?" asked Janet.

"Bubba gives me too much credit," said Harry bashfully. "Jack is a good player... and I'm just hanging in there."

"Well, I hear you can run pretty fast," said Janet.

"I do okay," said Harry, working up his confidence as he felt Janet sitting close to him. He wondered what to do with his arm. It felt awkward with the arm just sort of hanging there between him and Janet.

"Well," said Janet, "all the girls are talking about the new guy... Harry Quester!"

"Really?" asked Harry, embarrassed.

Janet looked up at him and smiled mischievously. "Sure! And I guess I get the first chance to see if you're for real!"

"For real?"

"Sure," said Janet impishly. "Some guys look great... but turn out to be jerks!"

"So," said Harry carefully, "how about me?"

"Oh, I don't know yet, Harry," said Janet. "But I will..."

Harry wondered how he was supposed to act to not be evaluated as a jerk. "I guess I have the chance to check you out too, Janet!"

"That you do!" said Janet with a little squeal in her voice. "But not too closely!"

Harry blushed and felt strange, thinking about the little naked angels on the clock. He wondered what it would be like to check Janet out closely. He guessed that would make him a jerk! He shook the thought off as Bubba parked the Dodge. Harry got out and opened the door for Janet. They went to the Commodore Theater and purchased tickets. The Commodore was Portsmouth's finest theater. They went inside and as Harry's eyes adjusted to the darkness, he saw murals on the wall of ships and shipyards and the dark crimson curtain that hid the movie screen. They walked up to the balcony where they had a grand view of it all and sat near the back.

The crimson curtains opened and they were subjected to a news reel. A bearded Ernest Hemingway received the Nobel Prize for literature. The French Army was being defeated in some strange place called Viet Nam. Segregation was abolished in American schools. It all seemed remote to Harry as he debated whether he should put his arm around Janet in the flickering dark of the theater. He had an image of her throwing his arm from her shoulder indignantly and calling him a jerk. He looked over at Bubba and Alice. Bubba was sitting back in his seat with his arm thrown around Janet in what seemed to Harry a sophisticated way. Why was he so unsure about girls? They seemed to like him but they remained a forbidden mystery... at least, so far.

Harry had seen Ray Milland before. He had not seen Grace Kelly, and as the main feature started, he stared at her. She was beautiful in an icy, delicate way. By the time Milland hired Robert Cummings to kill Grace Kelly, Harry bravely put his arm around Janet. She didn't move or say anything, so he leaned back relishing this first step. When Robert Cummings was killed and Ray Milland began to frame Grace Kelly, Harry was caught up in the suspense of the movie. His interest was distracted when he felt Janet relax and lean against his shoulder. After the movie concluded, Bubba and Alice, Harry and Janet walked out of the theater truly absorbed by the story they had seen. Harry held Janet's hand. Maybe this was going okay, he thought.

"Hey, it was really neat how all the clues build up to that final phone call," said Bubba.

"She deserved what she got," said Janet, her eyes flashing. "Ladies shouldn't run around on their man!"

"It's only nine thirty," said Bubba looking at his watch. "You wanna go out to the Dismal Swamp and see The Light?"

"That's an old fakey story…what's The Light anyway?" asked Janet as Bubba opened the door to the Dodge.

They all climbed in and Bubba started the engine.

"The Light is green and it floats above the swamp," said Bubba mysteriously as the Dodge rolled down High Street.

"Some people call it foxfire," said Harry. "It's really swamp gas that rises in balls of phosphorescence and glows… when the conditions are right."

"How do you know so much?" asked Alice.

"We studied it in chemistry," said Harry. "Swamp gas is made when leaves and other stuff decays in a swamp where the water is real acidic. It changes into luminescent gas that rises."

"Oh come on," said Janet dubiously. "It sounds like a big ol' story to me."

"There's a legend about the swamp… about an Indian maid who died just before her wedding," said Bubba in a theatrically hushed voice, "and she still paddles her white canoe across the waters of Lake Drummond in the Dismal Swamp looking for her lover boy! The light floats above her wherever she goes!"

"Oh phooey," said Alice. "The Light is just an excuse to go park and neck!"

"So?" laughed Bubba.

"So… let's go!" giggled Alice.

"I've read Thomas Moore's poem about the Lady of the Lake in Dismal Swamp," said Harry. "There's really a legend about The Light in The Swamp."

"A poem?" asked Janet looking at Harry's ruggedly handsome face suspiciously.

"Yeah," said Harry as Bubba bumped the car over the railroad tracks on High Street. "I read it in English last year."

"Well, what is it?" asked Janet anxiously.

"The first verse is like this," said Harry. He paused and then recited in a voice he hoped sounded artistic:

They made her a grave too cold and damp,
For a soul so warm and true,
And she's gone to the Lake of the Dismal Swamp,
Where all night long, by her fire-fly lamp,
She paddles her white canoe.

Harry felt a chill as he recited the verse. He paused for effect and looked at Janet.

"That's beautiful" said Janet listening intently. "What's next?"

"I can't remember it all," said Harry, "but it's about how her lover goes looking for her in the swamp."

"Come on Harry," laughed Bubba, "what's the rest of it?"

"I do remember the last verses," said Harry slowly.

"I still say it's just an excuse to go parking out near The Swamp," said Alice.

"Tell me the verses you remember!" said Janet breathlessly.

The Dodge turned to go through Cradock and head south toward Military Highway. Harry struggled to remember the poem he had memorized to recite in English class last year. He continued in a halting voice:

He saw the lake, and a meteor bright,
Quick over its surface played,
"Welcome!" he said, "my dear one's light!"
And the dim shore echoed for many a night,
The name of the death-cold maid.

Till he hollowed a boat of the birchen bark,
Which carried him off from shore,
Far, far he followed the meteor spark,
The wind was high, and the clouds were dark,
And the boat returned no more.

"Remember Harry," interrupted Bubba, "Shotgun don't like Poets."

"Well," said Harry, trying to not break the mood, "maybe he should learn to like them... he might enjoy it!"

"Uh Oh," said Bubba, "don't let that one get out!"

"Shut up, Bubba," said Janet in an impatient voice. "Let him finish!"

Harry continued the poem.

But oft, from the Indian hunter's camp,
This lover and maid so true,
Are seen at the hour of midnight damp,
To cross the lake by a fire-fly lamp,
And paddle their white canoe.

"It kinda makes you shiver," said Janet, putting her hands to her shoulders.

"It does," said Harry, nodding.

"So... what happened?" asked Alice suddenly interested.

"Don't you see?" asked Harry. "He died in the swamp looking for her... and found the maiden only in his death. And now they're spirits in their white canoe... still in love."

"And The Light follows 'em around," said Bubba dramatically.

"How romantic!" exclaimed Janet clasping her hands together.

"Yeah!" exclaimed Bubba licking his lips. "But it's more fun when you're alive!"

"Oh Bubba," said Alice disgustedly, "you ruin it all!"

"You know a lot of things, Harry," said Janet, "for a football player."

"Can't football players know things?" asked Harry.

"I guess so," said Janet.

Bubba laughed and drove on. "Harry is kinda a brain, ya know," he said.

"Not really," said Harry. "I just read a lot."

Harry got braver and put his arm around Janet, feeling a strange lift in his spirits from the story of the mysterious lovers who died together in The Swamp. They drove out Military Highway, the old Dodge winding up to sixty miles an hour.

"Isn't this too far?" asked Janet worriedly. "I have to be home by midnight."

"Don't worry, Cinderella," said Bubba, pushing the Dodge a little faster.

"Don't go so fast, Bubba," said Alice.

"This ain't fast!" said Bubba urging the old Dodge on.

They turned off on Washington Road and then onto a narrow blacktop.

"Where are we?" asked Janet with concern.

"This here is Route 604," said Bubba. "The swamp road!"

The land around them suddenly became swamp, lined with towering cypress, gum and juniper trees. There was the smell of stinking mud and slime combined with the rich scent of laurel and honeysuckle.

"It smells funny here," said Janet. "Sort of disgusting and sweet... at the same time."

"That's funny," said Bubba in a very serious voice. "That's what Alice says about me... disgusting and sweet!"

"Oh I do not," said Alice, slapping Bubba playfully on the arm.

They heard a dog howling in the dark night as the Dodge turned left on an old "gum road" running toward Lake Drummond. It was a dirt foresting road, deserted for many years. They could see where whole groves of juniper or cypress were cut down, the cleared land now grown into a jungle of impenetrable canebrake.

"Sounds like a bloodhound," said Bubba. "They used to bring 'em down here to chase runaway slaves… and people say some of 'em are still running wild… like… like… what was that Sherlock Holmes thing?"

"The Hound of the Baskervilles," said Harry. "It attacked people on the Moors!"

"Right! Like that!" said Bubba.

"I'm not so sure I want to go any further, Bubba," said Janet looking fearfully at the thick underbrush that lined the road.

"Oh, them bloodhounds won't bother us," said Bubba. "Just look out for them black bears, panthers, and water moccasins!"

"Now I know I don't want to go down here," exclaimed Janet. "What time is it, anyway?"

It's only 10:15, Janet," said Bubba. "Don't worry about the time!"

They came to the edge of a lake. The shores were covered with matted, twisted and broken roots arching out of the dark water. The water of the lake was as dark as blood, darkened by juniper sap and tannic acid from decaying leaves. The roots seemed as dry as the bones of skeletons. A partial full moon rose, casting its rays across the mirror of the black water and a gnarled tree with crooked branches that grew out of the lake. Bubba stopped the Dodge and turned off the engine. It was suddenly silent except for the chirping of crickets and the occasional howl of a dog. The comforting sound of the engine was suddenly gone, leaving an atmosphere of awesome silence.

"What is this place?" asked Janet, a shiver in her voice.

"It's called Deer Tree Road," said Bubba, stretching his arms.

"It sounds like you've been here before," said Alice in an accusing voice.

"Oh yeah," said Bubba mysteriously, wriggling his fingers at her, "we came down here a month ago… huntin' coons."

"Why is it called Deer Tree?" asked Janet.

"See that old gnarled, bald cypress tree down there in the lake?" asked Bubba.

"I see it," said Janet, feeling uncomfortable.

"That tree was a deer a long time ago," said Bubba, "a white tailed deer… a doe! The doe changed into a tree to escape the hunting dogs. She was really a witch in the form of a doe. She ran into the lake and turned herself into a tree… and couldn't change back!"

"You're pulling my leg," said Alice in a haunted voice.

"No, not really," said Bubba with an air of extreme politeness, "but I can do that too!"

There was a smack as Alice swatted Bubba, then a round of giggles as Bubba wrapped himself around her. The front seat creaked with their weight. Harry sat uncomfortably next to Janet in the back seat not knowing exactly what to do. An owl started hooting from a nearby tree, adding to the eeriness.

"What's that?" whispered Janet, looking cautiously out the car window.

"Just an ol' hoot owl," whispered Harry.

"Does he have to sound like... that?" asked Janet.

"He's just sitting up there in the tree looking for a mouse... or a frog or something to jump on and eat!" said Harry.

"Well, I wish he'd go hoot somewhere else!" exclaimed Janet.

They sat there together in the musty back seat of the Dodge, the owl hooting and the crickets chirping.

"You want to get out and look at the Deer Tree?" asked Harry finding the courage to break the silence.

"Get out?" asked Janet in frightened tones. "There might be snakes... or bears... or something out there."

"Nothing's going to hurt us," said Harry. "Come on!"

The back door of the old Dodge squeaked as Harry opened it. Janet snuck a glance at Bubba and Alice entwined in the front seat and got cautiously out. They walked toward the Deer Tree leaving Bubba and Alice to whatever they were up to. They walked to the edge of the reeds that separated the lake from the shore.

"It's scary out here," said Janet taking Harry's hand, "... but beautiful."

"It smells like mud and honeysuckle," said Harry feeling a thrill run up his arm from the touch of Janet's hand. "And... it's beautiful and scary at the same time... strange, you know."

"You sound like you're really some kind of poet," said Janet looking up at him. "Not a guy who just tries to play tough... like the rest of them."

"No, not really a poet," said Harry, "but I like poetry."

"So do I, Harry," said Janet. She squeezed his hand and stood close to him. "I really liked the poem about... the girl in the white canoe."

"I know some more..." began Harry.

"Why don't you just kiss me, Harry?"

"Well... okay," said Harry, embarrassed.

"You do want to, don't you?"

"Sure... yes," stuttered Harry.

Harry leaned over and found her pink lips with his. He kissed her gently and stood back hoping he had done it right. "You taste like strawberries," he said.

"Are you sure?" asked Janet.

"I think so."

"Better taste again to be sure."

Harry kissed her again, this time wrapping his arms around her. She moved close to him and he could smell the fragrance of her hair above the mud and flower smell of the swamp. He held the kiss and she held it with him. Harry felt a strange warmness and elation he had never felt before.

"Would you follow me into a swamp in a white canoe, Harry?"

"Golly," said Harry embarrassed. "I guess... if I really loved you I would."

"How do you know when that is?" asked Janet looking up at him with wide blue eyes.

"I don't know," said Harry. "I guess... I guess, the first thing is whether the kiss feels right... or something like that."

"Kiss me again," said Janet softly, lowering her eyes, "and let's see if it feels right."

Harry kissed her again and felt her open her lips slightly. She ended the kiss gently and opened her eyes. She gasped and stepped back.

"Look!" she cried out, her voice filled with fear and wonder.

Harry turned to look behind him. There in the lake, a shining green orb rose and floated mysteriously above the reeds near the Deer Tree.

"The Light!" exclaimed Harry in awe.

They watched The Light as it hung in the air, casting a ghostly glow over the black water.

"Listen!" exclaimed Janet. "I hear something in the water!"

Harry strained his ears. "It... it sounds like paddles in the water... like a canoe!"

"This isn't happening," said Janet backing away from the water. "It couldn't be the white canoe!"

"I don't know," said Harry breathlessly.

"I'm going back to the car," said Janet in a small scared voice. "It's time to go home... or we'll be late and my father will be mad."

Janet started hurriedly toward the car. Harry followed, glancing back at the green orb which still danced near the Deer Tree. The reached the car and got into the back seat.

"Hey, Bubba," said Harry. "Come up for air! We can see The Light!"

Bubba's head came up above the seat, his face smeared with lipstick. "The Light? Where?"

"Right over there... by the Deer Tree," said Harry. He looked and the light was gone.

"Damn!" exclaimed Harry. "It's gone!"

Suddenly the old Dodge started rocking.

"Eieee!" screamed Janet.

Terrible apparitions appeared at the side windows of the car, twisted faces illuminated by ghostly green lights. Harry recoiled and wrapped his arms protectively around Janet. She hid her face against his shoulder. Then a hilarious round of laughter burst out from around them echoing across the lake and into The Swamp. The door of the Dodge was pulled open and a deluge of muddy water swept inside. The water crashed over Harry and Janet.

"My sweater!" screamed Janet.

Allman Buddinger jumped inside the back seat of the car next to Janet. "Boogie boogie boo!" he shouted and wrapped his arms around her. "Ol' Harry is out here in the swamp hugging the girls... how 'bout that!"

Janet struggled out of his grasp. "Allman, you fool!" she shouted angrily.

Arnie Eberly stood outside the car laughing. It had a cruel sound to it. Big Jim Jensen stood next to Arnie in his usual stoic stance, his arms hanging loosely by his side. Allman made faces at them holding a flashlight covered with green paper under his chin.

"How's the little clarinet player!" teased Allman. "Playing kissy-face with Ol' Harry?"

Janet hit Allman on the arm with a small fist and began to cry. It was all too much for Harry. He crawled over Janet, grabbed Allman by the collar and pushed him out of the Dodge. They fell onto the damp, muddy ground beside the car wrestling each other. Allman grabbed both of Harry's arms and rolled over on top of him. Harry slowly forced Allman's hands away and broke his arms free.

"Now that ain't nice at all," grunted Allman.

Allman grabbed Harry's hands and they matched their strength, struggling for supremacy. Harry felt his muscles straining. Allman's face turned red with the effort.

"What the hell ya fightin' me for?" asked Allman through clenched teeth. "I'm your best Ol' Buddy!"

Harry wriggled out from under Allman and they rolled over and over in the mud. Harry ended up on top. He struggled to keep Allman pinned down.

"Buddies don't play tricks on each other, Allman," gasped Harry.

He felt large hands grasp him by the shoulders and haul him to an erect position. He spun around and faced Big Jim Jensen. Allman jumped up behind him. Harry started to charge at Big Jim, but Allman restrained him.

"Not a good idea, Harry," said Allman soothingly into his ear.

"This New Guy is breaking up the Team," said Arnie in a whiny, acidic voice. "Thinks he some kinda hot shit!'

Big Jim released Harry and stood in front of him like a solid juniper tree in the moonlight.

"By the way, Harry Ol' Buddy," said Allman. "What was that crap you put in my helmet?"

"It wasn't crap," said Harry, wiping the mud from his face, "it was chocolate pudding."

"It felt like shit, Ol' Buddy," said Allman in mock threat.

"Next time, I'll try that," said Harry angrily.

Bubba walked over, still smeared with lipstick. Alice walked slowly behind him.

"Bubba, ya look like you're bleedin' to death!" laughed Allman.

Bubba wiped at the lipstick. "Ya came at the wrong time, Allman... I was just getting started!"

"You weren't getting' anywhere, Bubba," giggled Alice. "You was just striking out!"

"You set me up, Bubba?" asked Harry in a puzzled voice.

"Who me?" asked Bubba in a voice filled with feigned innocence.

"Did you like the light, Harry?" asked Allman, wiping mud from his shirt. "It was pretty hard wading out in that water and getting the lantern and the green paper up the darn tree."

"I had to kill a snake," said Big Jim matter-of-factly without changing his stoic expression.

"We hope we helped with the romance of the evening," said Allman with a muddy smile, bowing to them with a flourish.

"Very funny!" snapped Janet climbing out of the car with a tear stained face. "Look at what you did to my new skirt and sweater!"

Harry looked at Janet. She was soaked with water, her brassiere showing through her white blouse, the pink sweater turned a muddy brown.

"Ol' Harry here," laughed Allman, "he's real cool, ya know... he'll be able to explain them muddy clothes to your Old Man... won't you, Harry?"

There was another round of laughter.

"Very funny!" shouted Janet, near tears again.

"By the way, Bubba," said Allman, "we need a ride back... Big Jim's jalopy broke down."

"Climb in," said Bubba with a grin.

Bubba and Big Jim got in the front seat. Alice jumped in on Big Jim's lap.

"Yick!" shouted Alice. "You guys are all muddy!"

Arnie and Allman got into the back seat.

"Where are we going to sit?" asked Janet in alarm.

"Right on my lap, honey," grinned Allman with a practiced leer.

"Slip over you creeps," said Harry pushing himself in. "Sit here on my lap, Janet," he said, holding out his arms.

"I don't want to sit on anybody's lap," shrieked Janet. "You're all muddy... and it stinks!"

"You can stay here and row your white canoe, sweetheart," said Bubba mysteriously.

Janet wrinkled her nose ferociously as if smelling something worse even than The Swamp. She crawled into the back seat of the Dodge and perched herself precariously on Harry's knee. The Dodge jerked forward along the bumpy dirt road.

"Ouch!" screamed Janet. "Cut it out Allman!"

"Me?" asked Allman in mock dismay. "I didn't do nothing."

"Stop pinching me, you big clown!" shouted Janet tearfully.

"Keep your hands to yourself, Allman," said Harry menacingly.

Big Jim turned around from the front seat and glared at Harry.

"Stop the car, Bubba," said Big Jim in a threatening voice.

"Naw... keep on going, Bubba," said Allman, "it's okay Jim."

"You're the only pincher in the car, Allman," said Janet heatedly. "I know you!"

"Keep the peace, Allman," said Harry with determination. "Keep your hands to yourself!"

Allman laughed and the old Dodge bumped along Deer Tree Road toward Route 604, its shocks fully compressed and its rear end dragging. Janet adjusted her position away from Allman and settled into the crack between Harry and the door of the car.

"I'm sorry, Janet," whispered Harry into her ear.

"I thought you were different," sobbed Janet trying to hold her temper.

Laughter and shrieks echoed through the Great Dismal Swamp as the Dodge bumped along. A low mist settled over Lake Drummond and a mysterious green orb rose and hung suspended near the Dear Tree.

****

The first day in the new High School was a blur to Harry. There were so many new faces along with Spanish, Math, English, Chemistry, and Government. He was glad to finally go to the gymnasium for the last class, the time when all football players had Physical Education. It gave Coach Braun and extra hour to work on them before practice officially started. Harry saw Allman coming toward him as he opened the gymnasium door. He ignored Allman and went through the door.

"Hey! Harry, Ol' Buddy," said Allman. "Let's find some mud and wrassle... that was a lotta fun!"

"Fun for you, Allman," said Harry grumpily. "Not me. Next time you pull a stunt like that, I'll finish it!"

"You're a tough man, Harry," said Allman with a laugh. "It took me more than I thought to take you down."

Harry glared at Allman. "Who took who down?"

"I took you down!"

"That's what you think?"

"Yeah, but we had some fun, didn't we!"

Harry smiled in spite of himself. "Yeah, yeah, Allman," he said, "and we'll see who ends up on top!"

"Too bad you didn't make first string," said Allman. "You did a good job at summer practice."

"Don't worry about me, Allman," said Harry nonchalantly.

"I worry about all my Team," said Allman coming up and slapping Harry on the back.

Harry stopped, spun around and faced Allman. "Is it your team, Allman?" he asked in a heated voice. "Is it your special property... your little group of worshippers?"

Allman looked surprised. "What do ya mean by that?"

"I mean you take advantage of all these guys," said Harry with emotion. "You think you can get away with anything you want! Worse... they let you get away with any thing you want!"

"Hey!" exclaimed Allman. "Back off! I'm just trying to talk to ya, Ol' Buddy. You letting that thing in the swamp get to ya?"

"Dammit, Allman!" exclaimed Harry with anger and frustration. "It's one thing to play tricks on each other... it's another to play tricks on a girl a guy is dating!'

"Whatsa matter, Harry," asked Allman with a leer. "Not getting any?"

"Come on, Allman," said Harry in frustration. "I dated Janet once... I brought her home late with mud all over her clothes... and now her father won't let me near the house!"

"Don't worry, Harry," said Allman with a practiced grin. "There's more where that came from... and it's only pussy!"

"You know Allman, I don't know about you," said Harry shaking his head in disgust.

"You will, Ol' Buddy," said Allman still grinning. "Just give it time!"

They walked on into the dressing room. Larry Kidwell was passing out game uniforms.

"Here's your number, Allman," said Larry, running up to him. He held up a white jersey with the numbers zero zero on it in black, shaded with bright orange. The long sleeves of the jersey had a broad orange stripe with a thinner stripe on each side.

"Thanks, Larry," said Allman, rubbing Larry on the head. "You're a good kid!"

"Thanks, Allman," said Larry, beaming in adoration, "and here's your trousers." He handed Allman a pair of solid black football trousers with two thin orange stripes running down the side.

"It's getting close to game time!" shouted Allman holding up his jersey. "Hot damn!"

"Yeah," shouted Karl Darby, "and it's about time!"

A cheer rose from the boys, all of whom had received their game uniforms. Harry went to his locker and found a white jersey with the number thirty-two and the black trousers with the orange stripes.

"Pretty sharp, huh?" asked Tony as he pulled on his black trousers.

"Yeah," said Harry quietly. "Pretty sharp!"

"We got the best game uniforms around," said Bubba.

"You screwed me, Bubba," said Harry indignantly. "I didn't think you'd do anything like that."

"Aw, come on, Harry," said Bubba, a hint of regret in his voice. "It was just a joke."

"Yeah… sure," said Harry.

"Anyway, you came running back to the car just when I was getting a little titty!" grinned Bubba.

"Aw, isn't that a shame!" said Harry in mock pity. "You know, Bubba, you're like this whole team… that clown Allman tells you to do something… and by damn you do it no matter how ridiculous or screwy it might be!"

"What do ya mean?" asked Bubba defensively.

"Give me a true aid, Bubba… a grape one," said Harry mimicking Allman.

"What's wrong with that?" asked Bubba, a combination of hurt and anger in his eyes.

"You know what I mean, Bubba," said Harry. "Let's just forget it and get ready to play some ball!"

Harry got up and ran out of the locker room to afternoon practice.

****

It was Tuesday afternoon after the second day in the new school. The Team was assembled in the dressing room. They stood, listening attentively to Coach Braun clad in their black and orange game uniforms with the white jerseys that they used for road games.

"Now the first game in our new stadium is with Gloucester," said Coach Braun in a surprisingly mild voice as he addressed the team. "They got a new school just like we do… and call themselves 'The Dukes'," said the Coach, his voice becoming more agitated. "I don't know a lot about this team, as we haven't played them before. They play the Tee formation just like we do. They have a quarterback who's supposed to be able to throw the ball. We're pretty good at defending the run… but we need to look out for this throwing guy."

Coach Braun paused and looked around the room at the assembled team. He folded his right elbow against his body and brought it upward with a ferocious motion. "The best way to defend the pass is to nail the passer before he passes! Nail his butt to the ground!" shouted Braun. "Make him afraid to pass! We've got two weeks before this first game to get ready… really ready!"

There was a murmur of understanding from the players.

"So when they have the ball," said the Coach, anger building in his hoarse voice, "I want to see a mound of black and orange on top of that quarterback every cotton picking play!"

"We'll get him, Coach," shouted Jack.

"I know we can beat this team," shouted Coach Braun, his face clouding. "I also know… that any team we play can beat us if you guys aren't ready for 'em… if you're not ready for 'em… if you don't hit 'em the way we've practiced!"

"We'll win 'em all, Coach!" said Allman with his big toothy grin.

"Get out on the field…go on over to the new stadium," shouted Braun. "We gotta have some pictures taken!"

The team and the coaches all ran full speed out the dressing room door and along the back of the new school building to the gates leading to the new stadium. The field was surrounded by tall poles on top of which sat an impressive arrays of lights. On one side of the field was a long set of bleachers twelve high. On the other side was another set of bleachers fifteen high, topped by a small press and announcer's box. On the field were the black and orange uniforms of the Churchland Marching Band. The trumpets and clarinets started the first bars of Sousa's *The Washington Post March*. Majorettes twirled their batons in front of the band, led by a statuesque girl with long curly brown hair.

Coach Braun took off his forlorn looking hat and slapped it against his thigh. "Damn band!" he exclaimed, hopping around like he had a hotfoot. "Where did they come from?"

"I don't know, Coach," said Eddie Fearless. "They aren't supposed to be out there!"

"Well get those hornblowers off the field... they're stomping on all the white lines!"

"Calm down, Coach," said Slate, "ya gotta have a band you know!"

"Just get them off the field!" said Braun his face darkening.

"They have a right to be there too, Cliff," said Slate facing Coach Braun.

"Get 'em off!" glowered Braun.

"I'll take care of it," said Slate starting toward the Band Director.

****

It was a cold and blustery Thanksgiving Day afternoon in 1941. Portsmouth Stadium was filled with ten thousand fans for the traditional football game between the Wilson Presidents and the Granby Comets. Granby had a team that was competing for the state championship. Wilson had four wins, three losses and a tie. Slate Phelps and Cliff Braun stood together in the dressing room waiting for the signal from Coach Wilder to run out on to the field.

"I guess this game decides whether we have a winning season for our last year," said Slate Phelps, wearing an orange jersey with the blue number fifty-five on it."

"Yeah," said Cliff Braun dejectedly.

"What's the matter with you, Cliff?" asked Slate. "We gotta get up for this game!"

"I know," said Cliff, his face filled with sorrow.

"Well then, what's wrong?" asked Slate.

"This morning," said Cliff reluctantly, "my father got hurt."

"What happened?" asked Slate with concern

"He fell off the roof of that new filling station," said Cliff. "... the one on High Street and Elm where he was working. He's in the hospital."

Slate's expression changed to one of concern. "I didn't know..."

"I went to see him this morning," said Cliff, tears filling his eyes. "He said to get on out here and play the game."

"How's your Mother?" asked Slate.

"She's over there with him," choked Cliff. "He's hurt pretty bad."

Slate knew that Cliff could be very emotional, but he seldom exposed it. Now, he couldn't control it. Cliff let the tears run from his eyes.

"Ya don't know how much... how much... ya know what I mean," sobbed Cliff, "'til something like this happens."

"He'll be okay, Cliff," said Slate putting his hand on Cliff's shoulder. "We'll go out there and win this game for him!"

"I'm working on it," said Cliff, clenching his fists and snorting back the tears. "When I get on the field... I'll be ready!"

The Wilson team hit the field, feeling the sting of a cold wind as they ran to the sidelines and prepared for the kickoff. The Granby team, in blue and white uniforms with gold trim, was already on the field doing calisthenics.

The game began with a kickoff that Slate fielded and returned to Wilson's thirty-four yard line. Slate and the other halfback, Les Caprio, banged the ball to the Granby thirty-five before they had to punt. The punt sailed high and was downed by Wilson on the Granby four yard line. Four plays later, Granby punted. It was a poor punt and Slate fielded it at the Granby thirty and returned it to the Granby thirteen.

"This is gonna be a touchdown," said Clay with confidence.

"This big guard is giving me some trouble," said Phil Joyton, the center.

"Well, crack the sonofabitch in the mouth!" advised Shotgun belligerently.

"Thanks for the help, Shotgun," said Phil sarcastically.

On the next play, the ball popped straight up in the air behind Phil Joyton, and Granby's big two hundred and thirty pound guard snatched it out of the air. Two plays later, Granby fumbled and Cliff recovered. It seemed that Wilson would finally score, but several runs produced no yardage and Wilson gave up the ball on downs. The first quarter ended with no score.

"Come on, guys," urged Slate as they assembled in defensive positions. "Get the ball... we're gonna score!"

Granby moved the ball to their thirty yard line and punted. Slate returned the ball to the Granby forty-five. Wilson tried a pass on the first play. Quarterback Clay Coggle lateraled to Slate who heaved a pass to Cliff who had streaked to the goal line. Cliff reached for the ball, knowing he had a touchdown, but an arm flew in front of him and a Granby man intercepted the ball and fell to the ground at the Granby one yard line. Cliff ran over to Slate.

"That bastard tackle and the end are double teaming me, Slate," said Cliff eagerly. "You can get at the quarterback through the tackle hole."

"Okay, Cliff," said Slate, setting his jaw. "I'll try it!"

Granby lined up to run the ball from their one. Slate charged through the line from his halfback position and crashed into the Granby quarterback two yards deep into the end zone. He wrapped his arms around the man and brought him to the turf for a two point safety. Wilson two, Granby nothing. The first half ended with that score.

During half time, Coach Wilder spoke to the team. "Okay, players, we've got the lead," he said in a calm voice. "It's not much, but we need to hang onto it… and get a few more points to be sure. We've seen they can't score on us… so keep it up!"

"Coach, we need to beat them up real bad," said Cliff emphatically. "We haven't, like Coach Ismail says… intimidated 'em yet!"

Coach Wilder started to say something and changed his mind. "Rest up and be ready for the second half," he said, glancing at Ismail scornfully.

Rest up? thought Cliff. What kind of coaching was that? He proceeded to work himself into a frenzied rage. By the time he took the field, he was boiling mad at the Granby Comets. The third quarter was a defensive battle. Near the end of the quarter, Slate threw a perfect pass to Cliff who charged to the Granby twenty, dragging a Granby back the last five yards.

"We can run the ball in from here," panted Cliff in the huddle. "We can't risk another interception… just run it behind me… I'm killing 'em!"

"Coach Wilder has called another pass from Slate," said Coggle, "Like the first one we completed."

"Naw… naw," said Shotgun. "That ain't what we wanna do!"

"That's what we're gonna do," said Coggle. "Except this time to McLatter."

They broke the huddle and lined up. Slate ran to the left and threw the ball to Clyde McLatter in a tight spiral. A Granby defensive back made a diving catch in front of McLatter for another interception. Slate stamped the ground in frustration.

"Damn it all," muttered Shotgun as they took up defensive positions. "I told 'em we should run it… run it… run it!"

As the fourth quarter began, Granby seemed to pick up steam. Their Coach was jumping up and down and yelling at them from the sidelines. Cliff glanced over at Coach Wilder who stood stoically on their sideline, clinging to his two to nothing lead.

The Granby punter kicked a towering punt from his forty yard line. Wilson's fullback, McLow, fielded it and was tackled at the Wilson nineteen.

In the huddle, Clay called the fullback's number.

"Ya know, Clay," panted Cliff, "we ain't gonna score with a buncha fullback runs."

"Coach says to grind it out," said Clay defensively. "We got the lead!"

"Two lousy points?" asked Cliff with disbelief. "Ya call that a lead?"

"Look… Shotgun," said Clay in exasperation. "Will ya line up and run the damn play?"

Disaster struck on Wilson's next play as Clay Coggle fumbled the hand off to McLow and Granby's giant guard fell on the ball.

"Damn!" exclaimed Slate. "We shoulda listened to Shotgun!"

Three plays later, Granby's big fullback ran the ball over for a touchdown.

"We really blew that one," muttered Cliff, a sinking feeling in his stomach.

"Yeah," said Slate mournfully. "We really did!"

Granby's fullback ran the ball for the extra point and Granby had the lead, seven to two. That's the way it ended. Slate and Cliff trudged off the field feeling as low as they had ever been.

****

Chapter Six
Summer Practice III

The team came running out of the locker room in good spirits wearing their smelly practice uniforms, shouting and grinning.

"Okay!" shouted Coach Braun. "Coach Fearless, take 'em through some laps and wind sprints out there on the field... to get 'em used to it... and don't mess up the lines. Then we'll go over to the practice field and scrimmage."

"Alright you Truckers," shouted Coach Fearless. "You heard the man!"

The team began to run laps around the cinder track that surrounded the field in the new stadium. They ran easily now, conditioned to the task by the trials of tryouts and summer practice. Coach Phelps walked with Coach Braun to the bleachers.

"The team is in pretty good shape," said Phelps.

"Yeah," said Coach Braun in a frustrated voice, "but they're not mean enough yet... they don't have winning in their gut yet."

"The passing game needs more work," said Coach Phelps.

"Yeah, I guess so," said Braun with a shake of his head, "but if we run and block well, we won't need it. The way to win games is to run and keep the ball... use up time, score points and keep the other guy's offense off the field."

'Don't forget the Maury game, Coach," said Slate reflectively. "You can't afford to be too cautious... ya gotta keep the momentum."

"Yeah, yeah," said the Coach grumpily. "I know."

Just below the Press Box was a short man with a prominent nose, clad in a snappy hat with a feather in the hat band.

"Hi Al," said Slate to the man with the prominent nose.

"Hi Slate... Shotgun," said the short man. "The Truckers look pretty sharp!"

"Sharp... and tough!" exclaimed Coach Braun.

"How do you like being Principal over at Cradock, Slate?" asked Gollen.

"It's good," said Slate, "but I miss the football... and that's why Cliff lets me come over here and bother him."

Braun snorted. "He ain't no bother... he keeps me in line."

"That takes some doing, as I remember, Shotgun," said Gollen.

Braun snorted again. "Heck, Al, I'm just a big pussy cat now... ya know that!"

"I don't know about that," said Al with a knowing smile. "Now what can I run about the Truckers in the Al Gollen column this week?"

"Heck, has the paper ever had anything good to say about the Truckers?" asked Braun. "I thought you just wrote about Pete Sacker and Wilson!"

"Come on, Coach," said Al, "I always find some room for the Truckers… but you guys are… well, Group II and Wilson is Group I, you know… and they've got a good team this year too!"

"Well, this year we ain't gonna lose a game," said Braun sticking out his jaw. "And ya can put it in your paper that I said it!"

"Well, now, Cliff…" began Slate.

"No… I said it!" insisted Braun. "We ain't gonna lose a single game! And we ain't playing second fiddle to Pete and Wilson no more!"

Al Gollen was writing furiously. "You think you could beat Wilson… if you played them?" he asked, leading Braun on.

"Damn right we could," said Braun, his face becoming more ferocious than usual. "We've got a bunch of really tough guys this year!"

"Can I quote you on that?" asked Gollen.

"Sure as hell can!" exclaimed Braun.

"We'd give Pete Sacker a good game, Al," said Slate, standing behind Cliff and waving his hand at Al to dampen the Head Coach's remarks.

"You know," said Cliff adamantly, "we taught Pete Sacker everything we knew when he was at ECTC with us. We can beat him!"

"You wanna play him?" asked Al anxiously.

"The schedules are fixed and the Superintendent will never agree to a post season game between us," said Slate diplomatically. "And, I think Wilson has a lot more depth than we can come up with at a small school."

"Suffolk plays them this year, I believe," said Al. "They're Group II."

"Yeah, and we're gonna beat Suffolk!" said Shotgun loudly.

"Pistol Pete Sacker and Shotgun Braun," mused Al with a smile. "It makes a good story!"

"Don't run it, Al," said Slate. "It's too early in the season for that kind of stuff."

"Go ahead!" exclaimed Coach Braun, "run it any time you like!"

"I'll think about it," said Al.

"You do that, Gollen," said Braun sticking out his lower jaw and squinting at the little man with the gold tooth.

A tall hefty man in the uniform of the Portsmouth Police walked slowly toward them.

"Hi Slate," said the tall man.

"Hi Grady," said Slate, "what brings you out here?"

Grady Spearman was six feet four and weighed in at over two hundred and forty pounds. His round, baby face did not match the power in his body.

"I'm just casing the new stadium, Coach," said Grady. "I'll be out here … to look out for you guys."

"Al… you know Officer Spearman, Portsmouth Police, don't you?" asked Slate. "He helps us with game security on Friday nights."

"I sure do," said Al extending a hairy hand to the policeman. "I remember when you played for Churchland, Grady… what was it... ten years ago?"

"More like twelve," said Grady, shaking Gollen's hand. "But we weren't so good then."

"How ya doing Grady?" asked Coach Braun.

"Doing great, Coach," said Grady. "I'm ready to see some good football!"

"We got a scrappy bunch this year," said Slate. "You're gonna see some hard hitting!"

"That's great," said Grady. "I'm ready!"

"I heard you were being promoted to Lieutenant," said Slate.

"It's in the works," said Grady. "But I still enjoy working the football games… so I'll be around."

"What about the Suffolk game, Coach?" asked Gollen. "You guys have never beaten the Red Raiders!"

"Like I said, we're gonna beat 'em!" said Braun removing his pork pie hat and twisting it in his hands. "Especially them!"

"You know they have a new coach, don't you?" asked Gollen, putting his finger on his prominent nose and widening his eyes.

"I knew they were looking for one," said Slate. "Who've they gotten?"

"His name is Fatso Hathaway," said Gollen with a sly grin. "Remember him… played tackle for Wilson a while back? Went on to play for Virginia? He left Wilson while you guys were still playing!"

Coach Braun stared at Gollen, complete surprise on his square face.

"Fatso told me he was going to beat Churchland and Shotgun Braun so bad they'd never come to Suffolk again!" said Gollen, watching Braun with a hint of humor.

Coach Braun threw his mangled hat to the ground, his face turning beet red. "Fatso Hathaway?" he shouted in astonishment. "That worthless sonofabitch!"

"That's not for quote, Al," said Slate quickly.

Gollen grinned, his gold tooth showing. "He never said it!"

"The hell I didn't!" muttered Coach Braun.

"You mean the Hathaway that played tackle for Wilson in the late thirties?" asked Slate seriously. "Ennis Hathaway?"

"Yep," said Gollen. "That's the one."

"They call him Fatso... in the press?" asked Slate in surprise while Cliff fumed and twisted his hat in his big hands.

Al Gollen grinned a big grin that wrinkled his face and showed the gold tooth in place of his left canine. "Well Slate... if your name was Ennis, wouldn't you rather be called Fatso?"

****

The next day, Harry walked the corridors of the new school toward first period English Class. The corridors had a new smell to them, and the lockers that lined the hallway were bright and shiny, their combination locks in a perfect line. Far down the corridor he saw the girl with the brown pony tail he had seen on Chandler Point that day in the boat. His heart skipped a beat. What was it about her that was so mysterious... so beautiful? He paused and watched her walk along the corridor toward him, her pony tail bouncing behind her. He wasn't sure that she saw him, or if she cared to see him. Maybe Paige Garnette wasn't interested at all, and he was imagining things when he saw her looking at him that day on the river. She turned abruptly into a classroom and disappeared.

Harry started forward again. He liked English class. He read a lot and English was usually easy for him. He saw Janet come up the steps and turn toward him. His heart jumped. What would he say to her? What could he say to her?

"Hi Janet," said Harry bravely. "What class have you got?"

Janet looked at Harry with a small smirk on her face. "Latin," she said. "By the way, my pink skirt washed out okay... but my Father still doesn't believe me."

"I'm sorry again, Janet," said Harry. "Can I come over and talk to your parents!"

"Great god... no!" exclaimed Janet, her blue eyes wide. "Mother mentioned your name and Daddy screamed and went outside... he kicked the lawn mower until it broke!"

"That doesn't sound too good," said Harry in a subdued voice. "What can I do?"

"Nothing," said Janet, "for now, you're off my menu... and Bob Porter asked me for a date."

"Yeah?" asked Harry feeling a hurt in his chest where his heart was. "Well, Bob is a good guy!"

"Maybe Mr. America won't take me out to a swamp!" said Janet with a little smile and a flip of her hair.

A woman with luxurious brown, curly hair, a brilliant smile and a striking figure appeared in the hallway walking toward them.

"Good morning, Mrs. Phelps," said Janet politely.

"Good morning, Janet… Harry," said Mrs. Phelps.

"Good… good morning," stuttered Harry, trying to keep from staring.

Mrs. Phelps smiled and walked on to her classroom.

"Who's that?" asked Harry in wonder, his eyes following Mrs. Phelps. "And how did she know my name?"

"Silly you," said Janet. "That's Mrs. Phelps… Coach Phelps' wife. She teaches English."

"Wow!" exclaimed Harry.

"She's real pretty, don't you think?" asked Janet.

"She's beautiful!" exclaimed Harry in awe.

Janet smiled. "You guys are all alike," she said, turned and walked away down the hall, her hips swaying. She glanced back over her shoulder and winked at him. "Don't give it up, Harry! Be sure to call!"

"I'll remember that," muttered Harry, feeling a little better. He turned back toward Mrs. Davison's English classroom.

Harry went into the classroom and pulled himself clumsily into a combination desk and chair. It was finished in a light maple color and had a metal shelf underneath for books. It was small and cramped for someone Harry's size. The thought of sitting in it for fifty minutes in the early September heat was frightening. He looked out the big windows which had panes near the bottom open to the outside. A slight breeze came through the open panes that only partially alleviated the heat in the class room. He could see the football stadium behind the school. How was he going to convince Coach Braun to let him play? The problem chased itself in his mind with no solution.

"Hi, Harry," said the girl sitting in the desk next to Harry.

The sound of the voice startled Harry and he turned abruptly. "Hi… Clara," said Harry looking at the pretty girl with the brownish blonde hair. She wore a blue skirt and a loosely fitting light yellow blouse with a lacy collar. She had the almost mandatory saddle shoes and bobby sox on her feet. Her smile radiated across the space between them.

"I saw you at football practice while we were practicing Cheerleading," said Clara. "Your uniforms are real spiffy!"

"Thanks," said Harry. He busied himself with his new English book, not knowing what to say. He glanced out of the corner of his eye at her. Clara sat erectly in her desk watching the other students come in. Harry only knew the ones that played football. There was Arnie and his buddies Bart and Bryan. Arnie sat on the other side of Clara, folding into the desk in his permanent slouched position. He glanced at Clara with a lifted eyebrow, then leaned back and closed his eyes. Bart sat behind Arnie. Mrs. Davison came into the room carrying a thick book in her arm. She was about forty years old, short and thin with a small scar on her forehead and a determined look on her angular face.

"Now, all of you sit down and pay attention!" said Mrs. Davison in a firm tone. "And you, Eberly... wake up or you'll be starting the morning in the Assistant Principal's office!"

Arnie opened his eyes slightly but remained in his elongated slouch position.

"And sit up straight!" said Mrs. Davison sharply, giving him her evil eye. "You can't think all stretched out like that!"

Arnie reluctantly sat up in the desk, somehow maintaining the appearance of still being in a slouch. His face held a look of contempt. He smoothed back his ducktails and ran a comb through his crew cut. Bart adjusted his slouch to match.

"Welcome to Junior English," said Mrs. Davison. "Welcome to Harry Quester who comes to us from Edison High in Alexandria Virginia."

Harry was embarrassed and nodded as the whole class, less Arnie and Bart, looked at him. "Thank you, Mrs. Davison," he said self consciously.

"Now this year we're going to begin with the classic works of literature," said Mrs. Davison, "and then we'll go into sentence structure and the way the classic authors used words and sentence structure to set their scenes and moods, and how they expressed themselves through their works. We'll look at how they used stories to illustrate morals and explore the issues of their day."

Mrs. Davison paused and looked around the room. "Are there any questions?"

"Which author are we going to study first, Mrs. Davison?" asked Clara.

"Why, who else but Shakespeare, the best of them all!" said Mrs. Davison with a smile. "Get out your books and turn to page thirty-four."

There was a rustling of feet and a shuffling of pages.

"William Shakespeare wrote three primary types of plays; tragedies, histories and comedies," said Mrs. Davison. "You will see a list of them on the page... and you should be familiar with his works. We will begin with a comedy... *The Taming of the Shrew*. Tonight you should read Scenes One and Two. Tomorrow, we will discuss how the Bard writes in a poetic rhythm that has a wonderful beauty. I shall expect you to be able to discuss the characters in these scenes and speculate on how the author is building the framework for the story."

Harry snuck a glance at Clara. She was looking at him cautiously. She smiled back and looked quickly away. The shape of her face and lips was intriguing to Harry, and he found himself wondering what it would be like to have a date with her.

"If there are no questions," said Mrs. Davison, "I would like for you to start reading the scenes from *The Taming of the Shrew* now. As you read, if there are questions, I will answer them. You will find that the Bard had an unusual writing style... and it will take some reading before you become accustomed to it."

Harry opened the English book in front of him, turned to *The Taming of the Shrew,* Scene 1 and began to read. Padua, A Public Place, it said. Harry had not read Shakespeare before. It began with a long, poetic dialogue from a character called Lucentio, who he eventually figured out was in love with a girl whose name was Bianca. It took Lucentio a long time to say anything, and he said it in a confusing jumble of words that mixed philosophical thought with flowery prose. It seemed that many of the characters were in love with Bianca, the daughter of Baptista, a rich man from Padua, but none of them wanted anything to do with her contentious sister, Katharina. Harry glanced over at Arnie. He was once again slouched and asleep. Bart was staring at the ceiling.

"What do you think, Harry?" whispered Clara.

Harry looked back at the bright blue eyes of the girl in the desk next to him. "I... I think Bianca is a lucky girl to have so many men in love with her," he whispered bashfully.

"No, I mean about Churchland," whispered Clara, confused. "How do you like Churchland... so far?"

"Oh!" whispered Harry, "I think it's great!"

Clara smiled at him and he turned back to *The Taming of the Shrew*. It would take some effort to learn to understand what was being said in Shakespeare's words... it was a new and different language, almost a poem but not a poem. He snuck another glance at Clara. It would take some effort to get used to Churchland High School too... that was for sure! After endless moments, the bell rang. The students filed out of class.

****

Harry ran out of the locker room for afternoon practice. Arnie ran up beside him, their cleats changing from clatter on the sidewalk to muffled thuds on the grass as they ran.

"Thank you Mrs. Davison," whined Arnie in an intended mimic of Harry.

Harry looked at Arnie with a question in his eyes. "What's wrong with that?" he asked.

"Ya got your nose up her ass already," said Arnie derisively, "and it's only the first day! She thinks you're a poet... or something!"

"Just being polite," said Harry defensively.

"I seen ya talking to Clara," said Arnie, his eyes fixed on Harry. "Don't get any big ideas, Poet!"

Harry looked into the watery eyes beside him. "Is that a threat, Arnie?" he asked.

"Call it what ya want," said Arnie looking away. "She's my girl, ya know!"

"I just met her," said Harry in an annoyed voice, "... and she asked me something about how I liked Churchland... that's all."

"Just remember what I said," muttered Arnie and ran on ahead of Harry.

Harry felt his anger rising as they ran to the practice field. It seemed he couldn't get anything right at Churchland... he couldn't even talk to anyone... to any girl without getting someone mad at him. He wondered what would happen if he ever worked up enough courage to talk to the girl with the brown pony tail. The team reached the practice field, ran two laps and went through the usual set of warm-up calisthenics. When they finished, Coach Braun blew a whistle.

"First string line up," shouted Coach Braun. "Second string on defense... we're gonna have a no contact scrimmage and run through some more plays... then we start the real practice... some real hitting!"

On the first play, Arnie ran a quick, short crossing route directly in front of Allman. Allman tossed the ball to him and he caught it. Harry tagged Arnie with a rough shove from his linebacker position.

"Hey, Poet!" shouted Arnie, animosity in his voice. "Godammit! This is no contact, remember?"

Harry grinned. "Just tagging you, Arnie... so you'd know I gotcha good! And don't call me Poet!"

"You a wise guy, Quester?" asked Bart in a rough voice.

"Naw, he ain't nothing but a Poet," said Arnie sarcastically. "He reads Shaky Spear ... and all that stuff!"

Arnie glared at Harry and pushed him with his hands. Harry stepped back. Arnie followed, his slack-jaw face contorted in anger.

"You think you're some kinda big shit from Northern Virginia, don't ya?" hissed Arnie. "Some kinda wise ass who knows everything... right?"

"Cool it, Arnie," said Harry, stopping and standing his ground.

Arnie swung at Harry. Harry ducked and caught the blow with his forearm. He felt his temper flaring and fought to control it. He didn't need a fight with Arnie. He didn't like to fight, and knew little about it. The team didn't need any fights among the players. He caught the next blow with his hand and held Arnie's arm away from him.

"Knock it off, Arnie," cried out Matt Pittinger running to where Harry and Arnie faced off, followed by Burt Noonan.

"Screw you, Pittinger," said Arnie, pushing Matt away. "You too, Noonan!"

"Come on Arnie," said Burt in his quiet drawl. "Don't start somethin' nobody wants!"

"We don't need no fights, Arnie!" said Hero, coming up behind Matt.

"Whatsa matter, Quester?" sneered Arnie. "You can't take a little joke in the swamp?"

"What about it, Quester… ya can't fight your own fights?" asked Bryan Muller in a belligerent voice.

Harry pushed Arnie away. Allman ran up and grabbed Arnie. He nodded at Big Jim who grabbed Arnie and pulled him away. Arnie struggled with Big Jim. Big Jim held him with ease in a powerful grip.

"Not a good idea, Arnie," said Harry with a wary smile.

"Okay, Harry Ol' Buddy," said Allman. "Be nice to my receivers, will ya?"

Harry frowned, his heart thumping in his chest. He forced a smile. "Okay, Allman… I'll be nice… for awhile!"

Coach Phelps came running over.

"What was that all about?" asked Phelps, a frown on his face.

"Nothing Coach," said Harry, "just a little disagreement… that's all."

"Come here, Arnie," shouted Slate.

Arnie walked to where they stood with his usual slouch. "Yeah Coach?"

"You got a bone to pick with Harry?" asked Phelps.

Arnie glared at Harry with his watery blue eyes. "Just keep him outa my way, Coach… he don't belong here… on this team!"

"You guys are team mates," said Slate angrily. "You can settle your differences off the field, but while you're out here ya get along and ya work together! You guys understand?"

"Shit," muttered Arnie.

"What did you say?" asked Slate, staring at Arnie with ice blue eyes.

"Nothin', Coach."

"That's what I thought!" said the Coach. "Now you guys figure out how to be team mates!"

"Yeah, Coach," said Arnie without emotion.

"Yes Sir," said Harry.

"Good," said Slate, "ten laps together after practice… both of you!"

"Awww man…" exclaimed Arnie shaking his head in disbelief.

The team went into its huddle. Arnie and Harry took their positions, still glaring at each other. The next play was a pass to Bud Darby, the right end, in the flats. Bud ran past Harry. Allman hurled the ball in Bud's direction in a wobbly spiral. Bud and Harry both leaped for it, but it was high and went out of bounds. Harry crashed into Bud and they both fell to the ground with a jarring thud.

"What the heck, Harry?" exclaimed Bud, pulling himself up painfully. "What are ya… some kind of headhunter or something?"

Harry jumped to his feet. "Just trying to get the ball, Bud… that's all."

Harry offered Bud his hand and pulled him up.

"If that's no contact," grinned Bud good naturedly, "I don't want to see you in full contact, Harry… unless it's with the other team!"

"We can do better than that," shouted Coach Fearless. "You're throwing too high, Allman, and you're leading him too much. Keep it down!"

"I'm gonna get out my shotgun and shoot some of those… darn wounded gooses, Allman!" shouted Coach Braun, making shooting signs into the sky. The team chuckled quietly. "That pass honked all the way to the sideline!"

"Here comes a perfect spiral, Coach," said Allman making passing motions as he ran toward the huddle.

Porter called the huddle. Harry watched the first string closely. This was bound to be another pass to Bud. He braced himself. The first string trotted to the line. The ball was snapped and Bud Darby faked at Harry and then turned outward toward the sidelines, running at full speed. Harry recovered from the fake and turned on a burst of speed. Allman's pass was short and nearly spiral as it hit Harry right in the number thirty-two. He gathered it in and ran toward the first string end of the field before slowing and holding the ball in the air.

"I'll take the wounded goose," shouted Braun hoarsely, "but don't throw any interceptions, Allman! It's a stupid way to give the other guy the ball!"

"Okay, Harry, just throw me the ball," said Coach Fearless, blowing his whistle.

Harry threw it to him in an arching spiral. Fearless caught it easily.

"Where'd you learn to throw, Harry?" drawled Fearless.

"I used to throw some… at the other school," said Harry.

Eddie Fearless threw the ball into the air in a little spiral and caught it. He looked at Harry curiously. Coach Braun came stalking over to where Coach Fearless stood.

"What kinda passing game is that anyway, Coach?" grumbled Braun so that only Fearless could hear it. "I think we'd better run the ball or we're in trouble."

"We need some more work, Coach," said Fearless.

"Yeah... yeah... keep working on it," said Braun.

****

"Harry," shouted Coach Fearless. "Come over here."

Harry ran to where Fearless stood with Bud Darby, Terry Moddy and Allman.

"I wanna see ya throw the ball," said Coach Fearless.

Harry looked at Allman, who shrugged.

"I can't throw long," said Harry, watching Allman closely.

Fearless tossed Harry a ball. "Go out about ten yards, Bud."

Bud ran five yards and then slanted outward. Harry threw a spiraling ball to Bud. It was on target. Bud jogged back and tossed the ball to Harry.

"Terry, go out twenty yards," said Fearless.

Terry ran directly out. Harry threw a high spiraling ball that was two yards beyond where Terry could reach it. Terry came back and threw the ball to Allman.

"Okay, Allman, throw twenty yards to Bud."

Bud ran the longer pattern. Allman threw a wobbly spiral that hit Bud in stride. Bud ran back and tossed the ball to the Coach.

"Okay, guys," said Coach Fearless. "Get back over there for scrimmage."

Harry and Allman jogged back toward where the rest of the team was setting up for scrimmage.

"What was that all about?" asked Harry.

"I guess the Coach thinks you can pass, Harry, Ol' Buddy," said Allman dolefully. "Maybe he thinks you oughta be quarterback!"

****

"Okay... you guys line up for scrimmage!" shouted Coach Braun, "Enough of this pansy stuff! I want full contact... and I want to see some hitting! "

Porter called the huddle for the first team. They huddled for a few seconds. Porter broke out of the huddle and ran to where the ball waited on the line. The others followed a short few seconds later. The first play was a run by Karl Darby. He took a lateral and tried to run around the end Tony Zee defended. Tony ran parallel to Karl, matching his speed. Karl turned up field and put a fake on Tony. Tony held fast, his arms spread wide and crashed into Karl, bringing him down.

Coach Braun jumped up in the air, jamming his fist toward the heavens. "That's a good tackle! Who're you, anyway?"

"Zee," said Tony climbing to his feet. "Tony Zee."

"Okay, Zee," said Coach Braun with a fierce expression. "Hit 'em again!"

The next play was another run by Jack Sanders. He ran around end directly at Benny Norwood. Benny backed away and tried to tackle Jack with his arms. Jack galloped though Benny's arms as though they were light brush in the forest and ran on to the goal posts.

Coach Braun's whistle blew. "Great gobs of crap!" he shouted. "What kinda tackle was that supposed to be, Norwood?"

Braun ran toward Norwood and stuck his chin into the boy's face. "You can't tackle a man with your doggone arms! Don't you know that? Huh? Huh? You have to hit him with your shoulders and wrap him up... knock him off balance and wrap your arms around his legs so he can't recover! Why don't you understand that? Huh? Huh?"

Norwood looked afraid and confused. "I don't know Coach."

"I tol' ya the same thing last year," shouted Braun.

Coach Braun backed away and ran at Benny. He hit him in the midsection with his shoulder, wrapped his arms around the boy's legs and lifted him high off the ground. He dropped Benny on the ground. Benny writhed in the grass, holding his shoulder and wincing.

"That's the way ya gotta tackle, Norwood!" shouted Coach Braun. Blood trickled from behind his left ear.

Braun looked at the frightened boy, his head cocked at an angle, staring at him.

"Ya afraid to take a hit?" asked the Coach, his eyes burning with intensity. "Is that it? Ya gotta be willing to take a hit to give one, ya know!"

"Yes Sir," said Benny, his eyes wide with fear.

"When're ya gonna be a football player, Norwood?" shouted Braun, more blood running from his ear. "Your ol' man said ya were ready to play this year! Are ya? Are ya? Or are ya some kinda scaredy-cat or somethin'?"

"I'm trying, Coach," said Benny, getting painfully to his feet.

"Well, stop trying and do it!" muttered Coach Braun.

Benny started running toward the dressing room, holding his shoulder.

"Where're ya going, Norwood?" shouted Braun.

"I gotta go in and see about my shoulder, Coach!"

Braun ran up behind Benny and gave him a kick in the trousers. "Go on… you're worthless out here 'til ya decide to play football!"

Harry couldn't take it any more. He ran between Coach Braun and Benny as the Coach wound up for another kick. He put his arm around Benny's shoulders.

"I'll give you a hand, Benny," said Harry, glancing apprehensively at the Coach.

Braun paused when Harry ran between him and Norwood.

"What're ya doing, Kester?" screamed Braun, his square face turning red. He wiped impatiently at the blood on the side of his face.

"I'm just helping Benny some, Coach," said Harry defiantly, his eyes intense, his anger building.

"You leave Norwood to me!" shouted Coach Braun, his eyes wide. "Get back over there where ya belong!"

The whole team watched as Harry walked along with Benny. Coach Fearless pulled Norwood out of Harry's grasp. "Go on and practice Harry," he said. "I'll take care of Benny."

"Okay, Coach," said Harry, pulling away and running back to his position

"You okay, Benny?" drawled Fearless.

"I don't know, Coach," said Benny, rubbing the soreness in his shoulders, "My shoulder hurts a lot."

"Go on in the dressing room," said Fearless. "I'll come in and check it out!"

"Thanks, Coach," said Benny. He turned and trotted off the field.

Coach Braun stood, his hands on his hips staring at Harry. Blood trickled slowly down the side of his face. Harry turned to face him, his heart thumping loudly in his chest. They stared at each other for a long moment.

"Hey Coach," said Harry quietly, "your ear is bleeding."

Braun wiped at his ear, not taking his intense eyes off of Harry.

"Coach, take this," said Slate handing Cliff a handkerchief.

"What?" exclaimed Braun. "My ear?"

"Yeah, Coach… wrap this on your ear," said Slate patiently. "You musta caught it on Benny's belt buckle."

Coach Braun took the handkerchief and held it to his ear. He took it away and glared at the blood. He jumped up and down, doing a little hotfoot dance.

"Damn it all!" shouted Braun. "That Boy almost took my ear off!"

Coach Braun stalked over to his 1950 Buick sedan parked by the practice field. He foraged in the trunk of the car, retrieved an old brown leather football helmet and stalked back to the practice. He took off his hat, folded it carefully and put it in his pocket. The team watched in wonder as he put the handkerchief behind his bleeding ear and jammed the old leather helmet onto his head.

"Well, don't just stand there!" shouted the Coach angrily. "Let's see those plays! Do ya know 'em? Huh?"

The teams lined up and ran another play. Allman faded back and raised his arm to throw one of his wobbly passes. Arnie darted out of the line, headed straight for Harry and at the last moment, changed direction to head downfield. Harry adjusted and ran close behind Arnie. Allman's wounded goose wobbled over their heads and into Arnie's outstretched hands. He caught the ball and kicked up his heels, beginning to run. Harry launched himself and hit Arnie, wrapping his arms around the tall boy's legs. They crashed to the ground with a jarring thud. Harry lay on top of Arnie for a second as the shock of the fall ran through him like electric energy. He willed himself to his feet and offered Arnie a hand.

Arnie sneered at Harry and got up on his own. He shoved Harry away. "You trying to hurt me, Poet? Is that it?"

Hal Newton ran up to them. "Nice tackle Harry," he shouted with a grin missing a front tooth.

"Shut up, Newton," said Arnie with a sneer. He took a step toward Harry, pushing Hal aside. "You stay outa my face, Poet… or you're gonna regret it!"

Hal grabbed Arnie's arm, a look of anger on his thin face. "Watch it, Arnie!" he exclaimed.

Arnie brushed Hal's hand away and took a step closer to Harry.

Coach Braun ran over to them. "You guys want more laps after practice than ya already got?" he shouted, anger in his voice. "What the… what the heck ya doing, Kester?"

"Learning to make hard tackles, Coach," said Harry. "The kind you like!"

"Cut out the fighting, Kester," said Coach Braun in a hasty, confused voice. "We're here to play ball!"

"Yes Sir, Coach," said Harry as the Coach stomped away.

Arnie glared at Harry. "Ya gotta have more than that, Poet, to stop me," he said with acrimony.

Arnie turned and trotted back to the huddle. They ran a dozen more plays and then Coach Braun blew his whistle. The sun was low in the sky, the bottom of its red orb touching the tree line.

"Eberly!" shouted Coach Phelps. "You and Quester start those laps!"

"You guys are gonna be out here until Eberly and Kester finish those laps," shouted Coach Braun.

A silent groan came from the players as the sun sank below the tree line. Harry and Arnie ran to the track around the practice field and began running. Slate ran up beside them.

"Run it side by side, fellows," said Slate firmly.

Harry moved up to run beside Arnie. Slate ran alongside matching them step for step.

"You guys run in step," shouted Slate. "You heard me… get in step and stay that way!"

"Aw, come on, Coach," moaned Arnie. "This ain't the Army!"

"Do it, Arnie," said Slate between his teeth.

Harry skipped until they were in step.

"Now you both run at the same speed and stay together… and in step!" said Slate. "Run together… like a team!"

Arnie glared at Harry. Harry winked at him. "Come on Arnie… stay in step!" he said with an edge in his voice.

"Screw you, Poet," said Arnie with a sneer.

"Screw you, Hood" said Harry trying to contain his anger.

Arnie glowered at Harry.

"We got some special shit for ass-holes like you, Quester," said Arnie.

"You guys knock off the crap," said Slate.

"I'm running, Coach," said Arnie. "And I'm in step. But I ain't gotta like this New Guy!"

"Remember," said Slate running alongside them, "your team mates can hit the showers as soon as you slowpokes finish!"

****

The players, tired from the grueling practice, clomped into the dressing room, their cleated shoes echoing around the locker filled room.

"How were the laps, Harry Ol' Buddy?" asked Allman.

"Okay," said Harry, "no sweat… but I don't understand what Arnie's problem is."

"You hit him pretty hard, Ol' Buddy."

"We're supposed to hit hard," said Harry with a frown.

"That's what the man says," agreed Allman.

"I've been practicing… hitting hard" said Harry wrinkling his brow.

"Yeah, you have!" acknowledged Allman.

"The only way I'm gonna get to play some ball is if I do what the Coach wants," said Harry defensively, "and that's hit people real hard."

"Seems like you might play some quarterback," said Allman lifting an eyebrow.

"I don't think so," said Harry worriedly. "I'm better at fullback… but I can throw short distances pretty well… if we need that kinda play."

"Maybe we do," said Allman, "but remember, ya gotta do things here, Harry… things to get the guys to accept ya… ya know what I mean?"

"I guess so, Allman," said Harry with annoyance. "But I don't have to put up with guys dishing out stuff… like Arnie… like you at The Swamp!"

"Get the chip off your shoulder, Harry Ol' Buddy," said Allman, his irritation beginning to show.

"I don't have a chip," said Harry vehemently, "just play it straight with me… that's all I ask."

Allman looked at Harry with a question in his eyes. "Ya know, ya came awful close to really pissing off Shotgun out there!"

"He shouldn't kick anyone," said Harry defensively. "It's not the way you make people want to play for you."

"Norwood is a screw-off," said Allman in a serious voice.

"You shouldn't kick the screw-offs either," said Harry determinedly. "If someone complained about it, the Coach could get in a lot of trouble… and we don't want that."

Allman looked at Harry strangely. "Okay, Harry Ol' Buddy," he said, thoughtfully, "just keep your sense of humor… if ya have one!"

****

Harry sat on the bench in front of his lockers and slowly undressed. He mulled over Allman's comment in his mind. Did he have a chip on his shoulder? He didn't think he had one. But maybe. Tony and Bubba sat down beside him. Rob Sonda sat on the bench across from them. He was a cocky boy with black hair, sleepy looking eyes and a permanent swagger.

"You were pretty tough out there today, Little Brother," said Harry.

"Thanks," said Tony. "So were you!"

"My cousin is outa his mind," said Bubba. "Why'd you take up for Benny? Ya really pissed the Coach off!"

"I don't care what Benny did," said Harry. "The Coach shouldn't be kicking the players… any of us!"

"He don't mean anything by it," said Bubba defensively. "It's… just the way he is!"

"What're you gonna do if he kicks you, Harry!" asked Rob, a taunt in his voice.

"I don't know," said Harry worriedly. "He'd better not kick me... or anyone else!"

"A big tough guy, huh?" asked Sonda sarcastically. "Gonna take on the Coach!"

"No," said Harry. "I don't wanna take anybody on... I just don't think the Coach oughta kick any of us!"

"You'd better cool it!" warned Rob. "Coach can get mean if he wants to!"

"Look, Rob," said Harry, his jaw set. "I'm going to do what I think is right... got it?"

"Yeah," said Rob, irritated. "I got it! Be as stubborn as you can be... and see if I give a damn!"

"I haven't figured Shotgun out, yet," said Harry. "Sometimes I think he's a great Coach... and other days..."

"Other days, what?" asked Rob.

Harry tried to capture his feelings, which were confused. "Well... other days, he just seems to be crude... and thinking only about winning... not so much about us."

"Yeah," said Bubba. "I know what ya mean."

"Coach Fearless thinks ya can pass," said Rob touchily. "I guess I have to sweat ya for back-up quarterback."

"Coach is just worried about the first game," said Harry waving off Rob's concern. "I think he thinks we can't pass and this other team in Gloucester can... that's all."

"Haven't they passed a lot before?" asked Tony.

"From what the guys say," said Harry, "Coach Braun has always relied on the running game."

"He's always been that way," said Bubba. "He'll run Sanders until he drops! Last year Jack was held together by nothing but tape by the last game!"

"Sanders is a tough guy," observed Harry.

"What got into you out there today, Harry?" asked Bubba.

"What do ya mean?"

"You know what I mean," said Bubba. "It's like you were pissed off at everyone... hitting people real hard and all that!"

"I've learned the secret," said Harry reflectively.

"What secret?" asked Bubba.

"The secret of... of hitting hard, like the Coach wants."

"Well, what's the secret?"

"It's not just the physical part... you gotta have it in your mind... in your game face."

"Your game face?" asked Tony.

"Yeah... you put it on when ya go to play ball," said Harry, "and it makes ya meaner... and willing to hit people hard."

"How do ya do that?" asked Bubba watching Harry with new perspective.

"You gotta psyche yourself," said Harry introspectively.

"What does that mean?"

"It means... well, become someone you're not normally... someone mean as hell who doesn't feel any pain."

"How do you do that?"

"I'm still working on it!" exclaimed Harry, making a mean face at Bubba, and then laughing.

Harry stood up and wrapped a towel around his naked body. He went into the shower room, followed by Tony. Soon the shower room was filled with boys and all the showers were spurting hot water. The shower was unusually quiet, each player wrapped in his own thoughts. Harry was left alone at one end of the shower room, except for Tony. He soaped himself and pretended not to notice the tense atmosphere. Arnie came in, walked haughtily by Harry and found a shower at the opposite end of the room.

"Yeehah!" a scream echoed through the shower room. Allman Buddinger appeared wearing only a jock strap, riding a blue bicycle. He had a water gun filled with ice water from the fountain in the locker room and squirted it as he wobbled the bike through the shower. Boys were ducking and jumping to avoid the stream of icy water.

"Hey! Allman!" shouted Benny Norwood. "That's my bicycle!"

"Don't worry, Benny!" shouted Allman as he squirted Benny in the face with the icy water. "I'm just borrowing it!"

Allman made a face at Harry and squirted water his way, but it was too far and the icy water fell to the tile floor of the shower room. He squirted Arnie in the chest. Arnie tried to push Allman off the bike, but he kept his balance and caught the fall with his foot.

"Allman, you ass-hole!" shouted Arnie.

There was a notable absence of anger in his voice. It sounded to Harry like the usual grab-ass shouting, almost a laugh. He wondered how Allman did it. Bubba grabbed the rear fender of the bicycle and stopped it. Allman put a leg on the ground to balance himself.

"Heeeyyy Bubba!" shouted Allman and squirted Bubba in the face.

Harry walked to a shower close to Allman, adjusted it to "cold" and turned it on him.

"Wooohooo!" shouted Allman with a screech as the cold water struck him. He swung the bicycle around and pedaled it at crazy angles out of the shower room while the cold stream of water followed him.

The team laughed together at Allman. It was a good sound, particularly to Harry.

"Wooohooo," shouted Allman insanely. "My nuts are gonna be pea size... pea size!"

****

It was a cool day, a week after the Granby game in late November. Slate and Cliff sat on the sea wall at the waterfront near the ferry dock and watched the orange colored ferries ply the Elizabeth River to Norfolk through the gray waters of November.

"I'm sorry about your Father," said Slate watching Cliff closely.

"Yeah," said Cliff mournfully, fighting to control the choke in his voice. "He shouldn't have been working on that roof... he shouldn't have fallen."

"It was just a bad accident," said Slate trying to comfort. "It wasn't your fault he died."

"I should've gotten outa school and worked," said Cliff. "Then we'd a' had some money... and he wouldn't have had to work on that damn roof!"

"Like I said... it wasn't your fault, Cliff."

"He had a heart attack! That's what killed him."

"I guess life is just unpredictable," said Slate. He tried to think what it would be like to lose his Father, who he loved very much. He struggled with it, not knowing how to understand such a loss. He didn't know how to comfort his friend.

"I should a' been working!"

"You need to be in school, Cliff," said Slate. "Your father knew that!"

"School is a buncha crap," muttered Cliff, "except for playing ball!"

"No it isn't," said Slate. "Ya gotta know stuff... to get ahead when ya grow up!"

"They're making me read poetry and shit," said Cliff bitterly. "What the hell use I got for poetry!"

"It expands your mind, I guess," said Slate.

"My mind works okay with none of that crap."

"What do you like in school, Cliff?"

"I dunno... I like to read 'bout history... some of it anyway... what happened in them wars and things like that."

"So there is something good about school?"

"Yeah, I guess... some of it."

"How's your Mother?"

"She's… a strong woman," said Cliff thoughtfully. "But now I gotta find a way to make enough money to keep us going."

"Don't worry," said Slate. "You'll figure it out… and I'll help you."

"We shouldn't have lost to Granby," said Cliff struggling to push the thoughts of his father from his mind, "We tried to pass too much… It's better to hang on to the ball and push it down the field!"

"Maybe," said Slate. "If ya got a big lead. I wonder what Coach Wilder could have done differently? We had a good team this year… we just didn't win enough!"

"I wanna have a team that wins 'em all!" said Cliff determinedly.

"I'm sure Coach Wilder felt the same way."

"Guys didn't want it enough," said Cliff, staring at the green water that ran beneath his feet. "Ya win the games mostly by defense, ya know… and we should have stopped 'em that last time."

"I wanted it," said Slate as if to himself. "We needed to be more innovative. You can't win games these days if you just run everything from one formation."

"I wanted it, too," said Cliff. "But Coach Wilder… he's just too nice a guy… maybe not tough enough!"

"Coach Ismail is tough," said Slate. "And he believes in defense!"

"Yeah… and he's a mean sonofabitch… but maybe not enough," said Cliff. "But… Wilder was the head Coach! Ya know, when you think about football, probably the most important thing is how tough ya are… how motivated ya are… I mean tough in your gut, and in your head! That's even more important than how much you practice and how good ya are!"

"Coach Wilder got us scholarships," said Slate.

"Yeah, I know," said Cliff. "What's the name of that place?"

"East Carolina Teacher's College… it's in Greenville… down in North Carolina," said Slate. "He treated us well!"

"I didn't say he wasn't a nice guy!"

"Being tough is good… but ya gotta have some skill, too," said Slate, "and be pretty smart to out-think the other guys."

"Yeah… yeah," said Cliff in a hard, insightful voice, "but ya can have all that… and if you're not in shape… if you're not tough… if you're not mean enough… and you don't want it enough, ya won't get it!"

"I suppose you're right," said Slate.

"Football isn't just how good ya are," said Cliff. "It's a game of intimidation… like Coach Ismail says!"

"Intimidation?" asked Slate in surprise.

"Yeah," said Cliff. "Ya gotta intimidate the guy in front of you… every play. How do ya think all them beautiful holes get opened up for you glory boy halfbacks?"

"I guess I never really thought of it that way," said Slate. He looked at Cliff thoughtfully. He wasn't used to Cliff thinking out loud like this.

"The Coach," said Cliff, "he can have assistants that know how to play football… but he has to be the guy that puts the fear of god in the players…and in the other teams… and the referees, too… someone the players know is gonna kick their tail if they don't want it enough! Someone they respect, someone they see wants it more than anybody else! Some ornery guy they're scared of, someone they can bullshit about… tell stories about!"

"That's the Shotgun philosophy of football?" asked Slate looking at his friend with new respect.

"If ya can call it that," said Cliff with a twisted grin.

"So… do you want to be a coach?" asked Slate.

"I don't know," said Cliff with a small grin. "I'd like to try… but right now I gotta figure how to make some money to help my Mother."

Slate was glad to see Cliff grin after the ordeal of losing his father.

"Look at that!" exclaimed Slate, pointing.

Cliff looked and saw the sleek form of a U.S. Navy destroyer coming down the channel from the Naval Shipyard. It passed in front of them and they studied every detail.

"Those destroyers are neat looking ships," said Slate.

"It looks real fast," said Cliff.

"Greyhounds," said Slate. "I read a book where they called 'em 'greyhounds of the sea'."

"Those guns look pretty big."

"Yeah… but not as big as the ones on cruisers and battleships!"

"Yeah," said Cliff without interest.

"I guess we're gonna need some of those guys with the big guns here soon," said Slate.

"What do ya mean?" asked Cliff.

"I mean, the Germans have taken over France," said Slate, "and we're already sending destroyers to help the British."

"Is that right?" asked Cliff in astonishment. "Way over there?"

"Don't you read the paper, Cliff?" asked Slate. "The Japs are all over China and the Germans are all over France!"

"Sure I read the paper… the sports page!" said Cliff honestly.

"You better start reading the rest of it," said Slate with a grimace. "We're gonna be drafted if a war starts, you know!"

"Drafted? Ya think so," asked Cliff, his eyes wide.

"Damn right! We may never get those football scholarships at East Carolina Teacher's College next fall. Our asses are gonna be in the army!"

"Naw!" exclaimed Cliff emphatically. "How is stuff in France and China gonna screw with us?"

"It's already affecting us, Cliff!" said Slate urgently.

"I'm gonna have to read the rest of the paper, I guess," said Cliff.

"I think I'm gonna volunteer for the Navy," said Slate. "I've been looking into it… and the recruiter guy says I may be able to go to school for awhile and get a commission as an officer."

"You really gonna join the Navy?" asked Cliff, disbelief in his voice.

"I guess it depends on what happens," mused Slate.

"Makes me seasick to think about it… I get sick just going out to catch them crabs."

"I like going out on the water," said Slate. "But I don't think I'd like to get shot at!"

"Well, whatever happens," said Cliff, standing up and stretching, "let's get it over with so we can play some ball!"

****

Chapter Seven
Gloucester

It was a clear, warm Friday night and the lights above A.P. Johns shown brightly down on the field at Churchland Stadium, creating an atmosphere of surreal excitement. Hurricanes Carol and Edna had brushed by them in the past few weeks, leaving the field damp and the grass very green. The white lines of the gridiron stood out vividly against the background of the rain fed grass. The band played the Churchland Fight Song and an electric feeling filled the air. The Cheerleaders, with their white skirts and jerseys with the big orange "C" jumped and shouted in shrill voices. Their skirts twirled about their legs enticingly. A.P. could see Officer Grady Spearman directing his officers to take position around the field. There were a number of Hoods lounging around the track smoking cigarettes and staring at the girls. The officers herded them up into the stands.

A.P. and his wife Patricia sat with two thousand other fans and watched the Churchland Truckers charge onto the field in their pitch black uniforms with orange numbers and trim. Charlton and Catherine Hawkins, Bubba's parents, sat with them. Next to her were Commander Ike Quester and his wife Helen, Catherine's sister. A.P. had known Catherine and Helen since they had gone to school together at the old Churchland Academy. He had pulled their pigtails since they were girls. It was almost like old times, except now he couldn't pull their hair… but he could still wink at them.

"Don't they look great!" exclaimed A.P with a wink.

The Churchland players didn't cheer or make a sound, but the energy they carried on to the field that September night radiated through the new stadium and sent chills up A.P.'s spine. He stood and waved a Trucker pennant as a thunderous cheer rose from the stands.

"They look good," said Catherine. "They ought to… as long as Shotgun keeps them out there for practice!"

"He works 'em hard," said A.P., "that's for sure!"

"I called Shotgun and told him to work 'em hard but let 'em loose in time for their dinner!" said Catherine.

"You didn't!" exclaimed A.P.

"Sure I did," exclaimed Catherine. "I'm tired of hiding the food so Charlton won't eat it all!"

The Gloucester team ran onto the field unheralded in their white jerseys with crimson numbers, gladiatoral victims to feed the hungry Trucker lions.

****

Harry felt a sense of wonder as he ran into the new stadium and onto the field with the Churchland Truckers. It was like running through some kind of time warp and into a stunningly different world populated with screaming fans under bright lights. The world shimmered with waving orange and black. The electricity in the air carried over to all the players. It was a moment that seemed intensely real, and yet unreal. They ran out to do warm up calisthenics. Harry went through the exercises automatically. They ran to the sidelines where reality suddenly confronted them… they were going to have to play a game! The eyes of all the people in the stands… and the newspaper men in the booth above them… would be on them and everything they did, or didn't do. Harry glanced across the field at the Gloucester Dukes. They seemed very big in their sparkling white uniforms with crimson numbers. They were an unknown to be confronted. Allman and Karl went out for the coin toss. The Dukes won the toss and elected to receive. The Truckers huddled on the sideline around Coach Braun.

"How bad do you guys want this game?" shouted the Coach in a hoarse voice. "I want ya to go out there and intimidate these boys… grind 'em down and stomp on 'em. You do that and we'll score… and they won't! Ya can do it… so do it! Get out there! Get out there!"

The huddle broke with a roar from the players and the coaches, followed immediately by a roar from the crowd that echoed around the stadium. The first team charged on to the field to kick off the ball to the Dukes.

"We got Wimpy Sawyer," said Coach Fearless, staring out at the men in the striped shirts. "He's the Referee."

"Where is that little wimp?" asked Coach Braun looking around the field with squinty eyes.

Fearless pointed toward the center of the field where a small man in a striped shirt stood, looking like a bantam rooster with a whistle in his mouth.

"Right there," said Coach Fearless.

"I hope he's better than he was last year," said Braun scowling at the referee.

Harry stood at the sidelines, suddenly faced with the fact that he wasn't charging on to the field. It was a frustration he had to deal with… at least for now. No one sat on the bench. All the second and third string guys stood up on the sidelines and cheered. No one wanted the Coach to catch him sitting down… there might be a chance to play! Harry watched anxiously as Arnie kicked the ball and it sailed through the night air to the Gloucester fifteen where a boy in crimson and white fielded it and began to run. He ran it to the Gloucester thirty yard line where he was tackled by Karl Darby.

"They're screwing off on the kick-off!" said Coach Braun heatedly to Coach Fearless standing next to Harry. "They should never get beyond their twenty on a kick off… and we're in trouble when our halfback has to make the tackle. What's wrong with those linemen and linebackers!"

"They're not getting down the field fast enough," said Coach Fearless. "A little too cautious, maybe. I'll get it fixed for the next kick off."

"Ya need a breaker to bust up the blockers… and a tackler," shouted Braun, "not just a buncha guys running around!"

Coach Braun watched the Dukes come up to the line. The quarterback faded back and threw a pass twenty yards down the field. A Duke end caught the ball and ran to the Churchland forty-five yard line. There was a moan from the crowd. Coach Braun did his hip-hop war dance and threw his hat to the ground.

"Well, here it goes!" muttered Coach Braun, stomping on the defenseless hat. "Who's that quarterback?"

"Adams," said Fearless. "Chester Adams is his name."

On the next play, Gloucester handed off to their left halfback and Jack Sanders tackled him for no gain. The next play was a sweep around left end. It made three yards after a jarring tackle by Bob Porter.

"That's the way, Porter," shouted Coach Braun, pacing up and down the sidelines. "Knock their jock off!"

The Gloucester quarterback faked a hand off to the fullback and dropped back for a pass.

"Oh no!" shouted Coach Braun shaking his fist in the air as the ball sailed downfield.

A Gloucester halfback caught the ball at the Churchland thirty yard line where he was nailed by Allman Buddinger.

"Time out!" shouted Braun.

Wimpy Sawyer called a time out. Allman came trotting to the sideline.

"What's wrong out there, Buddinger?" growled Coach Braun sticking his face into Allman's. "You guys are letting that Gloucester Dukey pass the ball!"

"I know, Coach," said Allman. "I'll get 'em fired up and we'll nail him!"

"I thought they were already fired up, Buddinger!" shouted Braun, as angry as Harry had ever seen him.

Harry stared up at the bright lights and absorbed their energy. He reached down into his psyche and pulled on his game face, feeling energy flow into him. He gritted his teeth and walked up to where the Coach and Allman stood. "Coach! I can get to that quarterback if you put me in at right end."

Coach Braun looked at Harry in surprise. "Who asked you, Kester?" he grumbled. He turned back to Allman. "Get those people going out there, Buddinger!"

"Coach! I can get that quarterback!" said Harry doggedly.

Coach Braun turned back to Harry irritably. "Dammit, Kester!' he growled, pushing Harry away. "Get back over there and stay outa this!"

Allman looked at Harry and winked. "What do ya see, Harry?"

"Whitely is handling his man at tackle," said Harry eagerly, "but Bud is getting blocked. I'm bigger than Bud. I can get through."

"What makes you so cock sure, Kester?" asked Braun heatedly.

"I want to do it... real bad, Coach," said Harry, between clenched teeth. "And I'm felling mean... real mean!"

"Harry did well at defense in practice," said Coach Fearless with his usual Carolina drawl. "He's been our best defensive guy!"

"Harry, Ol' Buddy, I believe you can do it," said Allman with a tight lipped grin. "I believe you can!"

"This ain't no time to experiment," said Braun, stepping away from Harry. "Kester hasn't shown me that much."

"Let's give it a try, Coach," said Allman stepping in front of the Coach.

Coach Braun looked at Allman with questioning eyes, one eyebrow raised. Then he glared at Harry, a fierce look on his face. Somehow, the boy looked different. There was a scowl on his face he had not seen before. "Alright... go in for Darby, Kester," he said irritably. "And I better see some blood... or you're coming outa there in a hurry!"

"Thanks, Coach!"

A thrill shot through Harry as he donned his helmet. He paused and inwardly adjusted his psyche... he pulled on his newly found game face. He accepted a sense of anger he knew only with the game face. He allowed it to pump him up and he felt the adrenalin flowing. He psyched himself... he hated everybody on the field in a white uniform! He felt like he was running on air as he charged out under the bright lights. "I'm in for you, Bud," he said as he approached the line of scrimmage.

Bud Darby looked a little disgusted. "Okay, Harry, good luck," he said. "This end's a big guy... and he gets help from the tackle."

"Okay, Bud," said Harry. "Thanks."

Harry turned to Jack Sanders behind him. "Jack... I'm gonna rush the quarterback real hard... can you cover the end in case they sweep?"

"Yeah," grunted Jack, assessing Harry with curious eyes. "I'll back ya up!"

"Bart, I'm going to rush hard. If I break in, it'll open it for you."

"Ya think ya can do anything, don't ya, hot shot?" grumbled Bart, a mean streak in his voice.

"I'll do it," said Harry determinedly. "You get mean, Bart!"

Bart looked at Harry with insulted eyes... he wasn't used to being told to get any meaner than he already was. The Harry Quester Bart saw was someone new to him... someone with a face that was familiar, yet unrecognizable... a face that was gripped in a tight scowl. Bart watched Harry out of the corner of his eye. Harry lined up and stared intently as the Gloucester end came jogging out from the huddle. He was taller than Harry and a bit heavier. The first play was a run off tackle to Harry's side. Harry ran full steam into the Gloucester end. He got under the boy's arms and pushed him back. He slid off and got an arm on the halfback coming off tackle. Whitely met the ball carrier head on with a resounding smack and they all fell into a jumble at the line of scrimmage.

"Good tackle, Bart!" exclaimed Harry.

Whitely snorted. "I don't need it from you, Quester!"

On the next play, Chester Adams fell back to pass. Harry charged at the big Gloucester end. He faked one way, went the other, knocked the end off balance and sprinted for the quarterback. He had Chester Adams in his sights and he knew he was going to get him. The quarterback raised his arm to pass as Harry launched himself and hit him hard in the midsection, bringing his arms up violently into the quarterback's solar plexus. Then he wrapped up the Gloucester man's legs to bring him down. The ball fell free. Bart Whitely fell on the ball. Chester Adams lay on his back and didn't get up. The Churchland crowd roared its approval. Time out was called.

Harry pulled himself up and saw Bud Darby jogging onto the field.

"Ya lucked out, Poet," growled Bart reluctantly. "But, thanks for the fumble!"

"There'll be more, Bart, "said Harry excitedly. "Just stay mean!"

"I'm in for you!" shouted Bud tapping Harry on the helmet. "Nice tackle there... I guess you really are a Headhunter!"

Harry jogged off the field, glancing longingly over his shoulder as Porter called the huddle. Chester Adams got up and limped off the field.

"Nice hit, Harry," said Coach Phelps, giving Harry a swat on the back as he arrived at the sidelines.

Time was started again. Harry stood silently as Jack Sanders began to bull his way down the field. It took only six plays and Jack was in the Gloucester end zone. Jack took it over for the extra point. Churchland seven, Gloucester zero. The roar from the fans was overwhelming.

"Okay Quester," said Coach Braun, coming up to Harry with an excited look in his eyes. "You're in for Darby for defense... including kick offs... get your butt in there! On the double!"

"Okay, Coach," said Harry, surprised to hear his correct name from Coach Braun.

The Truckers ran out to kick again to the Gloucester Dukes.

****

The Truckers ran excitedly off the field at half time leading the Dukes twenty to nothing. They clattered into the dressing room, all smiles. "Good tackling, Harry, Ol' Buddy," said Allman and gave Harry the Trucker salute... a thunderous blow to the chest.

"Yeah," said Bart Whitely eyeing Harry with suspicion, "you did okay."

They sat down on the cement floor and rested. The Coach came into the dressing room. They all got up. Coach Braun paced up and down in front of them slapping his mistreated hat on his leg with a vengeance.

"What're you guys smiling about?" yelled the Coach in a rage. "Ya think ya did a good job? You were lousy! Lousy! You're out there playing a game... a game! ...instead of hitting the other team until they're intimidated! Scared to death of ya! Now I didn't spend all summer showing you guys how to hit for nothing! If ya think twenty points is good enough, you're wrong! Twenty points means nothing! Nothing! Not a darn thing! You can score twenty points in two minutes if you have the other team scared to death of ya! And ya don't... ya don't! Some of those big old corn fed farm boys from Gloucester are intimidating you!"

Coach Braun stepped back and glared at the surprised Truckers. "What've you got, Coach Fearless?"

Coach Fearless stepped forward. "We're ahead because of two things. First, they can't stop our running game. Second, we've stuffed their passer... so far. But... we can expect them to do something different so that they can pass. They'll probably load up the side where we're getting through. So, we're gonna do something different. We'll go from a six-two-two-one to a five-three-two-one defense. We'll shift to that the first time they come up to the ball. Harry, you'll line up at center linebacker instead of end. You'll be a guard in the six-two-two-one if we shift back to that. We'll put you closer to the quarterback... and I expect you to get to him every time... every time! Bud will stay in on defense... Renny will come out... he and Bucky will alternate at nose guard. I want fresh legs in there. The nose guard will cream their center every time and make a hole for Harry to get in. Any questions?"

"We ain't never practiced that way, Coach," said Renny Dickson worriedly.

"If it doesn't work, we'll go right back to the way we've practiced, Renny," said Fearless. "Have I forgotten anything Coach Phelps?"

"No, Coach," said Phelps, "I think that covers it."

"Anything else you want, Coach Braun?" asked Eddie Fearless.

Coach Braun stepped forward. "We'll try this kind of defense," he said. Then his voice grew louder, "but it ain't no substitute for hitting… for intimidating… you got that?"

"We got it, Coach," said Allman with his toothy grin. "This second half is going to be really rough… for them corn fed farm boys called Dukes!"

"Then get out there!" shouted Coach Braun slapping his wrinkled hat on his leg. "And do it!"

The team roared its consent and charged out onto the field.

****

The Dukes kicked off to the Truckers. It wasn't long before Sanders scored his third touchdown. Churchland twenty-seven, Gloucester nothing. On the following kick off, Gloucester returned the ball to its own twenty-five where the ball carrier was tackled by Big Jim Jensen with a jarring thud. The ball carrier got up and limped off the field.

"Okay, Bucky," muttered Harry as he lined up as a guard next to Bucky Allison. "I'm coming in to your left."

"Cool, Man," whispered Bucky. "Their center is going to my right."

The crimson and white lined up. They had a very large boy lined up at the end position where Harry had been in the first half. A halfback was lined up behind him as a blocking back.

"Shift!" called out Harry.

The Truckers shifted into the five-three-two-one defense. Harry dropped back as center linebacker and Bucky shifted over center as nose guard. The Gloucester center snapped the ball. Bucky came up under him and stood him up. Harry paused a moment and charged at full speed through the hole made by Bucky. Big Jim knocked his man to the ground and Harry crashed into Chester Adams as he was trying to hand off to a halfback. The halfback never got the ball as the quarterback fell heavily to the ground with a grunt, Harry on top of him.

"Where the hell did you come from?" asked Chester, grimacing in pain and wiping mud and grass stain from his face.

"Don't you try to pass, Chester," said Harry with big grin, "or I'll hit you even harder!"

"Shit!" exclaimed Chester angrily. "I ain't buying none of that!"

The next play was an attempted pass. Harry squirted through the line and hit the quarterback even harder. He stuck his shoulder into the boy's belly and drove him backward for five yards and then into the ground. They hit with a thud and Harry felt all the wind leave the Gloucester player. Harry got up. Chester lay on his back gasping for air and holding his left leg. Harry walked back to the Churchland side of the scrimmage line. He saw Hayseed Parker, the Gloucester Coach running onto the field with an angry look on his face, shouting at the referee and pointing to Harry. Wimpy Sawyer shook his head and walked away. Hayseed continued to pursue the referee. Suddenly, Coach Braun was on the field shouting at the Gloucester Coach and Wimpy Sawyer, his face as red as a beet.

"It was a legal hit!" shouted Braun, crouching and sticking his square face into that of the other Coach, removing his pork pie hat and beating it against his leg.

"He drove my guy into the ground!" shouted Hayseed, not budging an inch. "It's unnecessary roughness!"

"You're a big pussy, Coach, if ya thought that was a hit!" shouted Braun, his jug ears getting red. "Wait'll you see the next one!"

"Who're you calling a pussy, Shotgun?" shouted the Gloucester Coach. "You're teaching your boys to hurt people… I know 'bout you!"

Wimpy looked from one angry Coach to the other.

"I didn't see no penalty," shouted Wimpy in a raspy, high pitched voice.

"What?" screamed Hayseed in rage.

"You heard the man!" shouted Braun.

"Now both of you get off the field or I'll penalize both sides!" shouted Wimpy, his face puckering up like a roasted prune.

"Those guys are playing dirty!" shouted the Gloucester mentor.

"Ya wanna get dirty, do ya?" shouted Coach Braun, balling up his fists.

The crowd roared. Coach Phelps showed up on the field. "Come on, Shotgun," said Slate putting his arm around Braun's waist. "Let's get off the field so we can play some ball!"

Coach Braun pulled away and stalked back to the sideline with Coach Phelps. His arms hung straight by his sides and his chin was stuck out like the beak of a fighting rooster. The Gloucester Coach walked to his sideline wringing his hands in frustration. Harry watched the Gloucester quarterback as he left the game limping. He never returned to the game.

Coach Braun paced the sidelines as the Truckers dominated the game, his hat jammed down on his head with the brims pulled down on each side. He glared at each player with an evil eye and cheered every hit. The final score was Churchland thirty-four, Gloucester nothing.

****

Bubba's 1947 Dodge bounced across the Churchland Bridge and onto High Street after the game. Bubba steered with the "necking knob" attached to the steering wheel, his right arm around Alice. Alice sat closely next to him. Harry sat in the back seat by himself. Perry Como was singing on the radio.

Solo Tu, solo Tu,
Are the dreams I have known,
Bringing love to my lonely heart,
Now there's heaven in view,
Now the dream has come true,
For tonight I have you alone.

"What does Solo Tu mean?" asked Bubba.
"It means 'You Alone'… in Italian, dummy!" said Alice.
"I guess I got you alone tonight!" smiled Bubba squeezing her shoulders.
"Not quite!" giggled Alice, pushing away. "Gimme some help, Harry!"
"You're on your own, Alice," said Harry with a grin. "I'm along for the ride."
The Dodge screeched to a halt for a stop light.
"You sure this thing'll make it to the Circle?" asked Harry.
"Don't insult Ol' Bessie, here," said Bubba in feigned indignation.
"Here comes Allman and the Red Rooster," said Harry.
The red jeep roared by the Dodge with Allman at the wheel and Georgia Blake snuggled up to his side. Allman waved and sounded his honky-horn which played the first two bars of "Dixie".
"There goes Georgia and her big you-know-whats!" exclaimed Bubba.
Alice swatted him on the shoulder. "Don't you stare at her you-know-whats!"
"I gotta have me some a' them you-know whats!" pleaded Bubba giving her another squeeze.
Alice swatted Bubba again. The jeep squealed wheels into the drive-in restaurant known as The Circle. It had a large parking lot on the side attended by curb side waitresses. A big sign over the lot showed a chicken playing golf with the inscription "Chicken-in-the-Rough". The

gray Dodge turned in to the drive-in and cruised down the front row. Bubba honked his old, tired horn at a new Ford sedan, white with a red streak on its side that dipped gracefully toward the round tail lights.

"It's those Wilson guys," said Bubba. "I heard they won tonight, too."

Harry looked at the Ford and recognized Linwood Honor and Dennis Aimsley, who he hadn't seen in a long time. They had dates with them, one of them in a Churchland Cheerleader's uniform.

"Ol' Linwood done stole Cathy Lawson from us," muttered Bubba.

"Who's the girl with Dennis?" asked Harry. "The one in the Wilson Cheerleader outfit?"

"Barbara something," said Bubba. "I can't remember her name."

Bubba drove around and pulled up in a parking place to the left of the Ford Sedan. There was a raucous honk and Arnie cruised the row in his 1939 chopped Chevy Coupe. Clara was in the passenger seat and waved at them. Johnny Calcione's red Studebaker with the bullet nose followed with Johnny, Carson, Bart and Bryan.

Big Joe Turner was grinding out a song from a loudspeaker on a pole beside the drive-in.

Get outa that bed and wash your face 'n hands,
Get outa that bed 'n make some noise wid dem pots and pans,
Well ya wear dem dresses dat de sun come shining through,
Can't believe my eyes all o' 'dat belong to you,
I believe you de devil dressed up in nylon hose,
Well all my workin' an' I don' know where my money goes,
I say SHAKE RATTLE AND ROLL,
I say SHAKE RATTLE AND ROLL!

The alternating beat of the bass saxophone and the drums had all the feet tapping. Allman and Georgia in the red jeep pulled up to the left of Bubba's Dodge and stopped. Allman stood up in the jeep and started gyrating to the rhythm of *Shake Rattle and Roll*.

"Yeeehahh!" shouted Allman, pulling Georgia up to dance with him. He jumped over the windshield of the jeep and lifted Georgia over with him, her skirt swirling up to her waist, briefly revealing her panties.

"Look at that fool, Allman," said Harry. "I don't see how Georgia puts up with him!"

"Come on, Harry," said Bubba with a chortle, "all the gals want a date with Allman!"

"Yeah?" asked Harry.

"That's what Allman told me," said Bubba with a wide eyed expression. "He said he's just swimming in pussy!"

"Oh Bubba!" said Alice, slapping him on the head. "Stop talking like that!"

"They all want to date him," said Harry. "And I don't have a date!"

"You can get a date anytime, Harry," said Alice. "But you gotta be cool and ask!"

"He's just too picky!" laughed Bubba.

"Heeey Bubba," shouted Allman, "need a tow truck for that thing?"

"For basic transportation," shouted Bubba with a flourish, "Ol' Bessie is all ya need!"

A waitress came to the car window. She was pretty with flounced blonde hair and a lot of lipstick. "What y'all want, honey?"

"Everyone for cheeseburgers and cokes?" asked Bubba with a flair, as though ordering at the very best restaurant.

"It's okay with me," said Harry, opening the back door.

"Me too," said Alice.

"Three cheeseburgers with fries and cokes," said Bubba, "and bring some catsup!"

"Okay, Honey," said the waitress. She bounced away in her short skirt and tight blouse.

"I'll have some of that stuff, too!" shouted Bubba watching her retreat with a lascivious eye.

The waitress turned, smiled and gave Bubba a big wave off.

"You couldn't handle it, Big Boy!" she said. "Come back in a few years!"

"Ha!" exclaimed Alice. "I guess she told you!"

The loudspeaker changed to Les Paul and Mary Ford.

Now the hacienda's dark, the town is sleeping,
Now the time has come to part, the time for weeping,
Vaya con Dios my darling,
May God be with you my love.

Allman and Georgia climbed down off of the hood of the jeep.

Harry got out of the car. He walked to the window of the Ford sedan. "Linwood?"

Linwood Honor looked out at him. He was a tall, well built boy with a blond crew cut. "I'll be damned!" he exclaimed as though he had practiced it. "Harry Quester!"

Harry stuck out his hand. Linwood reached across a tray filled with hamburgers and shook it. "Get in, Harry!" he said.

Harry climbed into the back seat next to a beautiful girl with dark brown hair in a blue and orange Wilson Cheerleader uniform who sat next to Dennis Aimsley.

"I'm Harry Quester," said Harry looking at the girl admiringly.

"Hi Harry," said the girl in a velvet smooth voice, "I'm Barbara Eason."

"I'm real glad to meet you," said Harry with one of his infectious smiles.

"Hey, take it easy there Harry!" exclaimed Dennis good naturedly. "Private property!"

"How ya doing, Dennis?" said Harry shifting his glance to Cathy Lawson in the front seat next to Linwood. "Hi Cathy… you're looking great tonight!"

"Hi Harry," said Cathy prissily. "You did real well out there tonight… for a second stringer!"

"Well, thanks… I guess," muttered Harry. "Dennis, I hear you guys won over Oscar Smith tonight."

"Yeah," said Dennis. "It was a good game. They were tougher than we expected. What're you doing here, Harry? Your old man back in town?"

"Yeah, we live in Green Acres," said Harry, "and I'm playing football for Churchland."

"Is that right?" asked Linwood in a sarcastic tone. "Playing for Ol' Shotgun? What position?"

"Fullback," said Harry, "I play behind Jack Sanders."

"How many touchdowns did Jack score tonight?" asked Dennis curiously.

"Three," said Harry. "We beat Gloucester thirty-four to nothing."

"Yeah?" asked Linwood with a sneer. "I hear you guys want to play us."

"Sure, we'll play you," said Harry confidently.

"No chance," said Linwood with an air of superiority. "You guys wouldn't have a chance!"

"Without Sanders they wouldn't," said Dennis thoughtfully. "He's a real horse!"

"We have a pretty tough team," said Harry. "I wouldn't put any money against us!"

Allman came up behind the Ford, put his foot on the fender and rocked the sedan. "Hoorah for Wilson… the next best team in Portsmouth!" he shouted.

"Oh no!" exclaimed Dennis in mock horror. "It's Buddinger!"

Allman came to the window and stuck his flat face into the car. "Hi guys!" he said. "Glad to hear you won tonight!"

"We gotta put up with your baloney tonight, Buddinger?" asked Linwood irritably.

"Naw… naw," said Allman squinting his eyes, "you ain't gotta put up with nothing, Linwood."

"Thank god," said Dennis with a laugh.

"Hi there, Cathy Sweetheart," beamed Allman, "what're you doing in here… you taking your stuff all over town now?"

"Well, that's about enough," said Linwood, pushing open the door.

Harry grabbed Linwood's shoulder. "Come on, Linwood… he didn't mean anything by it…"

"The hell he didn't," said Linwood heatedly.

Linwood crawled out of the car. Allman ran behind Bubba's gray Dodge.

"Help! Help!" shouted Allman in mock fright. "Da President is aftah me!"

Linwood tried to chase Allman around Ol' Bessie. Big Jim Jensen walked casually toward the Dodge, followed by Arnie. The scene was illuminated by flashing headlights from the back of the lot. Officer Grady Spearman walked toward Bubba's Dodge with a lumbering gate.

"You guys quit running around and get back in them cars," said Officer Spearman in even tones. "You can butt heads on the football field… but not here… got it?"

"Okay, Grady," said Linwood, walking back to the Ford Sedan. "Just keep that Allman character away from us!"

"Get back in the jeep, Allman," said Officer Spearman.

"Yes Sir!" exclaimed Allman, his eyes theatrically wide. "I'm 'a doing it!"

Allman scampered back and climbed in the jeep. Big Jim and Arnie faded behind the parked cars. Spearman stood for a minute watching them and returned to his patrol car. Linwood got back into the Ford sedan.

"I'm sorry, guys," said Harry with concern.

"That stupid sonofabitch!" said Linwood under his breath.

"Don't let him get to you." said Cathy, "He's… just that way!"

Harry climbed out of the Ford sedan.

"See you guys later," said Harry waving at Linwood and Dennis.

Harry got back into Bubba's Dodge. Alice handed him a cheeseburger.

"Thanks, Alice," he said.

"You know those guys?" asked Alice.

"Yeah… I know 'em," said Harry taking a big bite of the cheeseburger. Suddenly he realized how hungry he was after the game. "We used to play side lot football when I was a kid in Park View."

"They're big trouble," said Alice, "those Wilson guys… and that

Cathy… she's not a lot better."

"Now now…" said Bubba swallowing a cheeseburger and waving at the waitress for another. "No cat fights!"

"Allman made an ass of himself," said Harry.

"Naw," said Bubba, "he's already an ass… he's just being Allman."

Harry looked at Bubba and started to say something, but didn't.

The loudspeaker changed to The Drifters and *Honey Love*.

"Love me love me love me love me Lo,
Love me love me love me love me Lo,
Love me love me love me love me love me,
Love me love me love me love me Lo,
Do de do de do de doo
I need it… when the moon is bright,
I need it… in the middle of the night…

Harry watched as a white 1953 Cadillac convertible cruised the front row. It had a big chrome grill with dual rocket shaped bumpers projecting forward. Its rear end was graced with fins in which were embedded the tail lights. In it was a boy in a white sport coat, a red tie and wavy brown hair piled high on his head. With him was the girl with the brown pony tail.

"Who's that dressed up guy with Paige Garnette?" asked Alice, her eyes wide.

"That guy is Duane Starr," said Bubba. "He plays halfback for Suffolk. He's quite the dandy!"

"His daddy must be awfully rich," said Alice in awe.

"Peanuts," smiled Bubba. "He sells peanuts!"

"I wonder how many peanuts it took to buy that car?" asked Harry in wonder.

"Naw you don't, Harry," said Bubba. "What you really wonder is how to get a date with that girl with the brown pony tail!"

"Naw it's not!" said Harry self consciously.

Harry watched the Cadillac drive around the parking lot and cruise the front row a second time. The girl with the brown pony tail turned and looked at Harry. Her face broke out into a smile. It sent Harry's heart racing. He hoped it was meant for him!

"Get it Boy!" sang the bass singer of *The Drifters* over the parking lot loudspeaker.

"I'm going to have to do that!" muttered Harry to himself as *Honey Love* came to a harmonic end.

****

It was Saturday morning. Harry, Allman and Bubba sat on the drink cooler in A.P. Johns' Grocery Store drinking RC Colas and looking at the article from the sports page. There was a big picture of Jack Sanders running the ball next to the article.

SANDERS SCORES BIG IN WIN OVER GLOUCESTER
SHOTGUN INTRODUCES HEADHUNTER DEFENSE
By Al Gollen

Jolting Jack Sanders scored three touchdowns in Churchland's big win over visiting Gloucester Friday night in Churchland's new stadium. Sanders was unstoppable as he plowed through gaping holes opened by Big Jim Jensen and the powerful Churchland line. In the first series, it looked like Gloucester would make a game of it, as Chester Adams passed the Dukes to the Churchland twenty-five yard line. Coach Shotgun Braun was hopping mad and sent in his new Headhunter Defense. Harry Quester, a recent addition to the Truckers from Northern Virginia, went in as linebacker and rushed Adams hard, causing the talented quarterback to fumble. Bart Whitely recovered for Churchland. After the hard hit from Headhunter Quester, Adams left the game. Coach Hayseed Parker protested the hit, but to no avail as Shotgun Braun came to the defense of his team. After that, it was all Sanders and Churchland's powerful running game. Halfbacks Karl Darby and Terry Moddy also scored. Darby scored on a thirty yard scamper around right end with his brother Bud Darby leading the way. Moddy scored on a five yard burst off left guard behind Bucky Allison. Churchland's powerful line, led by Big Jim Jensen looks like a formidable threat for the Trucker's remaining opponents, beginning with Virginia Beach next week. Coach Braun said he believes that this team is the best he has coached. Time will tell if he's right!

"I'll be damned, Cuz!" said Bubba. "Your first game and you're in the paper... the Ol' Headhunter!"

"I don't know where they dreamed up that name," said Harry.

"I guess your game face worked," said Allman. "No longer the mild mannered Harry... now it's... the Headhunter. We're gonna have to get ya a red cape!"

"I don't want that to stick," said Harry with concern.

"Bud Darby put it on ya," said Bubba. "But if Al Gollen printed it... then you're the Headhunter, for sure!"

A.P. walked up to where the boys sat wearing the ever present white grocer's apron. His face was split in a big grin.

"You guys were awesome last night," said A.P. "Tell me, Harry, did Shotgun think up that Headhunter Defense before the game... or after that first pass Gloucester completed?"

"I don't know, A.P.," said Harry. "I just told him I could get to that quarterback… and he gave me a chance… the rest of it was something I guess he thought up."

"Shotgun is a stubborn cuss," said A.P. "But if he sees something that works, he's on it… right away!"

"Coach Phelps and Coach Fearless wanted to let Harry try," said Bubba. "And Allman wanted it, too."

"Allman was afraid Coach Fearless might give me a chance to pass," said Harry poking Allman in the ribs.

"You're absolutely right, Ol' Buddy," grinned Allman. "And it worked!"

"Shotgun told Coach Fearless to come up with a defense that let Harry move around and focus on nailing the quarterback," said Bubba, "and he did."

"Yeah?" said A.P. "That's interesting. Are ya gonna use it some more?"

"I don't know," said Harry. "I guess we will if we need it!"

"Shotgun better put ya in, Harry," said A.P. "Or I'm gonna start some Headhunter chants in the stands!"

"Please don't do that," said Harry. "That'll really piss off the Coach."

"Well, sometimes he needs pissing off," said A.P. with a conspiratorial smile.

"He came up with a good idea this time," said Bubba.

"And now we have… Ta Taaa! The Headhunter!" said AP, throwing his arms apart to match his fanfare.

Harry gave Bubba the Trucker salute and hit him full on the chest with a mighty blow. Bubba jumped off the drink cooler and limped around the store moaning.

"Don't say that word, A.P.," moaned Bubba, "it changes mild mannered Harry into a beast… a real beast!"

****

It was the end of October 1945. Slate Phelps knew that Cliff Braun had just gotten out of the Army and come back to Portsmouth. He drove over to Cliff's house on Maple Avenue in his 1942 green Ford Coupe and honked the horn. The familiar square face of Cliff appeared at the door.

"Hey, Cliff, you old Dogface," shouted Slate, "come on out!"

Cliff walked out of the house and up to the car. He opened the door and got in without saying a word.

"Welcome home," said Slate.

"How long ya been home?" asked Cliff, staring ahead of the car.

"I got out of the Navy in September," said Slate. "I've been home for a few weeks."

Cliff looked at Slate through squinty eyes. "It's good to see ya, Slate," he said emotionally. "I mean… it really is!"

"I'm glad you made it, Cliff," said Slate. "I was worried about you when I heard you went in at Normandy."

"Aw, that wasn't so bad," said Cliff. "I went in on one of the last waves with my truck… we got stuck there on the beach for a few days."

"Did you run into any Germans?" asked Slate.

"Naw," said Cliff, "my biggest problem was I couldn't find nothing to eat… an' man was I hungry! It was raining and miserable… that's all."

Slate started the car. "Let's ride around the corner to the grocery store and get some drinks," he said.

"Okay," said Cliff.

The Ford rolled away.

"What about you, Slate?" asked Cliff. "You was out there with all them Navy ships and them Japs… and all."

Slate laughed. "I never even saw a Jap," he said, "except for a few Prisoners of War."

"Yeah?"

"But I saw what they were doing to us… those ships and sailors would come into the Aussie Base at Milne Bay all shot up. It was pretty bad."

"Them atom bombs oughta shut them Japs up for awhile!" muttered Cliff.

"Yeah," said Slate. "That was scary, what those darn things did to Hiroshima and Nagasaki. I hope no one else learns how to build them!"

They rolled up in front of Hathaway's Grocery Store.

"Is Big Ennis still making book?" asked Shotgun.

"Why!" asked Slate. "You're not going to bet… are you?"

"Naw," said Cliff. "I was just wondering."

"Don't get involved with all that!" exclaimed Slate. "You'll blow your scholarship if you do!"

"I don't like betting," said Cliff. "I like winning… and betting don't give ya no control over winning."

Slate parked the Ford and they got out and walked inside. Old Mr. Hathaway stood behind the counter, a very large, fat man with a round, wrinkled face and several chins. He looked at them as if he had seen a ghost.

"Is that you, Shotgun?" asked Mr. Hathaway.

"Yeah… yeah, it's me," said Cliff.

"And Slate?"

"Yes Sir," said Slate, "we're both back from the war, now."

Slate remembered how old Mr. Hathaway had tried to bribe Alfonso Mays to get their paper route for Fatso. He watched the old man warily.

"Well, welcome home boys," said Ennis Hathaway Sr.

"Thank you Sir," said Slate.

Cliff walked to the drink cooler and withdrew two bottles of coca-cola. He handed one to Slate.

"Ya still got that barrel 'a tater chips?" asked Cliff.

"Yes… yes," said Mr. Hathaway Sr. "It's right over there."

"Thanks," said Cliff locating the barrel and starting toward it.

"How's Ennis?" asked Slate curiously.

"I reckon he's fine," said Big Ennis. "He worked for awhile up in Long Island. He's away at college now… Virginia… he got a scholarship to play football there."

"He didn't go in the Army?" asked Cliff, a tinge of anger in his voice.

"Well," said Big Ennis with embarrassment in his voice, "they wouldn't take him… said he was overweight! But he got a job working at the docks in Long Island… loading up them Liberty ships… said that was his contribution to the war."

"I'm glad Ennis could make a contribution," said Slate.

"Damn!" exclaimed Cliff. "I should've eaten up a lot of stuff before they come after me! Then I could've loaded ships instead of drive trucks around the Krauts!"

"Come on, Cliff," said Slate. "You know you're proud of what you did over there."

"Sure I am," said Cliff with a little smile. His eyes widened. "I drove a real mean… I mean a really mean… truck!"

"All I got is a fifty dollar bill, Mr. Hathaway," said Slate. "Can you change that? They gave it to me when I was discharged, and I need the change."

Big Ennis looked at Slate irritably. "Yes, I suppose I can," he said.

Mr. Hathaway went into a small room behind the store. They heard him rustling around there for several minutes. He came back with a handful of twenty, ten and five dollar bills. "Now don't you tell anyone I keep money in the back, Slate," said Big Ennis. "There are all kinds of thieves around here, ya know! And I don't have no Shotgun Braun here to keep them away no more!"

"Oh no, Mr. Hathaway," said Slate. "We wouldn't tell anybody."

"Thank you," said Big Ennis. "Your Daddy was one of my favorites, ya know, Cliff… he was a good man… a tough man!"

"I appreciate what ya did for Mother and me," said Cliff in a forced voice.

"Oh, I was glad to help," said Big Ennis as he counted out the change after charging for the drinks and chips. "Now you boys take all the chips ya might want... on me!"

"Thanks, Mr. Hathaway," said Slate.

Slate and Cliff took their drinks and several brown paper bags of chips, walked out on the front porch of the store and sat on a wooden bench there.

"This here is where my Father used to sit... with his shotgun," said Cliff emotionally.

"Yeah, I know," said Slate. "He'd be proud of what you did in the war."

"Maybe I'm proud," said Cliff, controlling his emotion, "but all I did over there in France was drive a truck. I got in some fights down at Fort Bragg and beat up some assholes there. The Sergeant said I was unreliable... so he sent me to the Transportation Corps to drive a truck."

"Well, that was important," said Slate.

"Yeah, we got to haul all of General Patton's stuff while he was running around Europe like a wildman!"

"I'll bet that was exciting," said Slate.

"In a way," said Cliff, "I ended up in what they called the Red Ball Express... which had a lotta nigras in it."

"What was that like," asked Slate.

"I didn't like it at first," said Cliff. "I never had much to do with the nigras around town here, ya know... but I got used to 'em... even had a coupla nigras who were good buddies... in a way."

"Is that right?" asked Slate.

"Yeah," said Cliff with a smile that spread slowly over his square face. "And they was good fighters... I mean I had some really good fights with some of them nigras!"

Slate laughed. "Did you win any?"

"Hell yeah!" said Cliff defensively. "Well... enough of 'em!"

"I was lucky," said Slate. "They had me all lined up to be an amphibious assault craft officer... you know, the Higgins Boats that carried the Marines in to the beaches?... I was gonna do that at the invasion of Hollandia there in New Guinea."

"Where the heck is New Guinea?" asked Cliff, sipping his coke and crunching a mouthful of chips.

"It's... near Australia," said Slate, "sort of northeast of Australia. The Japs took it in the early part of the war."

"Oh."

"Anyway, I met Gene Tunney... you know, the boxer?... when I was in Australia," said Slate, "and he helped me get a staff officer job with the

Captain in command of the Naval Base in Milne Bay."

"You met Gene Tunney?" asked Cliff in awe.

"Yeah," said Slate, "he was a Lieutenant Commander… a regular guy… we had some drinks together."

"Damn!" exclaimed Cliff. "I never met nobody like that in France!"

"Tunney is an interesting character."

"I'll bet! Did he look like a real slugger?"

"Not really… he just looked big!"

"So you never went to… what was it?"

"Hollandia?"

"Yeah."

"I went there after the Marines had taken it," said Slate. "We set up a new Naval Base there."

"What happened there?"

"Just more shot up ships coming in for repairs," said Slate. "But I did get to see General MacArthur… big old corncob pipe and all!"

"Yeah?"

"We had a Captain there in Hollandia who was a real arrogant pistol," said Slate, "The sonofagun had a brass rail at the bar in the officer's club, one side for senior officers, and the other side for us peons!"

"Oh, too bad! You had to suffer through the war on the wrong side of the brass rail at the bar. Shit! I was lucky to find a bar there in France!"

"Yeah… it was really tough," said Slate sarcastically. "Anyway, this Captain fell in love with this gal called Candy June… she was a touring New York model… with a bosom that would bowl you over! Candy went on to Buna and this Captain… he followed after her."

"Did he hook up with her?"

"Yeah, he did," said Slate, "but while he was gone, the General came by to tour the base… and he was really pissed that the Captain wasn't there!"

"So what happened?"

"The Captain came back with Candy and found out he'd been relieved… MacArthur sent another Captain there the day after he left!"

"No kidding?"

"Just like that!"

"I found a bar in a French tavern one night," said Cliff, his eyes far away. "There was women all over the place… I thought I was in paradise…it was dark and smoky and everyone was drinking red wine. Well, this French gal latched on to me after I was drunk as a skunk. She took me upstairs."

"And…?"

"The light was brighter in that bedroom," said Cliff making a horrid face, "and I was drunk and all... but I finally seen what she looked like."

"Pretty good, huh?"

"Oh my god!" exclaimed Cliff in horror. "I never seen such a damn ugly woman... she had a nose like a walrus... even had a beard!"

"Sounds really attractive!" laughed Slate.

"This gal was all cinched up in some kinda corset or somethin' like that, ya know... she pulls my trousers off and smiles at me," said Cliff rolling his eyes dramatically, "like a snake smiling at a rat, ya know... then she takes off her dress and this here corset!"

"It sounds like the Army in Europe wasn't all that tough!" said Slate with a wry grin.

"Tough? Let me tell ya!" said Cliff standing up, waving his arms, his face animated with the story, "When she pulled that corset off, her tits come rolling outa there and flopped down to her knees!"

Cliff made dramatic motions with his arms indicating the dynamic motions of the body parts he described. He continued. "And then her belly flopped out under them tits like a big ol' beach ball! Her legs and under her arms was all hairy and she grabs me and pulls me onto an ol' rickety bed!"

Slate laughed uncontrollably and shook his head.

"She smelled like some kinda greasy flower... it made me sick!"

"Well, what did you expect in a French Whore House?" laughed Slate.

"She grabbed me tight and nearly broke my damn neck!"

"So, how was she?"

"How was she?" exclaimed Cliff, his voice growing loud and his eyes rolling. "How was she? I'm telling ya... I wrassled free, got outa that bed, grabbed my trousers, pulled 'em on and beat feet outa there as fast as I could go! I wish I'd had a football, 'cause I sure as hell woulda scored! She ran down the steps yelling at me like some kinda wild woman!"

"What did you do?"

"I got in my truck and drove off as fast as I could go," said Cliff making wild driving motions. "The Sergeant was yelling at me to come back... but I wasn't gonna go back there... no siree!"

"War is hell!" exclaimed Slate, unable to control his laughter.

Cliff sat back down and took a big swig of his coke. "But don't ya worry none," he said with a lewd smile. "I found me some better French gals at the next town!"

"Made out okay, huh?"

"I worked my dick so hard I thought it was gonna fall off," said Cliff with a grimace. "I thought I'd caught the drip or something... but the

Doc said I just needed to give it a rest!"

Slate laughed as hard as he had ever laughed. "I'm glad you made it home okay, Cliff."

"Yeah… you too," said Cliff with a wink. "Now let's play some ball!"

****

Chapter Eight
Virginia Beach

The Virginia Beach Seahawks ran onto the field at Churchland Stadium clad in their white uniforms with green numbers. Harry crouched with the Trucker team around Coach Braun under the bright lights that bathed the gridiron.

"Now these here Seahawks are supposed to be tough!" said Coach Braun in a low voice.

Harry was on the outskirts of the huddle and had to strain to hear the Coach. Braun's voice rose as he spoke. "You guys were lucky to beat Gloucester last week!" said the Coach. "You weren't mean enough! You won, but you didn't intimidate! Now tonight I want you to put the fear of god into these beach bum guys! Tonight we'll see whether ya got the winning spirit... a real team or not! Let's go!.... Let's go!... Lets go!"

The huddle broke and the first team ran onto the field. Johnny Current was in for Terry Moddy, who felt sick before the game. Harry and Bubba stood side by side watching them run out and take positions to receive the ball. The ball sailed through the night air. It was a short kick, but Johnny ran up to the twenty yard line and caught it. A Seahawk ran at him and was leveled by Sanders. Another one tried to get at Johnny as he dodged back and forth. Big Jim came out of nowhere and knocked the Seahawk flat with nothing more than a forearm. Hero dodged a few more Seahawks and began running up the sidelines. Harry started yelling as he saw a clear lane between Johnny and the Virginia Beach goal line. Only one Seahawk stood in his way. Hero turned on the speed and ran right by him. Touchdown! Just like that, it was Churchland six, Virginia Beach nothing. Sanders bulled the ball over for the extra point. Seven to nothing!

"Look at that!" shouted A.P. Johns to his wife Patricia sitting on the fifty yard line as the crowd roared. "That was a perfect runback!"

Patricia nodded at him, smiled and continued knitting. The loudspeaker crackled. "Johnny Current takes the ball all the way for a Churchland touchdown!"

The three thousand fans in the stadium roared their approval. "Hero! Hero!"

Johnny ran back to the Churchland bench, prancing like a race horse, his face lit with a radiant smile. Hero ran in place holding up the ball and pumping his arms. His chest was puffed out like a toad in heat. Allman ran behind him and slapped him on the rear.

"Way to go, Hero!" grinned Allman, taking off his helmet.

"That really felt good!" exhilarated Johnny. "I'm not even tired!"

"Ya did good!" exclaimed Allman.

"Did ya see how I put the fake on that last guy?" exclaimed Johnny, his face beaming with exhilaration. "It was perfect… perfect!"

"Get back in there for the kickoff, Johnny!" shouted Braun with a snarl. "Ya think this game is over just 'cause you scored?"

"Nice run, Current," said Coach Fearless patting Johnny on the back.

"Thanks Coach," said Johnny.

"Okay, Porter," said the Coach. "I wanna see some of that speed getting downfield… and a big tackle! Run fast after the kickoff and get real mean!"

Bob and Johnny ran out on the field. Bob set up to hold the ball for Arnie on the kickoff. The referee blew the whistle. Arnie ran and kicked the ball. Porter jumped up and ran downfield. He timed his approach to the ball carrier just right, letting Arnie and Bucky absorb several blocks. Then he sliced through two more blockers and hit the ball carrier with a crack they could hear on the sidelines.

Coach Braun jumped into the air and did his little hotfoot dance on the sidelines. "That's that way to hit 'em, Porter!"

"Looks like Mr. America stole the spotlight from ol' Hero," said Bubba.

"Yeah," said Tony. "Shotgun likes the hits better than the points!"

"I don't know," said Harry. "I think he believes the hits make the points!"

On the next play, the Virginia Beach quarterback faked to the fullback off guard and lateraled to his halfback as the halfback ran at full speed around their right end. Arnie got caught between the end and the tackle and was turned in. Porter had been sucked inside by the fullback fake. The Virginia Beach halfback gained fifteen yards before Karl Darby brought him down with a lunge that tripped him up.

Coach Braun tore off his pork pie hat and flung it to the ground. He did his hotfoot dance, stomping on the unresisting, forlorn looking hat. "Darby! What kinda tackle was that? Eberly! Where in heck were you?"

On the next play, the Virginia Beach team ran the same play. Again, Eberly was blocked to the inside. This time, however, Porter didn't take the fullback fake. He crashed into the ball carrier after a five yard gain and landed on top of him. Bart flew through the air and landed on top of them. Porter and Whitely got up. The ball carrier didn't.

Coach Braun tore off his hat and waved it in the air. He screamed, "Good tackle! Ya killed him!"

Surfer Sam Jenkins, the Seahawk Coach, screamed and pointed at his downed ball carrier. "What about that?"

The Referee threw a yellow flag high into the air. "Unnecessary roughness! Piling on!"

Coach Braun threw his hat to the turf and jumped on it. "You blind or something? The whistle hadn't blown! What're ya doing? You live at the Beach or something?"

****

The Truckers sat on benches inside the Dressing Room at half time with a twenty-one to nothing lead. It had been Sanders left and Sanders right, slogging down the field in four to ten yard increments. Jolting Jack scored two touch downs after the one by Hero. He sat on the bench in the dressing room while Larry Kidwell re-taped his left shoulder. They survived the Virginia Beach end sweeps. After the first two, the Seahawks tried two more, but Porter sniffed both of them out and tackled the ball carrier for no gain.

"Ya think you'll get in, Harry?" asked Bubba. "How 'bout some of that Headhunter defense?"

"Not the way things are going," said Harry. "I think Coach will only use that if he needs it."

Coach Braun came into the dressing room. He stood in front of the team and jerked his crumpled hat from his head. "Now, that was a pretty good half... except for the Refs," he said with a grimace. "We had Hero dodge and prance his way to a score." The Coach dodged and pranced with an impish grin on his face, imitating Johnny. "... and we had Jack get real mean and plow his way for another coupla scores. The blocking was better than last week. Porter made some good tackles... so did Big Jim and Bucky. But... those guys are running around you on the end sweeps. They almost broke one there in the second quarter!"

Suddenly, as though a cloud passed in front of the sun, Coach Braun's expression changed. He threw his hat to the cement floor and walked around it in tight little circles, his hands clutched behind his back, eyeing the hat angrily as if it held a secret it was unwilling to release. He stopped abruptly in front of Arnie and turned a burning glare on him.

"They're running around you, Eberly!" shouted Coach Braun in a hoarse voice. "You're letting their end and that big tackle take you down! If it hadn't been for Bob and Karl there a few times, those bastards woulda had a score!"

"Yeah I know, Coach," said Arnie defensively. "It won't happen again!"

"Get mean, son!" shouted Coach Braun pumping his fist in the air in front of Arnie's nose. "You eat some sour pudding or something for dinner? Huh? Huh? Ya drink some bad juice or something? Ya just ain't mean enough tonight! Ya ain't running right!"

"I'm fixing that," said Arnie looking up at the Coach with watery, bloodshot eyes.

"Naw!" growled the Coach. "Ya ain't fixing nothing... you're worrying about some sweet little thing in tight blue jeans... or some glass of suds... or both... and staring at the pretty sky!"

Coach Braun grabbed Arnie by the shoulder pads and pulled him upright. He gave him a shake, and looked around at the team. "Anyone here know how to get Arnie mean tonight?" he asked with a questioning glare.

Harry got up and walked over to where the Coach stood with Arnie. "I can get him mean, Coach!" he said.

"Get outa here, Poet," growled Arnie defensively.

"I'm all ready to come in and play Headhunter defense, Arnie," said Harry, putting on his best game face.

"You ain't no damn Headhunter," shouted Arnie, his face growing red. "You're just a damn Poet!"

Coach Braun backed away, lifting his eyebrows, a surprised and satisfied look on his face.

"I told you not to call me that," growled Harry. He gave Arnie a little shove.

Arnie charged at Harry. Harry dodged away. Allman stepped in between them. He motioned for Big Jim. The big boy got up and wrapped his arms around Arnie, who continued to flail and shout at Harry.

"You Poet sonofabitch!" shouted Arnie.

"I think he's mean enough, now, Coach," said Harry smugly. He walked away from where Arnie flailed about in the grasp of Big Jim.

Coach Braun walked up to Arnie. "You ready to run fast and be mean, Eberly? Or ya want the Headhunter to come in?"

Arnie stopped struggling and glared at the Coach. "Yeah, Coach," he said, "I'm ready... just keep that damn Poet away from me!"

"You mean the Headhunter?" asked Braun glancing at Harry.

"Whatever he is!" said Arnie angrily, looking at Harry with confused eyes. "Keep him away from me!"

****

The second half opened with a run by Jolting Jack Sanders up the middle. Terry Moddy decided he wasn't so sick after seeing Hero's run and was ready to go. Terry ran a sweep around Arnie's end. Arnie ran as though possessed by demons. He launched a block at the linebacker that felled the player and ran on to make a glancing block on the halfback that threw him off balance. Terry saw daylight and ran for a score.

"Way to block out there, Arnie!" shouted Coach Braun, jumping up and down.

On the next Virginia Beach possession, they tried the sweep around Arnie's end once more. Arnie shoved the lumbering tackle away, dodged the end and slammed into the halfback for a three yard loss.

"Take that you Poet sonofabitch!" said Arnie as he got up, leaving the bewildered halfback on the ground.

The Truckers ran off the field that night with a thirty-four to nothing victory.

"Thirty four to nothing... again," said Bubba as they clattered into the dressing room. "It seems like a popular score... just like last week."

"Yeah," said Harry, "but it's only a matter of time before someone scores on us."

****

The football party was at Benny Norwood's house, a big two story brick colonial house facing on the Nansemond River north of Churchland. It was a Churchland tradition... the Football Party after the game. Some player each year volunteered his parents to host a Football Party. It always attracted a big crowd, most invited, some not. The Norwood estate had a big yard which was littered with vehicles of every imaginable size and shape parked on the lawn. Mr. Benjamin Norwood Senior's new beige Pontiac Star Chief sat majestically in the driveway, the five thin chrome stripes on its hood sparkling in the lights from the house. Benjamin, a tall, thin man in a white shirt and bow tie walked around the yard staring in horror at the many tire marks that now graced his manicured lawn. He made his considerable money as the downtown Pontiac Dealer, and he loved automobiles... but not the ones that tore up his yard. The house was ablaze with lights, but only a dim glow shone out over the pier that extended into the river among the bull rushes. In the house, there were punch bowls with Baptist punch and tables heaped with food. Mrs. Beverly Norwood, a tall, heavy lady with a determined look on her face, supervised the replacement of the food as it was gobbled down by the hungry crowd. A record player was rendering all the popular songs. Archie Bleyer was holding forth:

I know a dark secluded place,
A place where no one knows your face,
A glass of wine, a fast embrace,
It's called Hernando's Hideaway. Ole!

Benjamin came in and stood next to Beverly, watching the feeding of the teens with disdain. "An unruly crowd, if I ever saw one," he said in a prissy voice.

"Now Benjamin," said Beverly in a scolding voice, "we have to help Benny with his friends."

"From what I can see, his friends are mostly toughies trained by this Shotgun character!" said Benjamin with disdain.

"Benny says Shotgun is real mean and treats them all too rough," said Beverly, "but they do win the games!"

"Hrmmph!" said Benjamin competing for a chicken leg with an onrushing group of Cheerleaders. "I told the man he wasn't giving Benny a fair chance."

"What did he say?" asked Beverly.

"He said he'd push Benny and see what he can do."

"My goodness," exclaimed Beverly, "I hope he doesn't hurt him!"

In the yard were two pig cookers made from old fifty gallon drums. Each contained a well roasted pig ready for picking. Big tubs of Cole slaw and bowls of beans baked in cinnamon and brown sugar sat on a table next to the pig cookers. The aromas from the foods were intoxicatingly good. Large groups of people helped themselves amid the hubbub of the crowd. Arnie, Bart, Johnny, Carson and Bryan stood in aggressively posed positions, designed to show how "cool" and tough they were, smoking a cigarette next to the cookers.

Harry, Tony, Bubba and Alice stood next to the 1949 Chevrolet convertible that Harry's father had just bought. It was dark green with a tan top that lay on the car behind the back seat. The tires were white walled and the rear ones were covered by fender skirts. Harry had on his usual tan slacks and open neck sport shirt with a light jacket. Tony had adopted the "jeans" look used by most of the players.

"I see the Hoods are here again," said Harry nodding at Arnie and his gang.

"Yeah," said Bubba. "They think they're real cool."

"Yeah," said Alice, "some guys think it's cool being a Hood... I think it's stupid!"

"Johnny used to live in Long Island," said Bubba. "I reckon he was a Hood up there."

Tony backed away and looked at the Chevrolet.

"Not quite a Hood car, Harry," said Tony nodding his head, "but a really nice car. How'd you persuade your father to get it?"

"Yeah, it's a great car... I just asked Father to buy a cheese wagon," said Harry. "And he outdid himself... says he gets a kick outa driving it to work!"

"Well, I hope it attracts some cheese!" grinned Tony. "That's a good name for it... the Cheese-Wagon!"

"When are you going to get a date, Tony?" asked Bubba.

"Aww, I don't know," said Tony bashfully.

"I know a girl who wants to date ya, Tony," said Alice with a conspiratorial smile.

"Who's that?" asked Tony eagerly.

"Sherry Montgomery," said Alice. "She's a cheerleader!"

"Really?" asked Tony.

"Yeah... really," said Alice pointing. "She's right over there."

Tony looked at the girl Alice pointed to. Sherry was a vivacious girl with a grin that showed off perfectly white teeth against her fresh, pretty face. She was at the barbecue stand talking to Bucky.

"Is she Bucky's girl?" asked Tony hesitantly.

"Not right now, she ain't," said Alice, giving Tony a poke in the ribs

"Speaking of cheese," said Harry as he watched Allman drive up in his red jeep with Georgia.

"Yeah," said Tony, "she has it all packed in there, for sure!"

"She's probably wearing falsies," said Alice enviously.

"Just like you?" asked Bubba with a lewd grin.

"Oh Bubba!" said Alice as she swatted at him. Bubba ducked and ran for cover.

"I'll get you for that!" shouted Alice, giving chase.

Allman and Georgia jumped out of the red jeep laughing. He had on dungarees, a white tee shirt and a black Churchland "Varsity C" sweater with a big orange "C". She wore the white dress and jersey of the Churchland Cheerleaders, a big orange "C" across her quite obvious breasts. Allman paused, struck a match, lit something Harry could not see and ran wildly toward the crowd at the pig picking table. He faded back as though to pass a football and heaved a string of Chinese firecrackers to the ground near the crowd. The firecrackers began to go off with a rapid succession of pops and bangs. The crowd moved as a herd spooked by a wolf, then scattered in all directions as the firecrackers continued to pop. Allman jumped up and down and laughed, and then ran around with another string of firecrackers threatening to throw them at cowering groups of partiers.

"The Truckers are as hot as firecrackers!" shouted Allman, waving his arms and putting on a show for the crowd. Georgia ran up behind him and wrapped her arms around him, gyrating her body in suggestive ways.

"That darn Allman," said Tony in wonder, watching the show.

"That darn Georgia!" exclaimed Bubba, returning to the group with Alice still swatting at him.

Harry didn't hear him. He was staring at the big white Cadillac convertible that rolled into the yard. In it were Duane Starr in a blue blazer and striped red and white tie, and the girl with the brown pony tail... Paige Garnette. Starr parked the Cadillac and got out. He opened the door for Paige and she got out gracefully, her pony tail bobbing behind her. She had on a form fitting gray dress and a dark blue cashmere sweater under a fashionable gray jacket.

"How about introducing me to Paige, Alice?" asked Harry.

"I don't know her too well..."

"Come on, Alice," said Bubba. "You told me she's in your gym class."

"Well, she is, but... she doesn't talk much."

"Come on, Alice!" chortled Bubba. "Can't you see Harry is horny and needs a girl friend. Introduce him!"

"Oh, alright," said Alice reluctantly. "Come on, Horny Harry."

"Don't introduce me as Horny Harry!" exclaimed Harry in alarm.

Alice giggled. "How 'bout Headhunter Harry?"

"No, Alice," said Harry irritably. "Just Harry Quester will do."

"I'm going over here and try to talk to Sherry," said Tony, bashfully.

"Good luck, Little Brother," said Harry.

Harry, Bubba and Alice walked to where Duane Starr and Paige Garnette stood watching the finale of the firecracker episode.

"What in the world is going on over there, Duane?" asked Paige in a husky, velvety smooth voice. The voice surprised Harry, and he caught himself staring at the big brown eyes in the smoothly rounded face.

"Ah, just Buddinger screwing around," said Duane in an affected voice, "as usual!"

"Firecrackers?" asked Paige.

"Yeah," said Duane, dismissing it all with a wave of his hand.

"He got a rise out of them... that's for sure!" said Paige.

"Buddinger has a knack for that," said Duane smoothing back the mound of brown hair on his head. "It's good that he has something to amuse him."

"What do you mean by that?" asked Bubba with hostility.

Duane looked at Bubba as though he were a bug under a microscope. "Well, he's not much of a quarterback... so he must be good at something... like screwing around!"

"Allman's a pretty good quarterback!" said Bubba, insulted.

"Who are you?" asked Duane, looking down his nose at Bubba.

"Bubba Hawkins, a Trucker," said Bubba. "And who are you?"

"You know who I am," said Duane arrogantly.

"We won tonight you know!" said Bubba, uncharacteristic anger creeping into his voice.

"So did we," said Duane feigning amusement. "And very soon we'll show you Truckers again why we'll always beat you!"

"I don't think so," said Bubba bravely. "We're gonna smear you guys!"

"Hey, Bubba," said Duane sarcastically. "Why don't you come and play for a real team… we need some more blocking dummies!"

"Duane!" exclaimed Paige. "That isn't nice!"

Bubba balled up his fists and glowered at Duane.

"Save it, Bubba," said Harry, putting a restraining hand on Bubba's shoulder. He felt Paige's eyes inspecting him.

"You guys quit arguing," snapped Alice. "Hi Paige."

"Hi Alice," said Paige in a husky voice that made Harry shiver.

"Have you met Harry Quester?" asked Alice.

"Well, not really," said Paige holding out her hand. "I know who you are, Harry… and I'm glad to finally meet you."

Harry took her hand and held it briefly, feeling strong emotions as she squeezed it ever so gently. "Hello, Paige," he said, trying to make his voice sound deep and confident. He wasn't sure he succeeded. "I've been wanting to meet you, ever since…"

"You saw me on Chandler Point," finished Paige, a sparkle in her eye. "You looked so dashing out there in that red and white boat!"

"What the hell, Paige?" asked Duane insolently. "Who is this fellow?"

"Harry Quester," said Alice. "He plays… fullback… for the Truckers."

"I thought Sanders was the fullback," said Duane looking at Harry suspiciously.

"I back him up," said Harry straightforwardly.

"Oh… second string," said Duane arrogantly. "Or is it third?"

"Does it matter?" asked Harry taking an instant dislike to Duane Starr.

"I suppose not," said Duane with a staged sniff. "Come on, Paige, let's go sample this Churchland pork! It can't be as good as the peanut fed pork in Suffolk!"

Duane put out his arm and started to walk away.

"Look at that beautiful green convertible," said Paige admiringly.

"It's mine," said Harry. "Or… it's really my Father's."

"It's beautiful," said Paige.

"It's just a Chevrolet," said Duane with a sniff, "and an old one at that!"

Duane walked away, Paige holding on to his arm. She glanced back over her shoulder and smiled at Harry. Harry made driving motions with his hands and pointed at the Chevrolet. Paige's smile broadened and she nodded gently. Then she turned and walked away with Duane.

Bubba snorted. "Be careful, Harry," he said disgustedly. "I hear Paige is a big tease… and a cold fish… an ice berg! Worse than that… Duane has a nasty reputation of being really jealous."

"Are they going steady?" asked Harry.

"I don't think so," said Alice wrinkling her nose in distaste. "He's such a pompous ass I don't know how she stands him… unless of course, it's the football thing!"

"Or the money," said Bubba. "His old man has a lotta nuts!"

****

Harry was full of pork barbecue and bored with the people at the party. He tried to find a reason to approach Paige again, but Duane managed to keep her occupied with himself and a growing horde of people talking about the Suffolk and Churchland football teams. He saw Al Gollen munching on a barbecue sandwich, trying to talk to Duane at the same time. There was sure to be a piece in the paper about it all, tomorrow, thought Harry. Up by the house he heard loud laughter from Allman and Arnie. Then raucous shouting from Bart and Carson. He looked up and saw them staggering around chasing Allman. He felt isolated. Somehow, he just didn't fit in with all that tomfoolery. He wasn't sure he ever would fit in with the Churchland players. As Allman would put it, he was "too square". He turned and walked down to the pier. It was a beautiful night. Frogs croaked in the bull rushes and there was the occasional splash of a jumping fish or the swoosh of a hunting fish owl. He felt better sometimes just being alone. He stood there by the river for several minutes watching for the occasional splash of a fish leaping in the moonlight.

"Harry?" came a voice from behind him.

Harry turned to find Clara in her Cheerleader's uniform. "Clara!" exclaimed Harry. "What're you doing down here?"

"I just… needed to get away from all that," said Clara nodding back at the house.

"Yeah, me too," said Harry. "What's going on up there, anyway?"

"Allman and Arnie are chasing around making fools of themselves," said Clara. "Mrs. Norwood is about to have a fit!"

Harry shook his head in wonder. "You never know what Allman's gonna do next!"

"You wanna walk down on the pier with me?" asked Clara in a

hesitating voice.

"Sure," said Harry, wondering what this was all about.

They walked together out onto the rickety wooden pier. There was a light breeze, and though the mosquitoes had not quit for the year, the breeze kept them down. They sat on the edge of the pier and dangled their legs over the side. They could faintly hear Georgia Gibbs on a record from the house.

I touch your lips and all at once the sparks go flying,
Those devil lips that know so well the art of lying,
And though I see the danger, still the flame grows higher,
I know I must surrender to your kiss of fire.

"Are you wondering why Arnie isn't with me?" asked Clara breaking into his thoughts.

"Well... yeah," said Harry. "I guess I am."

"That's the problem," said Clara. "A girl gets tied up with a guy... and she isn't allowed to meet anyone new... and interesting."

"Well, Bubba told me that... you told him you were in love with Arnie... is that right?"

"Yes... I told him that!"

"Well... are you?"

"What?"

"In love with Arnie?"

Clara paused and stared at the glimmer of the lights from the house on the water below her. There was more loud laughing from the direction of the house. "I was... maybe I am," she said, the hint of a tear in her voice. "But he... sometimes he's just so difficult."

"Like tonight?"

"Yes... he's up there with Bart and Carson... and they're all getting drunk!"

"Drunk?" asked Harry. The thought astounded him, as it was not in his culture to drink as a high schooler... particularly when trying to be an athlete. Well, he and Bubba had drunk a beer this past summer at Virginia Beach... but that was last summer.

"Yes," said Clara, "they're there with Allman seeing who can make the biggest fool of themselves... except Allman has enough sense not to drink much... he's a fool without the whiskey!"

"No kidding?"

Clara sobbed. "No kidding."

"So... you just left him and came down here?"

"He started pushing me around... showing off that he sorta... you know... owned me."

"Did he hurt you?"

"No… I'm used to that… but I don't like it."

"What can I do?" asked Harry.

"Just talk to me," said Clara. "I feel so lonely."

"Okay," said Harry. "You know I had a little fight with Arnie?"

"I heard something about it."

"He and I don't get along too well," said Harry.

"You know they all think you're… well, sort of strange… don't you?"

"They do? Why is that?"

"You… you just seem to… to value different things than they do," said Clara. "Most of those guys just try to be nasty, so they can tell stories to their buddies."

"I hope I don't do that," said Harry, embarrassed. "Maybe I do value different things."

"And you don't give in to them," said Clara.

"I try not to."

"It gets under Arnie's skin… your being different."

"I can't help that. He sorta gets under my skin too with all that Hood stuff."

"Janet told me what happened down there at the swamp."

"She did?"

"Yes… and I would have been just as insulted as she was!"

"I know. It wasn't all the best."

"Don't let Allman and Arnie get away with stuff like that," said Clara seriously. "If you do, they'll do it forever!"

Harry turned to look at Clara. "I think that's good advice," he said. "Don't let Arnie worry you, Clara."

Clara looked up at him with a questioning look.

"I guess I don't have a choice," said Clara, looking away.

"Is being Arnie's girl what you want?"

"I don't know," she said, shaking her head from side to side.

Harry swung his legs over the side of the pier. "I met this girl, Paige Garnette," he said. "She… attracted me, but I don't know much about her. She's new here."

"I don't know her very well… but she seems sweet," said Clara. "I think she has the same problem I do."

"You mean Duane Starr?"

"Yeah… that arrogant guy from Suffolk."

There was a clomping on the bridge behind them. Harry got up and looked back toward the house. Arnie was weaving his way down the pier. He saw Harry and a rage came over his face. Then he saw Clara as she got up and stood next to Harry.

"Are ya… sittin' onna pier wit' my girl, Poet?" asked Arnie angrily, his voice slurred. "You still wanna make me look bad?"

"We're just friends, Arnie," said Harry bluntly. "And we're just talking."

"Talkin'… talkin'," said Arnie through blurry eyes as he staggered toward them. "How 'bout some kissin' kissin'?"

"Arnie!" exclaimed Clara forcefully. "You're drunk as a skunk!"

Arnie held out his hand. "Come on Clara," he said through thick lips. "Let this Poet alone. He ain't… worth a shit!"

Harry felt his anger rising. He had experienced the dark cloud of anger in him before. He had used it to develop his game face. Now, it was creeping over him involuntarily, numbing his sense of caution, his sense of what was right. He tried to control himself. Arnie grabbed Clara by the arm and pulled her toward him. "Goddam bitch… don't know when she got it good!"

Clara stumbled along the rickety pier as Arnie pulled her along.

Harry started toward Arnie and Clara. "Arnie, you bastard!" he shouted emotionally. "You can't treat girls like that!"

"Oh yeah?" sneered Arnie as he stopped, staggered and turned around. "And who's tellin' me whatta do…. some goddam poet?"

Clara held up her hand to Harry, agony on her face and tears in her eyes. "Stop, Harry," she sobbed. "Please stop! It's bad enough as it is!"

Harry stopped, doubt filling his mind. He ground his clenched fist into his hand nervously. There was a burning sensation in his eyes and the middle of his chest. His mouth felt dry and he gritted his teeth.

"I'll see ya… ya son'bitch… see ya at Teenage on Thursday," said Arnie, his words slurred. "That's when we fight! A challenge! I've had… enough of ya, Poet!"

****

Slate drove his Ford southward toward the North Carolina state line. The radio was on, playing *In the Mood* by Glen Miller. Cliff was sitting in the passenger seat. Pete Sacker was sitting in the back. Pete was a big man, six feet tall with broad shoulders and weighing over two hundred pounds. He was only eighteen, having just graduated from Wilson High School where he played tackle and excelled in school.

"I sure hope you guys are right about this East Carolina Teacher's College," said Pete. "I was All State, ya know… I gave up a lot to join you guys."

"Oh baloney… don't let that All State stuff go to your head," said Cliff. "We were All State too…what's the University of Tennessee compared to the chance to play with Slate and me?"

"I don't know," said Pete, doubt in his voice. "I just hope it works!"

"You'll be a lot closer to home than out there in Tennessee," observed Cliff.

"It'll work fine," said Slate, "and besides I need someone big to block for me… Cliff is too skinny!"

"Hey! Come on now," exploded Cliff. "I'm a hundred and sixty five now… that's bigger than I was in High School!"

"Yeah," said Slate, "you're a hundred and sixty five pound terror… but I need a two hundred pound terror!"

"Yeah, yeah… how far to Greenville?" muttered Cliff leaning back in the passenger seat and closing his eyes.

"About a hundred and fifty miles," said Slate watching the thick foliaged green trees beside the road flash by. "We should make it in four hours or so."

"I'm glad we got the scholarships to play ball," said Cliff. "My Mother is barely making it working at the department store downtown."

"I know," said Slate. "East Carolina Teacher's College isn't exactly the big time… but it'll do."

"Did we have a choice?"

"Not really."

"I could send her money when I was in the army," said Cliff, "but now I can't."

"We'll find some part time jobs or something down in Greenville," said Slate.

"And go to school… and play football, too?"

"We'll have to if we want any spending money."

"Yeah… I guess so."

"I hope they have good looking girls down here," said Slate hopefully. "I've heard that these North Carolina girls are beautiful!"

"I'll take a dozen or so," muttered Cliff.

"I just want to find the right one," said Slate.

"Find one for me too," said Pete.

"You're a one woman man, Slate," said Cliff. "I can tell."

"Right now I'm a no woman man," said Slate. "That's the problem!"

"Here we are, twenty four years old and just college boys," said Cliff. "I'm not sure I want to be anything else."

"I thought you wanted to be a coach," said Slate.

"Yeah, I guess so," said Cliff thoughtfully.

"Well, get your degree in physical education down here at ECTC and you'll be in line to be a coach."

"Maybe I'll go back and coach at Wilson," said Cliff. "Wouldn't that be a laugh!"

"Well, maybe it'll happen," said Pete. "Who knows?"

"It'll be good to see Coach Johnstone again," said Cliff.

"Yeah," said Slate. "We owe him a lot... getting us set up with football scholarships and Veteran's aid all at the same time."

"He did all that?" asked Cliff.

"Yeah, Cliff," said Slate in exasperation. "He and I did it all for you... and me, and Pete!"

"I'll be damned," said Cliff.

"It's his first year," said Slate. "You know ECTC hasn't played football since they stopped for the war... in 1941."

"I hope he has some fire in him," said Cliff, "not like old Eddie Wilder."

"Eddie was okay," said Slate. "He knew his football... he just didn't get worked up as much as some others. I remember Johnstone as having a lot of fire."

"Don't worry," said Pete, "we'll win our share of the games."

"I want to win all the games!" said Cliff. "All of 'em!"

****

Slate donned his purple football uniform with the gold number forty-four on it. He sat on the bench in the dressing room, his purple dyed leather helmet on his lap. It was the middle of October, 1946, and the big game this night at Guy Smith Stadium was between the ECTC Pirates and the Elon College Fightin' Christians. They had beaten Presbyterian College twenty to nothing in the first game and tied Atlantic Christian six to six in the second. Slate was optimistic about the remaining games. He tried to keep his mind on the upcoming contest, but thoughts of the girl he had met at a party after the last game filled his mind. Her name was Billie Eaton, and her wavy brown hair and penetrating blue eyes would not leave him.

"Ya ready to play some ball, Slate?" drawled Eddie Fearless, his fellow halfback sitting next to him on the bench. Eddie looked like the fellow next door, or the local drug store soda jockey, but he was a powerful and strong runner.

"Sure I'm ready, Eddie" said Slate.

"I wasn't sure," said Eddie in his North Carolina drawl, "ya looked like your mind was a thousand miles away."

Slate smiled. "Well, not that far..."

"How about only as far as Billie Eaton is up in the stands," said Eddie with a smile. "I seen ya last week mooning around her!"

"She… she's been on my mind," said Slate.

"Ya got a lotta competition for that filly," said Eddie slyly. "But right now, let's play some ball!"

"Yeah," said Slate slapping himself beside the head. "Let's play some ball!"

"I hope your boys Pete and Shotgun open up some big holes for us tonight!"

"They will," said Slate reassuringly.

"Shotgun better keep his temper this time out," said Eddie. "The referees are looking out for him after he clobbered that Atlantic Christian guy!"

"I'll keep an eye on him," said Slate. "He gets worked up over little things and flies off the handle."

Slate and Eddie got up and clattered to the center of the dressing room where the team assembled around Coach Johnstone.

"What can I say to you guys to tell you how bad I want this game?" shouted the Coach, his voice building in volume and intensity. "The question is, do you want it? Well do ya?"

"We want it!" shouted Cliff. He jumped up on a bench and stared at the team, his face turning red. He raised his hands.

"We want it!" shouted the team.

"How bad?" shouted Cliff.

"Real bad!" shouted the team.

"As bad as the Coach?" shouted the Coach.

"More than the Coach!" shouted Cliff, followed by the team. "More than the Coach!"

"Then let's go get it!" shouted Coach Johnstone, running from the dressing room and leading the team into Guy Smith Stadium.

Slate took the opening kickoff and returned it to the ECTC forty yard line. Paul Evergreen, the quarterback, lined them up in their split tee formation and barked the signals. Eddie Fearless ran off left tackle for five yards. Next, Slate ran off right tackle behind Pete Sacker and Cliff Braun… six yards and a first down. They marched down the field. Harry Pitt, the fullback ran for a few yards to the Elon twenty. In the ECTC huddle, Paul started to call the play.

"Wait a minute… wait a minute," said Cliff.

"What is it, Shotgun?" asked Paul. "We don't have much time here, ya know!"

"That big end in front of me thinks he has me figured out," said Cliff. "I can make him take the inside where Pete can take him… and I can get the linebacker leaving it all open for Slate around right end."

"How are ya gonna make him rush like that?" asked Paul wiping away the sweat on his brow.

"Just leave it to me, Paul," said Cliff impatiently.

"Okay," said Paul, "Forty-nine sweep... Slate around right end... on two!"

They ran up to the line and Paul began to bark signals. Cliff leaned just a little bit to his left. "Okay ass-hole," he said between clenched teeth, "we're coming right through tackle... and ya ain't got a chance!!"

"Ya think so, huh?" muttered the big end.

The ball was snapped and Elon's big end charged inside of Cliff's position. Pete caught him and pushed him further inside. Cliff ran into the Elon backfield. The linebacker had been sucked in behind the big end. Cliff heard Slate coming behind him.

"Get the halfback!" shouted Slate.

Cliff charged down the field. Open field blocks were just as hard... or harder than open field tackles. He had to be careful that he didn't extend his arms too far and be called for holding, and he had to not commit too early and let the halfback dodge aside. He ran straight at the halfback who was in a squat position, his arms extended, waiting to fend Cliff off and make the tackle. Cliff dodged to the right and then the left, his cleated feet kicking up turf. The halfback committed to the left and Cliff hit him with a resounding blow. His arms came up under the halfback's arms and crushed into his chest. The halfback fell backward. Cliff ran on, Slate close behind. The safety tried to catch then, but Cliff merely ran between the oncoming safety and Slate. Slate went over the goal line untouched. Elon called time and the halfback limped off the field.

"Touchdown!" yelled Cliff.

Coach Johnstone was dancing excitedly down the sidelines beside them. "Way to block, Shotgun! Way to run, Slate!"

Harry Pitt's run for the extra point was short, and the score stayed ECTC six, Elon nothing.

Elon scored late in the second half. Their extra point kick missed the goal posts and the score was tied six to six as the players ran into the dressing room at the half.

"Here we are again," shouted Coach Johnstone, "... tied! I hate ties! I really hate ties! We have to stop these guys in the second half and score... to win!"

****

Eddie Fearless took over in the second half. He ran four plays for fifty yards, but the Pirates were stopped on the Fightin' Christian's twenty yard line. They lost the ball on downs. Elon fought back but as the game neared an end, the score was still six to six. ECTC had Elon pinned down on their own thirty yard line where the Fighting Christians were forced to kick.

"Okay, guys, we got three minutes to get the ball and score," said Paul rubbing his hands together. "Let's block like hell for Slate and Eddie on the return!"

"Slate," said Cliff, "pump me up... I'm gonna get that punter this time!"

"What do you mean, pump you up?"

"You know, piss me off... get my juices flowing!"

"Ennis Hathaway is the punter," said Slate with a grimace. "And he called you a little, snotty punk!"

Shotgun's face turned beet red and he began to snort. His eyes closed to narrow, squinty slits.

"Why that Fatso sonofabitch!" shouted Cliff, crouching at the line.

The referee looked at Cliff strangely and reached for his flag. Then he changed his mind and the ball was snapped back to the punter. Cliff was off the line like a shot and ran around Elon's big end like a flash of hot lightning. He raised his hands and rushed at the punter.

"Ahhhhhhhh!" screamed Cliff as he leaped at the punter.

The Elon punter saw Cliff coming. He pulled in the ball and started running to the right. Cliff staggered, tried to follow him and fell to the turf. He watched in horror as the Elon Punter ran the seventy yards for a touchdown.

Cliff got up slowly. "Slate!" exclaimed Cliff. "Ya let that guy get away!"

"We got faked out, for sure," said Slate with a grimace and a shrug of his shoulders.

They lined up as Elon prepared to kick the extra point. The ball went to the holder. The holder sprung up and ran around right end for the point. Elon thirteen, ECTC six.

"Suckered again!" exclaimed Cliff, his face beet red. "That really pisses me off!"

The game ended with Elon the victor. In the dressing room, Coach Johnstone tried to console Cliff. "It was just a fluke, Shotgun," said the Coach. "Don't blame yourself... you were just... well, just too good on that play! You had the punter and we weren't ready for a run!"

"It ain't a fluke, Coach," said Cliff, tears in his eyes. "When ya lose, it's 'cause someone screws up... that's the way it is!"

****

Slate Phelps and Billie Eaton were married in June of 1947. Slate had a part time job in a hardware store in Greenville. Billie worked at the College Library, and with help from Billie's parents, they rented a small apartment near the college and continued their studies. Cliff was a frequent visitor. Fall football practice had begun. It was late afternoon and Cliff was in Slate and Billie's small living room drinking a coke.

"How'd you get the black eye, Cliff?" asked Billie sitting down on the sofa across from him.

"Aww, I had a fight with the guy at the shipping company where I work," said Cliff.

"What happened?" asked Slate with some concern.

"The… guy wouldn't let me use his hand truck," said Cliff. "And I had to walk down a long corridor and carry them big old boxes of barbecue sauce down to the loading dock… and put 'em on the trucks."

"Weren't there more than one hand truck?" asked Slate.

"Yeah, but mine broke."

"So you fought the guy for the other one?" asked Billie.

"Yeah."

"Who won?" asked Slate.

"Well… mostly I did," said Cliff, "but the guy in charge fired me."

"Uh oh!" exclaimed Slate. "You can't pay your rent without a job."

"Yeah, I know," said Cliff with a wicked smile. "All those gals will have to meet me out in the park!"

"I've heard about your line of gals, Cliff," said Billie. "You'd better watch out… you might find one you really like!"

"Well, some day, Billie," said Cliff. "But don't lasso me too soon!"

"What about a job?" asked Slate.

"Don't worry, Professor Franklin got me a job down at the school loading dock," said Cliff.

"You mean the Professor from the History Department?" asked Slate. "The one who's the big football fan?"

"Yeah… Marion Franklin," said Cliff. "He's a pretty good old guy… used to play some ball himself… at least that's what he says."

"That was good of him," said Slate.

"He's a good Professor," said Cliff. "He teaches history so we can enjoy it… not just a lot of blah blah bah like the others. I see him at every game."

"He must have taken a liking to you," smiled Slate, "though I can't imagine why!"

"Aw come on, Slate," said Cliff. "Lots of folks like Ol' Lovable Shotgun… he likes me 'cause of the way I can block… likes to think he can do it too... so I humor him."

"How are you doing on your studies?" asked Billie.

"I do great in history," said Cliff with a shrug, "with Professor Franklin... on the other stuff I get by. Some of them other Professors just make me mad... know-it-all bastards!"

"You know, Cliff," said Slate, "that chip on your shoulder is going to get you in a lot of trouble."

"I ain't got no chip!" exclaimed Cliff. "I just don't like people who try to put me down!"

"People aren't trying to put you down, Cliff."

"Yeah?" exclaimed Cliff. "They been doing it ever since we were kids, Slate... you know that!"

"Come on," said Slate, "we'd better get down to the Armory. Major Fuller doesn't like it when we're late."

"That Major guy thinks I'm still in the army," muttered Cliff, getting up and stretching.

"You want that Veteran's money coming in with the scholarship, don't you?" asked Slate.

"Yeah... yeah," said Shotgun impatiently. "But that tin soldier seems to have it in for me!"

Cliff went to the door. Slate kissed Billie goodbye.

"You won't be late?" asked Billie in a soft voice that made Slate feel all weak inside.

"No, dear," said Slate, "It's just a veteran's meeting... for all the guys who have Veteran money coming in."

"I'll wait up," said Billie sweetly.

Slate and Cliff walked down the stairs from the second story apartment and went to Slate's Ford.

"I'll wait up!" said Cliff in a teasing sweet voice. "Ya wanna go get a beer after the meeting?"

"Are you kidding?" said Slate seriously.

"Well, I don't see as much of you anymore," said Cliff as Slate started the car.

"Better get used to that," said Slate with a grin as he drove away. "You got heavy competition!"

"I know."

"You have a girl friend don't you?"

"I got more of 'em than I need," said Cliff wearily.

"Isn't there one you like best?"

"They all yabber too much," observed Cliff.

****

Chapter Nine
Deep Creek

Harry, Tony, Bubba and Allman were sitting in A.P. Johns' Grocery store looking at the headline on the sports page on the Saturday morning after the game.

CHURCHLAND BLANKS VIRGINIA BEACH
SUFFOLK HALFBACK SAYS THE TRUCKERS WILL NEVER BEAT THE RED RAIDERS
By
Al Gollen

The Churchland High School Truckers displayed complete dominance over the Virginia Beach Seahawks Friday night at Churchland Stadium in a Group II football game. Johnny "Hero" Current scored by taking the opening kickoff and returning it for eighty yards and a score. Jolting Jack Sanders plowed his way through the Seahawk defenses for two more scores in the first half. Terry Moddy and Sanders scored in the second half to make the final score thirty-four to nothing. This is the same score by which they beat the Gloucester Dukes last Friday night. Is there a pattern here? Coach Cliff Braun became agitated when the Seahawks picked up a first down on an end sweep. We don't know what the Coach said to the team at the half, but we do know that when the Seahawks tried their favorite play in the second half, they were thrown for a loss!

After the game, this reporter ran into Duane Starr, the hard running halfback for the Suffolk Red Raiders. Duane said that Churchland would never be able to beat the Red Raiders. They haven't in the past, and they won't in the future, according to the Suffolk star. The Churchland – Suffolk game scheduled for the first week in November is shaping up as a really important contest. The winner will likely be the District Group II Champions, and maybe have a record that will compete for the State championship. This paper will cover everything leading up to that exciting contest!

A.P. came up and looked over their shoulders at the paper. "That Suffolk guy has a lotta nerve," he said.

"I met him at the Football Party," said Harry with a frown. "He's an arrogant blowhard!"

"He's a real pill… hard to take," said Allman munching on a bag of potato chips, "but he can run!"

"Did you tell All Gollen that… about Starr being a blowhard?" asked Bubba with a twisted grin.

"Al Gollen doesn't talk to me," said Harry, "And I don't talk to him."

"What happened to the Headhunter?" asked A.P. "I expected to see you in the game after Eberly blew those two end sweeps."

"I guess Coach fixed it…another way," said Harry.

"Too bad," said A.P. straightening a row of doughnuts on a wire stand. "It was working great!"

"Coach Braun is the man," said Tony. "He'll figure it out!"

"Right," said Bubba. "Shotgun decides what works… and when it works… and he's mostly right."

A.P. walked behind the counter to answer a ringing telephone. Bubba pulled down a pack of donuts. He went to the cooler and took out three cartons of chocolate milk. "I guess my Old Man's tab can stand this," said Bubba with a grin. He handed the milk to Allman, Harry and Tony.

"What is Teenage?" asked Harry taking the milk and reaching for a doughnut.

"Shotgun says it's a den of in-iq-ui-ty!" smiled Bubba.

"Come on," said Harry impatiently. "What is it?"

"Over in Simonsdale, there's a little community center," said Bubba between bites and gulps. "They have a 'Teenage Dance' over there every Thursday night… everyone just calls it 'Teenage'."

"Arnie says he wants to fight me there," said Harry disgustedly. "What's that all about?"

"He challenged you?" asked Allman, a surprised look on his face.

"Yeah… I guess he did."

"What is it between you and Arnie?" asked Bubba with a frown.

"Clara and I were sitting on the pier… talking," said Harry. "She left Arnie because he was drunk!"

"Sitting on the pier talking… with Clara?" asked Bubba in amazement. "Harry, you're either dumb as a rock or braver than I thought!"

"Well," said Harry, "is there any law against sitting on a pier and talking… with a friend?"

"Yeah, I guess there is," said Bubba, "when the friend is a teammate's girl… and a Hood's girl!"

"There ain't supposed to be any challenges between the players," said Allman, uncharacteristic alarm in his voice.

"I don't really want to fight him," said Harry, shaking his head.

"You don't have a choice," said Bubba. "The Hoods have a sort of unwritten code about challenges and fighting. Once challenged, you have to fight… or you become nobody all of a sudden!"

"That's crazy!" said Harry in an irritated voice.

"That's the way it is," said Bubba with authority.

"I'm gonna have to talk to Arnie," said Allman introspectively.

"I've seen Arnie fight," said Bubba. "He fights dirty."

"Oh great," moaned Harry.

"And watch out for Bart."

"Whitely?"

"Yeah," said Bubba. "If you put Arnie down... you might have to deal with Bart... or Johnny Calcione."

"That doesn't seem fair," said Harry.

"Who said anything about these things being fair?" asked Bubba, a serious look on his face. "But... I'll back you up."

"Yeah! Me too," exclaimed Tony.

"I gotta get you and Arnie to shake hands and forget all this," said Allman worriedly. "If Shotgun hears about it, there'll be hell to pay!"

"Like I said," said Harry. "I have no reason to fight him."

"Ya willing to apologize?" asked Allman.

Harry looked at Allman and a cloud of anger came over his face. "Whatta ya mean? I don't have any reason to apologize to Arnie!"

"Sitting on the pier in the dark with his girl?" grinned Allman. "Ain't there something wrong with that?"

"No... I don't think so."

"So... how was she?" grinned Allman.

"Knock it off, Allman," said Harry, his anger growing. "We were just talking!"

"Harry... Harry," muttered Allman. "You take girls too seriously! Loosen up!"

"Look... Allman," said Harry containing his anger, "if Georgia came up to me and wanted to talk... and we were on a pier...at night... I'd talk to her. Anything wrong with that?"

"Ya can talk to Georgia anytime ya want, Harry Ol' Buddy," laughed Allman, "but ya won't make a score with her!"

"Why is it that talking to a girl means you're just trying to score?" asked Harry.

"Hey!" exclaimed Allman, his eyes wide. "Is there any other reason to talk to a girl?"

"Allman, you've got a warped mind," said Harry shaking his head. "Clara wanted to talk because Arnie was drunk and pushing her around. She felt real bad! Did you know Arnie was drunk, Allman? You were up there with him!"

"I knew he had a few drinks," said Allman worriedly.

"What does Shotgun have to say about that?" asked Harry.

"I don't know," said Allman, a look of confusion in his eyes.

"Well, you're the Captain of the Team... along with Karl," said Harry. "If you're screwing around with Arnie and Bart and they're drinking and pushing girls around... ya oughta do something!"

"Awww... they were just having some fun!" said Allman stepping close to Harry.

"That's the trouble with you, Allman," said Harry not retreating, "everything is a big joke to you!"

"Ya need to cool it, Harry Ol' Buddy," said Allman, his face turning serious.

"Where do these fights… these challenges… take place?" asked Harry worriedly.

"Out in front of the Community Center," said Bubba, "when Officer Eddie Spearman ain't looking!"

****

Harry went to his class in Algebra II. The teacher, Miss Gaskins, was an older woman who had never been married, and she was a bit odd… but smart. She wore long dresses and old style beads around her neck. She knew her math and wasn't too worldly, but she had a sense of humor and a quick mind. It was said that she had eyes in the back of her head! Harry went into the room and took a seat in one of the uncomfortable desk-chairs. It was a mixed class of juniors and seniors. Arnie and Clara came in, followed by Allman and Georgia. Arnie glared at Harry. Clara was careful to find a seat as far away from Harry as possible. Terry Moddy sat behind Harry.

"Now, Allman," said Miss Gaskins sweetly, "you and Georgia find seats way apart… waaaaay apart," she said with a swoop of her hands, "so you both can learn about algebra."

"Miss Gaskins," said Allman with his practiced smile, "you look really smashing today… those beads must be new, and just in from Paris!"

"Just sit yourself down, Allman," blushed Miss Gaskins. "And thank you for the compliment!"

"Yes Maam," said Allman walking to a desk.

"No… no!" said Miss Gaskins. "Over there! Further away from Georgia."

"Yes Maam," said Allman tiptoeing to a new chair. "Today feels like a good day for learning algebra!"

"There goes that darn Allman, again!" whispered Terry.

The class took their seats and opened their books.

"Now Class," said Miss Gaskins, "Today we will review linear equations before we move into quadratic equations, that is, equations that have an unknown with an exponent of two as well as one."

Arnie groaned and settled back into his chair. Miss Gaskins turned to the black board and produced a piece of white chalk which she wielded with a flare. She wrote the equation $(X-8)^{1/2} = 3$ on the board.

"Now does anyone remember from last year how to solve this?" asked Miss Gaskins searching the faces round the room. There was a deadly silence.

"You have to square both sides of the equation," said Harry, uncomfortable with the silence, "to get the X from under the radical."

The whole class looked at Harry as though he were an alien that had descended among them.

"Why, that's quite right," said Miss. Gaskins. "You are Harry… correct?"

"Yes Maam," said Harry, feeling embarrassed.

"Of course, Class," said Miss. Gaskins, "if we do what Harry has suggested, we get … $X - 8 = 9$. Now where do we go from there?"

"You move the 8 to the other side of the equation and reverse its sign," said Clara bravely. "Then X equals 17."

Arnie groaned again and put his hands over his face.

"Very good, Clara," said Miss Gaskins, ignoring Arnie. "Which is the same as adding eight to both sides of the equation!"

Miss Gaskins looked around the classroom, seeking faces that understood. She saw a few.

"I can see we have a lot of reviewing to do," said Miss Gaskins, "so let's try another one."

Miss Gaskins turned to the blackboard, selected a clean eraser and meticulously erased the equation on the board. She spun around suddenly and glared at Georgia.

"Now, Miss Blake," said Miss Gaskins in unforgiving tones. "Just what was that you handed to Bart?"

"Oh nothing, Miss Gaskins," said Georgia in an innocent voice.

Miss Gaskins went to Bart Whitely who was sitting next to Allman. He tried to hide the note, but she snatched it from his hand. Miss Gaskins opened it and read it aloud.

Allman, come to my house, tonight! I'll be alone and have the TV on and nothing else… just for you. Georgia.

There was a loud snicker from the class.

"Now Georgia," scolded Miss Gaskins, "you should save your invitations for after class… I'm sure that you can wait that long."

The snicker turned into a roar of laughter. Miss Gaskins looked confused.

"Now stop all that noise," said Miss Gaskins shaking her finger at the Class. "We have work to do!"

The laughter declined to the occasional snicker.

"Did you hear what I said, Georgia?" asked Miss Gaskins, rapping a pencil on her desk.

"Yes Maam," said Georgia demurely, sneaking a seductive glance at Allman, who just leaned back and smiled.

****

The Cheese-wagon cruised along Route 17 with its top down. Harry was driving. Allman was sprawled into the passenger seat.

"Thanks for the ride, Harry, Ol' Buddy," said Allman.

"You going to see Georgia?" asked Harry with a knowing smile.

"Sure, Harry Ol' Buddy," said Allman pretending to be serious. "Her TV is great! I like the knobs!"

They laughed together.

"You ready for Deep Creek Friday night?" asked Harry.

"No sweat!" said Allman. "Pieca cake."

"I hear they have a real heavy line."

"Yeah, I guess so."

"Think that'll slow Jack down any?"

"I doubt it."

"If it does, ya might have to pass more… we haven't passed much this year."

"I can pass it if I need to."

"Coach doesn't let you practice much on it."

"I do it enough."

"Come on by my house and throw me some spirals," said Harry. "I might even talk Mother into some lunch for us."

"I thought you were the only one who could throw spirals," said Allman resentfully.

"Come on, Allman," said Harry edgily. "Let's don't start on that again! Let's get some lunch."

Allman looked at Harry suspiciously. "At your house?"

"Sure," said Harry. "People are always welcome at my house."

"Not at my house," said Allman in a sulking voice.

"What do ya mean?" asked Harry.

"You old man is a big naval officer… right?"

"Well… I don't know how big," said Harry, "but he's a naval officer."

Allman sat quietly in the car for a minute as they turned into Sterling Point where Harry lived.

"Well… my old man is a drunk!" blurted Allman. "Last year, my Mother made enough money working at a garden shop to move us here to Green Acres. We lived over in Simonsdale near Arnie… and my Dad and Arnie's old man would get drunk all the time! Mother wanted to get Ol' Henry away from Clarence Eberly."

"You seem to manage okay, Allman," said Harry, not knowing how to respond.

Harry absorbed Allman's comment without saying anything further, sitting in the car staring ahead. They rode on and pulled up in front of Harry's two story brick home. They got out and went inside.

"Mother!" shouted Harry. "Allman and I are gonna play some pass in the yard."

Helen Carr Quester came into the foyer where they stood. She was a short woman with tightly curled dark hair and a pleasant smile.

"Okay, Harry," she said looking Allman up and down. "I'll fix you boys some sandwiches."

"You know, Allman, don't you, Mother?"

"Well," said Helen, "I've seen him play football."

"Yes Maam," said Allman with his best grin and a wink of his eye. "I'm glad to finally meet you… Harry always says what a great Mom ya are… and pretty too!"

Helen was taken aback by Allman's response, but she smiled. "Why… thank you, Allman… do you like liverwurst?"

"Oh Yes Maam," grinned Allman. "That's one of my ab-so-lute favorites!"

Helen turned and walked away. "I'll have some sandwiches ready in a half hour," she said.

"Thank you, Maam!" said Allman.

Harry grabbed a football out of the hall closet and whirled it in the air. "Come on!"

They ran into the front yard. Allman ran down the grass covered yard that faced the river. "Hit me short!"

Harry threw the ball to him in an acceptable spiral. The ball was just behind Allman, but he reached back and caught it on the run.

"Good catch," shouted Harry.

"Go long!" shouted Allman.

Harry ran about twenty yards toward the river. Allman threw the ball in his usual wounded goose wobble. The ball was a little long. Harry reached for it and pulled it in with one hand, staggering and falling to the grass in the process.

"Great catch!" exclaimed Allman. "Most fullbacks are bum receivers!"

"I've always been able to catch a good ball," said Harry, walking back to where Allman stood. "It's different when ya got someone defending."

Harry tossed Allman the ball in a tightly spiraled lateral. Allman caught it and began to toss it from hand to hand. "Coach Fearless says I gotta work on my spiral."

"Your throw is pretty accurate," said Harry. "You ever had a passing coach show ya how to hold it?"

"Fearless showed me."

"Lemme see your grip," said Harry. "In Northern Virginia, I tried to learn to pass... even hired a passing Coach for awhile... but I was never too good at it."

Allman reluctantly showed Harry his grip on the ball. "I know how to hold the damn ball, Harry, Ol' Buddy."

"Looks good to me," said Harry examining the grip. "Everybody does it different. Let's just pass back and forth some and you can try adjusting your grip and the way you throw it... without any pressure."

"Ya mean ya ain't gonna shout wounded goose and all that?" asked Allman in an annoyed voice.

"Naw... just throw it," said Harry backing away. "Get the spiral down... then work on the speed."

Allman threw the ball in a wobbly spiral. The next one was a bit tighter. They threw back and forth until Allman's throws were mostly tight spirals.

"What're ya doing different?" asked Harry.

"I dunno... I guess I'm just taking a little bit longer to think about putting the right twist on it."

"It's working."

Allman heaved the ball back to Harry. It was a tight spiral with good speed.

"I know what it is you're doing," said Harry.

"What is it?" asked Allman.

"You're relaxing and thinking about the pass... not the pressure of looking good... the great quarterback and all that!"

"Don't gimme that bullshit!" said Allman.

"No... I mean it, Allman," said Harry. "Because I have the same problem... letting my ego screw me up!"

"I ain't got no ego."

"Bullshit! I got a big ego... and yours is worse than mine!"

"I guess I got one."

"I wanna try something," said Harry. "I want you to throw the ball... not to me... but to a spot we both agree on."

"What?"

"Yeah... when you throw a ball to a guy, the defender always knows where to defend... right in front of the receiver... know what I mean?"

"Yeah... I guess so."

"And that puts a lot of pressure on the passer... to put it in just the right spot."

"Yeah... or it gets intercepted and Shotgun gets really pissed!"

"Now if we agree where you're gonna throw it... I can jink the defender out of position... and time it to be at the place we agree on at the right time."

"How will ya know when to get there?"

"Come on, Allman," said Harry impatiently. "I can see the whole field in my head most of the time."

"Aw bullshit, Harry!"

"Try it!"

"Okay... where ya wanna throw it?"

"Throw it twenty yards... right in line with that big pine tree near the river."

"Okay. "

"For timing," said Harry, "we'll count three seconds between the snap and your throw... that's three steps back and an arm raise for you... depending on how hard you throw it, the ball goes about 15 to 20 yards in a second. So, I have four and a quarter seconds to get to the place we agreed on. I can run twenty yards in about three seconds... which leaves me a second and a quarter for a jink to throw off the defender."

"Wait a minute... wait a minute," said Allman looking confused, "where'd ya get all a' them numbers?"

"Never mind," said Harry impatiently. "Just call signals... on two... drop back and pass it to the spot."

"This ain't gonna work," muttered Allman spinning the football in his hands.

"Yeah, it will," said Harry getting into a three point stance.

"Get down!... Get ready!" shouted Allman, "Hut one!... Hut two!"

Harry exploded from the imaginary line of scrimmage. He feinted left, turned to look over his left shoulder, and then abruptly shifted right. He looked up and to his right. He saw the football sailing in a near spiral toward the pine tree near the river. He put on his best burst of speed and ran under the pass, catching it and coming to an abrupt halt at the edge of the sloping lawn that led down to the bull rushes at the river's edge.

"Hey!" exclaimed Allman. "Great catch!"

"See?" exclaimed Harry. "I told you it would work!"

"Harry!" came the call from the house. "Come and get these sandwiches. You boys can eat out on the picnic table."

"I'm starving!" exclaimed Allman.

Allman tucked the ball under his arm and ran to where Helen stood on the brick steps leading into the kitchen. She held a platter covered with a white cloth towel. There was a pitcher of iced tea and two glasses sitting on the steps. Allman ran up to her with a big grin.

"Mrs. Quester, you're an angel in disguise," said Allman, his gray eyes wide, "just when I was about to starve!"

"Oh, go on, now, Allman," said Helen. "Take these plates over to the picnic table and enjoy the liverwurst."

"Thank you Maam!"

Allman took the plate of sandwiches. Harry grabbed the pitcher and glasses. They took them to the picnic table and sat down. Allman unwrapped a sandwich. It was thick with liverwurst, Swiss cheese and a thin slice of onion. He took a big bite. He rolled his eyes. "This is a great sandwich… just like a delicatessen… cheese and all!"

"Mother makes good sandwiches," said Harry taking a bite out of a sandwich and washing it down with cold iced tea.

"Hey… all that three second, four second stuff you rattled off out there…"

"Yeah?"

"Really… where did all that come from?"

"I just calculated it in my head," said Harry. "Numbers are easy for me."

"Along with poetry… and English?"

"You've been listening to Arnie too much," complained Harry.

"Speaking of Arnie… if I can't stop this fight between you two, we gotta keep Shotgun from finding out."

"I could just not go," said Harry, "to this Teenage thing."

"Naw," said Allman, "ya can't do that. That would do what Arnie wants… make you look like a jerk to the rest of the team."

"In my world, you can have a disagreement without fighting a guy," said Harry.

"That's your world Harry," said Allman. "Look around ya… this is your world… big house on the river and all… it ain't Arnie's world… and it ain't mine either."

"What is your world, Allman?"

"Like I told ya… my Pop's a drunk," said Allman disparagingly. "Arnie's Pop is his cut-buddy and he's almost a drunk… and we don't live in no big house on the river… and I don't drive a big convertible… and ya ain't gonna get no sandwiches at my house. My world is a rough place where guys are guys if they act tough and know how to fight… know what I mean?"

"You mean the world of the Hoods?"

"Sometimes, ya gotta go there."

"Yeah, I guess so," said Harry. "If you lived over there near Arnie, why aren't you one of the Hoods?"

"Hoods are fakes," said Allman. "I ain't no fake!"

"I guess I gotta learn to live in both worlds," said Harry.

****

Harry drove the Cheese-Wagon across the Churchland Bridge and through City Park to the Simonsdale Community Center early on a cool evening. Tony rode in the passenger seat. The Community Center was a small nondescript building surrounded by shrubs. There were cars of all descriptions parked around it. In the front of the building was a small lawn under a large sycamore tree. Harry saw Bob Porter and Janet pull up in the Yellow Peril. Harry pulled the green Chevy into a space next to the yellow Ford convertible.

"Hi Bob... hi Janet," waved Harry as he opened the car door.

"Nice car, Harry," said Bob, opening the door of the Ford for Janet.

"Yeah, it sure is," said Janet stepping gracefully out of the car.

"You look great, Janet," said Tony.

"Thanks, Tony," said Janet. "That's more than I get from Bob... or Harry!"

"Oh come on, Janet," said Bob with a tight smile, "I'll leave that gushy stuff to Tony."

"Harry," said Janet, concern in her voice, "are you really going to fight Arnie tonight?"

"He's the one who wants to fight," said Harry carefully.

"Clara told me what happened," snapped Janet, her eyes flashing. "It's pretty silly. I think you should tell the jerk to get lost!"

"Thanks, Janet," said Harry. "I won't fight him unless I have to."

"You'll probably have to fight him, Harry," said Bob. "Watch out... he's fast with his hands!"

"Oh, don't encourage him!" snapped Janet.

"Don't sweat it, Janet," said Bob, impatiently, "let's go inside and dance... Harry can handle it."

Bob and Janet turned and went inside. Harry watched Janet closely. He still had feelings for her, but he didn't want to have to fight Bob too. But, Bob was a member of his world. Arnie was not. He and Bob could agree to compete. But, with Arnie it was different. It was as much about saving face as it was about the girl... maybe more. He felt all of the eyes in the little dancing room turn on him as he went in. A record was playing Joni James singing:

Why don't you believe me? it's you I adore,

Forever and ever, can I promise more?
I've told you so often the way that I care,
Why don't you believe me? it just isn't fair.

The pure voice and haunting tune was one of Harry's favorites. He wished he had someone to dance with. Then he saw Paige come in the door with Gail Donaldson, Ken Darby's girl, the head majorette for the band. Paige wore a black and white dress that swirled out from her hips and dipped in a crescent across her bosom. Her red lips and brown eyes completed a picture that left Harry transfixed. His heart jumped a beat. He looked for Duane, but didn't see him. He hurried over to where Paige stood with Gail.

"Hi Harry," said Gail with a demure smile. "I hope you plan to dance tonight... and not fight that stupid Arnie."

"Hi Gail," said Harry. "I'm not in a fighting mood!"

"Ah," said Gail, "then you must be in dancing mood!"

"Sounds about right," said Harry trying to conceal his excitement. "Paige, would you like to dance?"

Paige looked at Harry with big brown eyes that made him feel weak.

"Sure, Harry," she said softly. "I was just waiting for you to ask!"

Harry offered Paige his hand.

"Treat her nice, Harry!" smiled Gail with a wink.

Harry blushed. He felt all the eyes in the little room on them as he led Paige to the dance floor. Harry put his arm around Paige's slim waist and held his left hand up. She put her hand in his and they began to move to the music. Her hand was warm and gripped his ever so slightly. The dance floor soon filled up and Harry felt less conspicuous.

"You... look wonderful tonight, Paige," said Harry self-consciously.

She squeezed his hand and moved a bit closer to him... just close enough that her body brushed his as they danced without really touching. "Thank you, Harry," said Paige in her husky, velvety voice. "I've wanted to come to one of these dances... and Gail offered to let me come with her."

"Where's Karl?"

"She said she was meeting him here... there they are!"

Harry looked across the room and saw Karl standing with Gail talking to Allman and Georgia. Karl led Gail onto the dance floor.

"Georgia says Allman doesn't dance," said Paige.

"He doesn't?" asked Harry. "I wonder why he comes."

Allman winked at Harry and gave him a thumbs up. Harry smiled and turned his attention back to Paige. Joni James sang on.

Here is a heart that is lonely,

Here is a heart you can take,
Here is a heart for you only,
That you can keep or break.

Harry wondered if Paige's heart was lonely. He knew his was. He had never had a real girl friend before… just post office girl friends… game kissing. He wanted a girl friend… he thought he might want Paige. He put his head beside hers and danced on, forgetting for the moment his problems with Arnie.

"Georgia says Allman is worried about this fight… you and Arnie," whispered Paige. "Gail and Karl are worried, too!"

"I know."

"Clara doesn't want you to fight Arnie," said Paige into his ear. The sensation of her voice close to his ear sent a shiver through Harry's body. Her message brought him back to reality.

"She told you that?"

"Yes," said Paige. "Everyone thinks you and Arnie are fighting over her… are you?"

"No… not really," said Harry, wondering to himself if it were so. "Arnie just doesn't like me for some reason."

"Clara said he challenged you because she asked you to walk out on the pier at the Norwood house with her… to talk… is that right?"

"Yeah, that's right… we just talked," said Harry hoping that Paige believed him. "But it's more than that… he resents me for some reason. I'm not going to fight him unless he forces it on me."

"She told me about her problems with Arnie," said Paige. "I feel sorry for her."

"She needs someone to talk to," said Harry. "I'm glad you listened."

"All this fighting," said Paige. "It's really unnecessary."

"Am I gonna have to fight Duane for dancing with you?"

"Don't be silly!"

"You're not going with him?"

"He might think so, but I never agreed to go steady… or anything like that."

"Good."

"Why is it good, Harry?"

"Because I really like you, Paige… would you go to the Sock Hop with me this weekend… Saturday night?"

Paige thought a minute. She knew Duane assumed she was going out with him every Saturday night. But this Harry Quester interested her. He was good looking… he had a nice car… and he knew how to dance! Better than that, he seemed to know who he was, not obsessed with himself like Duane. Her parents would be upset if she didn't go out with Duane. They were concerned that she, as they put it, should marry into an established family. Hah! By "established", she knew they meant rich. It was time she drew that line.

"I'll go with you, Harry," said Paige in a voice that almost purred.

"Great!" exclaimed Harry, his anxiety suddenly lifted.

Joni James ended the song;
How else can I tell you, what more can I do?
Why don't you believe me?
I love only you.

Harry stood with his arm around Paige's waist, not wanting to let go, the words ringing in his ears. Tony Bennett filled the room with his voice, singing *A Stranger in Paradise*.

"Want to dance some more?" asked Harry.
Take my hand,
I'm a stranger in paradise,

"Of course," said Paige with an enticing smile. "Like the man says… take my hand!"
All lost in a wonderland,
A stranger in paradise.

"That's me," said Harry, "a stranger in paradise… when I'm dancing with you, Paige!"

"You have a pretty good line, Harry."

"It's not a line, Paige," said Harry seriously. "If I say it, I mean it!"
If I stand starry-eyed,
That's the danger in paradise,
For mortals who stand beside,
An angel like you.

Harry felt a tap on his shoulder. He turned to see Arnie standing beside them, a sneer on his slack-jawed face.

"I'm cutting in, Poet," said Arnie gruffly.

Arnie grabbed Paige's hand and pulled her away from Harry roughly. He grabbed her and pulled her close to him and swung her around wildly. She looked at the surprised Harry with panic in her eyes. Harry took two quick steps to where Arnie held Paige and grabbed his arm. He pulled Arnie's hand loose from that of Paige with a powerful grip and swung him to the floor with a crash. Everyone on the dance floor stopped dancing and stared. Gail and Georgia ran to help Paige. The record played on.

Somewhere in space I hang suspended,
Until I know there's a chance that you care…

"Outside, Arnie!" shouted Harry, his face red with anger. "Let's get this over with!"

Arnie jumped to his feet and shoved Harry backward.

Won't you answer this fervent prayer,
Of a stranger in paradise?

Allman came running up to them and stood between them. "You guys take it outside if you gotta fight!"

Arnie spun around and stalked angrily out the door. Harry followed. Allman followed both of them outside and down the steps to the front yard under the old sycamore tree. The yard was dimly lit from the glow of a single light bulb on the side of the Community Center. The little dance hall quickly emptied as most of the boys and girls crowded outside to see what was going to happen. The lady who was chaperoning stood at the door wringing her hands. Suddenly the headlights of Arnie's 1939 chopped Chevy Coupe with the bomb shaped headlights and Johnny's red Studebaker coupe with the bullet nose flashed on, illuminating the yard. Arnie turned with his fists in the air to face Harry. Bart Whitely, Johnny Calcione and Carson Quinn stood behind Arnie with scowls on their faces and cigarettes behind their ears. Harry tried to calm himself and figure out how to fight Arnie. He wasn't very experienced in front yard brawls.

Allman and Karl walked to a position on the side of the fight arena. Big Jim stood behind them, his arms hanging loosely at his sides.

"You two guys are team mates… you don't need to fight!" said Allman worriedly.

"I need to fight… and he ain't no teammate of mine!" said Arnie with a snarl. "You stay out of this, Allman!"

Karl glanced at Harry. Harry grimaced and made a hopeless gesture with his arms.

"Okay," said Allman. "When its over, you're gonna shake hands!"

"Fat chance of that," said Arnie under his breath, his watery eyes focused on Harry.

Arnie circled Harry jabbing at him, looking for an opening. The only boxing Harry knew was what he had seen in the movies. He held his fists up and fended off Arnie's jabs. Arnie jabbed and swung a right hook. It hit Harry on the left cheekbone. The crowd of young people groaned and cheered. Pain shot through Harry's face and centered on the broken nose. He stepped back, tears running from his left eye.

"Ya got him, Arnie!" shouted Calcione.

Arnie continued to circle Harry, jabbing at him. Harry tried to protect his sensitive nose. Arnie swung another right, but Harry saw this one coming and blocked it with his left forearm. He countered with his own right hand and landed a glancing blow on Arnie's shoulder.

Arnie laughed. "Is that all ya got, Poet?"

Arnie swung his right arm again. The blow bounced off of Harry's arm and landed on his nose. Pain shot through him and he staggered backward, his vision blurred by tears.

"Ya got him now, Arnie!" shouted Carson shrilly.

Harry covered his face with his forearms while Arnie rained blows on his head and arms. There was only one way to handle this, thought Harry as his vision slowly returned. He reached into his gut and pulled up his Headhunter game face. He couldn't box… but he knew how to hit people… thank Shotgun for that! His face darkened and an angry scowl came over it.

Bubba recognized the game face instantly. "Come on Harry!" he shouted. "Put the Headhunter on 'im!"

"Punch him out, Harry!" shouted Bob, shaking his fist.

Harry saw Janet's anxious face behind Bob. Gail and Paige were next to Janet. Paige looked terrified as Gail held her arm. Arnie darted in and landed a right to Harry's head that stunned him momentarily. Then he grappled with Harry and kneed him in the groin. Harry groaned and fell backward, landing on his back on the hard ground. Arnie was on top of him in an instant and began pummeling Harry's face with his fists. The quickness of it startled Harry. He heard a gasp from the crowd around them and a few cheers from Arnie's buddies. He recovered and grabbed Arnie's flailing arms. He forced them away from his face, exerting his great strength. He pushed Arnie from on top of him, rolled over and struggled to his feet. Arnie got up and began circling Harry again, his fists jabbing out with lightning speed. Harry charged at Arnie and delivered a body block to Arnie's solar plexus that sent him crashing back. Arnie gasped loudly. Harry wound up and hit him in the face with his right fist so hard that blood spurted out of Arnie's nose and tears filled his watery eyes. Harry backed away, hoping that Arnie would stop fighting. Arnie just leaned on his car, stunned by the blow.

"Come on, Arnie," panted Harry. "Had enough?"

Arnie didn't say anything. Harry turned away and started to walk back toward the Community Center looking for Paige. Arnie charged at Harry's back.

"Look out Harry!" yelled Bubba and Tony simultaneously.

Harry turned and caught Arnie with another body block. He wrestled with the tall boy and drove him backward. Arnie spun around trying to evade Harry. Harry grabbed him from behind and wrapped his powerful arms around Arnie's chest. Arnie tried to dig his feet into the lawn as Harry shoved him along and drove him straight into the bullet nose of Johnny's red Studebaker. Arnie let out a cry of pain as his chest hit the tip of the chrome bullet, the winged hood ornament ripping into his chin. Blood dripped onto the red Studebaker as Arnie slumped to the ground. Harry stood over him, panting. Allman ran to where Arnie lay on the ground holding his chest and writhing in pain.

"Arnie!" exclaimed Harry. "Are you alright?"

"Ya sonofabitch!" moaned Arnie. "Ya broke my fuckin' ribs!"

Johnny Calcione ran to his car and wiped the blood off the red hood. "You'll pay for that, Quester, you bastard! You're gonna pay big time, Poet!"

The crowd scattered as Grady Spearman's patrol car pulled up, its headlights flashing and the red light on top spinning around. Grady got out and walked to where Arnie writhed on the ground.

"What's going on here?" shouted Grady.

No one answered.

****

Harry sat in the stands in the stadium at Deep Creek High School with his father and mother as the Truckers ran on to the field to face the purple and white clad Deep Creek Hornets. His face still hurt where Arnie had hit him. His left eye was deeply bruised from the first blow he had absorbed. He didn't like having a black eye. He was miserable, feeling rejected and as low as he had ever been.

"Don't worry, Harry," said Helen, "I'm sure the Coach will let you back on the team soon."

"I don't know, Mother," said Harry mournfully. "He just shouted at me and told me I was suspended."

"You shouldn't have fought that boy," said Helen. "We didn't bring you up to go out and brawl, you know."

"I know, Mother," said Harry. "I didn't have a lot of choice!"

"I don't understand that," said Helen.

"I understand it," said Isaac Quester, his square jaw set firmly. "And if Shotgun doesn't let Harry back on the team after this game, I'm going to see him… and we'll have it out."

"Oh, Ike," said Helen, "don't be like that."

"I am like that," muttered Ike, "and you, better than most, know it,

Helen."

"Don't you get into it, Father," pleaded Harry. "He suspended Arnie too."

"Arnie has two broken ribs," said Ike. "Of his own making!"

"I didn't mean to break his ribs," said Harry. "But he started it."

"I know, Harry, I know," said Ike, controlled anger in his voice. "A.P. and I both plan to talk to this Shotgun character!"

"He'll just yell at you, too," said Harry, "and then I'll never get back on the team."

"It's just terrible that boys are out there fighting like that," said Helen in an alarmed whisper.

Harry watched as the Truckers took the field. Benny Norwood ran out to replace Arnie at left end. Harry grunted to himself. Tony was a much better end than Benny. But... Benny had been around longer. Maybe he had finally decided to play football instead of complain! The opening drive was a long run by Sanders. Deep Creek couldn't do anything against the Truckers. Sanders scored thirty-five points.

"Joltin' Jack! Joltin' Jack!" roared the crowd.

Moddy and both Darbys scored a touchdown. The final score was fifty-six to nothing.

****

The gymnasium at Churchland High School was ablaze with Saturday night light and color as Harry and Paige walked to the entrance. There was a light drizzle outside and Harry carried an umbrella which he held over Paige's head. They checked their shoes at the door and walked on to the hardwood floor in their sock feet. There were black and orange ribbons hung all around the gym. Rocky Rawls, with his peroxided hair combed into a flashy pompadour, sat on a raised wooden platform in front of a piano with a microphone. There was a bass player, a saxophone player, a trumpet player, a man on a drum set, lead and bass guitar players. A shapely young lady with blond curls stood behind the piano in a sequined dress, holding a tambourine. There was excitement in the air as they began *P.S. I Love You* and the dance floor filled with shoeless couples swinging to the tune. Rocky sang out with a good mimic of the Hilltoppers, accompanied by the young lady who swayed her hips to the music and tapped the tambourine.

Dear, I thought I'd drop a line,
The weather's cool, the folks are fine,
I'm in bed each night at nine,
(P.S.-I love you).

Harry and Paige danced closely together. Harry twirled her about expertly and she responded as though she had been dancing with him for years. Harry watched her every move and marveled at her gracefulness.

"Your eye doesn't look too bad," said Paige.

"It looks like I should be wearing a steak!" said Harry with an embarrassed grin.

"That guy... Arnie," said Paige in a gentle voice. "He really scared me... I wonder how Clara stands it!"

"He's a no-good," said Harry, suppressing the anger rising in him.

The song ended and Rocky picked up the microphone.

"Hey! Truckers!" shouted Rocky, "I'll bet ya didn't know ol' Rocky could sing and play the piano... but here I am, playing and singing for sure... so be sure to listen to me on ol' WNV... 1150 on your radio dial... every day from four to seven. We'll be rocking and rolling and singing all the good ol' lovey dovey songs. Speaking of lovey dovey songs, here's our own Patty Parsons to sing the latest Doris Day hit."

The shapely young lady in the sequined gown stepped to a microphone and the band struck up the melody.

If I give my heart to you,
Will you handle it with care?
Will you always treat me tenderly?
And in every way be fair?

Harry grasped Paige's hand and drew her to him. They danced closer together than before, Paige responding to Harry's lead.

"You dance well, Harry," said Paige softly looking up at him with big brown eyes.

"Thanks," said Harry. "I guess it's just because I'm inspired!"

"You know how to flatter me," said Paige with a smile on her full red lips. "That's good!"

"It's true!"

"Harry," said Paige looking up at him, "what happened after the fight between you and Arnie?"

"I'm afraid I hurt him more than I wanted to," said Harry quietly.

"What about Clara?"

"I haven't seen her," said Harry. "I don't know what she's going to do."

Paige danced on, leaving the unanswered question of Clara hanging in the air. "Is it true that the Coach won't let you play?"

"Yes," said Harry. "For now, anyway."

"I think he'll let you back on the team," said Paige. "You're too good."

"You watch the games?"

"Sure," said Paige.

"I thought maybe, you'd be going to the Suffolk games," said Harry cautiously.

"Duane would like me to," said Paige, "but I'm at Churchland now. I told him I'd go to the games here."

"So he comes here to date you?"

"When I'm dating him, he does," said Paige coyly.

"Pretty good dancing for a Headhunter," hooted Allman, sitting with Georgia in folding chairs on the side, his legs propped up on a chair.

"I wish you guys would decide whether I'm a Poet or a Headhunter," said Harry in frustration. "Or maybe just Harry will do fine!"

"After Thursday night, you're definitely a Headhunter," said Bubba doing a block step with Alice nearby.

"That's for sure!" said Tony dancing with Sherry.

"Come on out and dance, Allman," taunted Sherry with a white toothed smile.

"He won't dance," pouted Georgia. "He won't even try!"

"Awww… dancing just makes me look stupid," said Allman. "I ain't no dancer."

"Ya get to put your arm around the girls, Allman," laughed Harry.

"I can do that right here," said Allman, putting his arm around Georgia.

Georgia wriggled out of Allman's grasp and whispered in his ear. Allman laughed and shook his head affirmatively. Georgia stood up.

"Harry, will you dance with me the next dance?" she asked.

"Sure," said Harry, "providing Paige and Allman won't beat me up!"

They all laughed as the young lady in the sequined dress finished the Doris Day song. Harry and Paige walked over to where Allman sat sprawled on a chair.

"Allman, will you get Paige some punch while I dance with Georgia?" asked Harry politely.

"Sure, Headhunter Ol' Buddy," said Allman, standing up and offering his arm dramatically to Paige.

"Why thank you, Allman," said Paige. She turned and smiled at Harry with one of the breathtaking smiles that bubbled up into her brown eyes.

"Georgia?" Harry offered her his arm as Patty Parsons started singing the *Song from Moulin Rouge*. The lights in the gymnasium darkened.

Whenever we kiss,
I worry and wonder,
Your lips may be near,

But where is your heart?

"Where is your heart, Harry Quester?" asked Georgia.

Georgia danced uncomfortably close to Harry, her body rubbing against all parts of him. She put her head on his shoulder and danced as though they were lovers.

"Uh, well," said Harry feeling a bead of perspiration break out on his forehead. "I guess I don't really know."

"Looks to me like you've fallen for Paige," whispered Georgia seductively in his ear.

"Maybe," said Harry awkwardly.

"I think she's got you hypnotized!"

"Uh… Georgia," said Harry under his breath, "should we really be dancing this close… and all?"

"I like to dance close, Harry," whispered Georgia in his ear, "and don't worry about Allman… he knows I'm hooked on him and all his foolishness."

"You really do dance close, Georgia," said Harry feeling her breasts press into him. Then he felt her legs against his.

"How else am I gonna check you out, Harry?" she asked in an ultra sweet voice.

"Check me out?"

"Sure… see what you're made of."

It's always like this,
I worry and wonder,
You're close to me here,
But where is your heart?

"Well, what am I made of?" asked Harry curiously.

"You're a hard man, Harry," laughed Georgia, pressing her body against him.

"I am?" asked Harry, embarrassed, hoping she wouldn't notice.

It's a sad thing to realize,
That you've a heart that never melts,
When we kiss, do you close your eyes,
Pretending that I'm someone else?

"I'll bet you're pretending that I'm Paige," whispered Georgia.

"Right now, I really don't know what I'm doing," said Harry in a confused voice.

Allman and Paige were drinking punch and watching them. He saw Allman laugh and make dancing motions with his arms. Paige had a worried expression on her face.

"Yeah," said Georgia, moving even closer, "it gets like that, don't it?"

The music ended. Harry put his hands in his pockets and moved his brown slacks down a bit. He took Georgia back to Allman and handed her over with a sigh of relief.

"Did she check ya out, Harry Ol' Buddy!" asked Allman with a grin.

Harry looked at Allman with a lifted eyebrow. "She… she's a real good dancer," said Harry, still embarrassed. He adjusted his trousers, feeling very uncomfortable, and grinned as best he could.

Allman let out with a loud guffaw and threw his arm around Georgia. Harry shook his head. "Allman… you didn't…?"

Allman grinned and handed Georgia a five dollar bill. She took it and winked at Harry with a big grin.

"You win, Baby," laughed Allman.

"Allman! You sonofabitch!" exclaimed Harry.

Allman guffawed and rolled his eyes.

Paige took Harry by the hand, looking embarrassed. "Come on Harry… let's go over here and dance some more."

They walked across the dance floor and stood waiting for the next dance. The music started, but Harry paused and calmed himself.

"What in the world did she do to you?" asked Paige, a tinge of anger in her voice.

"She… she just danced too close," said Harry uneasily.

"I don't like dancing dirty, Harry," said Paige. "She wasn't dancing close… she was dancing dirty."

"I know," said Harry feeling miserable, "I couldn't do much about it."

"You could've stopped," said Paige angrily. "You could've been a gentleman!"

Rage at Allman seethed inside Harry. It was a rotten thing to do… he and Georgia both! Suddenly, a boy dressed in a ridiculous Red Raider uniform with oversized shoulder pads ran up onto the raised platform in front of Rocky Rawls. There was a paper mache head between the pads with a very stupid look on its face.

"Truckers are Sissies! They wear pink panties and play patty-cake!" shouted the Red Raider in a falsetto voice. "We're gonna whip their tails!"

Allman jumped up on the platform and started sparring with the fake Red Raider. Then Bucky Allison dressed in Harry's number thirty-two ran onto the platform, sporting a long red cape. There was a big sign on the back of the cape that said "Headhunter". With one whack, Headhunter took off the Red Raider's paper mache head which rolled to the floor amid a drum flourish and a cymbal crash. A giant cheer rose from the crowd. Allman did a flip off the stage and landed awkwardly in Big Jim's arms on the dance floor. Allman and Big Jim took a grand bow and everyone laughed. The Red Raider, played by Bud Darby, was chased around by number thirty-two. The Red Raider found his head, grabbed it and ran off the dance floor. The Headhunter continued to whack at him as he left. The band broke into a jazzy Churchland fight song.

Oh when those Churchland Truckers fall in line,
They're gonna win this game another time…

The crowd sang the fight song and began jitterbugging to the jazzy beat. Harry looked at the exit and saw Duane Starr standing there in a red sport coat and tie, a grimace on his face.

"Speaking of Red Raiders," said Harry, "look who's here."

Paige glanced up, looked and then looked away. "Oh no," she said fearfully.

"What's the matter?" asked Harry. "You said you're not going with him."

"I'm not," said Paige apprehensively, "not really."

Duane Starr walked slowly to where they stood as Rocky Rawls finished the fight song and announced the next dance.

"May I have this dance, Paige?" asked Duane, a cutting edge in his voice.

"Harry?" asked Paige in a small voice.

"Sure," said Harry politely. "By the way Duane… how'd you get in? This dance is for Churchland people and their dates!"

"I go mostly where I want," said Duane with a sneer. "And you'll regret trying to date Paige, Quester."

"Is that a threat?" asked Harry, wondering if he'd ever get away from this constant friction.

"You can call it a threat if you want to, Quester," said Starr.

"Be nice, Duane," admonished Paige, putting her hand on his arm.

"Why did you come here with this guy?" asked Duane angrily. "You know how I feel about you!"

"He asked me, Duane," said Paige, "and you know I told you I didn't want to go steady!"

"Come on," said Duane haughtily, taking her hand. "Let's dance."

"Okay!" shouted Rocky Rawls with a toss of his hair. "We're gonna do the conga! Get in that line and let's see some grinning and kicking!"

Harry watched as Duane and Paige got in the conga line and the music started. Duane put his hands tightly around her slim waist. Harry felt the anger rising in him uncontrollably.

One two three kick!
One two three kick!

The line started to snake around the floor. Suddenly, there was a second, all male, all football team line... a double conga line, kicking and grinning. In front with a big silly grin on his flat face was Allman Buddinger with Big Jim Jensen next to him. Big Jim tried to grin but it only made him look meaner. Behind them were Bucky, Bubba, Bob, Jack, Tony, Karl, Terry and most of the team. Bart, Johnny, Carson, Bryan and some of Arnie's other friends slouched on the side watching, trying to put tough, "cool" looks on their faces.

Duane saw The Trucker Conga Line coming and watched them with trepidation. They conga'd up to Duane as he kicked and tried to ignore them. Allman and Big Jim snatched Duane out of the line and lifted him above their heads. Duane wrestled with Big Jim briefly. Big Jim, with Allman's help, passed him, kicking and screaming, to the top of the double conga line. The conga line passed him from one pair of players to the next.

"You damn guys!" shouted Duane angrily. "Let me down!"

The Trucker Conga line conga'd Duane out the exit and dumped him unceremoniously in the mud at the bottom of the gymnasium steps.

"You guys will pay for this shit!" shouted Duane. "Big time!"

Allman guffawed. Harry and Paige ran to the door. Paige ran out and helped Duane up, her hair becoming frazzled by the cold drizzle. Duane stood up, tried to wipe the mud from his jacket and grabbed her hand. Harry watched helplessly.

"Come on, Paige," said Duane. "Let's leave these ass-holes here!"

Paige looked at Harry with confusion in her eyes. "I can't leave Duane," she said tearfully.

"Why not?" asked Duane, hostility in his voice.

"I... I came with Harry," she sobbed.

Duane turned his back on her and stalked away.

"Duane!" shouted Paige, tears in her eyes. "Wait!"

Duane Starr kept walking. Paige looked back at Harry with apologetic, tear filled eyes. Then she ran after Duane.

"Paige!" shouted Harry. "Where're you going?"

She didn't answer. Harry watched them go into the parking lot. The white Cadillac drove away. Harry felt the eyes of the crowd on him. He turned to Allman who stood in the doorway with a big silly grin on his face. He felt rage come over him and possess him. He wasn't sure who he was mad at or why... but he desperately needed a target. He ran up to Allman and grabbed him by the shirt.

"What ya doing, Harry Ol Buddy?" asked Allman innocently.

"You can't treat people like that, Allman!" shouted Harry vengefully.

Harry wound up and hit Allman in the face with a powerful blow that surprised the senior quarterback. Allman reacted by driving Harry down the steps. They both fell into the mud, Allman on top of Harry. People came running out of the gymnasium to see the fight. Harry rolled out from under Allman and swung at him again, missing.

"You really wanna fight me, Harry Ol' Buddy?" panted Allman, rain and mud running down his face.

"Yeah, Allman," panted Harry in return, his anger in full bloom, "I really do… until you stop making me… and the girls I'm with… the butt of your goddam silly jokes."

"Aw hell, Harry," said Allman apologetically. "We was just having… a little fun, Georgia and I."

"It wasn't funny… to me or Paige," exclaimed Harry, a fierce scowl on his face.

Harry swung at Allman again, hitting him in the chest. The two boys struggled to their feet, grappling with each other.

"Okay, Harry," panted Allman reluctantly. "You asked for it!"

With a quick hand, Allman hit Harry in the forehead with a powerful blow. The blow stunned Harry and he fell backward, falling to one knee. Allman gave him a hand and pulled him up.

"Ya want another one, Ol' Buddy?"

Harry grimaced behind a muddy face and swung at Allman, missing.

"Ya know, Harry," panted Allman, stepping back, "we did that Headhunter thing with the band… to tell everybody we want ya back on the team. Now ya go and screw it all up!"

Harry charged at Allman and knocked him backward. They both fell into the mud, Harry on top. Harry felt a hand on his shoulder. He turned and saw Coach Phelps there. There was a serious expression on his face.

"What's this all about, Harry?" asked Phelps with concern.

Harry paused, and looked up, not knowing what to say. "It's just a… a friendly fight, between me and Allman," he said, feeling suddenly silly.

"Yeah Coach," said Allman with a grimace, lying flat on his back in the mud. "Just a real friendly fight… to see who's the biggest fool!"

****

Slate and Cliff parked in front of the Armory, a large Quonset Hut shaped building and went up the steep wooden steps to the cavernous interior. Major Buck Fuller stood waiting for them in full Army regalia standing next to a preserved Army M101A1 105mm towed howitzer. In front of him were thirty young men sitting in metal chairs around several folding tables. Fuller was a short man with a powerful build. He had a rugged looking face with a scar on his forehead. The gold oak leaves of a Major shone on the shoulders of the dark brown uniform jacket. A shiny leather shoulder strap crossed the front of the brown jacket above the light khaki trousers. Bronze Star and Purple Heart ribbons were on his left breast along with World War II campaign ribbons.

"Well," said the Major sarcastically, "now that Shotgun and Slate are here, I guess we can start our meeting."

Slate and Cliff sat down hurriedly. The others turned to look at them.

"The Veteran's paperwork for the fall season is in front of you," said Fuller gruffly. "Now that I have to wet nurse all you college boys, I want you to fill it all out right the first time… got it?"

There was a murmur and a shuffle of papers.

"You got that Braun?" shouted the Major in drill sergeant tones.

Cliff's face turned red, followed by his jug handle ears. He looked up at the Major with squinty eyes. "I ain't in the Army now!" shouted Cliff. "And now I'm Mister Braun… not Braun… okay?"

"Oh!" exclaimed the Major. "A wise guy huh?"

Cliff started to get up. The Major restrained him with a powerful hand. Cliff struggled with the Major and finally stood up. He stuck his square chin into the Major's face. "I never did like the Army," shouted Cliff. "And I ain't in it now!"

Major Fuller's fists clenched and he grew red in the face. "Sit down and fill out those papers, Shotgun!"

Cliff turned and stalked out of the Armory, strutting like a cock on the way to the fighting ring. His jaw was stuck out in front of him like a lantern leading the way. "You can stuff those papers up your big red Army ass, Fuller," shouted Cliff over his shoulder.

The Major stared after him in disbelief, whacking one fist into an open palm making resounding smacks that echoed around the huge armory room.

"Don't worry, Major," said Slate, "I'll fill out the papers for him… and get him to sign them."

"You tell Shotgun that if he wants those papers sent in, I'll expect him over here for an apology!" said Major Fuller, controlling his temper.

"I'll tell him, Major," said Slate dejectedly.

"And if he don't come with an apology," shouted the Major, "I'll have him thrown outa here… ya hear me?"

**********.

Chapter Ten
Smithfield

Harry drove the Cheese-wagon along Sterling Point Drive toward his home on Sunday afternoon. He was surprised to see Allman walking along the side of the road kicking a rock as he went. He started to pass him by, but changed his mind. He stopped the car ten yards in front of Allman.

"Where ya going?" shouted Harry.

Allman ignored him and walked on.

"Come on, Allman!" shouted Harry persistently. "Where ya going?"

"I ain't going nowhere," said Allman without his usual smile. "The same place I'm always going!"

"Want a ride to nowhere, ya Clown?"

"You ain't going to nowhere," said Allman dejectedly. "You're gonna go somewhere!"

"Come on!" exclaimed Harry, wondering what was wrong with Allman.

It wasn't like Allman to be so down and out. In spite of all that had gone on, there was something about Allman that was always likable. Harry felt good when he was around Allman even when he was mad at him... for reasons he didn't understand. Maybe it was the adventure of being around the guy. You never knew what was going to happen next.

"Get in!" said Harry. "We got things to talk about."

"Go on, Harry," said Allman irritably, waving his hand forward. "I don't need a ride nowhere... and I ain't got nothin' to talk to you about!"

Harry opened the passenger side door. "Then do me a favor, Allman... and just get in."

"So, you're my Ol' Buddy all of a sudden?"

"Yeah... all of a sudden!"

Allman got reluctantly into the car. Harry drove out to Route 17 and turned north toward the Nansemond River.

"Nice looking eye!" said Allman.

"Thanks! It doesn't feel too good," said Harry. "And you didn't help it any!"

"That was your idea, Ol' Buddy."

"Yeah, ya really pissed me off!"

"It's that shoulder chip again, Harry," said Allman. "It screws ya up! Where ya going?"

"Like ya said," said Harry, "... nowhere."

"Whataya wanna talk about?"

"Am I gonna get back on the team?"

"I told Shotgun what happened… with Arnie… and with me."
"You did?"
"I told him Arnie picked the fight. I told him I screwed up… and insulted your girl."
"You said that!"
"Yeah… Georgia and I will help ya get her back."
"Georgia?"
"She's sorry too."
"Good!"
"But she liked the dance!" said Allman, a grin breaking through his depression. "I guess I'd better watch out for ya!"
"It was embarrassing," said Harry stoically.
"We're sorry Harry," said Allman in a put-on pleading voice, the hint of a grin coming over him.
"Stop the bullshit," said Harry hastily. "Just don't pull any more of your stuff on me!"
"Naw, Ol' Buddy… I ain't gonna screw ya up no more," said Allman. "But it was a good fight! We'll have to do it again sometime… just for the heck of it!"
"Okay Allman… just for the heck of it!"
"Speaking of fights…I had a fight with my old man."
"What happened?" asked Harry, glancing at Allman with concern.
"He threw me outa the damn house," said Allman with a straight face, "Henry Buddinger, the neighborhood drunk threw me outa the house!"
Harry looked at Allman with concern. "No kidding? Did you fight him?"
"No kidding… but I don't fight with my Ol' Man!"
"So… where're you going?"
"Not back there!"
"What about your Mother?"
"She knows how to take care of herself."
"We got a spare room."
"Naw."
"Why not?"
"Naw."
"I'll wrassle ya!"
"Yeah?"
"And there's liverwurst left!"
"Yeah?"
"Yeah," said Harry. "Come on!"

****

Allman and Harry passed a football back and forth in the front yard of the Quester home on the river. It was Monday after football practice and the sun was setting. Harry had not gone to gym class or practice.

"Ya just about got the spiral down pat," said Harry, catching the ball.

"Shotgun'll never go to a passing game," said Allman. "Not as long as he has Jack!"

"Maybe he will," said Harry.

"I'll need to pass next year," said Allman, heaving the ball to Harry. "Coach says he can get me a scholarship to North Carolina. Ya gotta pass to make it in college ball."

"Hey, that's good news about the scholarship," said Harry jumping high to catch the ball. "I guess I get to be a Trucker for another year."

"Maybe Shotgun can get you a scholarship to Carolina, too," said Allman.

"Naw," said Harry. "Next year I take the tests to go to the Naval Academy."

"That what you wanna do?" asked Allman. "Or is that what your Old Man wants?"

"I guess both," said Harry. "I think I can play for the Navy team!"

"You wanna go stay out on ships for months and months?" asked Allman. "And get into wars... and all that kinda thing?"

"Ships go to some pretty good places," said Harry, "places with exotic women and all that!"

"Yeah?"

"I think it would be great to be a ship Captain," said Harry. "And if wars come along... I'll do what I have to do."

"Me... I don't want no part of the military," said Allman. "I don't want some Chief or Sergeant yelling at me and telling me what to do!"

"You're gonna have coaches yelling at you and telling you what to do!"

"That's different. I can mostly have it the way I want it. That's for me!"

"I hear Arnie will be out the rest of the season," said Harry.

"Yeah," said Allman. "He busted two ribs on his left side when he hit that Studebaker."

"I didn't mean to do that," said Harry regretfully.

"I know," said Allman. "But Bart and those Hood guys think you shoved him into that chrome bullet on purpose."

"I was trying to protect myself," said Harry. "He'd already beaten me up pretty bad."

"Yeah, Harry," said Allman, cocking an eye at him. "Ya ain't no fighter!"

"I do what I have to do."

"We're gonna have to go see Arnie," said Allman.

"What for?"

"Try to patch things up… for the team."

"Count me out!"

"Naw," said Allman emphatically. "Ya gotta go, Harry!"

"Harry! Allman!" shouted Helen Quester out the back door. "Come on in to dinner!"

Harry and Allman walked to the house and went inside where the smell of roast beef wafted to their nostrils.

"That sure smells good," said Allman sniffing deeply.

"Allman," said Helen, "I called your Mother to let her know where you are."

"What did she say?"

"I told her you and Harry were going over some football plays," said Helen. "She said that was fine… for you to come home as soon as you can."

"Was she okay?"

"She sounded fine, Allman," said Helen soothingly. "She said Henry was… feeling better."

"She said that, huh?"

"Yes, Allman," said Helen with an understanding smile.

"Is it okay if I stay another night?" asked Allman.

"Certainly," said Helen. "Why don't you call your Mother and tell her your plans."

"Mrs. Quester," said Allman, a hint of his big toothy grin coming back to his face, "you're not only beautiful, but you got a lotta good ideas!"

****

On Tuesday morning, Harry Quester trudged to Mrs. Davison's English Class feeling depressed. He had hoped to see Paige in front of her locker this morning, but she was not there. Clara walked down the hall toward him, a cloud on her pretty face.

"Hi Clara," said Harry cautiously. "How's Arnie?"

"He's in a lot of pain," said Clara coldly. "He has a big bandage on his chest."

"Will he be in to school?"

"Probably next week. He has pain whenever he moves right now."

"I gotta go see him."

"I wouldn't if I were you," said Clara. "He's not in his best mood."

"I know, but I still think I oughta go see him."

"Harry… you're a fool," said Clara emphatically.

"What do you mean?" asked Harry in a surprised voice.

"Oh… for goodness sake!" exclaimed Clara as people in the hallway stared at them. "You try to be… to be such a goody-goody!"

"A goody-goody?" exclaimed Harry, astounded. "I just want to make it all okay for the team… and be accepted by the team, that's all."

"Why? Arnie wouldn't take a second to do that for you!"

"There are still some people on the team… his friends… who are pretty mad," said Harry. "Allman says he wants to bring the team together before the next game… that's why I need to see him."

"Allman?" asked Clara. "That fool wants to bring the team together?"

"Don't underestimate Allman, Clara," said Harry, intensity in his voice. "He leads the team… in his own way… and playing the fool is part of it."

"Harry," said Clara shaking her blonde head, "you can sure see things I don't see."

The bell rang and Harry saw Mrs. Davison glaring at them from inside the classroom.

"Stop bothering the girls, Quester," said Mrs. Davison, giving him the evil eye, "and let her come in."

"Yes Maam."

"As for you, you already know Shakespeare's Julius Caesar," said the hard nosed English teacher, a hidden hint of humor in her voice. "Go to the Library and read something you don't know, so you won't pester the girls trying to learn something, will you please?"

"Yes Maam," said Harry with a small smile.

"And put some ice on that eye!" said Mrs. Davison, spinning about abruptly and heading back into her classroom. "It's repulsive!"

"Yes Maam!"

"Go on and see Arnie if you want, Harry," said Clara reluctantly. "At least he won't be able to start another fight while he's all bandaged up."

"Okay, Clara, I will," said Harry. "Is it okay now… with you and Arnie?"

"Heck, I don't know," said Clara mournfully. "I don't know how I feel."

"I hope you get what you want, Clara."

"Harry… I'm sorry I got you into all this!" said Clara softly, the cloud lifting from her face.

"It wasn't your fault, Clara."

"Are you going to the Library, Quester," asked Mrs. Davison from the doorway of the classroom in a steely voice, "Or not?"

"Yes Maam," said Harry apologetically. "I'm going right now!"

****

Harry went to gym class in the last period wondering what the Coaches would make him do as the others suited up for practice. He walked in and sat down next to Bubba and Tony on the bench in front of his locker.

"You heard anything, Harry?" asked Bubba with concern.

"Naw... nothing," said Harry.

"You should find out something today," said Bubba hopefully.

"Coach should have started you at end instead of Benny, Tony," said Harry. "You know you're better than he is."

"Harry's right, Tony," said Bubba. "Go out there today and bust Benny's chops!"

"Benny's been playing better," said Tony. "Maybe he finally woke up!"

"Benny's a prick!" said Bubba with authority. "Always has been... always will be!"

"I'll do the best I can," said Tony good naturedly. "I hope Coach sees it like you guys do."

Bubba and Tony started to put on their practice uniforms. Harry sat dejectedly on the bench. He took out his playbook and thumbed through it. He knew it by heart. He knew what every player was supposed to do on every play. The plays appeared in his mind as though on a movie screen... exes, ohs, arrows and all. It had always been like that. He found out in the second grade that it wasn't like that for everyone. Sometimes he wished it didn't happen for him. But it did. He could see how things fit together when others couldn't. He could see patterns of related objects that were obscure to most. Why was it?

"You know," said Harry, watching Bubba and Tony put on their practice gear, "you guys really stink!"

"Ha!" exclaimed Bubba assuming a dramatic pose, "As that famous Navy guy said, I ain't even begun to stink!"

"These practice suits do have a personality all their own," observed Tony, holding his nose.

Tony and Bubba clattered across the dressing room floor and out the door. Harry sat on the bench and shook his head. He thought about Paige. What was she going to do? He wished he'd never danced with Georgia. Now Paige was mad at him. The episode outside the Sock Hop showed him she still had feelings for Duane Starr. He wondered why. Duane was such an arrogant bore... at least he appeared that way to him. But, she had spent a lot of time in Suffolk before moving to Churchland. That had to make a difference... and, the Starr family had a lot of money. No, he thought. Paige was deeper than that... or was she?

"What in the heck are you doing, Quester?" shouted Coach Braun as he walked briskly up to where Harry sat on the bench.

Harry jumped up nervously. "Just waiting for... for whatever you... you want me to do in gym class, Sir," stuttered Harry.

"Why aren't you in your practice uniform, Quester?" shouted the Coach, a terrible scowl on his square face. "Sitting around here dreaming about girls in tight pants?"

"You... you..."

"You lost your cotton pickin' voice?" shouted the Coach.

"No... no Sir!"

"Then put on your uniform and get your butt out on the field!" shouted Coach Braun slapping his pork pie hat on his thigh. "I can't have the starting left end sitting in here thinking about girlies in tight pants!"

Harry wasn't sure he heard that right. "The what, Coach?"

"You heard me!" shouted Braun, with a little smile that looked out of place on his bulldog face.

"I'm playing end?"

"You got a problem with that, Quester?" asked Braun, an eyebrow lifted.

"No... no Sir! I can play end!"

"Then get out there... on the double," shouted Braun, his face turning red. "You run twenty laps for busting up Eberly... and no more fighting with Buddinger... or any of 'em! And I mean that! Understand?"

"Yes Sir, Coach," said Harry standing up to face the Coach.

"Then get on with it!" shouted Coach Braun. "Don't just stand there!"

****

Harry ran his twenty laps, feeling conspicuous as the team began to scrimmage. He finished the laps and jogged to where Coach Braun and Coach Fearless were running the team through scrimmage. Coach Braun was staring at some people standing at the side of the practice field.

"Who are those people over there with Calcione and Quinn?" asked Coach Braun in an irritated voice.

Eddie Fearless looked over at them. "I'm not sure," said Eddie. "Some of them are parents... I see Johnny Calcione's father... and

Buster's father... and that new fellow from Suffolk, Garnette is his name... and the lady is, I think, Benny Norwood's mother. I don't know about the others. "

"Well, damn it, get rid of 'em," said Coach Braun. "I don't want a crowd out here watching practice!"

"Okay, Coach," said Eddie, "I'll ask 'em to leave... but I don't know if we can keep 'em from watching."

"Get 'em off the field!"

Coach Fearless walked over to where the people were standing and began talking to them. Most of them walked away. Several retreated to the concrete roadway which was about fifty yards from where the team scrimmaged. Coach Fearless returned to the scrimmage area.

"Most of 'em left," said Fearless.

"Nosy people," muttered Coach Braun. "Stop the scrimmage... I got some things to say."

"Okay, enough scrimmage for now," shouted Coach Fearless. "Line up here in your positions and listen up!"

The team stopped scrimmaging and lined up in their positions, the first team on offense, and the second team on defense. Coach Braun swaggered over to a position beside the line of scrimmage.

"These here Smithfield Packers have a lot of real big guys on the line," shouted Coach Braun. "But they don't move well. So when ya see 'em, just remember to get mean... real mean! A few hard hits in their big ham bellies and they'll be begging ya to run over 'em!"

A laugh started among the team.

"It ain't nothing to laugh at!" shouted Coach Braun. "Remember... any team can beat ya... if ya let 'em!"

Coach Braun turned to Harry. "Well, don't just stand there scratching yourself Quester! Get into the line up!"

Harry trotted over to where Benny Norwood occupied the left end position. Benny looked at Harry with angry eyes.

"What now?" asked Benny.

"Coach says I'm playing left end, Benny," said Harry.

Benny looked at Coach Braun who ignored him. Coach Fearless pointed at him and then at the second string. "Come on, Benny, move over," said Fearless with a stern look.

Benny moved over to defense. "Thanks a lot, Harry," he said grudgingly.

Harry ignored Benny and took the left end position.

"Ya know the end plays yet, Harry?" asked Coach Fearless.

"Yes Sir, I know them," said Harry confidently.

"Already?"

"Yes Sir!"

Harry knelt down beside Big Jim. Big Jim held out his hand to Harry, which surprised him.

"Ya did good," said Big Jim in guttural tones.

"Thanks Jim," said Harry staring into the stoic face of the big man.

"Okay," yelled Coach Braun. "We got a new line-up… I wanna see all the plays run now without hitting… to make sure you hot shots all know what you're supposed to do… and haven't forgotten while prancing around at some fancy sock hop!"

"And then the second team is gonna run some a' Smithfield's plays at ya," shouted Coach Fearless. "We gotta keep serious about our defense!"

****

Allman's red jeep pulled up in front of Arnie's house in Simonsdale late in the evening. It was a small, white shingle house with a screened side porch. A pickup truck was parked in the drive way. Arnie's Chevy was parked on the grass. There was an old refrigerator standing and rusting near the side porch. Big Jim pulled up in his black thirty-two Ford souped-up jalopy. They all got out and walked to the door.

"Now, remember," said Allman, "let me do the talking… and follow my lead."

"Okay, Allman," said Harry worriedly.

Big Jim only nodded his massive head. They knocked on the door. It was opened by a tall man with a mop of gray hair. His face was creased with age and his eyes dull. He was in his undershirt, holding a beer can.

"Is Arnie here, Mr. Eberly?" asked Allman cheerfully.

"Yeah… in his room in the back," grumbled Clarence Eberly taking a swig of the beer. "When's your Ol' Man comin' over?"

"I don't think he'll be over," said Allman testily.

They went in. The house smelled like beer. There must be a Mrs. Eberly, but of her there was no evidence. They walked through a darkened hallway to a room in the back. Allman opened the door and went in. Arnie sat in a dilapidated blue easy chair next to a single bed. He wore no shirt and had a cigarette behind his left ear. His chest was in a tight bandage from the bottom of his rib cage to under his arms. Arnie looked up with his watery eyes, which became immediately hostile when he saw Harry.

"What do you guys want?" asked Arnie angrily.

"Did ya hear abut the new book, *The Ruptured Chinaman*?" asked Allman with a straight face.

"Aw come on, Allman," grimaced Arnie. "Not more of that crap!"

"Written by that famous award winning author… One Hung Low!" shouted Allman.

"That's pretty corny," said Arnie without a smile.

"Where's your sense of humor, Arnie?" asked Allman.

"It hurts to laugh, ya sonofabitch!"

Allman guffawed. "Let's hear ya laugh, Arnie!"

"Why'd you bring that sonofabitch?" asked Arnie nodding at Harry. "I hear he's taking my place… is that right?"

"I'm playing end until you can get back!" said Harry evenly.

"You ass-hole," muttered Arnie.

"Let's call off the fighting!" said Harry half heartedly.

Arnie sighed, grimaced in pain and adjusted his position in the chair.

"Not a chance, Poet," grimaced Arnie. "As soon as I get these ribs well, I'm coming after ya!"

"Ya don't have to do that!"

"You gonna stop me?" asked Arnie with a glare.

"If I have to," said Harry defensively.

"I'll stop you," said Big Jim matter-of-factly.

"Naw ya won't, Jim," said Arnie. "Ya can't beat all a' my guys!"

"Why don't you two sonsabitches shake hands?" asked Allman walking to a position beside Arnie.

"Are ya kidding me?" asked Arnie. He took the cigarette from behind his ear, lit it with a zippo lighter, blew out a cloud of smoke and dangled the cigarette from the side of his mouth.

"Hey!" exclaimed Allman. "Harry and I had a fight… and we kissed and made up!"

Allman grabbed Harry and planted a big kiss on his cheek.

"Arghh!" exclaimed Harry pushing Allman away and wiping his cheek with a disgusted look on his face. "Allman, you bastard… stay away from me!"

Arnie smiled in spite of himself.

"Shake his hand, Arnie!" said Big Jim.

Arnie shook his head and snickered.

"What're ya laughing at?" asked Allman.

"Shake his hand, Arnie," said Big Jim with a fixed stare.

"Forget it!"

"For the team!" said Big Jim.

Harry held out his hand. "I'm sorry your ribs were broken Arnie."

"Yeah?" said Arnie under his breath, eyeing the hand. "What did ya expect?"

"You were beating me up! I had to do something!"

Arnie sat still, his watery eyes fixed on Harry.

"Come on, Arnie," said Jim. "You wanted the fight… Harry gave it to ya!"

"I'm sorry you wanted that fight," said Harry, lowering his hand. "I'm not chasing after your girl."

"You're not huh?" said Arnie, a waiver in his voice.

"No," said Harry. "If she weren't your girl I might be. You're lucky to have a girl like Clara."

"You're a real cool guy, aren't ya, Poet?" asked Arnie with a sneer.

"Except when I'm headhunting!" laughed Harry.

"When I get outa this bandage," said Arnie restlessly, "we're gonna have us another fight!"

"Okay," said Harry evenly. "On one condition."

"What the hell is that?" asked Arnie angrily.

"You give me some boxing lessons first," smiled Harry. "You see, that's the first time I ever tried to box… so it wouldn't be a fair fight unless I had some lessons!"

"You're a pieca work, Quester," said Arnie shaking his head.

"And in exchange, I'll show you how to pass Mrs. Davison's quizzes about Shaky Spear real easy."

"Yeah?"

"Yeah," said Harry offering his hand again.

Arnie took the proffered hand and shook it briefly, turning it loose like a hot potato. "It's a deal!" he said with a secretive smile.

"Did ya hear about the new book called The Churchland and Suffolk Game?" grinned Allman in triumph.

"There's a book like that?" asked Big Jim in amazement.

"Okay, Allman," sighed Arnie, a look of patient disgust on his face. "Who wrote the damn book?"

"Written by that famous winner of the Noble Noble Award for Russian Literature… Trucka Knockyajockoff!"

Arnie sighed in disgust and lit another cigarette. "You guys can't beat Suffolk!"

"Why the hell not?" asked Allman in surprise.

"'Cause I ain't there to help ya… that's why!"

****

Friday morning, Harry read the sports page as he was eating his cereal for breakfast.

CHURCHLAND LOSES EMERSON TO INJURY
QUESTER TO PLAY END
By Al Gollen

Churchland High School lost its starting left end, Arnie Eberly, to injury this week. Eberly reportedly accidentally broke two ribs. No details were available on how the injury occurred. No one was willing to talk about it, which leaves open the question, what happened? Coach Braun had no comment. He reacted to the loss immediately, however, moving Harry Quester, better know as The Headhunter, from reserve fullback to end. Braun, who played end at Wilson, ECTC and Memphis State said that Quester was a more natural end than fullback. He should know!

Churchland plays Smithfield this evening at eight PM in Churchland Stadium. Churchland is a heavy favorite. A large crowd is expected to see it the beefy Packers can score on the high flying Truckers who have not lost or been scored upon to date. Churchland's big, athletic line, led by "Big Jim" Jensen should prove to be more than the Packers can handle, in spite of their size.

There was a picture of Arnie in the paper, posed catching a football over his shoulder. Harry put down the paper. He sat reflectively drinking his orange juice. What had Shotgun promised Al Gollen to keep him from printing what really happened? Most people knew anyway. It was no secret. Ol' Harry Quester broke Arnie Eberly's ribs so he could play first string! That's what Harry thought people thought, anyway. He got up and went out the door, walked to the bus stop and waited. Tonight, he would have to show he could play end… first string end. It made him nervous… but he felt ready.

****

The Smithfield Packers ran onto the field at Churchland Stadium clad in blue trousers and white shirts with blue numbers framed in gold. Their helmets were a solid gold color. The crowd stood and screamed as the Churchland Truckers took the field in their menacing black uniforms with the orange numbers and trim. The band played the fight song and the crowd enthusiastically joined the singing. Georgia led the Cheerleaders in a big "Gimme a 'C' cheer", jumping onto the air with each letter, their white skirts flying around them. It was a chilly night, the eighth of October. A.P. Johns stood on his tiptoes to see over the tall man in front of him.

"There he is, Ike!" shouted A.P. to Ike Quester standing next to him. "Number Thirty-two!"

"I see him, A.P.!" shouted Ike over the noise of the cheering crowd.

"I'll bet there are at least four thousand people here tonight," screamed A.P. in an excited voice.

"At least that many," said Ike.

Harry and Tony stood side by side waiting for Allman and Karl to come back from the coin toss.

"I wish we could both start, Little Brother," said Harry, clapping Tony on the back.

"You've earned it, Harry," said Tony, "and I got two more years to start."

Allman and Karl ran back to the sideline. "We receive, Coach," said Karl. "And we got the goal near the school."

"Alright, Truckers!" exclaimed Coach Fearless. "Huddle 'roun the Coach!"

Harry jumped into the huddle, his arms around Big Jim on one side and Bud Darby on the other. Coach Braun squatted on the ground in the middle of the huddle and stared up at the players, intensity and anger written all over his face.

"Are ya mean enough tonight?" screamed the Coach. "I wanna carve up these Smithfield hams and have 'em for lunch. Load up some hams in our trucks and take 'em off to market. I wanna push these fat slobs all over the field until they yell for mercy. I don't care if the score is a hundred to nothin'! Take no prisoners! Do ya guys understand me?"

There was a murmur of agreement among the players.

"Then let's hear it. I want ya to come out of this huddle with a sound that puts the fear of God in everyone on the field right up to the last row in the… darn stadium! Now break!"

The huddle exploded into boys racing onto the field as though possessed by demons. A sound came from them that was half cheer, half blood lust… a roaring screaming sound that made the stadium shake. In the middle of the huddle, the veins sticking out in his neck like blue pipes, was Shotgun Braun screaming with them! Harry ran onto the field. He reached down into his belly and pulled up his game face. Jekyll and Hyde, he thought as he put it on. Or was it just Hyde and Hyde? Maybe this game face thing was warping his personality for good. He snorted, took his position and pawed the turf with his cleats, his eyes narrowed and focused on the man he was to block. Harry ran swiftly down the field, hearing the roar of the crowd as the ball sailed high. Karl Darby took the opening kickoff. Harry ran directly into his man and bowled him over. Karl ran to the Smithfield forty yard line before he was tackled.

On the first play, Harry lined up in front of a big, tall boy with an enormous gut that hung out over his belt. Next to him was an even larger boy, so big that he bulged out of his uniform from all angles. The play was a run off left tackle by Sanders. Harry's assignment was to block the end out as Big Jim did the same to the tackle. Bucky was to get the guard and block him in. Harry saw a chubby looking linebacker standing right in the hole.

"Get down! Get ready!" shouted Allman. "Hut One... "

The ball was snapped. Harry hit the end with a forearm that stood him up straight and pushed him out. Allman handed the ball to Jack who was coming on like the freight train that he was. Harry rushed at the linebacker and cracked him in the head with another forearm. The linebacker fell like a heart shot deer. Sanders flashed through the hole at tackle. Harry overtook him and ran in front. He could sense the movement of all the players on the field. It played like a theater short subject in his mind. A Smithfield halfback stood in their way. Harry motioned to Jack to go left. Harry ran between Jack and the halfback, dipped his shoulder and hit him. The halfback careened out of Harry's view as he saw Sanders run over the safety and on to a touchdown.

"Joltin' Jack! Joltin' Jack!"

Harry turned around and saw the yellow flag lying on the field.

"Unnecessary roughness, number thirty-two, Churchland," shouted Wimpy Sawyer, blowing his whistle.

Harry ran up to the Referee. "Hey, Ref! What did I do?"

"You hit that linebacker in the head!" said Wimpy in his raspy voice that sounded like a hoarse woman.

"His head just got in the way, Ref," said Allman running up behind them.

Coach Braun was on the field, his face red. "What kinda call is that, Wimpy?" he shouted. "That was just a heck of a good block!"

"He hit him right in the face, Shotgun," said Wimpy in an excited voice.

"So?" exclaimed Shotgun.

"So, you can't hit a guy in the face like that!"

Braun took off his symbolic hat and slammed it to the turf, glaring at it as though it had called the penalty. "Where does it say that... where, Wimpy? Where does it say that?"

Wimpy blew his whistle loudly, his cheeks puffing out like a toad defending his leaf pile. "Touchdown comes back! Penalized fifteen yards!"

Coach Braun picked up his hat and stalked off the field, his arms stiff beside him, a nasty scowl on his face.

"Don't you come out here yelling no more, Shotgun," said Wimpy, "or I'll have to kick ya out!"

Coach Braun kept on walking and began slapping his often abused hat on his leg. The noise of the crowd was overwhelming.

The Truckers huddled. "Okay, gang," said Allman wrinkling his snub nose. "Same play.... Harry, this time hit the guy in the chest, will ya?"

"Okay, I will," said Harry, a scowl on his face.

They ran the same play. Harry hit the linebacker in the chest, knocking him backward. He ran on to the halfback and heard Jack thundering along behind him. The halfback tried to fend him off with his hands, but Harry launched at his legs and took him down. Touchdown!

"Joltin' Jack! Joltin' Jack!" shouted the crowd, exuberant in the repeat performance.

The teams lined up for the extra point. Harry could see the look of shock on the face of the big end with the paunch in front of him. Sanders barreled over left guard for the extra point. Seven to nothing! Jack ran to the sideline holding his shoulder.

Harry lined up for the kickoff feeling pretty good about that single play that produced their first touchdown. Jack was still on the sideline getting his shoulder re-taped. Chip Gross was in for him. Bud Darby kicked the ball. It sailed end over end to the Smithfield twenty yard line. A smallish halfback took the ball and began to run to Harry's right. Harry didn't follow. He had contain left on this play. He watched for any trick reverses or the like. The smallish halfback ran afoul of Bart Whitely who crushed the fellow to the ground.

Harry ran over and smacked Bart on the rear. "Nice tackle, Bart!"

Bart looked at Harry with narrowed eyes. "Keep your rah-rah crap to yourself, Headhunter! I don' need your stuff!"

"Okay, Bart… if that's the way you want it."

Harry ran to his position as left defensive end. The Smithfield team lined up.

"Why don't ya just lay down now, Packer Boy?" snarled Harry through his game face. "Ya don't have a chance… ya know!!"

****

A.P. opened the morning paper to the sport page. He put on his spectacles, adjusted them to the end of his nose and read.

THE TRUCKERS DO IT AGAIN!
SANDERS ROLLS FOR FOUR TOUCHDOWNS
SCORES ON THE FIRST PLAY
By Al Gollen

Will anyone ever score on the Truckers? The Smithfield Packers tried and ended up at the bottom of a 41-0 score. This is the fourth straight game this season in which the Truckers have won with no one scoring on them. Karl Darby, the speedy halfback who specializes in break away scores, took the ball back forty yards on the opening kickoff to the Packer's forty yard line. On the first play, Jolting Jack Sanders rumbled off left tackle, and with blocks from Big Jim Jensen and Headhunter Harry Quester smashed over the last man between himself and the goal and made it six to nothing in the first minute of play. The play was called back as Quester was called for unnecessary roughness. As usual, Shotgun Braun had something to say about that, but the penalty stood. The Truckers ran the same play for another touchdown, demonstrating that they could run on the Packers at will. That set the pattern and the Packers never recovered. Shotgun Braun's team went on to win 41-0, with scores by Sanders and halfbacks Karl Darby and Terry Moddy.

Assistant Coach Slate Phelps, when asked what made this team so good, said it was the right combination of toughness and smartness, a brew boiled up by Shotgun, Slate and Assistant Coach Eddie Fearless, all of whom played ball together at ECTC. He also said that they were "a scrappy bunch" competing among themselves, but when Friday night came, they were one team. The Captain of the Team, Quarterback Allman Buddinger, known as The Ball Fox, put it quite simply. When asked what made the team so good, he said "hand it to Sanders and watch the other guys mow 'em down... it almost makes me a spectator!" It is rumored that he will play for the Tar Heels next year. Stay tuned for Trucker exploits as next week they take on the Matthew Whaley Colonials from Williamsburg. Can the Colonials do it? If not, the Great Bridge Wildcats will get the next chance!

Gollen has it all about right, thought A.P. ... except that part about Buddinger being modest. That crazy loon doesn't have a modest bone in his body! And where did that "Ball Fox" thing come from? Gollen was working over time to give the players nicknames he could use in his column. The telephone rang. A.P. put down the paper and went to answer it. He lifted the receiver from its place on the wall.

"Johns' Groceries," said A.P., a sparkle in his voice. "Yes Maam, Mrs. Taylor... Yes Maam, I'll pick you out some good steaks and have them delivered before three o'clock. Oh, Yes Maam... I did see the game last night! It was terrific wasn't it? …. Yes Maam, they're good boys... the Coach?... You heard what?"

A.P. listened intently, a pained expression on his face.

"No Maam, I haven't heard about that."

A.P. listened and a dark expression came over his face. "I'm sure Coach Braun treats the boys right," he said. "And... he has to be tough if he wants them to win!"

A.P. listened some more and began to shake his head in concern. "Yes Maam… thank you!"

A.P. hung up the telephone. Where did these ladies get their stories? Shotgun too tough on the boys? Swearing at them! Oh my goodness, thought A.P. He'd probably swear at those goons too! But Patricia would think he was being terrible…. just terrible! He thought he'd heard it all! Where did Mrs. Taylor get this stuff? He went to the butcher cabinet to find Mrs. Taylor's steaks.

****

The fall festival dance at ECTC was held in the armory. The big hall was decorated with purple and gold ribbons and banners. The tables were filled with food and covered with brightly colored fall leaves and jugs of apple cider. The vinegary smell of North Carolina barbecue filled the air as the band started playing.

Slate and Billie went to the hardwood floor and began to dance. Slate watched as Cliff led a young lady onto the floor. Slate put his head next to Billie's and held her close as they danced.

"You know how much I love you, Billie?" asked Slate into her ear.

"Just keep on telling me, Slate," she said. "Never stop."

"I won't... I promise."

"Your friend, Cliff," said Billie, "how did the two of you become friends, Slate... you're so... so different."

"That's a long story..."

"Sometimes he really gets on my nerves," said Billie in a concerned voice, "it's like he's always wanting to fight someone... like he always wants you to be afraid of him... or something."

"I've been more worried about him lately," said Slate. "He's been depressed about something."

"He doesn't act depressed," said Billie. "He just acts like he's in a frenzy about something... all the time!"

"He's just bothered because I don't go out and drink beer with him as much," said Slate. "Maybe that's it... or maybe it's his love life... he complains all the time about his women!"

"I don't think so. He's in love with football... and himself," observed Billie. "Not much room for a woman there!"

They stopped dancing and turned toward a ruckus on the dance floor a short distance away. Major Fuller, in dress Army blues, stood facing Cliff Braun.

"Ya laughing at me, ya crum?" shouted Cliff angrily.

"No, Braun" said the Major, embarrassed as everyone around them stopped and stared. "Stand back from us... and try to have some respect for a change!"

"You bumped into me pretty hard and started laughing," shouted Cliff. "That ain't too polite, ya know!"

"Hit him, Shotgun!" shouted Cliff's girl friend.

"Back off, Braun," said Major Fuller, turning away from him.

"You wanna go outside with me, Fuller?" asked Cliff, red in the face.

"I won't fight you," said the Major haughtily, turning to face Cliff.

"You're not worth the effort!"

Cliff swung, but Slate caught his arm before the blow landed.

"Knock it off, Cliff!" said Slate softly.

Cliff struggled with Slate. Major Fuller turned his back on Cliff and stalked away. Slate pushed Cliff away and faced him.

"You want to fight, Cliff?" shouted Slate raising his fists. "Fight me!"

Cliff looked at Slate in total amazement. "I don't want to fight you, Slate," he said, "you're my friend!"

"Well, friend," said Slate, "you're gonna have to stop trying to fight everybody... the world and everybody in it!"

"Okay, Slate," said Cliff, backing away. "Okay."

****

It was the night before the first football game. Slate and Billie joined Cliff for dinner in the college cafeteria. Slate and Billie went through the serving line and sat at a table waiting for Cliff. Cliff turned up his nose at the smell of the food. The menu was turkey and ham with yams and green beans. The turkey was in trays in chunks and smelled less than fresh. The yams and the beans had dried up in the trays.

"What kinda soup is that?" shouted Cliff at a startled server.

"It's cream of potato," said the serving lady, her eyes wide.

"Is that right?" shouted Cliff angrily. "It looks like it's a year old... like paste water! Put some of that stuff in a bowl and let me taste it!"

The Serving Lady ladled out a bowl and handed it to him. Cliff took the bowl just as a big, young student in the line behind him jostled Cliff's arm. Soup spilled onto Cliff's sleeve. Cliff turned to the man behind him.

"What're you doing?" said Cliff angrily. "You spilled soup on me!"

"Big deal, Pop!" said the young student with a laugh.

"Pop?" shouted Cliff incredulously. "Who ya calling Pop, ya squirt?"

The big, young student poked a young man behind him. "Look at Pop, there," he said with a laugh, "he thinks he's still got it!"

"Who're you laughing at, Sonny?" asked Cliff, his anger growing.

Cliff dumped the hot soup on the young man's shirt, grabbed him by the collar and started to shake him. The young man struggled in his grasp and tried to hit Cliff.

"That all ya got, Squirt?" shouted Cliff.

Cliff slapped the young man beside the head and shook him harder. He pushed him away violently. The young man fell to the floor. Cliff stood over him angrily, his fists raised and cocked, waiting to land another blow when the boy got up.

Major Fuller came up behind Cliff and grabbed him by the shoulders.

"Hold your temper, Braun!" said the Major, his face filled with anger.

Cliff broke free of the grasp and turned to face the Major. "I thought I told you I was Mr. Braun to you... not just Braun, soldier boy!"

Major Fuller stared at Cliff in amazement. Then his face clouded and he reached for Cliff. Slate came up behind him.

"Cliff was just leaving, Major," said Slate. "Come on, Cliff!"

Slate grabbed Cliff's arm and tugged at it.

"This soldier boy thinks I'm still in the Army," muttered Cliff.

"Come on, Cliff," said Slate. "It's time to go!"

They walked out of the cafeteria together. Billie followed. Major Fuller stomped along behind them.

"Tomorrow morning in the President's office, Braun," shouted Major Fuller. "We'll see about you then... with Coach Johnstone!"

****

The next morning, Cliff walked into the President's office unannounced, his face and ears red. The President's secretary ran after him trying to restrain him, to no avail. President Robert Holland, a trim man with an equally trim beard looked up at Cliff through thick glasses with astounded eyes.

"I need to talk to ya," said Cliff in a loud voice.

Holland recovered his poise and addressed the distraught man. "What can I do for you?" he asked. "It's Shotgun Braun... isn't it?"

"I'm glad you watch football, Doctor Holland," shouted Shotgun, "we have a good team... but the food here is lousy... lousy! I can't get nothin' decent to eat here! And that tin soldier you got running us veterans around is a classic son of a... you know what!"

"I assume then that you have a complaint," said Holland, his face clouding over, his well known temper starting to rise.

"That I do!" shouted Cliff much too loudly.

"Mary," said Doctor Holland addressing his secretary, "would you please ask Coach Johnstone and Major Fuller to my office immediately... and bring me Mr. Braun's academic record."

"Bring my football record, too," said Cliff abrasively.

"Sit down, Braun," said Doctor Holland authoritatively.

"I'm Shotgun... or Mister Braun... or Cliff!" shouted Cliff, feeling put down by the use of his last name alone.

"Sit down... whoever you are!" said Holland in a loud voice.

Cliff sat down in a chair reluctantly and looked around nervously. The office was paneled in glowing dark mahogany and lined with bookshelves that contained a number of leather bound volumes.

"People around here are out to get me, Doctor Holland," complained Cliff. "Everywhere I go, there's another one… like that Major… and the cooks that make that lousy food... and the professors here that don't know how to teach!"

"That's interesting," said Doctor Holland, looking at Cliff with intense eyes as if examining a bug under a microscope.

"Are you out to get me too?" asked Cliff squinting his eyes.

Mary returned and laid a folder on the President's desk.

"Thank you, Mary," said Doctor Holland, adjusting his glasses and studying the papers in front of him. "Mr. Braun! Physical education, all As… I see that last year you made a C in history and four Ds in first term… then, after football season of course, you did better… a B in history… and four Ds."

"Yeah… I think that's right," said Cliff. "Professor Franklin teaches history real well… he's the only decent Prof around here!"

"Is that a fact?" asked Holland belligerently.

"And we won most of our football games!" exclaimed Cliff.

"Five, one and one so far, I believe," said Holland, lifting his eyebrows. "Mediocre at best."

Coach Johnstone and Major Fuller came hurriedly into the office. Fuller's face was red. Johnstone's brow was wrinkled with concern.

"Gentlemen," said Doctor Holland sarcastically, "I have… enjoyed discussing Mr. Braun's complaints with him. Could you accompany him now and let him fill in the details?"

"Yes Sir," said Coach Johnstone. "Cliff was wrong, and he's sorry."

"I ain't sorry 'bout nothin'," muttered Cliff.

"If he's sorry, he can apologize," said Fuller holding his temper with visible effort, "and even if he does, he doesn't belong here at ECTC… or at any university!"

"See what I mean," said Cliff, his eyes wide in innocence. "They're all out to get me!"

"Coach, you and the Major, please take Mr. Braun to a proper place and listen to his grievances," said Doctor Holland. "I would then appreciate your recommendation regarding his future at ECTC."

Coach Johnstone grimaced and motioned for Cliff to come with them. Cliff grudgingly complied. Major Fuller looked at Cliff with eyes fit to kill and followed them out of the office.

"Wait a minute, Major Fuller," said Robert Holland.

Major Fuller came back into the office.

"Now just what was that all about?" asked the President tersely.

"That guy," said Buck Fuller, "he's some kind a' psychotic nut… the biggest bully with the worst attitude I've ever seen."

"He seems to be violently angry about something," said Holland trying to calm himself. "What happened?"

"Oh, last night… just one of many things," said Fuller, "some kid jostled him in the chow line and Shotgun tried to beat him up."

"Sounds a bit extreme!"

"He's gotta go, Dr. Holland," said Major Fuller in a polished voice, containing his anger. "He's a real nut case!"

****

Slate and Cliff drove along a narrow road in Slate's Ford through the countryside outside of Greenville. The leaves on the trees were orange and red with a sprinkling of green. They made beautiful hanging canopies over the winding road.

"Cliff, is something wrong?" asked Slate. "I mean… you can't act the way you've been acting. People will think you're nuts!"

"I ain't nuts," said Cliff glumly.

"Maybe not," said Slate, "but sometimes you act as though you are… I always knew you had a chip on your shoulder, but it's gotten bigger… and bigger! What's going on?"

"I ain't got no chip," said Cliff. "I just… I don't know… I just…"

"You just beat up on people for no good reason," said Slate.

"I got a reason," said Cliff. "I can't stand people making fun a' me… or laughing at me. It makes me… do stuff!"

"Sometimes you think people are doing that," said Slate, "but maybe not… you don't give people a chance!"

"They got a chance," said Cliff with a toss of his head. "One!"

"Cliff… you were a bully at times back when we were kids… I thought you'd grow out of it!" said Slate. "But you enjoy intimidating!"

"A bully?" exclaimed Cliff. "You think I'm a bully?"

"Sometimes you are, Cliff," said Slate bluntly.

"Ennis was a bully," said Cliff to himself. "Not me!"

They drove on in silence. Cliff looked out the window at the passing forests, seeing only a blur of red and orange as he brooded over events.

"I found out this morning," said Cliff without emotion. "I'm being expelled!"

"I was afraid that would happen!" exclaimed Slate.

"Coach Johnstone and Professor Franklin told me," said Cliff as the Ford bumped along at a leisurely speed. "They said I was being expelled for demonstrated lack of academic potential… and behavior not befitting a gentleman… or some horseshit like that!"

"You brought it on yourself, Cliff."

"I never knew ya had to be a gentleman to go to college and play football!"

"You don't, Cliff," said Slate, "but you have to be civil to other people… the world isn't a football field… you can't be running around hitting people… in the world."

"I never thought about it like that."

"So… what are you going to do?" asked Slate.

"I don't know. Coach told me that Fuller swore I'd never play ball again in the North Carolina… or anywhere else!

"That's not good," said Slate, "because he can blackball you."

"And the government money has disappeared."

"Yeah, I guess it has," said Slate shaking his head.

"Professor Franklin says he knows the President at Memphis State," said Cliff, "and they have a good football team. He thinks he can get me in on a scholarship… he says he'll take up for me."

"The Professor is a brave man," said Cliff.

"He knows I can play football!" said Cliff defensively.

"Yeah, Cliff," said Slate with concern in his voice, "but can you live in the world?"

Cliff looked at Slate, his eyes dulled as if looking far away. "I can, Slate," he said. "But I need you as my friend."

"I'll always be your friend, Cliff," said Slate emotionally. "But I can't take up for you all the time."

"You know, you and Doc Franklin are the only two people who've taken any interest in me… except for football coaches."

"You scare everyone else away," said Slate.

"I don't mean to," said Cliff, "it's just… well, all the coaches like me to be… you know tough."

"It's time to start thinking, Cliff," said Slate. "Why is it that you get along with this Doctor Franklin so well?"

"He's a funny guy, ya know," said Cliff introspectively. "He can take some guff without getting upset… and without backing down. I know because I tried to give him some guff."

"He sounds like an interesting guy."

"He's… tough in the mind… not such a big guy… but real tough in the mind."

"Cliff," said Slate, "you can't just live on the football field… the world isn't the football field. You have to live in the world… and you have to do it yourself!"

"I know that," said Cliff. "I'm gonna work on it!"

****

Chapter Eleven
Hurricane Hazel

The headlines on the sports page of the Thursday, October 14, Virginian Pilot Sports Page caught Harry's eye as he ate breakfast with his Father and Mother.

WILL CHURCHLAND BE SCORED ON?
WHO WILL DO IT?
By
Al Gollen

The unbeaten, untied and unscored upon Churchland High Truckers football team, coached by Cliff "Shotgun" Braun is building extraordinary expectations. The question each week seems to be not will they win, but will they be scored on? Meanwhile, Pistol Pete Sacker has taken the Wilson Presidents to an unbeaten record so far in the season, though their opponents have scored. Both teams are now in the running for the State championship in their respective Groups, I and II.

It is likely that the game between Churchland and Matthew Whaley will be postponed due to the passage of Hurricane Hazel, scheduled to hit the Tidewater Area sometime tomorrow and pass rapidly up the coast. The Wilson game with Newport News is also threatened. If Matthew Whaley doesn't get a crack at the Truckers this week, the Great Bridge Wildcats are up next. Bobby O'Briar has built a good team and they have a chance to score and give Churchland a good game!

Coach Shotgun Braun of Churchland says he is not concerned about being scored on. His goal is to win all of the scheduled games this season, and he says that the Truckers will remain unbeaten. Yet, the pressure builds on Shotgun and his team to maintain the unscored upon pace. If a team manages to score on them, it will be a moral victory for that team even if they lose the game.

Fatso Hathaway and his Suffolk Red Raiders have sworn they will beat Churchland again. Churchland has never beaten the Red Raiders. The drama builds for the Truckers! Can they do it? Can they beat all their opponents? Can they do it without being scored upon?

Meanwhile speculation builds on how Arnie Eberly broke his ribs. Some have said that Shotgun broke the ribs showing Eberly how to block. Shotgun has endured criticism before that he is too rough on his players. Shotgun denies anything to do with Eberly's injuries. Last year, parents complained that Shotgun roughed up their children and, in some cases bruised them unnecessarily. As Shotgun's successes build, will his methods stand the scrutiny? Time will tell.

"Did you see this thing on the Sports page, Father?" asked Harry.
"Sure did," said Ike Quester sipping a hot cup of coffee.
"What do you think, Sir?"
"I think Shotgun Braun has a problem," mused Ike. "If someone

scores on you fellows, it'll be almost like you lost a game."

"That's not really fair," said Harry.

"Are you guys worried about being scored on?" asked Ike.

"I guess I really haven't given it much thought," said Harry. "We just go out and play the game… and everybody focuses on their assignments."

"I'm sure that's what the Coach would tell you to do, Harry," said Ike. "Is he as rough on the players as it says here?"

"He's pretty rough," said Harry, "but it's a rough game. He's trying to teach us… and get us in the right frame of mind… as he sees it."

"Has he ever roughed you up?"

"Nothing I can't handle, Father."

****

"The game with Matthew Whaley has been postponed," announced Eddie Fearless to the team on Thursday afternoon in the dressing room. "This hurricane… I think its name is Hazel… is supposed to come up the coast on Friday and pass near here. The game'll be played on a Saturday after the regular season is over."

"We gonna practice today, Coach?" asked Allman hopefully.

"What do you think?" smiled Coach Fearless.

"We're gonna practice," said Allman nodding his head.

"We got things to work out before the game with Great Bridge," said Coach Fearless.

"Say, Coach," said Terry. "Did ya see the thing in the morning paper?"

"Yeah Terry," said Coach Fearless. "I saw it."

"Does Coach Braun really expect us to go without anyone scoring on us for the whole season?"

"Well," drawled Fearless, "Why don't you ask him?"

"What about you, Coach?" asked Karl. "What do you think?"

"I think that if each of you does your job and doesn't worry about things in the paper, that things will take care of themselves… now get ready for practice!"

"Is the Coach in some kind a' trouble about showing people how to block?" asked Tony.

"Naw," drawled Eddie Fearless. "Now stop asking questions and get on out there on the field."

The boys opened their lockers.

"Special treat today," said Coach Fearless with a little smile, "washed practice jerseys!"

There was round of laughter and cheering.

"I don't know how I'll get it on," shouted Allman. "I'm used to the thing walking out to meet me!"

There was more laughter.

"Don't faint from the smell of a fresh shirt, Allman," shouted Harry.

Allman pulled out the fresh shirt with the big black number zero-zero on it and swooned, falling onto the floor. Big Jim yanked him to his feet.

"We gotta practice," observed Big Jim dryly as he propped Allman up. "Ain't no one gonna score on us!"

"Alright alright" shouted Coach Braun as he strode briskly into the dressing room, "what's all this… screwing around? Get into those uniforms and get hoppin'… or you'll be running extra laps!"

****

The wind howled around Allman's red jeep as it ran east along Virginia Beach Boulevard headed for the ocean front. Bart rode in the front seat. Harry, Buster and Bubba rode in the back. Buster and Bubba hung over each side and Harry sat cramped in the middle. Light rain beat against them as they bounced along in the open jeep.

"The waves ought to be great!" shouted Bubba over the howl of the wind as they rode along through the rain. "We'll bust some big ones!"

"Where ya gonna get on the beach?" shouted Bart.

"Down there south of Rudee Inlet," shouted Allman. "At Sand Bridge!"

"Gimme a beer!" shouted Bart.

"No beer drinking on the road!" shouted Allman. "Ya want the police to haul us in?"

"Here, Bart," said Bubba handing him a jar, "check out this wine… it'll warm you up!"

Bart took the jar and took a big gulp. "Wow!" he gasped. "That's got some kick!"

"Want some, Harry?" asked Bubba. "Best moonshine in Churchland!"

"No… no thanks," said Harry as he bounced on another bump in the road.

"Ya sure?"

"Yeah! I'm sure," said Harry. "We're supposed to be in training you know!"

Bubba laughed. "Well, this here is training wine! Kickapoo Joy Juice… it makes ya real mean… just like Shotgun wants ya!"

"Gimme some!" said Buster.

Bubba handed Buster a jar. The red jeep turned onto the beach near Rudee Inlet and ran along the beach south toward Sand Bridge. The waves towered ten to fifteen feet high, crashing onto the sand with frothy fury. Gobs of sea foam blew in the air as the wind whipped by them.

"Yeehah!" screamed Allman, standing up in the jeep behind the wheel, the wind whipping though his hair.

"Sit down, for christ's sake!" shouted Harry.

This was all crazy, thought Harry. He was in the company of mad men! What was he doing here? Yet, as he put his face into the wind and felt the sting of the rain and the exhilaration of speed, he began to feel a wild abandon. It felt good, he acknowledged guiltily. They ran the beach for at least a mile. Then Allman turned down wind. He drove the jeep into the white surf that surged back and forth from the crashing waves. He ran in and out of the surf, the jeep careening crazily from side to side. Harry gasped as he saw Allman drive directly at a gigantic wave that was rolling in to the beach. Water splashed up from the tires, making fountains at the sides of the vehicle.

"Watch out for that wave!" shouted Harry.

At the last moment, Allman turned away. The wave crashed and Allman drove up the beach toward the dunes, the surge of the wave chasing them with foaming fury. Allman turned and shook his fist at the wave.

"Got ya that time!" shouted Allman in a crazy voice.

"Crack some of them beers, Bubba!" shouted Bart.

Bubba opened a waterproof sack on the floor of the jeep, extracted five beers and handed them out. He took a Church key from his pocket and opened them. Allman stood up, swigged the beer and started toward another incoming wave. Harry chased the opening in the beer can with his mouth as the jeep swayed about crazily. He managed to get a sip. It was salty and tasted good. Bubba drank the strawberry wine and followed it with the beer.

"Bubba! You're gonna have a big headache!" exclaimed Harry.

"Yeah, I know," said Bubba with a crazy grin. "Ain't it great?"

Harry didn't see the wave coming. It crashed into the jeep, knocking the little vehicle on its side in the surf and washing them all into the water. Harry surfaced, tasting the salt of the ocean, the back surge of a wave pulling at him.

"Aw shit!" exclaimed Bart. "There goes our beer!"

Harry saw the water proof sack surging out to sea with the tide. Bart plunged after it and grabbed it. A big wave crashed over him and knocked him down. Harry pushed himself through the water and grabbed Bart by the shirt. He held him tightly.

"I can't swim!" gurgled Bart as another big wave washed over them.

"Hold on, Bart!" shouted Harry over the howling wind. "We'll get you out."

Harry turned and saw Bubba struggling through the surging surf toward them. He held out his hand.

"Grab my hand, Bubba!" shouted Harry. "Buster! Allman! Come here! Quick!"

The tide surged forward and then abruptly reversed and surged back toward the ocean, tugging at Bart and Harry. Another big wave came crashing in. Bubba grabbed Harry's hand and began to pull. Buster grabbed Bubba's hand and pulled. Allman latched on to Buster and they slowly pulled Bart ashore. He lay on the sand burbling salt water like a beached whale. Victoriously, he held up the water proof sack.

"I saved the beer!" shouted Bart triumphantly.

"Come on!" shouted Allman. "We gotta get the Red Rooster!"

The red jeep lay on its side in the sand, the surge of the waves rushing by it, pulling it further seaward. They ran to one side. Bart staggered into the surf and joined them. Allman, Buster, Harry, Bubba and Bart reached into the sand and grabbed the side of the jeep.

"On two!" shouted Allman. "Get down! Get ready! Hut One! Hut Two."

They all heaved together. The red jeep popped up out of the soft sand and rolled drunkenly upright.

"Get behind it and shove!" shouted Allman.

Bart and Buster got behind the jeep. Harry took the left side, Bubba the right. Allman took position where he could grab the wheel.

"Okay, you guys," shouted Bart, "Heave! Heave!"

Together they pushed until the jeep broke loose from the soft sand. Once it hit the hard sand of the beach it rolled freely. They pushed it until it was free of the water and near a large sand dune.

"Okay Allman, you Genius!" said Buster irritably. "What now?"

"Where's the beer?" asked Allman, looking around with concern.

"I threw it up there by that sand dune," said Bart.

"There's an old World War II defense bunker right along here somewhere," said Bubba.

"Yeah?" said Allman. "Get the beer, Bart... and come on!"

****

The boys sat sheltered from the wind behind a sand dune in a trench dug fifteen years past to defend the beaches of Virginia against the Germans. The rain let up, at least temporarily, and now was a drizzle mixed with salty spray from the raging ocean. The old trench was reinforced with salted timbers, weathered by the wind. Harry made a fire from pieces of the timbers and some driftwood he found. They stripped, wrung out their clothes and hung them on sticks stuck in the sand around the roaring fire to dry. They sat naked, warming themselves, listening to the howl of the wind above the dunes. It was still strong, but diminishing.

"Harry! The Eagle Scout!" said Bubba. "I knew that Boy Scout stuff would come in handy someday… who would've thought you had matches in a metal container?"

"It was in my jacket pocket, thank goodness," said Harry. "I put it in there a few weeks back when we were burning some leaves."

"Open the sack and see if the sandwiches are dry," said Allman. "I could eat a horse!"

"They're mostly dry," said Bart, opening the sack, "and the beer's cold!"

They cracked the beer cans and opened the sandwiches. Bubba's mother had made the sandwiches thick with fatty, greasy country ham you could only get in A.P.'s store. Each sandwich had a thick slab of American cheese on top of the ham.

"Ya think that jeep is gonna start?" asked Bubba with concern.

"Sure!" exclaimed Allman. "The Red Rooster just needs to dry out a little."

"The Red Rooster had better start," said Buster in mock horror, "or we'll be having sand sandwiches for dinner!"

"It'll start," said Allman. He took a big bite of the sandwich and a swig of beer. He tilted back his head and howled at the threatening sky above. "Ya know, it jus' don't get any better than this!"

"We could be home and dry, you asshole," muttered Bart.

"Aw… that ain't no fun!" exclaimed Allman giving Bart a shove on his hairy shoulder.

"I knew when ya said to come with ya, Allman," muttered Bart, "that we'd end up doing somethin' crazy!"

"Yeah, but… what a bullshit adventure!" exclaimed Allman. "Where else can ya be with your buddies and have a big-ass adventure!"

"Let's see," said Buster, wide eyed, "we smashed down a tidal wave, sunk a German submarine, captured their Nazi crew… and survived days in the surf fighting to get ashore! How's that?"

Allman guffawed and held his side. "That's good Buster! Real good!"

"And then the sharks came!" narrated Buster, a terrified look on his face. "They were American sharks, so they ate the Germans first… we just got ashore before they got around to us!"

"Okay, Buster," laughed Allman, "but I'll have to work on it some!"

"You're fulla shit, Buster," said Bart, "like always!"

"Hey!" exclaimed Buster. "It's a helluva story! But I forgot to mention the beach nymphs!"

"The what?" asked Tony, a puzzled look on his face.

"The beach nymphs who did exotic things to us when we washed ashore!" said Buster with a lewd grin.

"What kinda exotic things?" asked Tony.

Buster leaned over and whispered in Tony's ear.

"You're crazy!" exclaimed Tony, giving Buster a shove.

"Will ya shut up, Buster," grumbled Bart. "You're so fulla shit your eyes are brown!"

"It's all true!" exclaimed Buster, his eyes wide.

"I like the part about the sea nymphs!" said Allman seriously, licking the grease from his fingers.

Bart snorted in disgust and looked at Harry. He stared at him while Harry hungrily stuffed down a sandwich and reached for another.

"Well, Headhunter," said Bart reluctantly, "I guess… anyway… thanks for grabbing me!"

"No sweat, Bart," said Harry. "Thanks for grabbing the beer! I'd never have gotten us out if it weren't for these other guys!"

"And we'd have never gotten the jeep out without you and Buster," said Bubba nipping on the strawberry wine.

"Yeah, guys," said Allman with uncharacteristic intensity. "We're a team… and no matter what happens… nothing changes that… nothing!"

"We were lucky," said Harry wiping the ham grease off his face.

"All good teams make their own luck, Harry Ol' Buddy!"

****

Harry and Allman sat in the dressing room on Monday afternoon before practice taking off their shoes. The other players were just coming into the room.

"I'm glad the Red Rooster started," said Harry. "I'd have had a hard time explaining to my Father why he had to come dig us out of a beach bunker in a hurricane!"

"The Red Rooster always starts!" said Allman with a confident wave of his hand.

"You know, Allman," said Harry reflectively. "I figured it out."

"What's that, Harry Ol' Buddy?"

"You planned it all," said Harry. "All that stuff down at Sand Bridge in the storm… you planned it all!"

Allman laughed. "Well, not quite all of it!"

"You wanted to get Bart to be with us," said Harry.

"Yeah," grinned Allman, slapping Harry on the back, "that and loosen ya up some. Ya gotta be flexible!"

Harry laughed a short laugh. "I guess you made some progress!"

"I heard the story going aroun' that we got washed out to sea and had to be rescued by the Coast Guard," said Allman with a wry grin.

"The way I heard it, we were attacked by female pirates who took us off to their lair!" said Harry.

They both laughed.

"Hey!" exclaimed Allman. "I like that last one!"

"Buster's been hard at work," said Harry. "That's' for sure!"

Coach Fearless came to where they sat. "What's this I hear about you guys running around in a jeep during the hurricane?" he drawled.

"Golly, Coach," said Allman. "I don't know who told ya that!"

Fearless smiled and then a serious look came over his face. "Don't you go getting anyone hurt with some a' your pranks, Allman! We can't afford to get any more guys hurt!"

"Oh, no Sir," said Allman, innocence spreading over his face. "Not me!"

****

Cliff Braun went to Memphis State in 1947. He played end on the football team with his usual vigor and determination. He once again gained a reputation as a fierce competitor and a crazy, tough guy. In November of 1948, he dislocated his shoulder while making a viscous tackle on a big fullback. Professor Marion Franklin came to see him in the hospital. He was a man of about fifty with thick gray hair and a short, well trimmed beard. There was the same twinkle in his eyes that Cliff remembered from ECTC. Cliff was sitting in a hospital chair with his right shoulder bandaged and his arm in a sling, looking out the window at the leaf strewn hospital lawn.

"Well, Cliff," said Marion Franklin in a slow drawl, "I guess you're going to have to hang up the shoulder pads for awhile."

Cliff stood up favoring his sore shoulder, plainly happy to see Doctor Franklin. "Doc! It's great to see you," said Cliff holding out his left hand.

"And I'm glad to see you too, Cliff," said Marion. "You were always my favorite football player, you know!"

"Sit down... sit down," said Cliff offering a straight back hospital room chair. "Why was I your favorite, Doc? I never could figure it out... I tried to give you a hard time, but you just smiled and used something in history to make me laugh."

"History is full of humor," said Doctor Franklin. "I dug out your sense of humor, and used it to shape you."

"Yeah?"

"At first, I didn't think you had a sense of humor... wasn't sure you could take a joke," said Marion. "But I found it... your sense of humor, that is."

"Yeah," said Cliff. "I can laugh at things."

"But it's hard to laugh at yourself."

Cliff looked at Marion strangely. "I guess it is."

"Can you laugh at yourself?"

"Yeah," said Cliff with a frown, "I guess I can, but it's hard."

"You have a hard time laughing at yourself?"

"Well, you know, I don't really like people laughing at me! So, I don't laugh at myself... much."

"I was here for interviews when you dressed up at half time in the tuxedo, the Panama hat and the big green bow tie," said Professor Franklin. "Remember that?"

"Yeah," laughed Cliff, "and I carried a little umbrella and smoked a big ol' cigar."

"You were laughing at yourself then," said Marion. "It's called the humor of the ridiculous!"

"Yeah."

"And others were laughing at you."

"Yeah... but that was different... I was just showing off. I wanted them to laugh at me."

"You wanted the attention."

"I guess that was it."

"You also have to learn to laugh at yourself even when you're not trying to be ridiculous."

"Whataya mean?"

"I mean... sometimes we all do ridiculous things... even when we don't intend to!" laughed Marion.

"Yeah," said Cliff reflectively, "I guess so... but not too much... for me."

"Cliff... defending what others see as ridiculous just makes you more ridiculous."

"That's when I get mad... real mad."

"Don't get mad," said Marion. "Laugh with them... and they'll think you're wonderful!"

"Yeah... I guess so... but it's hard to do that... real hard!"

"You understand that, then?"

"Sure," said Cliff, "so you found out I could laugh... but that wasn't the reason I was your favorite."

"No," said Marion reflectively, adjusting his position in the straight backed chair, "I reckon you were my favorite because you played football with such great intensity... the way I would have liked to play it."

"You did play, though, didn't you Doc?'

"Sure," said Franklin, "I played guard for a little High School near Durham... they were surprised that I tried out. I was always the last guy picked for back yard football games... the little guy named... Marion, of all things!"

"But you made the team?" asked Cliff.

"Sure did," said Marion, "I got bigger... even played first string my senior year."

"Hey! Making the team and playing is what counts!"

"Yes, I know," said Marion, "but I never really made the headlines. I think I played because the Coach needed to fill a hole and he didn't have that many players."

"But you loved the game!"

"You're correct," said Marion. "I do love the game. It provides a sense of heroics that you can't get anywhere else, except in the reading of history... except for men like you who fought in the war... and made history!"

"I didn't fight none... except with the other soldiers," said Cliff. "I drove a truck and never saw any Germans, except prisoners."

"But you were there, Shotgun!" exclaimed Professor Franklin. "You were a part of history... you saw history... I only teach it."

"Yeah, I guess I saw some history," said Cliff with a wry grin, thinking of the French woman who had chased him out of the bar. "I guess I did."

"That's also why I love history," said Marion, great passion in his voice. "Reading about the decadence and the nobility of man... and how some men and women... some heroes always rise above the rubble and make sense of the world... and understanding the dynamics of it all... that's why I love history."

"You make it sound like a big adventure."

"It is... it is!" exclaimed Doctor Franklin with bubbling enthusiasm. "That's what I mean, Shotgun... you have to find a passion for the adventure of your studies! Sometimes a Professor can do this for you. But alas... all of us do not have that ability. The passion must come from you... from you, Shotgun! You must attack a book with the same passion you attack a halfback!"

"Yeah... I guess so," said Cliff. "But some of that stuff is just real hard to understand… and boring."

"That's where the passion must translate to long hours at the books, Shotgun," said Marion. "You have to want to study… to enjoy it! You can't just read the words… or listen to the words! You have to read and listen and write things out until you understand! For some, it comes quickly… for others, like myself, it takes longer."

"How do ya know when ya understand, Doc?"

Marion smiled. "You, better then any I have seen, understand the game of football. You're not just an end. You see the whole field… you know what every man is supposed to do… you see it when it breaks down… you see it when it all works… you understand, and you know you understand!"

"Yeah, yeah," said Cliff, nodding slowly, "I do."

"Then," said Professor Franklin triumphantly, "when you see English… and Biology, and Mathematics in the same way, you will know that you understand."

"Gosh, Doc," said Cliff, "I don't know if I can ever understand all that stuff the way I do football!"

"You'll never understand anything as well as you understand football, Shotgun my friend… but you will understand many things. That's what education is!"

"Heck, Doc," exclaimed Cliff with a smile, "I thought education was just something ya had to do to play football!"

"Now, Shotgun," said Marion twitching a finger at him. "You're trying to give me a hard time again!"

Cliff laughed. "See… there you go again! You just won't let me give you a hard time!"

"No, I won't," said Marion stroking his gray beard. "Now tell me, how's the shoulder, Shotgun?"

"Hurts a lot," said Cliff, rubbing his shoulder. "They operated on it yesterday… I guess I'll be here a few more days before I can go back to classes."

"How are the classes going?"

Cliff smiled and looked up in the air as if the answer hovered there somewhere. "Oh, the usual," he said, "okay in history… not so good in the others."

"I'm coming to Memphis State," said Professor Franklin. "They want me to be Dean of Arts and Sciences. I would like to help you get through and get your degree… is that alright?"

Tears came suddenly and uncontrollably to Cliff's eyes. He struggled with his words. "You… you want to help me?"

"Of course," said Doctor Franklin," but I can only help you if you help yourself! Now that you won't be able to play football, you can concentrate on your studies."

Cliff brushed away the tears, embarrassed that they existed. "I know that, Doctor Franklin," he said. "But I won't know what to do if I can't play football anymore."

"Concentrate on graduating and getting your degree... and go on to get your master's degree," said Marion. "With that in hand you can get a job for sure... and be a fine football coach somewhere."

"Yeah... yeah," said Cliff as though to himself. "I could do that!"

"You are an intelligent and very vibrant young man," said Marion, "and I believe you have the potential to do great things... you have a genius for football... but you must learn to enjoy your studies... and learn to be tolerant of others, no matter that they may be fools... or be you the fool!"

"What do ya mean by that?" asked Cliff, fighting a sudden irritation.

"I mean that most irritating situations... things that make you mad... are created by someone being foolish," said Doctor Franklin patiently. "Sometimes it's the other person... sometimes its you... but most won't see it... or admit it when it's them!"

Cliff paused and forced the irritation out of his mind. "I think I understand that," he said.

"You understand the words, Cliff," said Marion with a smile that parted his gray beard. "You do not yet understand what the words mean... but you will!"

****

It was June of 1950. Slate and Billie Phelps both graduated from ECTC, he with a degree in physical education and education management, she with a degree in English. They crossed the Tar River and headed north to Virginia in Slate's 1942 Ford. It was a hot day and the windows were open, the smell of pine and honeysuckle wafting in.

"I hate to leave Greenville," said Billie passionately. "It's been so wonderful... being with you and... being able to study... and seeing you play football, and all..."

"Well, I'm lucky to get a job with Jack Ryder at Great Bridge," said Slate. "Coach Johnstone has known Jack a long time, and he got it for me."

"Assistant Football Coach," said Billie, her eyes bright, "it sounds exciting!"

"You'll be able to get a job teaching English I hope."

"Oh I will... or something else until I can."

"I'll be coaching other things too, I guess... basketball, track, baseball..."

"Can you do that?"

"I'll figure it out..."

"Is this what you want to do... coaching?"

"I'm not sure that's all I want to do... but for now, yes."

"What else would you do?"

"Oh, I don't know... maybe go into education management... be principal of a school... that kind of thing."

"I guess this North Carolina girl can learn to live in Virginia," said Billie, pausing to inhale the smell of the sweet pine forest.

"You'll like Portsmouth," said Slate, "it's a small town with a lot of nice people."

"Whatever happened to Shotgun?" asked Billie.

"I thought you didn't like Shotgun," said Slate.

"Oh, don't be silly," said Billie. "I love Shotgun. He's a wonderful character. He just scares me, not because I'm afraid for myself, but because I'm afraid for him, or for what he might get you into."

"I know what you mean," said Slate thoughtfully. "He's been a bully all his life... it seems to be built into him. I've stayed in touch with him. I talked to him last month... he's doing okay. He's brought his grades up and managed to stay mostly out of trouble."

"Mostly?"

"Well, last fall, he beat up some guy who tried to date a girl he liked," said Slate. "I guess he talked his way out of that... says he just lost control!"

"That's unusual," said Billie.

"What?"

"That he admitted that he lost control."

"Yeah, that's progress. He says a Professor there... someone he knew at ECTC... Professor Franklin... has helped him a lot."

"I'm glad for him."

"He says he's going to graduate next year... had to make up a few courses to bring his grade point average up."

"That's wonderful! Where will he go?"

"I don't know," said Slate. "I think he's going to graduate school, and then probably come back to Portsmouth. He wants to be a coach."

"Is Shotgun married?" asked Billie.

"No," said Slate, "You know better than that! Shotgun... married? Didn't you say once he was in love with football... and there was no room there for a woman!"

"Yes... I remember saying that," said Billie.

"Shotgun has different standards for his women, I think," said Slate. "But, he'll find the right one eventually."

"Where will he live?"

"I think he plans to live with his Mother. They're real close… and she's getting along in age."

"Do you think he can get a job coaching?" asked Billie. "I mean… after being thrown out of ECTC and all that?"

"I don't know," said Slate. "But if he ever does get a coaching job… look out!"

****

The 1950 football season at Great Bridge High School under Jack Ryder was a real learning experience for Slate. He walked into the Coach's office on an early summer day in June of 1951. Jack was a man in his fifties who had been a coach a long time. He was tall, balding, ruggedly handsome and in good shape for a man of his age. His office smelled of analgesic balm and was littered with sports magazines and newspapers.

"Jack, I've got an offer from Principal Fred Beckler at Churchland High School to take over as Head Coach for the 1951 season," said Slate bluntly.

Jack looked at Slate with a frown which he changed into a smile. "That's great!" he said. "It's a good school!"

"Fred also wants me to be the Assistant Principal," said Slate.

"At the same time?"

"Yes Sir," said Slate. "I can handle it."

"I know you can," said Jack. "Is that what you want to do?"

"It sure is," said Slate, "and Fred says Billie can teach English there, also."

"Sounds like a great deal," said Jack. "We'll miss you and Billie!"

"I need to make a decision about my future," said Slate. "I love coaching, but I think I want to try to be a Principal and get into school management."

"It sounds like Fred Beckler has given you the right deal to let you make up your mind."

"Yes, he has," said Slate. "And about my replacement… I have a suggestion."

"Who ya got in mind?"

"Cliff Braun."

"Shotgun? You mean Shotgun Braun?"

"Yes sir. He'd be great with you here… and you could teach him a lot, just like you have me."

"I remember him from his playing days at Wilson," said Ryder thoughtfully. "He played with you…was a tough guy… a little rowdy as I remember him."

"That's the guy," said Slate, "but he's mellowed some and wants to get into coaching real bad. I'd appreciate it if you'd give him a try… he has a degree in physical education from Memphis State and a Master's Degree in Education, too.

"Really? I'll be damned!"

"What do you mean?"

Ryder laughed. "If ol' Shotgun hadn't gone to college… he'd a' probably gone to jail!"

"Well… he went to college!" exclaimed Slate.

"I'm glad for him," said Coach Ryder. "What's he doing now?"

"He's working in the shipyard… waiting for a break to get into coaching."

"He knows football… that's for sure," mused Jack.

"How about it, Coach?"

"I'll do it, Slate."

"Thanks, Jack"

****

Slate walked in to the office of Fred Beckler on the second story of the old brick schoolhouse in Churchland Village in May of 1952. In the preceding 1951 season Slate's Truckers finished with a five, three and one record… not bad, for a first year Coach. The Principal was in a good mood. He didn't know much about football, but he enjoyed winning. More than that, he enjoyed having a winning football team because it brought the little school more revenue to buy library books and other things he needed, like new instruments for the band. Fred was a tall man with a round body, a balding head, a jovial disposition and a small, well manicured moustache. He liked Slate Phelps and he smiled broadly as Slate came into the office.

"Well, Slate, congratulations on your first year here," said Fred. "You've done well!"

"Thanks, Mr. Beckler," said Slate.

"Sit down… sit down!" said Fred jovially.

Slate took a chair and sat to the side of the Principal's desk next to the window that looked through tall sycamore and pine trees toward the Baptist Church. The leaves were almost all off the trees now but the scene had its own stark beauty.

"Mr. Beckler," said Slate, "I feel like I wasn't able to put as much time into the Assistant Principal job as I should during the football season."

"Oh, I know what you mean," said Fred Beckler, "but we managed... and you did well!"

"I know, Mr. Beckler," said Slate, "but I'd like to bring in an Assistant Coach next year... it'll help the team, and it'll help me have a little more time to take some of the burdens off you as Assistant Principal."

"It makes sense," said Fred, "but I'm not so sure I can get Superintendent Hobbs to approve it."

"Can we try?" asked Slate. "I think we can bring in even more fans next year with a better team... and they have an Assistant Football Coach at most of the other High Schools."

"Sure," said Fred Beckler agreeably. "I'll ask Doctor Hobbs when I see him next week."

"Thank you, Sir," said Slate.

"You got anyone in mind for the job?"

Slate paused. He wondered how Fred Beckler would react to Shotgun Braun.

"Yes Sir," said Slate, "I want Cliff Braun... he's over at Great Bridge as an Assistant now."

"You mean Shotgun Braun?"

"Yes Sir. I played with him at Wilson and later at ECTC. No one understands football better. And he's got the fire in his gut to win!"

"I know, I know," muttered Fred. "He's also got a reputation as a trouble maker. Didn't he get into some kind of trouble at ECTC?"

"He... had a disagreement with an Army Major in the Veteran's program," said Slate, "and decided to transfer to Memphis State. He got a degree in physical education there... and a master's in education."

"Hmmm," mused Fred Beckler. "Is he still a troublemaker?"

"He's mellowed a lot," said Slate. "and... like I said, he really understands football... and how to win. With him, I think we can win the Group II District title... maybe even the State title."

"You think so, huh?"

"Yes Sir," said Slate. "We've got the raw talent in the boys around here... and with a District Title, we'll sell a lot of tickets... and make money for the team... and the band!"

"Yes... yes, we would," said Fred rubbing the ends of his moustache.

That was a good sign, thought Slate. Fred always rubbed his moustache when he was thinking about money.

"Yes sir," said Slate, "we might beat Suffolk! What do you think,

Sir?"

"What would Jack Ryder think about that... taking Shotgun away?"

"He's retiring this year," said Slate. "So it won't make much difference to him."

"I guess we can get Shotgun over here, Slate," said Fred. "See what you can do."

"Yes Sir," said Slate with a grin. "I'll talk to Shotgun. Please let me know if the Superintendent okays it."

"I will, Slate," said Fred. "I will."

****

The spring in Churchland was always beautiful. It was May of 1953 and the trees erupted in green and the dogwood flowered in white and pink splendor. Slate sat in his little office in the old traditional brick two story school building and looked out at Route 17 where it passed the school. He had a good second year as Head Football Coach, but he itched to do something different. He talked it over with Billie. She agreed to his plan. Having Cliff with him for the 1952 season meant a lot... but they hadn't beaten Suffolk.

Pete Sacker called the past month and asked for a recommendation to become Wilson's Head Football Coach. Slate sent his endorsement knowing that Pete would get it. He was not only a great football player, but also smart! It was ironic that Pete would be at Wilson while he and Cliff were at Churchland. The telephone rang. Slate picked it up.

"I'm free now, Slate," said Fred Beckler.

"I'll be right up," said Slate.

Slate ran up the stairs to the Principal's office and walked in.

"What is it, Slate?" asked the Principal.

"Sir... I want to promote Cliff Braun to head Football Coach and spend full time as Assistant Principal," blurted out Slate, felling relieved to get it out.

Fred Beckler looked surprised. "Why is that, Slate?"

"I want to compete for a Principal job, and I don't think I'll get serious consideration while I'm the Football Coach. I can be the Assistant Coach. But I need more time being Assistant Principal."

Fred scratched his bald head and paused. "You're probably right, Slate. Is Shotgun ready to be a Head Coach?"

"Yes Sir. He really is!"

"He won't get out of control, will he?"

"No Sir," said Slate. "I'll be there to help him."

"Okay, Slate," said Fred. "Let's give it a try!"

****

Slate caught Cliff as he exited the classroom where he taught the health class. Cliff had an amused expression on his face.

"What's so funny?" asked Slate as they walked toward the gymnasium.

"Aw… those guys give me a hard time when I get to the sex part of that class."

"Well, I'll vouch for you," smiled Slate. "You're well qualified to teach that part… but I don't know about those other parts."

"Yeah… I'm not so hot on the di-ges-tive system and that other stuff."

"You do okay," said Slate.

"It's hard to teach sex without saying it, ya know," said Cliff. "Ya gotta talk all aroun' it without saying it!"

"I think with that bunch, you don't have to say it," said Slate. "By the way, are you ready to be Head Coach?"

"What?"

"You heard me!"

They went into the gym, their voices echoing around the walls.

"Where're you going?" asked Cliff inquisitively.

"Nowhere," said Slate. "I'll be here as your Assistant… but I'll be spending more time as Assistant Principal."

"Why?"

"I'm applying for several jobs as Principal… and I need more experience on my resume."

"I'm ready," said Cliff, trying to hold back his eagerness.

"Okay, Coach," grinned Slate. "You got it!"

****

The 1953 football season was a good one. Cliff was an exceptionally tough coach, and Slate made progress toward his goal to be a Principal. The Truckers won eight games and lost one… to Suffolk! Fred Beckler was happy about the team. He bought new band uniforms. Slate had to spend a lot of time keeping Cliff's enthusiasm within bounds, but he was successful. Fall passed on to spring of 1954 and Slate became anxious to hear about the application he had submitted to be Principal at several local schools. He walked into his office as the telephone rang.

"Hello?"

"Slate?" asked Fred Beckler.

"Yes Sir."

"The Superintendent just called to tell me that Slate Phelps is the new Principal at Cradock Junior High School, starting in the fall," said the Principal. "Congratulations!"

"That's… that's great!" exclaimed Slate.

"Do you know anyone who can take over as Assistant Coach?"

"Well, yes sir," said Slate, "I do!"

"Well," said Fred, "go hire him!"

Slate hung up, picked up the telephone again and put through a call to Eddie Fearless in North Carolina.

****

Slate Phelps, Cliff Braun and Eddie Fearless sat in the little Coach's office near the gymnasium in the new Churchland High School. It was Friday morning before the Great Bridge Game, the undefeated, unscored upon 1954 season to be tested once again.

"I told Buddinger and Darby they'd better get the team together in a hurry," said Cliff worriedly. "Quester is a good player… but all that fighting… with Eberly and then Buddinger… has got the team thinking about other things… instead of the game."

"Did you lay down the law to Quester?" asked Eddie.

"Yeah, I did," said Shotgun with a frown. "I put the fear of God in him! I told him to stay away from that den of in-iq-ui-ty over there!"

"You never went to a place like that, did you, Cliff?" asked Slate with a sly grin. "Or had a fight like that?"

Cliff looked at Slate with a frown. "That was different!"

Slate and Eddie laughed. Cliff didn't see the humor.

"What's so funny?" asked Cliff, a cloud coming over his face.

"Quester's a good kid," said Slate. "Those guys gave him a lot of New Guy stuff… and he stood up to them."

"He'd better be ready to play some ball!" said Shotgun gruffly.

"You should like the guy, Cliff," said Slate. "He's a fighter!"

Shotgun grimaced. "He's a troublemaker!"

Slate grinned at hearing the word from Cliff. "Yeah," he said, "we don't know any troublemakers, do we Eddie?"

Cliff looked at Slate strangely, his eyebrow lifted. "Ya trying to give me a hard time, Slate?"

There was a knock on the door.

"Come on in," said Cliff gruffly.

Al Gollen walked into the room with a serious look on his face.

"We have a problem, Shotgun," said Al hesitatingly.

"What's that?" asked Shotgun.

Gollen put a piece of paper on Shotgun's desk. "This goes in the paper tomorrow," said Gollen.

Shotgun picked up the paper.

SHOTGUN ACCUSED OF ABUSING PLAYERS
WILL HE STAY AT CHURCHLAND?
By
Al Gollen

Coach Cliff "Shotgun" Braun has been accused of abusing his players at practice. Reportedly, he has injured several players with his rough and tough style of coaching. Further, the Coach is accused of using curses and abusive language unfit for a high school environment. Specifically, it is said that Shotgun hits the players and hits them hard, and that in one or more cases, he has broken a nose and bruised the players unnecessarily. Anonymous documents have been sent to Principal Frank Beckler at Churchland demanding the removal of Shotgun as Coach. Superintendent Hudson Hobbs has also received a copy. These documents allege that Coach Braun has a long history of a violent temper. According to the documents, Braun was ejected from Eastern Carolina Teacher's College for fighting and ungentlemanly conduct and should have never been awarded the Head Coach job.

Shotgun's face grew redder and redder as he read the paper. Slate and Eddie read it over Shotgun's shoulder.

"How'd you get these papers… documents or whatever you call 'em?" asked Cliff Braun.

"Someone mailed me a copy," said Gollen. "A typed copy without a name or signature!"

"What the heck, Al?" exclaimed Eddie. "You ain't gonna print this stuff… are ya? Can't ya see someone's trying to smear the Coach?"

"You went to ECTC, Eddie," said Al. "Is all this true?"

"You don't want to print that stuff, Al," said Eddie, an edge one did not normally hear in his easy North Carolina drawl.

"It's the news, Eddie," said Al apologetically.

"Who's doing this… this letter thing?" asked Cliff, standing up, his fists clenched at his side.

Al Gollen retreated to the door. "I don't know, Shotgun," he said. "Like I said… the documents were sent anonymously!"

****

Chapter Twelve
Great Bridge

The school bus bounced along Military Highway toward Great Bridge High School near the North Carolina line. The sound of a harmonica echoed through the bus. It played *High Noon* with a wailing sound that only Bob Porter could get from a harmonica. The words ran through Harry's mind almost automatically.

Oh don't forsake me now my Darling,
On this our wedding da-ay,
Oh don't forsake me now my Darling,
Wait, wait along…

He had to find a way to get back together with Paige. At first, he thought he could shake her out of his mind. After all, Churchland was full of pretty girls. But, for some reason, this one… this Paige Garnette wouldn't get out of his mind. But… had she forsaken him? Was she back again with that stupid guy from Suffolk?

"Knock off the music!" shouted Bucky. "How the hell do ya expect a guy to get some sleep?"

The harmonica stopped. There was a moment of silence. A deep voice came from the back of the bus. "I like it," said Big Jim.

There was a silent pause and then the harmonica started again. The haunting sounds of *Cry of the Wild Goose* echoed around the bus.

My heart knows what the wild goose knows,
And I must go where the wild goose goes,
Wild goose, brother goose, which is best?
A wanderin' fool or a heart at rest?

Harry wished his heart was at rest… but it was wandering. Maybe he was a fool! How could one girl make it hurt so much? The bus pulled into the parking lot at the stadium at Great Bridge High School. The team piled out and headed for the dressing room.

"Nice harmonica, Bob," said Harry as they climbed off the bus.
"Thanks!" said Bob. "I'm glad some of you like it."

****

The lights in Great Bridge Stadium were very bright. The grass on the field had begun to turn brown. The stands were full, and there was a lot of black and orange along with the green and gold. The Churchland Band traded marches with the Great Bridge Band as the teams ran onto the field amidst the roars of the fans. Jack Sanders sat on the bench while Larry Kidwell adjusted the tape wrapped around his chest and left shoulder. Harry stared across the field and wondered if the Great Bridge Coach, Bobby O'Briar, remembered coaching a skinny little kid on the vacant lot in Park View.

"Hey Jack," said Bubba. "What happens if we pull all that tape off?"

"I just fall apart, Bubba," said Jack with a straight face.

"That's what I thought," laughed Bubba, giving Larry a hand as he wrapped more tape around Jack's chest. "I think I'm gonna invest in a tape factory."

Allman and Karl went to center field for the coin toss and came back motioning that the Truckers were to receive.

"Get 'roun me here," shouted Coach Braun.

The team gathered around the Coach. "These guys are fast... but we can beat 'em," shouted the Coach, a look of intensity and anger on his square face. "Cut 'em off before they can get up to speed! Don't worry about them scoring on us! If you do your jobs, they won't score... but we're here to win... not worry about who scores and who doesn't! And watch that number forty-five... Sam Horseback! He's fast! Now get out there... I wanna see some in-tim-i-da-tion... some real hustle!"

The huddle broke with a roar and the first team ran out on to the field. Harry stared downfield at the green and gold clad Wildcats. They were big... but not as big as Smithfield. The Coach said they were fast. Harry wondered how fast they really were as the Wildcat kickoff sailed into the waiting arms of Karl Darby. Karl broke left and Harry blocked one Wildcat to the ground and ran on. A second man challenged him. He lunged at the player, but missed as the Wildcat brought Darby down on the Churchland thirty-five yard line.

The first play was the usual... Sanders off guard. Harry knew they were in trouble when they lined up. He knew Great Bridge would do something new... now he saw it. There were four linebackers, all lined up close behind a five man line. Sanders took the ball from Buddinger and crashed through a hole between Renny and Bob. Two linebackers met him just beyond the line of scrimmage and brought him down. Sanders gained two yards and came back to the huddle shaking his head.

"They got too many linebackers," said Harry. "We need to pass... there's only two guys in the backfield!"

"Coach says run," said Allman, gritting his teeth.

"Let's go off tackle," said Jack.

Sanders ran off tackle and met with the same result... two yards.

"We need to suck those linebackers inside and go outside," said Allman in the huddle. "You ready for an end around, Harry?"

"Sure," said Harry, clenching his fists.

"Fifty-eight end around, fake to the fullback... on set," said Allman. The team ran to the line of scrimmage.

"Get down!... Get set!"

The ball was snapped on the word "set". Harry faked a block on the man in front of him and then pulled back and ran to the right. Allman faked the ball to Jack up the middle and handed it to Harry in full stride. He heard the Wildcats yelling "end around" and turned on the speed, looking for the right place to cut up-field. He saw the outside linebacker charging at him and Sam Horseback running up. There was a small gap between them and he turned into it, taking a bead on the goal posts. He ran straight ahead and as the linebacker closed, he lowered his shoulder and bowled the player over. He turned back and was seeking his stride as the halfback hit him. He crashed to the ground at the fifty yard line. First down!

"Way to run, Harry," said Jack Sanders slapping Harry on the butt.

Allman called a time out and jogged to the sidelines. Harry watched him as he talked to Coach Braun. Braun's hat was jammed tightly down over his jug ears and he was gesticulating wildly to Allman. Allman ran back to the huddle.

"Okay, guys," said Allman, "here's the plan. We're gonna run Jack most of the time... but change the blocking assignments to get those extra linebackers!"

On the sideline, Shotgun was seething. "That's just what that Coach... Bobby O'Briar... is trying to get us to do," he shouted at Coach Fearless. "... make us pass... get us out of what's worked for us so far... we'll fool the sonsabitches!"

"If the guys can adapt to new blocking," said Eddie, "maybe it'll work."

"They're smart guys," said Shotgun. "They'll figure it out."

Back in the huddle, Bucky asked the question. "How're we gonna change our assignments?"

"Use your head, Bucky!" said Allman emphatically.

"Look... look, Allman," said Harry, "we can't just leave it up to everybody... someone has to say what assignments are changed... or we'll screw it up!"

Allman looked at Harry and winked. "Okay, Headhunter," he said. "You say you can see the whole field in your head... you call the blocking changes."

"Okay," said Harry. "I'll try. What do you want to run?"

"Let's try thirty-four... fullback through left tackle," said Allman.

The Xs and Os popped into Harry's head. "Big Jim... the tackle, take him in... me, take the end out... Terry, you lead Jack and take the inside linebacker in... Renny... you pull left and take the outside linebacker out. Jack, you just run through the halfback."

Allman looked at Harry in wonder. "That's gonna work?"

"I'm not used to pulling that much," said Renny.

"You can do it," said Harry. "Someone's got to get that outside linebacker. I'll give you some help if I can get the end out quickly."

"We'll try it!" said Allman. "Any questions?"

There was a brief silence. "Okay... on one!" said Allman.

They ran up to the line. Harry hoped the guys could remember the new assignments. Coach Braun had drilled them in their plays so many times that the regular blocking assignments had become almost automatic. The ball was snapped. Big Jim crushed the tackle. Harry shoved the end out. Terry ran directly at the inside linebacker and got in front of the boy. Renny pulled from his right guard position, followed Terry into the hole and hit the outside linebacker. Harry knocked the end down and hit the outside linebacker from the side, knocking him down. Jack crashed through the hole, ran down the field toward Sam Horseback and tried to run on but stumbled down. It was a first down!

Coach Braun turned to Eddie Fearless. "See? I told ya they'd figure it out!"

The first half ended with Churchland ahead twenty-eight to nothing.

****

The Great Bridge visitor's dressing room was small and crowded. The Churchland team sat on small benches and listened to Coach Braun.

"They tried to screw up what got us here with all those linebackers," shouted Coach Braun. "We didn't fall for it... we kept running! You guys figured out the blocking ya needed... and we kept jamming it down their throat. That's what we're gonna keep on doing!'"

"It was the Headhunter," said Bart. "He figured it out!"

Shotgun looked at Bart in surprise. Then he looked at Harry, a frown on his square face. "What do ya mean, Bart?"

"Harry," said Bart. "He looks over at the other team and calls the blocking assignments... don't know how he does it, but he does."

"Well... that's good! You guys just use your heads and figure out how to block," muttered Braun, not convinced that Harry could figure out the blocking assignments that quickly. "We got time now to talk about it now."

"Just let the Headhunter call the blocking assignments," said Bart.

"It's working, Coach," said Allman with an enthusiastic nod.

Coach Braun glared at Harry. "You can do this, Quester?" he said with a furrowed brow.

"Yes Sir," said Harry. "So far, I've been able to."

"Well, ya holler when ya can't!"

"Yes sir!"

"They're going to change something, for sure," said Eddie Fearless.

Coach Braun turned and looked at Eddie. "If I were the Great Bridge Coach, I'd keep the four linebackers … but drop one or two back every now and then to watch out for the run or pass."

"Yeah… they probably will do that," said Eddie. "What else Coach?"

"They've been laying back waiting for the run," said Coach Braun. "They may start trying to rush the holes… be ready for that!"

"Okay, Truckers," said Eddie. "You know what to watch out for. Now these guys haven't been able to run on us… so you can bet they'll try the pass. That quarterback, Freddie Foote… he'll probably try to pass to Horseback. Don't let him get in the open!"

"Yeah," grumbled Coach Braun, "and I know they want to at least score on us… so Coach O'Briar will try every trick play in the book. Look out for reverses, fake kicks, laterals and all that kinda thing!"

"You sure you're okay with calling blocking assignments, Quester?" asked Coach Braun, still in doubt.

"Yes Sir," said Harry. "But if they move around when we come to the line, it'll be harder."

"We haven't faced a defense that changes around," said Eddie Fearless. "But we may have to."

"You guys just sitting there listening… get off your butts and get mean!" shouted Coach Braun, his voice rising, his face turning red. "All this fancy talk will mean nothing if ya hit 'em so hard they don' wanna play no more! So I wanna see some real hitting! I don't care what the score is… a zillion to nothing! Grind 'em into the dirt! Now get out there!"

****

Harry pulled on his game face and began snorting and stomping the brown grass on the field. He knew the game face was on when he felt like a different person… not nice guy Harry… but angry Harry, a real mean guy. He felt the adrenalin flowing and thought about the satisfying thud of a good hit and watching the other guy fall to the ground in pain. Bud Darby kicked a long end over end kick to the Great Bridge Wildcats to open the second half. A Wildcat fielded it and started to run to the left. Number Forty-five ran behind him headed right. The ball was handed off to Number Forty-five and he sprinted toward the right sideline at full speed. Harry saw the whole play develop, almost as though looking down at it from above. He held his ground when the back started left and watched Sam Horseback take the ball. He charged toward the sprinting halfback, fully prepared for the fake he knew was coming. He disciplined his mind to not take the first juke. Horseback came at him, juked left and then right. Harry stayed with him. Forty-five tried to stiff arm Harry, but Harry crashed through the stiff arm and hit the fast halfback with a blow that could be heard in the stands. He wrapped his arms around Horseback and drove him backwards until he fell on top of him, his helmet digging into the halfback's belly at the Wildcat twenty-five yard line. He heard a whoosh as Horseback's breath came out in a rush.

Harry got to his feet and heard the chant from the fans on the Churchland side. "Headhunter! Headhunter! Headhunter!"

Harry looked own at Sam Horseback who was struggling to regain his breath and offered him a hand. Forty-five took it reluctantly and Harry hauled him up.

"Thanks," said Sam Horseback.

"Don't come my way again, Horseback!" said Harry menacingly. "I'm gonna knock the crap outa ya every time!"

Horseback looked at Harry strangely. "Screw you, Headhunter!"

Number Forty-five turned his back and ran to the huddle. The first play run by the Wildcats was an attempted pass. Harry saw the quarterback fade back. He broke through the end and rushed the passer, but was beaten there by Big Jim. Jim picked the quarterback up by the legs and dropped him to the ground.

Harry stood over the fallen Wildcat, his face contorted into a fierce mask. "Don't you try any more passes, Freddie! We got your number!"

"Yeah!" snorted Big Jim.

The Wildcats ran two running plays that produced no yardage and lined up to punt. The ball was snapped to the punter. Harry held back. He thought he knew what was coming. The punter pretended to kick but held on to the ball and heaved it downfield toward a streaking Number Forty-five. The ball was almost in Horseback's hands when Allman Buddinger flew at him and crashed him to the ground. A yellow flag flew right after him. The referee gave the signal for pass interference. Coach Braun did a hotfoot dance on the sideline and threw his pork pie hat to the ground. He got a running start and jumped into the air, landing on the forlorn hat. He stomped it several times then stuck his jutting jaw out onto the field.

"You refs are blind as bats!" shouted Coach Braun. "He had the ball when he was hit! How can that be interference? That's a cotton pickin' fumble!"

Coach Braun started out toward the middle of the field, but was restrained by Coach Fearless, who began talking earnestly to him. Coach Braun acquiesced to only stomping on his hat some more. Suddenly, the Wildcats had a first down on the Churchland forty.

"Headhunter! Headhunter!" chanted the Churchland fans.

"Zee!" shouted Coach Braun. "Get in there at left end! Tell Quester to move to middle linebacker and play the Headhunter defense! Pull Dickson out!"

Tony jumped to his feet, and put on his helmet. "I got it, Coach!" he shouted.

Tony ran in and Renny Dickson came out.

"Go for the Headhunter defense, Harry," said Tony patting Harry on the butt.

Harry shifted to middle linebacker. "You ready for some headhunting, Bucky?" he asked.

Bucky turned a dirt smeared face to Harry. "Damn right! Let's do some headhunting!"

"Okay," said Harry. "Move that center to the right. I'm coming by you."

"I got it," said Bucky in a fierce tone.

The Wildcats came to the line looking cocky. Freddie Foote began to bark signals. Harry edged forward. The ball was snapped. Bucky cracked into the Wildcat center, grappled with him and shoved him back and to the right. Harry crashed through the line and grabbed the quarterback just as he attempted to lateral the ball to Sam Horseback. The ball flew crazily through the air. Sam reached back and tried to field the wobbling ball with one hand. Harry crashed into him and the ball fell to the ground. Harry turned to recover the fumble just as Bucky scooped up the ball and started running. Horseback pursued Bucky and overtook him quickly. Harry flew through the air and knocked Horseback off balance and away from Bucky. Harry fell to the ground and looked up in time to see Bart Whitely throw the block that let Bucky into the Wildcat end zone. Bucky jumped into the air in glee. Harry got up and ran to him, giving the thumbs up signal. He hit Bucky on the chest with a Trucker salute.

"Way to run, Bucky!" shouted Harry.

"Hey… just like a glory boy halfback… right?" shouted Bucky.

"You'll be right up front in Gollen's column!" shouted Bart excitedly.

The extra point made it thirty-five to nothing. The play took the wind out of the Wildcat sails. After that, Jolting Jack Sanders ran amuck.

Toward the end of the game, Coach Braun put in some of the second string. Bubba, Buster, Tony and Matt got to play a whole quarter. Rob Sonda played quarterback. Hero got in and scored a touchdown. The final score was Churchland sixty, Great Bridge nothing.

****

Harry ate breakfast hurriedly early Saturday morning. He was going dove hunting with Bubba, Buster, Tony and Allman. Bubba would be by to get him in a few minutes. The sports page had big headlines.

GREAT BRIDGE FAILS TO SCORE ON CHURCHLAND
TRUCKERS WIN 60-0
By
Al Gollen

The Great Bridge Wildcats gave it a valiant effort. On a fake punt early in the second half, Great Bridge got to the trucker forty and it seemed the momentum had shifted to the Wildcats. Coach Shotgun Braun, however, was having none of it, and he put in his Headhunter defense. Harry Quester broke through the Wildcat line on the next play and caused Great Bridge to fumble. Guard Bucky Allison picked up the fumble and ran it sixty yards for a touchdown, with blocks from Quester and tackle Bart Whitely. Coach Eddie Fearless said "I didn't know ol' Bucky could run like that!"

Jolting Jack Sanders scored thirty-five points. Karl Darby and Terry Moddy each scored a touchdown. Churchland showed an uncanny ability to execute its plays in the face of defensive change-ups introduced by Great Bridge. The Great Bridge Coach, Bobby O'Briar, was disappointed that the change-up fifty four defense didn't work well on the Truckers. He also said he didn't like the way the Truckers ran up the score. Coach Shotgun Braun responded by saying "Heck... we couldn't help it. Everybody we played scored on 'em!"

****

Bubba drove Ol' Bessie along the stone and gravel streets of Green Acres. Harry sat in the front passenger seat. Tony and Buster were in the back. They went by to pick up Allman, but he wasn't there. His Mother said that he would meet them later. They went on without him, out to Route 17 and into the country. They drove along a dusty dirt road near the Nansemond River north of Churchland past corn fields that had been harvested. The brown stalks lay on the ground with the dried ears of corn that the harvester had missed. Flocks of mourning doves flew gracefully in and out of the fields eating the leftover corn. Harry watched their unique wing movements with fascination. Their wings were in perfect harmony with their bodies and their flight. It was one of those brisk, sunny fall days that made the blood run warm and the spirits high. The leaves on the trees were spectacular; orange, yellow and red against a background of green pine and cedar. The pungent smell of rotting corn stalks filled the air. Most of the fields had been hunted out, but Bubba had persuaded Harry to hunt the fields on old Mr. Hargood's land.

"Last year, Old Mr. Hargood caught us hunting his land and chased us off," said Bubba.

"That sounds great," said Tony sarcastically.

"Yeah," smiled Buster, "... got his shotgun after us!"

"You sure you want to go hunting, Bubba?" asked Harry.

"Ah hell," said Bubba, "Hargood is just a big bag of wind. Everybody hunts around here! Look at all those doves out there!"

They approached the Hargood land with caution. Bubba looked around, but no one was to be seen. He parked the Dodge beside the road. They got out and walked about a half mile to a field where the birds were feeding on the remains of the harvested corn. They sat in the brush at the edge of the field. On the other side of the field about a quarter mile away was the Hargood farm house. Harry cradled his Grandfather's old single barrel twelve gauge shotgun. Bubba and Tony both had double barreled shotguns. Buster had a new pump shotgun. Bubba also had a twenty-two caliber pump rifle.

"What's the rifle for?" asked Harry.

"Just get ready to shoot," said Bubba. "I'll go over there and fire the twenty-two into the field to flush the birds toward ya... then ya pick 'em off."

"I've never done this before," said Harry.

"Me neither," said Tony.

"Just lead 'em a little and... bang! Squeeze it off!" grinned Buster adjusting the floppy Marine issue hat on his oversized head. "Just don't shoot me!"

"Where'd ya get that ugly hat, Buster?" asked Bubba.

"Hey!' exclaimed Buster. "That's my lucky huntin' hat... my Ol' Man got it from some Marines he knows!"

Bubba grabbed the hat from Buster's head and threw it high in the air over the corn field. He raised his shotgun and fired. The hat jerked in the air as the bird shot ripped through it. Buster jumped on Bubba and wrestled him to the ground.

"That was a good hat, Bubba, ya sonofabitch!" shouted Buster.

Bubba pushed Buster away and struggled to his feet. "I was only showing Harry and Tony how to shoot a dove!" said Bubba with a chortle.

Buster stalked off into the corn field and returned wearing a somewhat tattered hat and a triumphal smile. He nestled down into the brush with the others. "I hope you guys know how to shoot, now!"

"How long we gotta wait?" whispered Tony.

"We flushed the birds when we shot Buster's hat," said Bubba with authority. "We gotta wait another twenty minutes or so for 'em to fly back in and settle down."

"Okay," said Tony.

"I'm gonna move down here a ways and set up to flush 'em," said Bubba.

Bubba got up, bent low and walked silently off into the multicolored tree line. Harry, Tony and Buster crouched in the brush next to the field.

"That was a great game last night," whispered Tony. "I even got to play!"

"Yeah," said Buster in his best narrative baritone voice. "Me too. I put the hurt on that guy in front a' me. He was pleading for me to go easy on him!"

"Really?" asked Tony.

"Yeah," said Buster with feigned modesty, "and he weighed about three hundred pounds… tried to punch me out, but I fixed his ass!"

"You both did great!" whispered Harry with a smile.

"Harry… you really had your game face on," said Tony admiringly.

"Yeah," said Harry. "I did. I had a hard time taking it off!"

"Whatta ya mean?"

"I got pissed at the waiter when we went to Nick's to get pizza after the game," said Harry seriously. "I'm not normally like that!"

They waited patiently in the brush and watched as the birds came back to feed. There was the crack of Bubba's twenty-two rifle. The birds flushed. Harry, Tony and Buster raised their 12 gauge shotguns and fired. One bird fluttered down. They heard the distant report of a shotgun. Harry stared across the field trying to see who had fired the shot. Suddenly, there was a burning pain near his neck as a 12 gauge shotgun pellet penetrated. He grabbed his neck and stumbled to one knee. He could feel the gush of blood and see Tony running to him. Tony ripped off his shirt and stemmed the flow of blood with his hand. Then, with a strength that did not match his wiry frame, Tony picked Harry up and carried him out to the road and toward the Hargood farm house. Bubba caught up to them.

"What happened?" asked Bubba in alarm.

"Harry got hit in the neck," shouted Buster, fear in his voice.

"Someone was shooting from the other side of the field," panted Tony.

Bubba looked up and saw the Red Rooster bumping along beside the field. Allman was in it, his shotgun protruding above the windshield. The jeep drove up to them and stopped.

"What's going on?" shouted Allman.

"Harry's been hit!" shouted Bubba.

Allman jumped from the jeep, his face knotted in alarm. They helped Harry to the side of the jeep. Tony looked at the wound.

"It's just above his collarbone on the left side," said Tony. "It's bleeding, but not too bad."

Bubba ripped off his shirt. "Hold that shirt to it to keep it from bleeding more," said Bubba, "How do ya feel Harry?"

The initial shock of being hit had faded. Harry felt better. "I'm okay," he said. "Someone was firing across the field… not up at the birds!"

"Ya think so?" asked Buster.

"It sounded like it," said Harry.

"We can take him to Old Mr. Hargood's house," said Bubba.

"Naw," said Allman quickly, "that sonofagun probably shot him! Put him in the jeep and we'll go down to Maryview Hospital."

"I'm alright!" exclaimed Harry getting to his feet, "I'm okay… I can walk!"

"You're going to the hospital to make sure," said Tony. "No boy scout first aid for this!"

Harry climbed into the back of the jeep. Tony sat with him and pressed the shirt against the wound. Bubba ran to Ol' Bessie and got in. Allman drove the jeep at breakneck speed along the dirt roads, followed by Ol' Bessie. Harry sat quietly, holding on. He saw a plume of dust rising from a dirt road across the cornfield from them.

"Who's that over there?" asked Harry.

Buster looked at the dust plume. "It's a Studebaker," he said, "and it's hauling ass!"

"Is it Calcione's Studebaker?" asked Harry staring at the car with the bullet nose.

"It's red," said Allman. "Only one I know drives a red Studebaker is Johnny Calcione."

"I wonder where that sonofabitch is going in such a hurry!" exclaimed Tony.

"Or what he's running from," said Allman reflectively.

"Maybe he's the one that shot Harry!" exclaimed Tony.

"Hood revenge?" speculated Harry. "Would he really do that?"

They turned onto the two lane tarback road that led to Route 17 with screeching wheels.

"Slow down, Allman," said Harry as they bumped along. "You'll kill us all before we get to the hospital!"

Harry was irritated that this freak shotgun pellet had interrupted his life. He didn't want any Doctor telling him not to play football. Not now! He wondered who had been hunting on the other side of the field.

"I'm really okay," said Harry. "I don't need to go to any hospital!"

"Shut up, Harry," said Tony with authority. "You're going to the hospital!"

Bubba, Tony and Allman went to the emergency room and took Harry inside. They took him immediately to an examining room. They all went with him. A Doctor in a white gown showed up.

"I'm Doctor Goldstein," said the Doctor, a middle aged man with saggy jowls. "What happened?"

"Shotgun pellet," said Tony pointing to the wound. "Right there!"

The Doctor laid Harry down on a table and rubbed the wound with antiseptic and a numbing agent. He took out a long silver set of tweezers and a probe and began probing the wound. Harry grimaced and held his breath.

"You mean that one?" asked the Doctor holding the tweezers up in the air. They contained a small round, gray shotgun pellet.

"Yes Sir," said Tony, feeling woozy.

"Probably a spent shot coming down," said Doctor Goldstein. "The pellet grazed your collarbone and lodged in the muscle. It looks like birdshot... not too big."

"Are ya gonna have to operate?" asked Allman anxiously.

"No," said Doctor Goldstein. "That's it. The Nurse will come and give... what's your name?"

"Harry Quester," said Harry weakly.

"She'll give Harry some antibiotic and tetanus and treat the wound," said the Doctor. "We'll keep you here overnight ... just to avoid shock or anything... then you should be good to go!"

"Whew!" said Allman. "That was a scare. We can't afford to lose Harry."

"I know you, Allman Buddinger," said the Doctor staring at Allman. "Good game last night, Ball Fox!"

"Thanks, Doc."

"Are you Headhunter Harry Quester?" asked the Doc.

"Yes Sir!"

"Hell of a game!" said the Doc. "We go to them all, you know."

"Thank you Sir," said Harry. "And thanks for coming to the games."

"Wouldn't miss 'em," said the Doctor. "Now how did this happen?"

"Hunting accident, Doc," said Buster. "That's all."

"Well, come with me," said Doctor Goldstein. "There'll be some paperwork."

Bubba, Tony, Buster and Allman went with Doctor Goldstein. Harry was wheeled away to a room where a middle aged nurse took great joy in making him put on a hospital gown. She dressed the wound and stabbed him in the butt with a tetanus shot.

"Now you just let me know if there's anything you need, Harry," said the Nurse with a knowing smile. "I'll be just right down the hall."

****

Helen Quester came to visit Harry with her sister Catherine that evening. Ike Quester was at sea. Harry sat up dutifully in the bed.
"Are you alright, Harry?" asked Helen worriedly.
"Yes, Mother," said Harry. "I'm fine."
"Who in the world shot you?" asked Catherine.
"We don't know," said Harry. "It was a spent shot fired from the other side of the field."
"I guess it was Old Man Hargood," said Catherine. "I've told Bubba a hundred times not to hunt out there!"
"That's where the good fields are," grinned Harry.
"Are you sure you feel alright, Harry?" asked Helen.
"Yes Maam," said Harry, "I'm okay."
"I'm glad your father isn't here," said Helen worriedly. "He'd probably get his rifle and go hunting for this… Mr. Hargood."
"Just forget it, Mother," said Harry. "It could've even been from our own shells… it was just a freak accident."
"When will you be home, Harry?" asked Helen.
"They said the Doctor will check me after lunch tomorrow," said Harry. "If everything's okay, I'll be home in the afternoon."
"Bubba's going to pick you up, Harry," said Catherine.

****

Harry couldn't sleep that night. Was it really Mr. Hargood that shot at him? Or Calcione? Or… he didn't want to think about it… was it one of Allman's pranks… shooting into the air from the other side of the field… or was it Allman aiming at a bird? It could have been anyone from the Nansemond area out hunting doves. Johnny assuredly had been there with his red Studebaker. Bubba said he didn't shoot… the birds were flying away from him. So, who was it? Harry decided he didn't want to know… at least for now. There were more important things… like the upcoming games with Princess Anne, and then Suffolk!

Harry woke the next morning at seven o'clock. The Nurse took his temperature while an attendant wheeled in a tray of scrambled eggs and bacon. There was a small pot of coffee, a plate of toast and some fruit.

"Looks like you're normal, Harry," said the Nurse.

"Good!" said Harry. "I've got football practice Monday."

"You just take it easy, young man," said the Nurse.

The Nurse left. Harry ate his breakfast hungrily and was drinking his coffee when Bubba came in with Coach Braun and Allman.

"How ya doing, Harry?" asked Coach Braun, glancing around at the mysterious trappings of a hospital room. He had been in them before and didn't like being in another one. It reminded him of his dislocated shoulder at Memphis State. Memphis State reminded him of being expelled from ECTC... and now someone was trying to use that against him. God, he thought, don't do this to me now... right when I'm about to be somebody... somebody more than a kid trying to play football... a Coach with a championship team!! It didn't happen to just anyone. And now, this thing with Quester!

"I'm ready to go, Coach," said Harry.

"Doctor say it was okay to practice?" asked Allman.

"He said to take it easy for a few days," said Harry. "But I'll be out there... and ready for Princess Anne Friday night."

"That's good," said Coach Braun in a hoarse voice. "We need ya out there, Harry... not smelling daisies in dome darn hospital!"

That made Harry feel really good. He smiled. "Thanks for that, Coach!"

"And stay away from them... shotguns!" said the Coach with one of his rare smiles. "Officer Spearman is gonna look into all this."

"He doesn't have to," said Harry worriedly. "It was just an accident!"

"We'll see ya later, Harry," said Allman with a wink "We got a little surprise out here for ya!"

"What..." began Harry, but Allman and the Coach were out the door before he could finish.

The door burst open and Georgia Blake and all the Churchland Cheerleaders crowded into the room in their white skirts and jerseys with the big black and orange Cs.

"Gimme an H!" shouted Georgia jumping high, her skirt swirling above white panties.

"H!" came the response.

"Gimme a Q!" shouted Georgia.

"Q!"

"Harry Quester Rah Rah Rah! The Headhunter!!"

Harry looked at them in embarrassment, not knowing what to say.

"Come on, Harry," said Georgia with a radiant smile. "Stand up and model your hospital gown for us!"

The Cheerleaders all giggled and smiled. Harry felt suddenly vulnerable at the thought of his skimpy, open backed gown and pulled the sheets up around himself protectively.

"Awww… come on Harry," pleaded Georgia mischievously.

"Wait'll I get outa here, Georgia, then you can model something for me," said Harry self consciously. "But I appreciate you girls coming over here… I really do!"

"Okay, Harry," said Georgia with a wink of her eye. "We'll see you later… out on the field. But we have another surprise for you!"

"I don't know if I can stand another one!" exclaimed Harry.

"Well, stand by, Harry!" shouted Georgia as she and the other Cheerleaders ran out the door.

Harry sat in the bed not knowing what to expect. Knowing Allman and Georgia, it could be anything… anything! There was a quiet knock on the door.

"Come on in," said Harry.

Paige Garnette peeked into the room. "Is it okay if I come in, Harry?" she asked in her soft, husky voice.

"Golly!" exclaimed Harry in surprise. "Sure… come on in, Paige."

Paige walked into the room, her warm brown eyes fixed on Harry. She wore a stylish light pink suit with a frilly white blouse. She was always meticulously dressed in the latest fashion. Her brown pony tail was held back with a pink bow. Harry's heart jumped at the sight of her.

"Sit down, Paige," said Harry, searching for words.

She sat in a straight backed chair close to the bed. Harry felt self conscious with only the sheet and the flimsy hospital gown between him and Paige.

"I'm sorry you got hurt," said Paige looking into his eyes.

"I'll be okay," said Harry self consciously. "I should be out of here by this afternoon."

"That's wonderful," said Paige. "You played a really great game Friday night."

"You were there?"

"Yes," said Paige. "I went with some girl friends."

"I thought you might be going to the Suffolk games," said Harry bashfully.

"Georgia apologized for that night at the sock hop," said Paige. "And I… well, I've been thinking a lot…"

"About what?"

"About… you. I don't want to go back with Duane."

Harry's heart beat faster. "You mean I can ask you for another date?"

"Sure," smiled Paige. "And I'm sorry I left you that night… at the sock hop. I don't know what I was thinking."

"Well, how about Pizza after the Princess Anne game?"

"Sounds great," said Paige with a relieved smile. "But there's something else I need to tell you."

"What's that?" asked Harry.

"Duane has a Churchland Playbook," said Paige reluctantly.

"A Playbook… a Football Playbook?"

"Yes," said Paige. "Duane was bragging about it… he said it was your Playbook!"

"Mine?" asked Harry, astounded. "How'd he get it?"

"I don't know," said Paige. "I asked him about it. He just laughed and said that there are people who don't like Shotgun… at all. He said you were one of them… because the Coach broke your nose."

"He's a liar!" exclaimed Harry. "Coach Braun and I manage to get along… even if he did break my nose!"

"Duane is telling everybody that you gave the book to him," said Paige. "To get even with Shotgun!"

"That's a buncha baloney!"

"I told Duane that he must wrong," said Paige, "because I know you wouldn't do that!"

"That…."

"I know," said Paige. "That sonofabitch, that's what I called him."

"You did?"

"Yes," said Paige. "And I told him not to call me."

"Can I call you?" asked Harry.

Paige reached across the sheet and took Harry's hand. Her hand was warm and she squeezed his hand ever so slightly. Electric currents ran up Harry's arm and through his body. He sat up and adjusted the sheet over his body. He squeezed her hand.

"Please call me real soon, Harry," said Paige softly.

Paige leaned over and kissed Harry lightly on the lips. The electric currents became high voltage charges. It was all Harry could do to stay in the bed.

****

With his Father at sea, Harry had the 1949 Chevrolet to himself. He was in the car on the way to school on Monday morning. He had a small bandage on his neck and shoulder. He had to go back for a check up on Tuesday before the Doctor would let him practice. His strength had come back. He flipped the radio on. Rocky Rawls' voice filled the car.

"Well," said Rocky on the radio, "everyone is wondering about Shotgun Braun and the Truckers. As I'm sure you heard, an anonymous letter has been submitted accusing Shotgun of being too rough on his players… someone wants to remove Shotgun as Football Coach. They've dug up some old stuff about him being expelled from ECTC for fighting. And worse! Shotgun even curses at the players! Oh me oh my! Shotgun! Shotgun! Shame on naughty you! The world is aghast to find that Shotgun Braun has uttered a curse word! Come on, Gang! What's this all about? Who dreamed this stuff up? Anyway, let's root for the Truckers! They have some big games coming up… and they don't need a distraction like this! Now for some music!" Billy Ward and the Dominoes hit the airways:

Look a here girls I'm telling you now,
They call me "Lovin' Dan",
I rock 'em, roll 'em all night long,
I'm a sixty-minute man!

What was going on? It was bad enough that he was going to have to tell the Coaches about the Playbook. Now this!

****

Coach Braun, Coach Fearless and Coach Phelps sat in folding metal chairs in the gymnasium, their voices echoing across the hardwood floors. Coach Braun looked at the Monday morning newspaper article.

"Well, he did it," said Braun.

SHOTGUN ACCUSED OF ABUSING PLAYERS
WILL HE STAY AT CHURCHLAND?
By
Al Gollen

Coach Cliff "Shotgun" Braun has been accused of abusing his players at practice. Reportedly, he has injured several players with his rough and tough style of coaching. Further, the Coach is accused of using curses and abusive language unfit for a high school environment. Specifically, it is said that Shotgun hits the players and hits them hard, and that in at least one case this year, he broke a nose. It is said that last year he broke several player's noses and beat up other players under the guise of "showing them how to block". Anonymous documents have been received by the Principal at Churchland demanding the removal of Shotgun as Coach. The documents allege that Coach Braun has a long history of a violent temper. According to these documents, Braun was ejected from Eastern Carolina Teacher's College for fighting and ungentlemanly conduct, credentials that do not support his appointment as a Head

Coach. The documents arrived in the office of Churchland Principal Fred Beckler on Friday, the day of the Great Bridge game.

When contacted, Shotgun had nothing to say. Principal Beckler said that he would discuss it with the Superintendent. School Superintendent Hudson Hobbs said that if the situation merited it, there would be a hearing. In the meantime, Shotgun Braun continues to coach the Truckers.

Pistol Pete Sacker, the Coach at Wilson, who has known Shotgun a long time, said that Shotgun is a tough Coach, but he has always known him to be fair and to have the best interests of the players at heart. Coach Fatso Hathaway at Suffolk says that the documents do not surprise him at all, that Shotgun has always had a terrible temper and engaged in fights throughout his childhood, at Wilson High School and later on in College. Fatso says he personally had to fight Shotgun in self defense when growing up in Prentiss Park. When asked who won, he said the same one who'll win their upcoming game. Fatso says his Red Raiders will beat Churchland badly whether Shotgun is there or not!

Coach Braun got up and paced up and down the hardwood floors, a grim look on his face.

"Come on," said Slate. "Al has agreed to meet us at Rodman's Barbecue for lunch… to discuss this whole thing further."

"I wish I knew who sent this cotton pickin' letter!" exclaimed Shotgun, his eyes fierce.

"What're you going to do, Cliff?" asked Slate wryly. "Beat them up?"

****

The Coaches pulled into the parking lot at Rodman's Barbecue on High Street near The Circle Restaurant. It was a one story white shingle building. The lot was nearly full. They went inside. The restaurant was filled with small tables on stainless steel legs with red porcelain tops, and matching chairs. Waitresses in white dresses shuttled back and forth to the tables with steaming plates of barbecue, Smithfield ham, beans and slaw. Slate saw Al Gollen sitting at a table with Pete Sacker and Fatso Hathaway, sipping coffee. All eyes turned on them as they walked in.

"What are those guys doing here?" asked Coach Braun, momentarily taken aback.

"I don't know," said Slate.

"Gollen has pulled a fast one," whispered Eddie Fearless.

They paused and surveyed the situation.

"Come on," said Slate. "We need to go sit with them."

They walked toward the table where Gollen and the Coaches sat. Gollen and Sacker stood up. Fatso remained seated, munching indifferently on a bag of potato chips.

"Good to see you, Shotgun, Slate… Eddie," said Gollen.

Coaches Braun, Fearless and Phelps shook hands with Al Gollen and Pete Sacker.

"Good to see ya, Pete," said Braun. "Ya got a great team this year!"

"Good to see you, Shotgun," said Pete, clasping Cliff's hand warmly. "You're doing pretty well too!"

Cliff turned to Hathaway. Fatso was as big as he always had been, though taller. He had a ponderous gut and oily, greasy hair, slicked back on his head. Braun grinned, raised his left fist, drew back his right hand and faked a punch at Fatso, ducking his head like a boxer and putting the famous bulldog scowl on his face. Fatso flinched and drew back instinctively, the chair nearly tipping over. Braun dropped his hands and laughed hoarsely. A suppressed chuckle ran around the restaurant.

"Got ya that time, Fatso!" exclaimed Cliff triumphantly.

Fatso recovered and adjusted his chair, which creaked and complained at the load. "I don't know why I'm here with the likes of you, Shotgun," moaned Fatso angrily.

"You're here 'cause I asked y'all to come… remember?" said Gollen. "Let's sit down!"

They all sat down. A waitress in a bulging white dress came to the table. "What'll y'all have?" she grinned over a double chin.

"More coffee and your special barbecue all around," said Gollen.

The waitress scribbled something on her pad and waddled away.

"That your girl, Fatso?" asked Cliff, lifting an eyebrow.

"Just shut up, Shotgun," growled Fatso irritably.

"Come on, guys," said Al. "We know about someone trying to smear Shotgun. I want you guys to support him in whatever hearings follow."

"I'll support you, Shotgun," said Pete Sacker seriously. "But… you did get in a lotta fights… and they did expel you from ECTC… we can't deny all that."

"I don't expect you to, Pete," said Braun in a rough voice. "I am what I am… and if that ain't good enough for people, they can find another Coach!"

"We all know that to build a football team, you have to be tough on the players!" said Pete. "I like to think I'm pretty tough, too."

"Ya had some good teachers, Pete," said Slate.

"I know that, Slate," said Pete. "And I appreciate everything!"

"We got the toughest bunch of guys I've seen for a long time," said Cliff proudly. "They want every yard of every game… real bad!"

"We beat Petersburg Friday night," said Pete, "and we're still undefeated… I'd say my guys are as tough or tougher… and against

Group I teams!"

"You're right, Pete," said Slate. "You've got a really super team."

"And we're gonna play ya!" growled Shotgun, "... and beat ya."

Pete Sacker smiled and nodded. "We'll see about that, Shotgun!"

"Let's get through all this," said Gollen, "and I'll do some stuff about Churchland and Wilson having a post season game."

"If we're both undefeated," said Pete eagerly, "we can sell it to the Superintendent, and the profits go to something he needs."

"We'll be undefeated," growled Braun.

"Like hell ya will," said Fatso, bits of potato chips spattering the table in front of him.

Cliff glowered at Fatso. Slate put a restraining hand on the Coach's arm. "Ignore him, Cliff," said Slate. "He's trying to get you mad!"

"The point is, you Coaches have to stand together on these things," said Gollen, looking warily at Shotgun and Fatso. "I'd like to do a piece about what it takes to build a good team... with comments from all of you about coaching styles and the like... and something in it about Coaches standing together. Can we do that?"

"It's not for me," said Fatso grumpily, slurping his coffee.

"I thought you agreed to it, Fatso," said Al Gollen, surprised.

"I agreed to come here," said Fatso watching hungrily as the waitress brought their lunch. "That's all!"

The waitress put more coffee and their lunches in front of them. Fatso dug into his, stuffing great gobs of barbecue into his mouth. Grease ran down his chin. Coach Braun stared intensely at Fatso, got up and shoved his chair back with a scraping noise that turned all eyes in the restaurant on him.

"I ain't eating with that fat, sloppy sonofabitch!" exclaimed Coach Braun in a loud voice. He walked toward the doorway with a swagger. Coach Fearless followed.

"Nice try, Al," said Slate. He got up and followed Coach Fearless.

"Go get your girls ready to get beat, Shotgun!" said Fatso, his mouth full of sugary red beans.

Coach Braun turned and started to say something but Eddie Fearless pushed him out the door.

"I'll be going, Al," said Pete Sacker, pushing aside his plate and standing up.

"You get ready to get beat, too, Sacker!" said Fatso between gulps of slaw. "We get to play you fancy Group I guys, ya know!"

"We'll see you in November, Fatso!" said Pete, anger in his voice.

****

Chapter Thirteen
Princess Anne

Harry reported to the gymnasium for the last period Monday. He would have to watch out at practice today... if he did what the Doctor said to do. He saw Coach Fearless in the Coach's office. He went and knocked.

"Come on in," drawled Eddie.

Harry went in. "Coach, I got something to tell you."

"Is it about the Playbook?" asked Eddie.

"Yes Sir," said Harry, surprised.

"Well, it's all over school that you gave a Playbook to that Duane Starr guy at Suffolk... you know?"

"It is?" asked Harry, astounded. "It's a lie. The book is missing from my locker... but I don't know who took it!"

"The story going around is that you planned all this stuff about Coach Braun... that you and your parents sent the letter... and you gave Suffolk the Playbook to get even with Coach Braun for breaking your nose," said Eddie.

Harry looked astounded. "Sir, you know that's wrong. I wouldn't do that!"

"Did Coach Braun really break your nose?" asked Eddie.

"Yes Sir," said Harry, "I think he did. But Bubba snapped it back in place and I went on."

"Have you complained that Coach Braun treated people too rough?" asked Fearless with a serious look.

Harry paused and thought. "I guess I have... back in the summer. I wasn't used to it... the way he hit people... the way he kicked people around... like Benny Norwood... I tried to stop him before it got out of hand."

"I remember the incident with Benny, Harry," said Fearless. "You were right. Coach Phelps and I have to sorta... tone Coach Braun down from time to time. He has a great football mind... but you know how he gets... sometimes."

"Coach is rough," admitted Harry, "but I got used to it."

"That's what you're gonna say at the hearing?"

"I wasn't planning to say anything at any hearing, Coach," said Harry.

"Well, you may have to, Harry," said Coach Fearless dejectedly.

"Does Coach Braun think I'm behind all that?"

"I don't know, Harry... what he thinks," said Coach Fearless. "But I know it isn't like you."

"Thanks, Coach," said Harry worriedly.

"And I'll say so," said Fearless, "before this stuff gets outa hand!"

"Thanks, Coach."

"When are you gonna be able to practice, Harry?"

"The Doctor says Wednesday, Coach," said Harry. "But I'm working out at home to stay ready!"

"What the heck happened out there?" asked Fearless skeptically. "I heard some story about you guys being ambushed by a buncha poachers... and one of 'em shooting Buster's hat off before the next one shot you! Supposedly, Buster winged one of 'em!"

Harry shook his head in exasperation. "I think that's just one a' Buster's stories, Coach. It was a freak accident... that's all."

"Oh... Buster again!" said Fearless with a wry grin. "That explains it."

"Yes Sir."

"Don't ya bust somethin' loose, Harry," drawled Fearless. "We're gonna need ya!"

****

Tuesday morning Coach Braun and Coach Fearless went to the door of the gymnasium dressing room.

"We gotta be up in the Principal's office at nine o'clock, Coach," said Eddie.

"I know... I know," said Coach Braun in disgust. "I guess he's gonna read me the riot act!"

They unlocked the door to the dressing room, opened it and were greeted by wall to wall peanut husks six feet high. Dust and residue from the husks floated around the room as the wall of shells rolled over them.

"What's all this stuff!" exploded Coach Braun, stepping back and brushing shells furiously from his face and shoulders, his face turning red.

Coach Fearless waded into the husks, sneezing and coughing. "Peanuts!" he drawled. "It's a buncha cotton pickin' peanut shells!"

Coach Braun did his hotfoot dance and slammed his often abused hat into his thigh. "That goddam Fatso!" he shouted.

"I don't think Coach Hathaway would do this," said Eddie, "even if he is a classic no-good!"

"Yeah he would!" shouted Coach Braun. "If he didn't do it, then who? Who? Who did this?"

"Probably those Suffolk kids," said Eddie, sneezing again amidst the peanut shell dust.

Allman walked up behind them, staring at the head high pile of peanut husks. "What's going on, Coach?" he asked, his eyes wide.

"It seems we've been visited by the Red Raiders," drawled Eddie sarcastically. "Or some elephants with a lotta nuts!"

Coach Braun stalked away. "Get the goddam custodians up here and clean this crap up before practice this afternoon!" he shouted.

****

Cliff Braun, Eddie Fearless and Slate Phelps all stood in front of Fred Beckler's desk in the Principal's office. Principal Beckler sat behind the desk with an uncharacteristic glum look on his moustached face. When Slate left as Head Coach, he tried to get used to Shotgun. It hadn't worked. The jovial and the rough just didn't mix well. But, Shotgun won games and brought in money… so he adjusted. Now, the Coach had become a problem!

"Coach Braun, I don't like this anymore than you do," said Principal Beckler. "The Superintendent has asked me to look into this matter… about the anonymous documents we received. He wants to hold a hearing in his office next week."

"The week before the Suffolk game?" asked Eddie Fearless in astonishment. "We have a lot of things to do that week."

"I know, Eddie," said Fred shaking his head, "I know. We'll just have to make it all work!"

"What does the Superintendent plan to do at this here hearing?" asked Cliff Braun, his face a square mask.

"Well… frankly, he said he'll decide whether you can stay on as Coach or not," said Fred. "Can you clear any of this up for me?"

Coach Braun paused, his face taking on an aggressive look. "Well, Mr. Beckler, I did get expelled from ECTC… Slate was there… he knows what happened. I was wrong, and I admit it. I was young and… well things just happened. As for fighting…. sure! I've had a lotta fights. That's just the way I am."

"What about this thing of breaking a boy's arm last year?" asked Beckler.

"Well," said Cliff. "I broke Calcione's arm… didn't mean to… but it happened."

"And Sanders? Did you break his nose?"

"His nose is such a mess, ya can't tell if it's broke or not," said Cliff. "Anyway, if it got broke he never said anything 'bout it to me."

"And at summer practice?" asked Fred. "What's that all about?"

"I never knew I broke any noses this year," said Coach Braun.

"Did you… hit the players?" asked Fred in a careful voice.

"He was showing 'em how to block," said Eddie. "That's all."

The Principal waved his hand at Eddie. "Let Cliff answer, Eddie."

"I was pretty rough on a few of 'em," said Coach Braun. "I showed 'em how to block… how to be tough like I wanted 'em when they played.

"Do you have to hit them, Shotgun… to make them… tough?" asked the Principal.

"It's hard to understand what I'm trying to teach 'em with just words, Mr. Beckler… it takes more! They have to feel it… ya know what I mean? They have to take a big hit to understand how to give one!"

"So, you might have broken a nose," said Fred.

"I guess so," said Coach Braun, "but no one ever complained 'bout no noses."

"Broken noses are part of the game," said Eddie under his breath.

The Principal waved at Eddie to be quiet.

"What about Eberly?" asked Beckler.

"Arnie picked a fight with Quester at one of those dances over in Simonsdale," said Cliff. "When it was over, Harry had a black eye and Arnie had broken ribs… I never said nothing 'bout it 'cause I didn't want no newspaper stuff to screw up the team."

"What did you do about it, Coach?"

"Quester was suspended for a game and had to run laps," said Cliff. "The fight was mostly Arnie's fault… according to Buddinger. And Arnie's off the team for the season."

"What've you got to say about all this, Slate?" asked Fred, confident that the former Coach that he liked and trusted would help him understand.

"Coach Braun is a bit unorthodox in his ways," said Slate carefully, "but he's effective… and the players all respect him. I think someone has a bone to pick and is coming up with all this stuff to smear our Coach… and ruin our season!"

"Yes," said Fred. "It does appear that way. If the letter were signed… I would give it more credence… but it isn't."

"The disappearance of the playbook has something do with it all," said Coach Fearless.

"Tell me more about that," said Fred.

"Some lousy bas… someone… stole one of our playbooks," said Coach Braun, his eyes intense with anger. "And we have the word that a guy on the Suffolk team has it."

"Someone also tried to put the blame on Quester," said Coach Phelps, "but he denies it… and I can't find anyone who believes Harry would do that!"

"That thing when Harry Quester was shot... is that related to all this?" asked the Principal.

"We need to look into it some more," said Eddie. "Officer Spearman is helping... and we'll let you know what we find out!"

"And the peanut shells?" asked Fred with a grimace.

"They'll be gone by practice," said Coach Braun, his ears turning red.

"That may have something to do with it, too," said Eddie.

****

It was Wednesday afternoon. Bubba, Tony and Harry walked together down the halls in the school toward the gymnasium.

"Well, let's see," said Harry, "who would have reason to be pissed at Shotgun?"

"It's a long list," said Bubba. "And it goes back to the days when I was the Water Boy!"

"He broke my nose," said Harry. "He kicked Benny Norwood and Buster...and some other guys... in the tail a lotta times. He gave Benny a big bruise on his shoulder. He busted Buster in the gut... and made him puke!"

"And that's just this season," said Bubba.

"What did he do last season?" asked Tony.

Bubba grinned. "He kicked Benny Norwood and some other guys in the tail a lotta times, he busted Jack Sanders in the gut until he puked... and broke his nose... he kicked Buster all around the field...and he broke Johnny Calcione's arm."

"What happened with Johnny Calcione?" asked Harry.

"Shotgun showed him how to block! Johnny said he was really hurt," said Bubba. "He had to go into the hospital to have his arm set."

"Did he play any more?" asked Tony.

"He came back near the end of the season," said Bubba, "but Bart had replaced him and Shotgun didn't let Johnny play any more."

"Why was that?" asked Harry.

"Johnny was a complainer... even though he's big, and did okay playing tackle," said Bubba. "But, he was always bitching about something... I think it pissed Shotgun off."

"What does he do now?" asked Harry.

"He works around here somewhere," said Bubba. "... has some kinda construction job."

"Was he pissed off at Shotgun enough to start something like this?" asked Harry.

"Who knows?" exclaimed Bubba with a shrug of his hands. "You gonna practice today?"

"Yeah," said Harry, "the Doctor said it was okay... just watch the wound so it doesn't open up... or anything like that."

"Was that really just a freak accident?" asked Bubba. "I wonder who fired that shot?"

"I don't know," said Harry. "I'm not sure I want to know."

****

Coach Fearless called a team meeting in the dressing room before practice. "Okay," said the Coach standing in front of the assembled players, "we got a lotta things going on... and we can't afford to let 'em distract us from these upcoming games!"

Eddie paused and looked at the players one by one. He continued. "Now anyone want to get anything off their chest on this thing going 'roun 'bout Harry?"

"Someone's putting out some lies about Harry," said Bucky.

"And someone took Harry's playbook!" exclaimed Bud.

"Anyone know anything about that missing playbook?" asked the Coach.

There was silence.

"How did it get to Suffolk?" asked Renny.

"No one really knows," said the Coach.

"Is it gonna hurt us to have Suffolk with that book, Coach?" asked Big Jim.

"Maybe a little," said the Coach. "But you can beat those guys anyway... and we'll make some adjustments."

"What's gonna happen with Coach Braun?" asked Bart.

"There's a hearing next Tuesday with the Superintendent," said Coach Fearless. "Is there anyone here who doesn't support Coach Braun to continue as our Coach?"

There was a prolonged silence.

"We all support Coach Braun," said Allman looking at the players with a serious expression, something new for him. "If there's someone who doesn't, see me or Karl and turn in your uniform... right now!"

Harry watched the players as Allman looked around the room. They all looked back... expect for Benny, who stared at the floor.

"Are we gonna have a say at the hearing?" asked Terry.

"I don't know," said Coach Fearless.

"They'd better let us!" exclaimed Bucky.

"We'll see," said Coach Fearless. "Now about those peanut shells..."

"Just leave that to us, Coach," said Allman, his voice filled with resolve.

"I don't want any retaliation," said Coach Fearless. "Things are too sensitive right now!"

"Like I said, Coach," said Allman with a grim grin that showed no teeth, "leave that to us!"

****

The practice was unusually grueling that Wednesday. It was as though Coach Braun wanted to show them that no accusations could make him let up on them.

"Now I guess ya heard that a buncha pantywaists think I'm too tough on you guys," shouted Coach Braun. He started to shout again, but his voice failed him and he stopped shouting, coughing violently. He regained his voice and continued hoarsely. "These here pantywaists ain't never had to win a football game! Remember… ya win games because you're tough. You guys know that! Now run! Run! I want you to be able to run circles around these here Prissy Anne Cavaliers… while they're lying in the dirt gasping for breath! Run! Run faster!"

Harry ran faster. He hoped the exertions wouldn't open the wound. It had a good scab on it, and he had it bandaged and taped down. He felt his nose. It seemed to have healed well. They finished the run and Coach Braun grouped them all around him.

"Now anyone who wants his cotton pickin' nose broken," growled Braun, a slight smile on his rugged face, "just line up over there… and I'll get to ya!"

There was a round of laughter. Allman strutted toward the designated spot with an exaggerated swagger.

"Get back over here, Allman!" shouted Eddie Fearless. "Your nose ain't big enough to break!

Allman came trotting back, a big happy look on his face.

"Ya know, I always got more… more dates after my nose was broken a few times," said Coach Braun. "Them gals like them crooked noses!"

There was more laughter.

"We might have some volunteers later on," said Allman, wiggling his nose with his hand. "I ain't getting enough!"

More laughter.

"But we ain't thinking about the girlies out here," growled the Coach. "Princess Anne is a bigger school than we are, and they'll have some good players. They can run and they can pass. They got a fullback who claims he's better than Jack… Number Thirty-nine, name is Newman… but he ain't that good. We gotta look out for him, though… and a right end, Number Forty, a guy name a' Fish... that's real fast. But... they ain't as good as you can be when ya want it bad... and they won't be in shape the way you guys are! And they won't be as mean as you guys are! So... the way we win is to grind 'em down... run the ball and keep it outa their hands... and make 'em afraid you're gonna hit 'em even harder than the last time you hit 'em!"

"They got any trick plays, Coach?" asked Renny.

"Same kinda thing," said Coach Braun. "Reverses... end arounds... fake punts... and all that fakey stuff! Play your position and don't get faked out and you'll do okay. If they score... they score... but we'll win!"

"They ain't gonna score!" said Big Jim, expressionless as usual.

"I don't think they will either," said Braun. "But it's up to you guys!"

"What about Suffolk?" asked Bud.

"I ain't saying nothing 'bout Suffolk," said Braun taking off his pork pie hat and twisting it again and again. "We got someone here who passed 'em a playbook. Some people say it was Quester, but I ain't buying that! And I ain't saying anything 'bout Suffolk 'til we find out who it was and get rid of 'im."

"Anybody who knows how Suffolk got that playbook," said Coach Fearless. "Come see me right away."

****

Harry, Bubba, Allman, Tony and Buster leaned against the Cheesewagon parked in front of A.P.'s Grocery Store drinking chocolate milk.

"We gotta find out who the traitor is," said Allman. "Any ideas?"

"The candidates," said Harry, "are me, Benny Norwood, Jack Sanders, and Calcione."

"How 'bout me?" asked Buster. "Shotgun kicks me around a lot! And my Ol' Man gets pissed about it... 'cause he thinks I'm some kinda great football player... which I am, of course!"

"Okay, Buster," smiled Harry. "We wouldn't want to leave you out!"

"Good!" said Buster with a broad smile on his oversized face. "Calcione is dirt mean. "He's my choice! He's the one that probably fired that shotgun that hit Harry."

"Yeah?" asked Bubba. "I thought it was a buncha poachers!"

Buster grinned proudly. "Ya liked that one, huh?"

"It was okay, Buster," said Allman condescendingly. "But I'll hafta work on it."

"You think Calcione fired the shot, Buster?" asked Harry.

"Could've been anyone," said Allman quietly.

"Yeah," said Bubba with a chortle, "but Calcione was really pissed at

Harry when he stuck Arnie on the nose of that red Studebaker."

"Naw, I don't think so," said Harry. "We don't even know that the two things are related! But since I know I didn't give away the playbook, that narrows the field for me."

"What about those Wilson guys?" asked Tony. "They're jealous about our being unscored on!"

"If you mean Linwood and Dennis... no," said Harry. "They may be hard to take at times... but they wouldn't do anything like that. And Pistol Pete is Shotgun and Slate's Buddy."

"I guess it's not them," said Tony.

"What about Eberly?" asked Buster. "He's pissed at you, Harry... and maybe at the Coach too."

"Arnie and Harry shook hands," said Allman.

"Yeah," said Bubba, shaking his head "but that don't mean a damn thing for Arnie."

"Ya don't think so?" asked Allman with concern.

"Come on, Allman," said Bubba. "You know Arnie better than I do!"

"We'd better put Arnie on the list, too," said Harry.

"Ya do that," said Bubba, "and ya put Carson and all the Hoods on the list... including Bart."

"Probably not Bart," observed Allman.

"Why not?" asked Bubba. "Just 'cause we drank some beer together in the hurricane... and rolled around in the surf... don't make him one of us!"

"We can eliminate Sanders," said Harry, "that's for sure. He wouldn't do anything like that... and he's got nothing to gain. He's closing in on a State scoring record!"

"That leaves Benny Norwood, Johnny Calcione, Buster, Arnie and the Hoods," said Allman. "Whatta ya think?"

"Buster's ol' man is pissed at Shotgun," said Harry, "but he wouldn't do it!"

"Benny's a pussy," said Bubba. "He ain't got the guts!"

"I wouldn't want to accuse any of them," said Harry, "without something to go on."

"We got nothing to go on," said Tony. "What're we gonna do?"

"I'm gonna talk to Horace Holly," said Bubba. "He's that kid out in Suffolk that manages the Suffolk team. Maybe he's heard something!"

"Good idea, Bubba," said Harry.

"By the way, you guys," said Allman. "I need sixty bucks to buy a pig."

"What?" exclaimed Buster.

"Yeah," said Allman, "ya don't think we're gonna let those Suffolk guys get away with that peanut shell trick, do ya?"

"What're ya gonna do with a pig?" asked Tony.

"Play some Pig Football," said Allman merrily. "Now come on, put up some money so I can buy this farmer's pig!"

"I got thirty dollars," said Harry.

"Ah! The rich man," said Allman holding out his hand.

"I got ten," said Bubba.

"I have fifteen," said Tony.

"I got five," said Buster. "Count me in!"

"Good!" exclaimed Allman. "We're in business!"

****

It was a crisply cool night in late October as the school bus filled with the Churchland team rattled along Virginia Beach Boulevard toward Princess Anne Stadium. Harry, Allman, Bubba and Tony sat huddled in the back of the bus.

"The documents have got to have been sent by Benny," said Harry. "His Father is a car dealer downtown… they have money, and maybe some influence with the Superintendent."

"If Mr. Norwood had sent it, he woulda signed it… wouldn't he?" asked Bubba.

"I think you're right," said Allman. "I think the Calcione Family had something to do with it."

"You think so?" asked Tony.

"Yeah," said Allman, "His old man was Mafia on Long Island before they came down here a few years ago."

"You're kidding!" said Tony

"Naw," said Allman, "I ain't kidding. Calcione told me last year that Big John, his father, worked on the waterfront docks at the ports up there… and he works at the docks down here."

"That doesn't mean he was Mafia, does it?" asked Harry.

"Ya seen that movie… *On The Waterfront*… where they beat that guy Brando up?" asked Allman.

"Yeah."

"Well?" asked Allman. "All them waterfront guys are hooked up with the Mafia!"

"Calcione is doing more than working at the docks to live out there on the Nansemond River where he does," said Bubba. "Grady Spearman thinks he's taking book on the games!"

"You mean betting on the games?" asked Tony.

"Yeah, Tony," said Bubba impatiently, "that's what I mean!"

The bus pulled up in the parking lot next to the Stadium. The Truckers clattered out of the bus and ran onto the field... all except for Jack Sanders who followed Larry Kidwell into the dressing room for more tape on his shoulder.

****

The Princess Anne Cavaliers ran onto the field to the cheers of the home crowd. Harry and Allman stood waiting at the sideline for the Coach to call the pre-game huddle.

"Alright, team, gather 'roun the Coach!" shouted Coach Fearless.

They all gathered around, Coach Braun squatting in the center of the huddle. He seemed unusually somber, his square face almost placid. Then they could see it come over him. His face took on a ferocious visage and started to turn red, his lips wrinkled into a snarl. "Tonight I'm really... really ready to smash this bunch of Prissy Anne Cavaliers out there in their fancy-dancy red, white and blue uniforms! You know what their Coach said... that you guys were nothing more than a buncha dumb farm boys? Does that piss ya off?"

"Yeah," came the shout in unison from the Truckers.

"I wanna take these guys apart and plow 'em under... show 'em what a buncha tough, mean farm boys can do!" shouted Coach Braun. "Are ya ready to do that?"

"Yeah," came the second shout in unison from the Truckers.

"Then get out there! Kick their butts! Make 'em wish they were somewhere else... anywhere but on a field fulla Truckers!" shouted Coach Braun hoarsely.

The huddle broke with a tremendous roar from the players, echoed by the Churchland fans in the stands. Jack Sanders ran onto the field just in time for the kickoff.

"Nice ya could join us, Sanders!" shouted Braun.

"Thanks, Coach," said Jack with a grin, putting on his helmet and adjusting to the new tape on his shoulder and ankle.

Harry felt a great surge of excitement as he ran onto the field. He had watched Shotgun put on his game face. He looked up at the bright lights of the stadium. They blinded him and he felt his game face coming on. He reached down into his soul and body, transforming himself into the man they called Headhunter. The two teams lined up on the brightly lit field for the Trucker kickoff. Bud Darby kicked the ball and it sailed to the Princess Anne fifteen yard line. A halfback took the ball and started to run right up the middle. Harry held his outside position and watched Renny Dickson bring the Cavalier down at their twenty five yard line.

Harry lined up at left defensive end. The Cavalier team broke their huddle and ran to the line of scrimmage. There were loud cheers from the Princess Anne fans. A tall boy with wide shoulders and thick calves lined up in front of Harry at right end… number forty… Hanson Fish. The ball was snapped. Harry waited a moment to see what the play was going to be, absorbing a block from Fish. He saw the ball handed to Sam Newman. Newman started off right tackle. Harry held his position and slid off the block by the big end. Harry and Big Jim hit Number Thirty-nine at the same time. There was a thud that could be heard in the top row of the stands. Newman was driven backward and landed in the Cavalier backfield with a mound of white, black and orange jerseys on top of him. There was a moan from the home crowd.

"We got your number, Newman," said Harry ferociously as he got up from the pile.

"Ya got nothing, Headhunter!" exclaimed Newman angrily.

Princess Anne tried two more running plays which gained very little. They punted and Terry ran it back to midfield. The Truckers huddled.

"Okay," said Allman. "These guys ain't so tough! Thirty four on three."

Bob Porter left the huddle.

"You ready Jack?" asked Allman.

Jack Sanders nodded.

"Thirty-four on three. Hut!"

"Get Down… Get set!… Hut One… Hut Two… Hut Three!"

The ball was snapped. Allman handed off to Jack who went crashing though the line. Number Thirty-nine was waiting for him on the other side at the linebacker position. Jack lowered his head and shoulder and tried to butt Sam Newman out of the way. The Princess Anne player lowered his head and lunged forward. Number Thirty-nine's helmet hit Jack on the shoulder and then crashed into his helmet with an explosive sound heard in the top row of the stands. Jack's helmet came off as he fell, as did Sam Newman's. The helmets rolled crazily around on the gridiron. Jack staggered to his feet, picked up his helmet and jogged painfully back to the huddle.

"Call another number," said Jack. "I gotta shake that one off."

"Okay, Jack," said Allman. "Twenty-eight, on one."

Bob jumped out of the huddle.

"Get that big end, Harry," said Terry worriedly.

"Consider it done," said Harry. "Renny, can you pull and lead around to get the halfback?"

"Sure," said Renny, "but I'm supposed to block the guard."

"Don't worry about the guard," said Bart. "I'll get him and the tackle both!"

"Okay," said Renny.

Harry ran up to the line. "Okay, Fishy Ol' Buddy," he said to the big end. "We're coming right around you this time!"

"Try it!" said Hanson Fish in a surprised voice.

"Get down... Get ready... Hut One!"

The ball was snapped. Harry hit Fish head on, his legs pumping. He banged into the big end's chest and face with his forearms, driving him back and in. Renny came charging around left end, Terry running behind him. Terry flashed by Harry and faked toward the linebacker. Renny got between the halfback and Terry, and it was all over. Terry ran into the end zone for a touchdown. At the end of the half, it was Churchland fourteen, Princess Anne, nothing.

****

In the visiting team locker room, there was a hubbub of chatter. Jack Sanders sat on a bench, silent... obviously in some pain. Kidwell was once again adjusting the tape on his shoulder and left ankle. Then there was silence as Coach Braun walked in.

"What's wrong with ya, Sanders," asked the Coach. "That's the first half ya haven't scored!"

"I'll be alright, Coach," said Jack. "They got a lucky hit on me, and I've been shaking it off."

"Ya wanna come out?" asked Coach Fearless.

"Naw, Coach," said Jack determinedly. "I'm okay."

"You're sure?" asked Fearless. "You're wearing a lotta tape!"

"Yeah... I'm sure, Coach."

"Alright, now listen," said Braun pacing back and forth in the dressing room, twisting his battered hat in his hands. "Terry and Karl have both scored. We've stopped their running game. I expect 'em to open up and pass to that big end... Number Forty, whatever his name is!"

"His name is Hanson Fish," said Harry. "He's big and fast, but not so tough!"

"I think they've been holding back the pass to this Fish guy," drawled Coach Fearless, "hoping they'll catch us off guard."

"Quester," said the Coach, "I want you to hit that Fishy guy hard at the line of scrimmage before he ever starts running. Porter, if he gets by Harry, I want you to run with him and keep him off balance... then Karl, you pick him up and stay with him... you and Porter. You understand?"

"We got it, Coach," said Karl.

"On offense, I wanna keep running," said Coach Braun. "Just like we're gonna run it and run it when we play Suffolk. Jam it down their throats. Run out the clock. They can't score if they ain't got the ball! And I wanna see some of what got us here… Sanders running over people… blocks that can be heard up in the stands!"

"I'm ready, Coach," said Jack testing his arm and shoulder.

"You're sure?" asked Coach Braun.

"I'm okay," said Jack, his face distorted with pain, "just someone block that Newman guy!"

****

Princess Anne kicked off to begin the second half. Hero fielded the ball and returned it to the Churchland forty-two yard line. On the first play, Sanders took it to midfield, following a crunching block that Harry made on Sam Newman. Then on two successive plays, Sanders took it to the Princess Anne thirty-two. He returned to the huddle holding his shoulder.

"What's wrong, Jack?" asked Allman.

"Nothing," said Jack. "My shoulder is sore, that's all… nothing new!"

"We'll give you a breather," said Allman. "Harry… how 'bout an end around?"

"Yeah, sure," said Harry. "They'll be looking for it… I'm sure they've scouted us on that… so I'll be looking to cut it back off tackle."

"Just cut it back," said Bart, "I'll be there. Follow me."

"I'll do it," said Harry.

"Okay then," said Allman, "sixty-nine on set."

The play worked to perfection. Harry took the ball from Allman and ran at full speed toward their right end. He saw Bart out of the corner of his eye. As he thought they would, the Princess Anne team was running at full speed toward their left end, matching Harry's pace. Harry cut back toward tackle, following Bart. The Cavaliers were caught off guard and struggled to reverse their field as Harry followed Bart. Only Sam Newman stood between Harry and the goal line. Bart crashed into Number Thirty-nine and knocked him down without missing a stride. Harry ran on unmolested and crossed the goal line. Jack Sanders ran the extra point over and the score was Churchland twenty-one, Princess Anne zero.

The score broke Princess Anne's will. Hanson Fish caught two passes, but posed no serious threat. The closest Princess Anne came to the Churchland goal line was the thirty yard line. Late in the game, Jack Sanders scored from the three yard line to make it Churchland, twenty-eight, Princess Anne nothing.

"Joltin' Jack! Joltin' Jack!"

****

Paige was waiting in the Chevy when Harry came out of the Princess Anne dressing room. She slid over as Harry climbed into the driver's seat. The engine was running and the heater felt good on the cold evening.

"Well, you guys did it again," said Paige happily, snuggling up to Harry. "It looks like no one will be able to score on you!"

"Shhh!" cautioned Harry. "We don't want to tempt luck!"

Harry put the car in gear and weaved his way through the post game traffic. He drove down Virginia Beach Boulevard to Military Highway and took Route 17 in to Portsmouth.

"What's going to happen with the Coach?" asked Paige with concern.

"I don't know… a lot depends on the hearing next week."

"Can you win without him?"

"Maybe," said Harry, "but it would be hard."

"Why's that?

"It's hard to explain. Shotgun somehow makes you win… just him being there makes you feel like you'll win… that you gotta win!"

"How does he do it?"

"I wish I knew," said Harry thoughtfully.

Nick's Italian Restaurant and Lounge was on Crawford Street in downtown Portsmouth. It was an old brick building set in a row of stores. It emanated the most delicious odors. There was a flashing red, neon sign outside that said "Nick's". Harry parked the Chevy on the street, got out and opened the door for Paige. She got out. Harry put his arm around her waist and walked her to the door of the restaurant. He looked around them cautiously as Crawford Street was known to be a rough part of town… sailor town some called it. But… Nick had the best pizza! They went inside to face a rowdy scene. Seated at one end of the room, like some Italian Mafioso was Arnie Eberly and his gang of Hoods. Johnny Calcione, Carson Quinn, Bart Whitely, Bryan Muller and others all lounged in their chairs smoking cigarettes and drinking cokes. Arnie had bandages around his chest, displayed through his open shirt. He unabashedly took a flask from his coat pocket and poured some whiskey into his coke. Waiters brought steaming bowls of spaghetti to the tables where the Hoods sat. Harry wondered where Clara was.

"Hey! Harry! Over here!" shouted Bubba.

Bubba, Tony and Allman sat at a table at the opposite end of the room from Arnie. There was a pitcher of coke on the table with many glasses. Alice was with Bubba. Georgia was with Allman. Tony, looking smug, had his arm around Sherry. Harry held a chair for Paige and she sat down gracefully. He sat next to her. A jukebox played Dean Martin.

When the moon hits your eye like a big-a pizza pie,
That's amore,
When the world seems to shine like you've had too much wine,
That's amore!

"We ordered," said Bubba with a flourish.

"Well, order some more," said Harry with a twisted grin on his face.

A waiter came and put four big raised plates on the table. Each one contained a steaming pizza pie, rich with mozzarella cheese and the flavor of oregano. Each one had a different topping... pepperoni, sausage, mushrooms and anchovies. Bubba grabbed a slice of sausage pizza and handed it to Alice. She took a bite and a long piece of plastic-like cheese strung out between her mouth and the pizza. Bubba bit the cheese string in two and took a gigantic bite of the pie Alice held.

"Bubba! You like that old pie better than me," complained Alice.

"The pizza now, you later!" exclaimed Bubba mischievously.

Alice swatted Bubba's shoulder. "Pizza now, you wish later!"

Harry reached for a piece of the pizza. "You like pepperoni or sausage, Paige?" asked Harry.

"Either one is fine," said Paige, trying to adjust to the surroundings. She wasn't used to places her father called "dives". She hoped he wouldn't find out she had been at Nick's... but it was exciting!

Harry gave Paige a piece of pepperoni pizza and took one himself. She tasted the pie daintily.

"Wow! This pie is hot!" said Paige, reaching for a glass of Coke.

They ate the pizza pie, watching the Trucker victory scene swarming around them. Buster was one table over with Bob Porter, Janet, Matt Pittinger and several girls from the band. Buster was holding forth with his latest story, his arms waving wildly.

"We're all in the water," shouted Buster, a look of absolute sincerity on his face, "and the sharks came after us! I took off my belt and stuck it in a big one's mouth... cinched it up and rode the sonofabitch right up to the beach!"

"I don't believe that, Buster," said Janet, wrinkling up her nose.

"It's what happened!" exclaimed Buster, wide eyed. "I got tooth marks on my ass where the shark bit me... wanna see?"

"Never mind, Buster," said Janet with disgust.

Harry saw Hero, Bucky, Karl and Gail at the next table. Jack Sanders was notably absent.

"Where's Jack?" asked Harry.

"He said he didn't feel good," said Allman. "I guess he went home."

"He didn't have too good a game," said Bubba.

"Yeah," said Tony sarcastically, "only one touchdown!"

Allman stood up with a slice of pizza in his mouth. He put his hands behind his back and began chomping at the pizza. Everyone in the restaurant stopped and watched him. Even Nick, with his bald head and white apron came out of the kitchen to watch. The slice of pizza slid into Allman's mouth until his cheeks puffed out.

"Sit down, Buddinger, ya clown!" shouted Arnie caustically from the other side of the room.

Allman turned to Arnie, his mouth stuffed with pizza and made valiant efforts to yell back at him, pieces of cheese and tomato flying from his mouth. He gave Arnie the finger, politely shielding it from the girls at the table with a cupped hand. Then with several gigantic swallows, he downed the pizza, his eyes wide and rolling about theatrically.

"You'll get yours, Allman," shouted Johnny Calcione, returning the finger salute.

"Oh Allman," said Georgia watching him adoringly and laughing. "You did it!"

"Okay, Bubba," shouted Allman wiping tomato sauce from his mouth, "What was the time?"

"Fifty seconds," said Bubba.

"Okay!" shouted Allman raising his hands for applause, which he received. "Pay up, Bubba!"

"Hey Nick," said Bubba, "bring this pig here a pizza with double cheese and some pickled pork!"

"I gotta no pickle pork," said Nick in hurried frustration. "I never hava no pickle pork! Whatcha want?"

"Okay," said Bubba leaning back and stretching. "Put some mystery meat on it… something really hot!"

"Okay," grinned Nick through a five o'clock shadow, fingering the thick gold chain around his neck. "I canna do that!"

Allman laughed boisterously. "Thanks Bubba… you're just a sweetheart!" He leaned across the table and patted Bubba on his prominent gut.

"Hey Allman," said Bubba, sucking in his gut, "Whatta ya call a Coke bottle fulla bees?"

"I don't know, Bubba," said Allman grinning. "What do ya call a Coke bottle fulla bees?"

"A Suffolk vibrator!" said Bubba with a straight face.

Alice slapped Bubba on the shoulder. "Bubba, you're awful!" she exclaimed with a giggle.

Nick scurried back into the kitchen to prepare the mystery pizza, shouting orders to the cooks in Italian.

"Hey Allman, what goes HA-HA… thud-thud?"

"Come on, Bubba, give us a break!" pleaded Tony.

"Okay, Bubba… what goes HA-HA… thud-thud?" asked Allman with a grin.

"A guy laughing his balls off!" said Bubba triumphantly.

"That one wasn't funny, Bubba," said Alice with another giggle.

Harry saw Linwood Honor and Cathy Lawson come in the door. Cathy still had on her Churchland Cheerleader uniform. Harry waved at them. Linwood came over to the table where they all sat.

"Pull up a chair and have some pizza," invited Harry.

"I guess I won't get killed if I sit with a bunch of Truckers," said Linwood eyeing them with caution.

"Hi, Cathy," said Sherry. "Come on, sit down!"

"Let's sit here, Linwood," said Cathy, waving to Sherry.

Linwood held a chair for Cathy and sat down next to her.

"Hey Bubba," exclaimed Alice with a silly grin. "What do boys and beer bottles have in common?"

"Uh oh," said Bubba, wide eyed. "Now I got her started!"

"Well," said Alice, "do ya know?"

"No, Alice," said Bubba with a condescending grin. "What do they have in common?"

"They're both empty from the neck up!" said Alice triumphantly.

"She got ya that time, Bubba!" laughed Allman.

"Cathy tells me you guys are still unscored on," said Linwood handing a piece of mushroom pizza pie to Cathy.

"Yeah," said Allman. "We lucked out again! How'd you guys do?"

"We beat Maury," said Linwood. "We beat 'em thirty-three to thirteen… at our homecoming!"

"Linwood scored a touchdown!" said Cathy proudly.

"Congratulations, Linwood," said Harry extending his hand.

Linwood took Harry's hand and gripped it firmly. "Thanks, Harry," he said. "I hear you're playing end now."

"Whatever the man wants!" said Harry. "I do it… if I can!"

"Harry scored a touchdown, too," said Paige.

"Congratulations to you, too," said Linwood, once again extending his hand.

Harry shook Linwood's hand again. "Thanks, Linwood. It looks like you guys are going to go undefeated."

"Granby, Roanoke and Suffolk to go," said Linwood. "Roanoke's gonna be tough!"

"That'll make the Presidents state champs," said Allman, tomato sauce smeared across his face,"... if ya win 'em all!"

"I hope so," said Linwood smugly.

"We play Suffolk first," said Bubba, "so we'll soften 'em up for you!"

"By the time we play Suffolk, we'll have beaten all the Group I schools," said Linwood arrogantly, "and the championship!"

"So little old Group II Suffolk won't matter, huh?" asked Allman sarcastically.

"Sure it'll matter, Allman," said Linwood with a smile. "After Suffolk beats you guys, we'll have to beat 'em real bad to shut you Truckers up!"

"That'll be the day!" said Bubba.

"We're gonna beat the pants off Suffolk," said Allman. "Then we're gonna play you guys!"

"You think you can win without Shotgun?" asked Linwood.

"Shotgun'll be there," said Bubba. "You can count on that!"

"He's in a lot of trouble from what I hear."

"He'll be there," said Allman. "You can't beat Ol' Shotgun!"

"Well, either way," said Linwood condescendingly, "we'd like to play you guys... if they can get the game scheduled! It would be a blast!"

"We're working on it," said Allman, winking at Linwood. "Tell Willy Scooter to stand by for a dose of the Headhunter!"

Linwood glanced at Harry. "I've handled Headhunter Harry before," he said confidently.

"That was before I was a Trucker!" exclaimed Harry.

"Duane Starr told me he knows all your plays by heart," said Linwood, looking nervously at Harry. "What's that all about?"

"He can have our plays," said Harry. "We'll still beat 'em!"

"I guess we'll have to see about all that," said Linwood reaching for another piece of pizza.

The waiters brought four more pizzas on elevated plates and set them on the table. One waiter brought in a plate with the mystery pizza. He sat it in front of Allman. It was piled high with cheese and mounds of sausage flaked with little red pieces of pepper. Allman grabbed a piece and wolfed it down. His eyes got wide, his face got red and he jumped up and danced around the floor, whooping. He grabbed a glass of water and poured some of it down his throat, most of it on his face.

"Yeehah!" shouted Allman. "That mystery pizza is really good... give some to The President's star end over there!"

"No thanks," said Linwood holding up his hands defensively. "I'll just have the regular."

Allman, Bubba, Harry and Tony helped themselves to the mystery pizza. The plate was soon empty. They sat around the table gasping and drinking water, tears rolling down their faces.

"You guys are nuts," said Linwood with a broad grin. "And Allman's an idiot!"

"Yeah," said Harry wiping away his tears. "You're absolutely right!"

"Ain't it great?" exclaimed Bubba, tears rolling down his cheeks.

"Excuse me, guys," said Paige, motioning to Alice.

Paige started to stand up. Harry stood up and held her chair. Paige and Alice walked to the back of the restaurant to the lady's room.

"You guys cool off and behave," said Alice with a wink of her eye. "And we'll be back!"

Georgia came over and sat in Harry's lap.

"No you don't Georgia!" exclaimed Harry. "Not that again!"

"No… no, Harry," said Georgia giggling. "I'll be nice!"

Harry glanced at where the Hoods were sitting. "Where's Clara?"

Georgia tickled Harry on the chest. "She broke up with Arnie," she giggled. "You wanna see her?"

"No… no," said Harry, embarrassed. "I just wondered."

"How are you and Paige making out?"

"We're doing fine," said Harry uncomfortably as Georgia squirmed in his lap.

"Is she, you know… treating you right?" asked Georgia impishly.

"Come on, Georgia," said Harry. "I'm not going to talk about what Paige and I do… you know that!"

"Oh shucks, Harry," teased Georgia. "I just wanted to know if the little ol' iceberg had warmed up any!"

Harry stood up and dumped Georgia from his lap. "We're doing just fine, Georgia… so help me out and stay clear!"

"Okay… okay, Harry," said Georgia, winking at him and walking away with swinging hips.

Harry took the opportunity to go the men's room at the back of the restaurant.

"Hey Harry!" shouted Allman. "Whatsa matter… ya gotta pee?"

"Go to hell, Allman!" said Harry with a grin.

Harry walked through the door of the room marked SIGNORES. He was using the urinal when Bart Whitely came in.

"Harry," said Bart. "I want you to know something… something important."

"What's that, Bart?" asked Harry, flushing the urinal.

"Calcione is behind all this playbook stuff," said Bart stepping to the urinal. "So watch your ass!"

"Johnny?" asked Harry in a surprised voice. "What about Arnie?"

"I don't know about Arnie," said Bart. "Johnny usually does what Arnie tells him to do… but I don't know."

"I think Arnie is okay… after we went to see him… and all."

"Arnie ain't never okay if ya make him look bad," said Bart. "He'll wait until the time is right and get back at ya!"

Harry shook his head worriedly. "Thanks, Bart. I'll remember."

****

Harry and Paige sat in the Chevy parked in front of the Garnette home in Green Acres. He worried that Paige had been uncomfortable with the scene at Nick's. He was coming to understand that she was… somehow different from most of the girls.

"I enjoyed the Pizza," said Paige. "Thank you."

"I'm sorry about all the noise and stuff," said Harry. "I hope you had a good time."

"Oh," said Paige, "I did… I'm just not used to all the guys being so…"

"Rowdy?"

"Yes, I guess that's it… but it was fun!"

"I'd like to take you somewhere real nice… maybe after the Suffolk game?"

"You won't eat any more mystery pizza?"

"Naw… I'm sorry about that."

"Whatever you say, Harry," said Paige.

Harry sat nervously. Was he supposed to kiss her now? He wished someone had explained how to do this dating thing. He had never been very good at it. He took her hand and kissed her lightly on the cheek.

"You're the prettiest and sweetest girl I've ever met, Paige," said Harry. His mind detached, floated up and looked down on the bumbling fool in the Chevy trying to talk to this beautiful girl.

"Well, then… kiss me again!" said Paige through parted lips that even in the dark shown in a subdued red.

Harry leaned over and put his lips against hers. Her lips were full and moist. He kissed her and she kissed him back, stirring feelings in him that made him feel strong and weak at the same time. They held the kiss for a breathless moment. Her lips felt right on his… as if they had been made to fit together… like the couplings of the cars in his electric train, like the shear pin in the propeller hub of his outboard. Their lips parted wetly and Paige squeezed Harry's hand.

"I guess its time to go in," said Paige softly.

"I guess so," said Harry, hurriedly opening the door.

He ran around to the other side of the car and opened the door for Paige. She stepped out gracefully, a mysterious crinkling sound from the petticoats under her dress. They walked to the front door.

"Goodnight, Paige," said Harry self-consciously.

"Don't I get another kiss?" asked Paige in her soft, husky voice.

"Well sure," said Harry glancing around him.

"Don't worry," said Paige, "there's no one around."

"You don't mind tasting pizza?"

"Not if it's your pizza, Harry."

Harry kissed Paige gently on the lips and felt her body move ever so briefly against his.

"Goodnight, Harry," said Paige softly. She went inside and closed the door gently.

Harry staggered back to his car wiping away smudges of lipstick that tasted like candy. He got in and drove away wondering what it felt like to be in love.

****

Coach Braun sat in a late diner on Military Highway with Slate and Eddie drinking coffee after the Princess Anne game.

"When is that hearing, Slate?" asked Cliff.

"Wednesday morning at ten o'clock downtown in the Courthouse Building on High Street... in the Superintendent's office," said Slate.

"What are we gonna say?" asked Eddie.

"Just tell the truth," said Slate.

"I think I'm gonna get canned," said Cliff emotionally. "Just when I'm about to do something... something good... I'm gonna get canned. It ain't fair!"

Slate watched Cliff's square face and thought he saw a tear in the corner of his eye. He hadn't seen that since Cliff's father died.

"Whatever happens, Cliff," said Eddie emotionally, "everybody will know about what you've done with these boys."

"Maybe... maybe," said Cliff wrinkling his brow. "I just wish we knew who stole that playbook," he said, sounding frustrated. "I got some plans for that game with ol' Fatso, that sonofabitch... but I can't let the word leak out if we got us a traitor."

"We'll find out who it is," said Eddie. "Allman told me they were working on some clues."

****

Chapter Fourteen
Pig Football

Harry drove the Cheese-wagon through the countryside into the farm lands around the small city of Suffolk. It was after ten o'clock. Bubba was in the passenger seat. Larry Kidwell was in the back. They drove to a small farm house and pulled into the front yard. They got out of the car. Larry went to the door and knocked. Chickens clucked under the house at the disturbance. A pudgy boy with red hair came to the door.

"Whatta ya want, Larry?" asked Horace Holly glancing anxiously at the Chevy containing Harry and Bubba.

"Come on out, Horace," said Larry, "We just wanna talk."

"Yeah?" asked Horace in a hesitant voice. "Who're them guys?"

"Bubba Hawkins and another guy," said Larry. "They won't hurt ya... they wanna know about the playbook."

Harry and Bubba got out of the Chevy and stood beside it.

"I don't wanna talk to Bubba," said Horace defensively. "He picks on me all the time!"

"Come on, Horace," said Larry, "I know ya know about the playbook. Now come on out!"

"Who's at the door, Horace?" came a voice from within.

"Just some friends," answered Horace nervously.

"Well, get in or out," said the voice, "you're letting the cool air in!"

"Come on out, Horace," whispered Larry. "Or I'll tell Duane ya talked to me!"

Horace hesitated and then came cautiously out the door. He closed it softly. They walked out into the yard and stood next to Harry's Chevy.

"Harry," said Larry, "This here is Horace."

Horace looked up at Harry apprehensively.

"And this here is the Headhunter, Horace," said Larry.

Horace quickly averted his eyes.

"You gave the playbook to Duane Starr, didn't you, Horace, ya little twerp!" said Bubba.

Horace looked at the ground and shuffled his feet nervously. "Well... Duane said he wanted it... ya know!"

"And what Duane wants, Duane gets," said Bubba. "Right?"

Horace glanced at Bubba nervously. "Bubba... ya know what goes on," he said. "If Allman asked ya for somethin'... you'd get it!"

"And Duane gave the playbook to Fatso... right?" asked Harry.

"Yeah, I guess so," said Horace. "But I don' really know."

"Who gave you the playbook, Horace?" asked Bubba stepping close and clamping his hand on the boy's shoulder.

"Ow! That hurts!" whined Horace, wriggling from Bubba's grasp.

"Just tell him who gave ya the book," said Larry. "Ya know it's not right to steal the playbook!"

"Ya wanna get thrown in jail for stealing, boy?" asked Bubba with a practiced frown.

"I didn't steal it," choked Horace. "Someone gave it to me!"

"Who?" asked Bubba, a fierce expression on his face.

"I didn't wanna do it," whined Horace.

"Who gave it to you, Horace?" asked Harry.

"Are you really the Headhunter?" asked Horace bashfully.

"That's what they call me," said Harry. "Why?"

"Duane Starr is really mad at you for stealing his girl," said Horace fearfully.

"She wasn't his to steal!" exclaimed Harry irritably.

"Be careful, Horace… ya pissed off the Headhunter!" exclaimed Larry.

"Come on, Horace," said Bubba impatiently. "Who gave ya the playbook? Was it Calcione? Ya wanna piss off the Headhunter again?"

"Yeah… yeah… okay," said Horace reluctantly. "Johnny Calcione gave it to me after the game Churchland had with Smithfield."

"How'd he get it?" asked Harry.

"I dunno," said Horace looking at the ground.

"I think ya know, Horace," said Bubba. "And you'd better tell us!"

Harry took a menacing step toward Horace, playing Bubba's game.

"Wait a minute, Headhunter," said Bubba in a devilish voice. "Don't beat the snot outa this kid yet… I think he wants to help us!"

Bubba put a restraining hand on Harry's arm.

"Johnny said that… that…"

"That what?" asked Harry menacingly, feeling silly playing the role Bubba had set up for him.

"That Benny took it," said Horace. "He made Benny Norwood do it! He and Benny were going to get even with Shotgun and make it look like the Headhunter did it!"

"Thanks, Horace," said Bubba. "Just keep your mouth shut and we won't tell Duane ya told us."

Horace ran back to his house and went inside quickly. Harry and Bubba got back in the Chevy and drove away.

"I'm gonna get hold of Grady Spearman," said Bubba. "There's something real fishy going on… and Grady will help us."

****

It was a starlit Sunday night after the Princess Anne game. A frost was in the still air. A low mist hovered over the fenced fields. Bart drove his old, beat up black 1935 Ford pickup truck at breakneck speed along a dirt road near a farm in Suffolk. It had a small cab and a short truck bed in the back, each adorned with multiple dents and rust. There was a spare tire mounted on the right side of the truck bed that rattled a lot. Buster Stanley sat in the passenger seat. Jack, Harry, Bubba, Allman and Tony were bouncing along in the back of the truck.

"Where'd ya get this thing?" asked Buster as they bounced along.

"Got it outa a junk yard," said Bart proudly. "I just got the ol' flat head engine to run yesterday, but the body is still pretty beat up and rusty."

"I'll say," muttered Buster. "And there's a spring in this seat that's goosing me every time we hit a bump!"

"Hey!" said Bart with a wicked smile. "Don't complain! Lean back and enjoy it!"

"Now where's this pig?" asked Bubba impatiently.

"Hell!" exclaimed Allman. "There's a whole field of 'em up here. Mister Ebergreen said we could take one and he'd never tell anyone."

"For sixty dollars," said Jack.

"That old fart charged too much," said Bubba.

"Well," said Allman, "it took seventy bucks to keep him quiet… but I found it."

"Just what is this latest hare brained plan, Allman?" asked Jack.

"It ain't hare brained!" grinned Allman. "Just some Pig Football!"

"You never had any other kinda plan… 'cept hare brained," said Jack with a laugh. "Your brain is zero-zero… just like your number!"

"Aw Jack," sobbed Allman, "ya really hurt my feelings!"

"What's Pig Football?" asked Tony.

"That's an easy one," exclaimed Allman. "Pig Football is… whatta ya think?… ya play football with pigs! And they always have the ball, so ya gotta tackle 'em!"

"Six points for every tackle!" laughed Bubba.

"See?" said Allman. "Bubba knows how to play Pig Football!"

The black truck made an abrupt turn into an even narrower dirt road that ran beside a fence made of rough hewn timber.

"You know where you're going, Bart?" shouted Jack watching the fence fly by.

"Right here!" exclaimed Bart and slammed on the brakes. They held on as the truck rattled violently, kicked up a cloud of dust and stopped with a cough and a cloud of black smoke. They all clambered out.

Harry looked around in the dark night. "Where're the pigs?"

"Right out there in that field!" exclaimed Allman. "All we gotta do is find 'em."

"Somewhere in that field," said Bubba grimly. "That's pretty good!"

"I hear they got a good team!" shouted Allman. "They call themselves the Big Pig Raiders!"

"How much pig crap do we have to step in… in the dark, before we find a pig?" asked Tony with disgust.

"A lot!" said Allman jumping from the Jeep and running toward the fence. "That's what makes it so much fun!"

"Ugh!" said Tony in disgust.

Allman jumped the fence. He had a burlap sack and a coiled rope slung over his shoulder. "Come on!" he yelled. "Spread out and listen for them pigs!"

"What do pigs sound like?" asked Tony.

"You'll know 'em when ya hear 'em," said Bubba with a snort.

"What do we do if we find one?" asked Tony.

"Ahah! You tackle the critter!" said Allman. "Remember… Pig Football… that's why it's called Pig Football!"

"Yeah?" asked Harry. "Then what?"

"We tie up the pig's legs, sack him, and put him in the pickup truck… whatta ya think!"

"Or, we could just have us a pig picking barbecue right out here on the farm," laughed Bubba.

"No eating the pigs!" said Buster with a snicker.

"Come on, spread out," shouted Allman.

"I just stepped in some pig shit," said Bart matter-of-factly.

"Hey! That's a good sign!' said Allman encouragingly. "They must be near!"

"I just stepped in some too," said Tony, disgust shrouding his voice. "It smells like shit!"

"What did ya expect, Tony?" asked Buster sarcastically. "Ya want pig shit to smell like something else?"

"I guess not," said Tony, embarrassed.

"One night I scored twenty-four points on the pigs," whispered Buster. "Everywhere I ran there was a big pig just wantin' to get tackled."

"Bullshit, Buster," said Allman. "Ya ain't never scored any points against the pigs!"

"Yeah I did, Allman," said Buster convincingly, "and I didn't even step in any crap!"

"Listen!" exclaimed Harry holding up his hand.

They all froze in place and listened. Ahead of them came a gentle snorting sound.

"Pigs!" whispered Tony.

"Sneak up on 'em!" whispered Bubba, crouching low and creeping forward.

They went ahead slowly through the hovering mist until they could see dark gray humps in the muddy grass.

"There they are!" whispered Allman.

They crept forward. Harry felt something gooshy under his feet and stepped more carefully. Suddenly Allman broke into a full run toward the dark gray humps in the field. The pigs were on their feet in an instant. They started running away. Allman launched himself at the nearest one.

"Ooeeee!" squealed the pig as Allman tackled it.

They all charged toward where Allman lay on the ground struggling with the pig. Suddenly, the pig squirted from Allman's grasp with another squeal and ran away.

"Damn!" exclaimed Allman. "Some bastard musta greased that pig!"

Allman stood up, covered in mud and pig excrement.

"I've never seen ya looking so shitty, Allman," laughed Buster.

"Listen, Buster," said Allman wiping his face. "Next time I jump a pig, ya get your lard ass on top so it don' get away!"

"Next time ya jump a pig," said Buster with a serious face, "I'm gonna tell Georgia on ya!"

Bart snickered.

"Come on, Buster," laughed Allman, giving the squarely built boy a rough shove, "be a nice guy!"

"Where did the pigs go?" asked Jack looking around in the dark.

"Over this way," said Bart. "I can still see 'em."

"Lead the way," said Allman.

Bart started in the direction of the pigs. They got closer and heard more grunting sounds. Bart ran at a pig. The pig started running around in circles, with Bart stepping high, running close behind and grabbing at the offended porker.

"Get that pig, Bart!" screamed Allman waving his hands in the air.

"Ooeeee!" screamed the pig.

Bart danced through the field of pig droppings, followed by Bubba, Harry and Tony high-stepping along behind. Bart launched himself at the pig and missed, falling into a mud sink. Harry put his best fake on the pig, but it evaded him. The pig ran directly at where Jack was standing. Jack crouched and tackled the surprised pig amid a chorus of squeals. Jack fell to the ground and the pig escaped. Jack lay there in the mud holding his shoulder.

"Jack!" exclaimed Harry. "You okay?"

Jack got slowly to his feet. "I'm alright," he said with a pained grimace. "That damn pig hit my sore shoulder, that's all."

Suddenly there was a thud behind them and a new set of squeals.

"Ooeeee! Ooeeee!"

"You guys looking for a pig?" asked Buster nonchalantly.

They stared through the darkness and saw Buster get to his feet holding a pig up by its back legs. The pig's front legs were kicking wildly and squeals of porcine panic filled the crisp night air.

"Ooeeee! Ooeeee!"

"See!" said Buster, puffing out his barrel chest. "I told ya I could tackle pigs!"

"Quick!" shouted Allman. "I got the sack!"

Allman ran to where Buster held the squirming pig. He quickly tied the pig's feet together and Buster slipped the porker into the burlap sack. Allman tied off the top of the sack.

"You guys pick up this pig!' exclaimed Allman. "We gotta get it back to the truck!"

"Whatta ya mean we guys pick up the pig?" exclaimed Bubba, looking with concern at the wriggling burlap sack.

"Hell!" said Allman. "Buster caught it… I tied it up… now you guys can carry it!"

****

Suffolk High School was dark as the beat up black truck turned off the main road, pulled up and parked near the Gymnasium. It was an older building surrounded by trees and very few street lights. There was a big sign out front that said "Home of the Suffolk Red Raiders".

"They got a night watchman?" asked Harry.

"I don't think so," said Allman.

They got out of the truck as its lights went off and the engine shuddered to a halt. They unloaded the burlap sack containing the grunting and squirming pig from the truck bed.

"You guys really stink!" whispered Buster, making a face.

"You ain't smelling like a rose yourself, Buster!" said Bubba with a grin through his muddy face.

"How're we gonna get in?" asked Tony.

Allman grinned and held up a key.

"Where'd ya get that?" asked Harry.

"Horace gave it to me," said Bubba.

"Horace Holly?" asked Harry. "But he'll tell on us!"

"I don't think so," said Bubba.

"Bubba gave Horace a deal he couldn't refuse," said Allman.

"What was that?" asked Harry.

"Horace has some pet chickens," said Bubba, rubbing his muddy belly. "I got a big frying pan!"

"You wouldn't…" began Harry.

"Yeah he would," said Buster wiping his hand across his lips and smacking them loudly.

Harry shook his head in disgust.

"Now pick up this fat ol' pig," said Allman with authority.

They walked the twenty yards from the street to the gymnasium carrying the complaining porker. It squirmed and snorted and made little squealing sounds. Tony carried a sack of carrots they had brought along for the pig. Harry's heart beat wildly. It felt good to be on the delivering end of Allman's stunts instead of the receiving end. But what if they were caught? There'd be hell to pay!

A pair of headlights came toward them on the main road. They all ducked behind some bushes near the school as the car turned into the school road. The lights came closer. Suddenly, a spotlight swept over the old black truck.

"Ooeeee!" A muffled squeal came from the pig in the burlap sack.

"Shut that pig up!" whispered Buster.

"How do ya shut up a pig in a sack?" asked Tony as he struggled with the struggling pig.

"Rub his belly," said Bubba expertly. "Pigs like that!"

"Shhh!" cautioned Allman as the spotlight swept by the bushes. "It's a cop car!"

The spotlight was turned off and they all watched the police car as its lights went out and it sat idling near the curb in back of the black truck. A policeman got out and walked to the truck. He walked around it.

"I ain't got no license plates," muttered Bart.

"Oh great!" said Tony.

"Don't worry," said Bart. "They'll never trace it back to the junk yard I found it in."

"You bought it in a junk yard?" asked Tony.

"Well," muttered Bart, "Not exactly."

"What happened to the pig?" asked Buster. "He ain't squealing no more."

"I'm rubbing his belly," said Tony, "like Bubba said."

"You must be a good belly rubber, Tony," chortled Buster. "I'm next!"

"Get in the sack, Buster," laughed Tony. "I'll fix ya up!"

The policeman went back to his car and they saw him talking on his radio. They crouched behind the bush for fifteen minutes before they saw a tow truck come, hook up and tow Bart's unlicensed truck away. The police car followed the tow truck.

"Oh great!" muttered Buster. "Now how we gonna get home?"

"Ya got legs, don't ya?" asked Allman.

"Yeah… yeah!"

"Good! Then we'll run home!" said Allman.

"We can hitch-hike," said Bart.

"Matt Pittinger lives out this way," said Harry. "We can go to a gas station, find a phone, and call him… he'll come get us."

"Good idea," said Bubba. "His Ol' Man bought a new Plymouth."

"Ya got that sack of carrots, Tony," whispered Allman. "We want this pig well fed during his stay with the Red Raiders."

"Yeah, I got it."

"Well, come on!"

Allman stepped cautiously from behind the bushes. They opened the door to the school and carried the pig inside the dressing room. They went further until they found the door to the main Gymnasium. The polished hardwood floors shone dully in the dim light.

"Okay, lay out the carrots over there," said Allman pointing. "We want piggy here to have a lotta crap for this here floor!"

Tony dumped the carrots on the floor.

"Okay," whispered Allman. "Release the piggy!"

Buster pulled the burlap sack loose, reached in and released the rope that bound the pig's legs. The pig ran out of the sack and promptly expelled excrement on the shiny hardwood floors. "Ooeeee!"

"I'll never eat another pork chop!" exclaimed Tony in disgust.

****

Coach Braun sat in his little office on Monday morning feeling lower than he'd ever felt before. He hadn't been able to sleep. He felt irritable and out of synch with his being. Early in the morning he had experienced feelings of claustrophobia, as if the whole world was generating just too much for him to handle at one time. He hadn't felt that way since those nights driving Army trucks in France when it had seemed that the Germans were everywhere and the Sergeants were lining up to shout at him. He had gotten out of bed during the night and paced the floor for hours. Now he was tired. The telephone rang. The Coach picked it up.

"Whatta ya want?" he growled.

"It's me, Coach, Fred Beckler, can you come up and talk right now?"

"Yeah, Mr. Beckler," said Braun trying to rid himself of the depression that stalked him. "I'll be right up!"

Coach Braun walked through the empty halls of the school and went to Mr. Beckler's office. Frank Beckler sat behind his desk appearing to be in a more than normally frustrated state of mind. He was twirling pencils on his desk when Coach Braun knocked.

"Come in, Coach," said Fred, standing up.

"What is it, Mr Beckler?" asked Coach Braun trying to conceal his nervousness.

"I just had a call from the Principal at Suffolk High School," said Beckler in a stern voice.

"What's Fatso done now?" asked Braun worriedly.

"Coach Hathaway has done nothing that I know of," said Fred, "but it seems that a... a pig has been roaming the gymnasium at Suffolk High School over the weekend!"

"Fred," said Coach Braun with a hoarse laugh. "I've known that all season... and his name is Fatso!"

"No! No... I mean a real pig!"

"How'd it get there?" asked the Coach, suddenly quiet.

"I don't know," said Fred Beckler. "Do you know anything about it?"

"Naw," said the Coach indignantly, "I don' know 'bout no pig!"

"The police found an old Ford truck abandoned at the school. You know anyone who has one of those?"

"No... no. I don't."

"The Principal said that it was an unpleasant situation," said Beckler a smile beginning to form beneath his neatly trimmed moustache. "It seems that the pig relieved itself all over the gymnasium floor!"

Cliff Braun laughed until he was red in the face and began to cough hoarsely. Fred Beckler laughed with him and then sought to regain the proper décor of a Principal.

"Well, Coach," said Fred straightening his tie and combing back his receding hair, "please find out what you can about this pig... and truck!"

"Yes Sir," said Coach Braun.

"And oh yes, Shotgun," said Fred. "I'll do everything I can for you at the Wednesday morning hearing. I've been bombarded with calls from parents and fans that support you."

Coach Braun looked relieved. "Thanks, Mr. Beckler!"

Shotgun left feeling a little better. But not much! That night he couldn't sleep once more and lay awake most of the night thinking about the upcoming hearing... and the Suffolk game.

****

Monday afternoon before practice, Benny Norwood went to his

locker to find that it had been cleaned out. Harry, Bubba and Tony sat in front of their lockers near Benny's.

"What the hell?" exclaimed Benny. "Where's my uniform?"

"We know you took my Playbook, Benny," said Harry, standing up and confronting Benny. "You've been invited off the team!"

Benny stared at Harry with unbelieving eyes. "I didn't… "

"Yeah you did, Benny," said Bubba standing up and glowering at Benny.

"You guys are nuts!" said Benny, panic in his voice.

Allman walked to where they stood confronting Benny

"Better get on over and see the Coach, Benny," said Allman, a threat in his voice. "The guys here are pretty pissed already!"

Benny looked around the dressing room searching for a friendly face. There weren't any. Tears came to his eyes. "You guys are all wrong," he sobbed. "You can't prove I took anything."

"Yeah we can, Benny," said Allman, his gray eyes penetrating through the tall boy in front of him. "And tell your peanut pickin' friends we don't care if they have our playbook! We're gonna run the ball right down their throats!"

"You're making a big mistake," glowered Benny.

"Move it out of here, Benny," said Allman with the most serious face Harry had ever seen on his friend. "On the double!"

Allman walked threateningly toward Benny. Benny backed away on unsteady legs and disappeared through the door.

"Good riddance," said Tony opening his locker.

They dressed in their practice uniforms. Larry Kidwell came in, staggering under the load of a stack of black three ring binders.

"You guys come sign for your new playbooks," shouted Larry. "And turn in your old ones."

"Do I get one too, Larry?" asked Harry.

"Sure, Harry," said Larry, "'cept we all know where your old one is."

Larry handed playbooks to Harry, Bubba and Tony. "Coach says don't take 'em outa here," said Larry. "And here are new combination locks for your lockers. Lock 'em up whenever you're not in here… including when you're at practice."

Coach Fearless came into the dressing room. "Now listen up, guys… take about thirty minutes in here to look over the new plays," he said. "You'll find that they are similar to the old ones, with about a dozen new ones. And… don't let the word out that we have new playbooks. We want the Red Raiders to think they got 'em all and we don't know! Be out on the field not later than three forty five… and know your plays!"

"Damn!" exclaimed Bubba. "A half hour to memorize all this stuff."

"Pieca cake," said Harry, opening the playbook.

****

Coaches Braun and Fearless stood beside the line of scrimmage with copies of the new play books.

"Anyone here know anything about a pig running 'roun inside the High School at Suffolk?" drawled Coach Fearless, a smirk on his face.

Coach Fearless looked around at the faces of the players, all of whom looked unbelievably innocent.

"I didn't think so," drawled Fearless, a twinkle in his eye. "Anyone here have an ol' black truck?

There was silence and innocent stares.

"It seems this pig had a bowel problem." A snicker ran through the assembled players. "If ya know anything, you're 'spose to let me know!"

Coach Braun stepped forward. He looked haggard, his face strained and tired. The players had never seen him that way.

"Now if ya really can't remember what your assignment is in these new plays… speak up," snapped Coach Braun impatiently. "Don't fake your way through it! We gotta know these plays down pat by end of practice tomorrow."

"Another thing we're gonna do," shouted Coach Fearless, "is get used to adjusting blocking assignments… like we did in the Great Bridge game. If Suffolk shifts defenses on us, Quester will call the changed blocking assignments in the huddle."

Jack Sanders came running on to the field.

"Nice ya could make it today, Sanders!" exclaimed Braun, an angry expression on his face.

"Sorry, Coach," said Jack, taking his place in the line up.

Allman called the plays and they walked through them all. Coach Braun watched impatiently. He jammed the pork pie hat down on his head and pulled the brim down over his jug ears. After a half hour, he began to pace up and down as Coach Fearless continued to call out the plays to be walked through.

"Okay, enough of that," shouted Braun hoarsely. "I wanna see some football! I wanna see these plays now with full contact. I wanna see how you're gonna get mean and hit these… these Peanut Heads!"

"Okay guys, full contact!" shouted Fearless.

"Line 'em up… line 'em up… and no pussyfooting around!" shouted Braun hoarsely.

The first team went into a huddle. "We'll run thirty-four pull, on two," said Allman. "This is the way the new play works… I'll fake to

Karl... Jack will come through the four hole, but Renny will pull and lead him through, getting the linebacker. You guys at the four hole move the guard and tackle to open the hole. Got it?"

Bob Porter left the huddle.

"Thirty-four pull on two," said Allman. "Break!"

The huddle broke and they ran to the line.

"Get down! Get set! Hut one! Hut two!"

The ball snapped into Allman's hands. Harry shoved the end out. Big Jim and Bucky opened the four hole. Allman faked to Karl running to the three hole and handed off to Jack. Renny pulled behind the center and ran to the four hole. Jack followed Renny, and charged forward. He hit the four hole just as Renny was blocking the linebacker. Jack stumbled and fell to the ground.

Coach Braun came running over to where Sanders was picking himself up painfully from the ground. "What wrong with you, Sanders?" screamed Braun. "We ain't got enough tape holding you together? You been screwing off so much ya can't stay on your feet?"

"I'm okay, Coach," said Jack, pain and fatigue written on his face.

"I taught you how to butt these guys when you come through the line," shouted Braun. "You forgotten everything I taught ya to do?"

"Naw, Coach," said Jack. "I remember it all."

"Get down and come at me," said Braun strapping on his old leather helmet. "Ya need a refresher... that's what ya need!"

"Coach," said Eddie Fearless. "I think..."

"Stay outa this, Eddie," shouted Braun looking at Fearless with blood shot eyes. "Well, Sanders... ya gonna get down or not? Ya gonna play ball or just sit there and rest?"

Jack got down and charged at Braun. He lowered his shoulder and tried to butt the Coach the way he did when he floored most opposing players. Braun came up under Jack's forearms with a blow that sounded sharply around the practice field. His forearms struck Jack's shoulder and bounced up to hit him in the face. Jack staggered forward and fell to the grass unconscious. Braun fell over him and bounced on the turf.

"Oh no!" groaned Eddie Fearless as he ran to where Jack and the Coach had fallen.

****

"This guy really is a Wildman," observed Ike Quester as he read the morning newspaper.

"He... gets out of hand," said Harry. "But he understands football... and how to make us win!"

Ike handed Harry the newspaper. He read Al Gollen's column.

SHOTGUN BREAKS SANDERS' COLLAR BONE AT PRACTICE
WHAT'S NEXT FOR THE CHURCHLAND COACH?
By
Al Gollen

Jack Sanders, the Truckers' superior fullback suffered a broken collar bone during practice yesterday afternoon. When questioned, Coach Eddie Fearless said that the incident occurred when Coach Shotgun Braun was showing Sanders a new technique for breaking through opposing players. Sanders is temporarily hospitalized. It is expected that he will be released this afternoon, but will be out for the upcoming Suffolk game. Will the Truckers be able to move the ball against a tough Red Raider team without Sanders, their stalwart runner for all of the season?

Shotgun Braun has been accused of abusing his players in anonymous documents that will be reviewed by Superintendent Hudson Hobbs on Wednesday morning. How will this incident affect the hearing? When asked who will replace Sanders in the line up, Fearless had no immediate answer. "It's up to Coach Braun", he said.

****

"Damn it all, Cliff!" exclaimed Slate as they sat in the Coach's office before practice Tuesday afternoon. "Sometime I think you enjoy getting yourself into hot water!"

"I know," said Coach Braun showing uncharacteristic emotion, his face tired and drawn. "I screwed up!"

"You're letting this hearing thing get to you, Shotgun," accused Slate.

"I ain't getting' much sleep," said Braun wearily. "That's for sure!"

"Coach was only trying to make a point," said Eddie. "Jack has been slowing down."

"Don't make excuses for him, Eddie!" said Slate angrily.

"Yeah," said Braun miserably, "just let me rot in hell!"

"I've spent the last few days tracking down Professor Marion Franklin," said Slate.

"Professor Franklin… at Memphis State?" asked Cliff, his eyebrows raised.

"Yeah, he's retired now… we've got to have something to say tomorrow about how you got kicked out of ECTC… he may be able to help," said Slate.

"Professor Franklin will help me," said Cliff hopefully. "He always has. I'll be glad to see him!"

"What're we gonna do about someone to fill in at fullback, Shotgun?" asked Eddie.

"Can Chip Gross do it?" asked Braun.

"Not against Suffolk," said Eddie.

"You know what to do!" exclaimed Slate impatiently. "The solution is right in front of you, Shotgun!"

"The solution is... that sonofagun, Quester," said Cliff slowly.

"You don't like Quester much, do you, Coach?" asked Slate.

"He's a good player," said Braun, "but you're right... there's something about him that pisses me off."

"He stands up to you, Shotgun," said Slate. "That's why... and that's okay... if you can handle it!"

"I can handle anything," said Cliff grumpily. "Including Quester!"

"He's your man for fullback," said Eddie.

"I know it... I wanted to hear you guys say it!" said Braun irritably.

"He already knows all the plays," said Slate.

"What about left end?" asked Cliff. "I think Zee can do it."

"Zee's been looking pretty good," said Fearless. "He's learned how to hit... and he's faster than most."

"So, we'll move Quester to fullback and Zee to left end," said Coach Braun. "I agree."

"Quester is good, but he's no Sanders," said Fearless.

"Eddie's right," said Slate. "We'll have to adjust to the new lineup."

"We've run Jack too hard this year," said Coach Braun, "and it's my fault! I haven't been fair to Jack! Now, without him, I think we'll need to pass some to beat Suffolk!"

"Pass?" asked Eddie as though he couldn't believe his ears.

"Yeah," said Cliff. "And we'll pass to Quester... as well as Zee and Darby and the halfbacks."

"Pass to a fullback?" asked Eddie, his eyes wide.

"Why not?" said Coach Braun with wink of his eye. "He can catch the ball... and that'll be sure to fool ol' Fatso."

"Okay Coach," said Eddie. "Let's do it!"

"Also, Eddie," said Coach Braun, "I want to have the Headhunter defense ready."

"Now you're talking!" said Slate.

****

Superintendent Hudson Hobbs had a large office in the Court House Building on High Street. In it was a long table around which sat the Superintendent, Fred Beckler, Cliff Braun, Eddie Fearless and Slate Phelps. Hobbs adjusted his spectacles and looked at Coach Braun.

"If what these documents say is true, it's serious business, Coach Braun," said Superintendent Hobbs. "You've read it... what do you have to say about it?"

Cliff Braun licked his lips. His mouth was so dry and his throat so hoarse he wasn't sure he could say anything... but the words came out. "I was expelled from ECTC," said Cliff. "I'm what they call... aggressive, I guess!"

"So you don't deny any of this," said Hobbs, looking at Fred Beckler. "It makes me wonder how you were selected for Head Coach."

"That's where I come in, Superintendent," said Slate. "I've known Coach Braun all my life... and I recommended him to Mr. Beckler."

"You recommended him in spite of this record?" asked Hobbs.

"Yes Sir, I did," said Slate, "...and I still do. Cliff understands football... and how to win, better than anyone I've ever known!"

"It says here, Coach, that you broke Johnny Calcione's arm and Jack Sanders' nose last year," said Hobbs, "and a boy named Harry Quester... you broke his nose this year. It says you kicked Benny Norwood, pushed him down and bruised his shoulder. It says you kicked Buster Stanley and shoved him down trying to humiliate him."

"Yeah... Yes Sir," said Cliff slowly. "I broke Johnny's arm last year showing him how I wanted him to block hard! I didn't mean to... but... he was goofing off. I never knew anything about breaking Sanders' nose. I showed Quester the same thing this year, but I never knew I broke his nose either... and I ain't trying to humiliate anyone."

"Sanders never complained?" asked Hobbs

"No Sir," said Cliff Braun. "And as for Norwood and Stanley, I never hurt 'em... more than necessary. They both need toughening up!"

"And this boy Jack Sanders... the most recent incident?"

"That was all my fault, Sir," said Cliff, his voice breaking. "I get real emotional about these players, and I..."

"Emotional?" asked Hobbs in a questioning voice.

"Well, Yes Sir," said Cliff, choking and becoming hoarse. "I want 'em to do well. I... I care for them... as football players... and I try to show 'em what it takes... what it takes to win!"

There was a pause as Coach Braun regained his voice.

"Are you ready to assume duties as Head Coach, Coach Fearless?" asked Hobbs.

"No Sir," said Eddie calmly. "I won't take the job."

Hobbs looked at him over his spectacles, surprise written on his face. "And why not?"

"Sir, with all respect, Coach Braun is the Coach of the Churchland Truckers," drawled Eddie. "He's the heart and soul of the team."

"And the players...?"

"They play well... and win because Shotgun won't let 'em do

anything else," said Eddie forcefully.

"And you can't do that?" asked Hobbs skeptically.

"It's not the same," said Eddie. "This is Shotgun's team. Someday I'll have my team. I'll have it 'cause of what I've learned from the Coach!"

"I suppose you can turn it down if you want to," mumbled Hobbs.

"Did you ever play football, Sir?" asked Eddie, his eyes intensely focused on Hobbs.

"Well... no," said Hobbs after a brief hesitation.

"Then maybe you haven't experienced what I mean," said Eddie emotionally.

Superintendent Hobbs shifted his weight in the chair and looked uncomfortable.

"But," interrupted Slate quickly, "you probably had a Professor in the School of Education at William and Mary who inspired you.... in a way none of the others could... one who gave you the passion to learn!"

"Well, yes, as a matter of fact, I did," said Hobbs regaining his composure. "I had a professor like that... his name was Doctor Albert Rosser... he had a great passion for learning which he passed along to us all. He was an inspiration to many people who have done well."

"It's the same thing, Sir," said Slate with a winning smile. "The passion... the passion that Doctor Rosser has... it's the same with Coach Braun and football!"

"I see, said Hobbs, rubbing his chin. "I think I understand. Thank you for that, Principal Phelps."

"Yes Sir," said Slate with an inward sigh of relief.

The door to the Superintendent's Office opened with a bang. Allman came in, the whole team squeezing in behind him.

"Hi, Mister Superintendent," said Allman with a careful grin. "We're here to tell you we want Shotgun to be our Coach!"

"And you are?"

"Me?" asked Allman in surprise. "I'm Allman, the Team Captain."

"I'm Jack Sanders," said Jack stepping forward wearing a sling on his left arm and shoulder. "And Coach didn't break my collar bone!"

"What did you say?"

Jack took another step forward. "I said Coach didn't break my collar bone! I broke it myself on Saturday... but tried to hide it."

"That's a little strange," said Hobbs looking somewhat flabbergasted. "Just how did you break it?"

Jack looked at Allman and then at Harry behind him. He looked embarrassed. Allman looked anxious. "I was... playing around with the guys... and I broke it. I thought I could get it taped up and play like I always do... and make those school scoring records I've been aiming at... so I hid it."

"What happened Monday?" asked the Superintendent.

"I ran into Coach running through the line, and that broke it worse," said Jack looking straight at the Superintendent with unflinching eyes.

Harry stepped forward. "I'm Harry Quester, Sir... and Coach Braun didn't break my nose. I broke it running into the Coach. It wasn't too bad, and I kept on playing."

Superintendent Hobbs looked curiously at Harry's nose. "I t doesn't look broken to me."

"Bubba there," said Harry nodding at Bubba, "he snapped it back to the middle of my face."

Hudson Hobbs visibly winced and looked as though his nose had been broken and snapped back to place. "And what about this fellow... Calcione?"

Allman walked boldly to the Superintendent and whispered to him as though taking the older man into his confidence. "That Calcione guy deserved to have his arm broken, Mr. Superintendent... Sir," he said. "He's just a no good worthless skunk... that's what he is. You've seen guys like that, I know!"

"Well.... hrmmph... yes, I suppose I have," whispered the Superintendent.

Superintendent Hobbs looked up and realized he was whispering to Allman and recovered. "This is very difficult," he said.

Allman walked back to where the team stood, a big toothy grin on his face.

"Sir, in spite of these documents," said Fred Beckler, "I've had numerous calls from parents and faculty supporting Coach Braun."

"You have?" asked Hobbs.

"Yes sir," said Fred, "and they all support him quite strongly."

Hudson Hobbs rubbed his chin thoughtfully. "Then there's the matter of Coach Braun's qualifications for the job... and this thing about being thrown out of ECTC for fighting."

"Doctor Hobbs," said Slate diplomatically, "I have invited Doctor Marion Franklin, retired Dean of the School of Arts and Science at Memphis State to come and shed more light on Coach Braun's expulsion from ECTC. He was a Professor there at the time and can tell you what really happened."

"Really?" asked Hobbs. "Where is he?"

"He is currently indisposed and asked that you see him next week," said Slate. "He can be here next Tuesday."

"Hrrmmph," grunted Hobbs. "Well, I suppose I should listen to Doctor Franklin."

"Yes Sir," said Slate in his best professional manner.

Hobbs sat silently staring at the table. "Are you boys ready to play Suffolk?" he asked, lifting his head suddenly.

"Yes Sir!" came the answer from the team in chorus.

"Coach Braun, you will be on probation until this matter is completely cleared," said Hobbs. "So go and coach this team… and I'll see you with Professor Franklin next Tuesday morning."

"Yes sir!" exclaimed Coach Braun.

*****)|(****

Coach Braun and Principal Phelps walked out of the Courtroom Building and to Slate's tan 1953 Chevrolet sedan, parked along the curb on High Street near the Commodore Theater.

"You're a smooth sonofabitch, Slate," whispered Braun out of the side of his mouth.

"Yeah, I am," said Slate confidentially. "And what about that emotional thing in there? That could've won the Academy Award!"

They both stopped, faced each other and laughed.

"Ah come on, Slate," said Cliff. "I really do get emotional about the guys on the team… I just don't let 'em see me get all gooshy!"

"I know, Cliff," said Slate. "I know!"

"I care about 'em all. But I can only… ya know… show that by teaching 'em how to win!"

"You're not the kinda guy who's gonna hold their hand, Shotgun… I understand… but everyone doesn't."

Grady Spearman was sitting on a bench in front of the Court House watching the Coaches. He wore civilian clothes. He got up and walked to where they stood.

"Hi Grady," said Slate. "Not on duty today?"

"Actually, I am," said Grady. "I got my Lieutenant's badge… going plain clothes for awhile."

"Hey, congratulations, Grady!" said Slate enthusiastically.

"Yeah!" said Cliff.

"How'd it go in there?" asked Grady nodding at the Court House.

"I'm gonna coach the Suffolk game," said Cliff.

"There's a follow-on hearing next week!" said Slate. "With another fellow coming in to vouch for Shotgun."

"Good!" exclaimed Grady. "I been looking into things… and I may have something that'll help by then."

****

Chapter Fifteen
Suffolk, First Half

It was a brisk Friday night in early November. The crowd started coming to Churchland Stadium for the Suffolk game long before the stadium lights came on. By seven o'clock, there was standing room only as over five thousand people packed the stadium. The lights came on, flooding the gridiron with light as a roar from the crowd went up. The players heard the noise of the crowd all the way into the dressing room.

"What's going on out there?" asked Tony sitting in front of his locker.

"The fans are getting rowdy," said Bubba excitedly. "This is the biggest game in the history of the school!"

The players put on their pads and black trousers and pulled the black home jerseys with the orange numbers over their heads and shoulder pads.

"You guys look pretty tough," said Harry with a nod of approval.

"You'd better be tough, Harry," said Bubba pounding his cousin on the chest. "The whole team is counting on ya!"

"Yeah, said Matt. "I'm countin' on ya to explain to my old man why his new Plymouth smells like pig crap!"

"Hey Matt," chuckled Bubba. "Ya went beyond the call a' duty the other night!"

Matt laughed. "I was glad I could rescue you guys," he said.

"Or we'd still be running home," said Harry.

Jack Sanders came to where they sat and plopped down beside them. He was in his street clothes, a sling on his left shoulder. "Whatta ya think, Harry?"

"I think I'm pissed at that pig that took ya out, Jack!" said Harry nervously.

Jack grimaced. "It was bound to happen," he said. "They been patching me up all year. Sometimes I felt like only the tape was holding me together!"

"You had a helluva season, Jack," said Harry.

"Yeah, I did," said Jack proudly. "Now it's time for you to have a helluva game!"

Jack extended his hand. Harry took it and shook it. "I'd give ya a Trucker salute," said Jack, "but I don't want one back with this shoulder!"

"Consider it given and returned, Jack."

"Okay!" shouted Coach Fearless. "Huddle up 'roun the Coach here!"

They all gathered around Coach Braun in the center of the dressing room. The Coach knelt on one knee, looking up at them. His face was haggard. He made eye contact with every player before he spoke.

"This game is very important, guys," said Coach Braun evenly. "I'm a little up tight about it. I know you are too. So… let's all of us shake it off. It's a game! We're gonna go out there and have some fun beating these Peanut Heads! So, shake off the jitters and put on your game faces!"

Coach Braun shook his shoulders and arms visibly as if shaking away an evil spirit. The players stared at this new side of the Coach in wonder. The Coach stopped shaking and looked at the eager faces around him.

"I appreciate you guys showing up at the Court House," said Braun, a catch suddenly in his voice. He cleared his throat. "I'm proud of ya… real proud!"

"We're not gonna play any games without ya, Coach," said Karl.

"That's right!" said Allman.

There was a murmur of agreement from the Truckers. Coach Braun shook his head and pumped a clenched fist.

"We got another problem," said the Coach. "Bart Whitely is in the hospital with some knife wounds. I don't know what happened. But right now, Bubba, you're the starting right tackle!"

Bubba took the news with wide eyes. Harry clapped him on the back.

"Is Bart okay?" asked Allman with concern.

"As far as we know, he is," said Coach Fearless. "He's got cuts on his arm and some in his side… that's all we know."

"Who cut him?" asked Bubba.

"We don't know right now," said Fearless.

There was a round of concerned voices.

"I'm ready to go, Coach," said Bubba as if in a trance.

The team clapped for Bubba. Harry looked at his cousin and gave him a big thumbs up. He had never seen so serious a face on Bubba.

"Bubba Hawkins has gone from Water Boy to starting tackle," said Coach Braun, his intense eyes focused on Bubba. "It's a story worth a book, for sure. He'd better be tough in there tonight!"

"I'm getting my game face on right now, Coach!" said Bubba with a fierce scowl.

The Coach stood up in the middle of the huddle. "We're gonna start off playing ball just like we always have. Then we're gonna gradually shift to the new things we've practiced… I'll call 'em when we need 'em. Any questions?"

The players maintained an ominous silence.

"The Suffolk players to watch out for are this guy Duane Starr," said Braun, "… some of you know him… and their fullback, a guy they call Hunk something or 'nother… Hunk Swanson… that's it. Their quarterback is okay... Foster Hunt... and he can pass, mostly to the halfbacks... some to the ends. I wanna smother him if he tries to pass."

"Like the other teams," said Fearless, "these guys are gonna pull everything they can to score... and score early! So get yourselves ready! There isn't any warm-up in this game!"

"Okay, team!" yelled the Coach. "Shake off them jitters!"

Coach Braun started vibrating and shaking as he had before. "Shake off the jitters and get your head screwed on right!" shouted the Coach.

The team started shaking, laughing and pushing. Coach Fearless started shaking, looking somewhat embarrassed. Even Coach Phelps did a dignified shake.

"Alright!" shouted Coach Braun with a snarl that grew in volume with each word. "Now get on them game faces! I want you guys to be mean! Really mean! Extra mean!! Run these Peanut Pigs into the ground! Hit 'em clean, but hit 'em so hard they don' wanna get up!

"Hit 'em hard!" said Big Jim in his bass voice.

"You guys are hard and tough! I know it, 'cause... like ya said... ya keep running into me!" shouted Braun thumping his chest with two closed fists. "Show these Peanut Pancakes how hard and tough ya are! Make 'em wanna go back to Suffolk. And remember those cotton pickin' peanut shells in the locker room! Now get out there! Get out there! Get out there!!"

"Pig football!" shouted Allman jumping into the air. "Get mean and bust some Peanut Pigs!"

The huddle broke with a roar that matched the roar coming from the field.

****

A.P. Johns sat on the fifty yard line midway up the stands near the Press Box munching a bag of peanuts. Ike and Helen Quester, Charlton and Catherine Hawkins sat with them. Bobby Tom and Monique Zee, Tony's parents had joined them. Commander Bobby Tom Zee was a tall man with dark eyebrows and a rugged face. Monique was a petite woman with dark black hair and classic beauty.

"I'm glad they gave us all these peanuts," said A.P. "They're pretty good."

"You're supposed to save the shells and throw 'em in the air every time we score," said Catherine excitedly.

"I got bags of extra shells," grinned A.P. "Seems Fred Beckler had 'em left over... or something!"

"We all got 'em," said Ike holding up a big sack. "Everybody in the stands has 'em!"

The Churchland Trucker Band was marching smartly on the field in their black and orange uniforms, new sousaphones gleaming in the cool, crisp night air, purchased by Fred Beckler with funds from the previous games. They broke into the Churchland Fight song as they marched off the field, the sousaphones producing vibrating bass blasts. The fans started singing.

Oh when those Churchland Truckers fall in line,
They're going to win this game another time!
And for old Churchland High we'll yell and yell,
And for Old Churchland High we'll yell and yell and yell,
And then we'll fight fight fight for every yard,
Knock 'em to the ground, we'll hit 'em hard,
And run down the field for another score,
Churchland Hi-i-gh!

There was a wild cheer as the Truckers took the field. They ran as though chased by demons, their menacing black and orange uniforms catching the bright lights of the stadium. Black and orange pompoms waved in the stands. Cheerleaders yelled and jumped.

"There's Tony!" exclaimed Monique, poking Bobby Tom in the ribs as she caught a glimpse of number thirty-nine.

"He looks good!" said Bobby Tom proudly. "There's Harry, Ike!"

"I see him," said Ike. "There's a lot of pressure on him tonight."

"Oh, you know he'll do well!" said Helen, patting Ike's arm.

On the field, the Coaches ran into the stadium behind the team.

"We got Wimpy Sawyer as the Ref," said Coach Phelps as they ran.

"Where is that little fart?" asked Coach Braun glaring around the field.

"Right over there!" said Coach Phelps pointing to the scrawny little man in the black and white striped shirt.

"The starting line up for the Truckers," said the announcer over the loudspeaker, echoing loudly around the stadium. "At left end, Terrible Tony Zce... at left tackle, Biiiig Jim Jensen... at left guard, Battling Bucky Allison... at Center, Mr. America, Bob Porter...at right guard, Roughneck Renny Dickson... at right tackle, Baaad Bubba Hawkins..."

The crowd cheered loudly as each name was announced. Catherine Hawkins leaped from the stadium bench when Bubba's name was called. "Bubba's starting!" she exclaimed.

"This is really exciting!" exclaimed Helen. "They're both starting... and Tony too!"

"At right end," continued the announcer in an excited voice, "Bustin'

Bud Darby... at left halfback, Tough Terry Moddy... at fullback, Headhunter Harry Quester... at right halfback, Co-Captain Killer Karl Darby and at quarterback, number zero zero, Co-Captain, Allman Buddinger, the Ball Fox! And their Coach... your Coach! Cliff 'Shotgun' Braun!"

When the announcer finished, the crowd roared with a noise that could be heard in downtown Portsmouth. The Suffolk Red Raiders ran on to the field in their red trousers and white jerseys with bright red numbers. Their helmets were red with a white stripe. There were cheers from the Suffolk fans on the other side of the field. They were drowned out by the Churchland fans yelling and throwing clouds of peanut shells into the air.

"The Suffolk Red Raiders," shouted the announcer trying to be heard above the noise of the crowd, "and their Coach, Ennis 'Fatso' Hathaway."

Cheers erupted from the Suffolk side of the field where red and white pompoms rustled in the night air.

"That sonofabitch!" muttered Braun as Coach Hathaway rumbled clumsily onto the field. "He can't even run!"

"Naw," drawled Coach Fearless. "But he ain't dumb!"

Harry stood with Tony and Bubba on the sidelines watching the Suffolk team, feeling the excitement of the evening coarse through them.

"Where'd they get all those nicknames?" asked Tony.

"Hey, Terrible Tony,... the Announcer just made them up," said Bad Bubba.

"Okay... okay... you ready to go Baaaad Bubba?"

"Yeah!" said Bubba with a snarl. "I'm feeling badder and badder!"

Allman and Karl came running back from the coin toss. "We're gonna kick off," said Karl eagerly.

The players all gathered around the Coach. Jack Sanders was there, his arm still in a sling. He walked around among the players slapping them on the butt and growling encouragement. Arnie Eberly stood alone, aloof and stiff, still bandaged around his broken ribs.

"Hey Coach," said Allman, beginning to shake violently. "Let's see that shake again!"

Coach Braun grinned and did his "loosen it up shake". The team laughed.

"Enough of that laughing stuff!" said the Coach abruptly. "It's time to put that game mask on! It's time to intimidate them Peanut Pigs! Is everyone ready?"

"Yeah!" came the chorus of replies.

"Then get out there! Get out there! Get out there!" roared the Coach.

The huddle burst. Players shouted and pumped their fists as they took the field. The fans in the stands responded and a noise with a life of its own lifted from the field and vibrated the forest around Churchland Stadium. Harry ran on to the field with more adrenalin rushing in him than he had ever felt before. He glanced up into the stands, knowing that Paige and his parents were there watching him. It made him feel warm. He looked up at the lights, absorbed their energy, and quickly adjusted his game face to "full fierce". He lined up for the kick-off with trepidation and anticipation waging a battle in his soul.

****

The ball sailed high into the crisp night air. Harry watched it as though it were a slow motion picture against the glare of the lights. He ran down the field as fast as he could, knowing that he was the "breaker"… the player with the responsibility to break apart any blocking that formed in front of the opposing runner. Bob Porter was running slightly behind him as the "prime tackler", the player who would try to exploit the actions of the breaker and make the tackle. Tony and Bud had "contain" responsibility on each end. The rest of the Truckers ran in a broad line, sweeping down the field. Harry saw Duane Starr, number eleven, catch the ball as a wall of blockers formed in front of him. Duane faked to the left and ran to the right, the blockers staying in front of him. Harry pumped up his game face and crashed into the wall of blockers, taking two of them down. He fell to the ground and saw Bob flash through the hole in the blocking wall and grab Starr by the legs. Harry jumped to his feet, ran and crashed into Starr, knocking him backward. He rolled over and looked at the sidelines. They were at the Suffolk thirty yard line.

"Nice try, Duane," said Harry offering Starr a hand.

Starr ignored the hand and jumped up. He looked at Harry with anger in his eyes. "Stuff it, Quester!" he exclaimed and ran back to the red and white huddle that was forming.

"Friend of yours?" asked Bob sarcastically.

"You might say that," said Harry as they ran back to their defensive positions.

The Suffolk team came to the line of scrimmage. Harry surveyed them from his position as right linebacker in a six-two-two-one defense. They were big… very big. He knew Duane was fast… but he was also worried about the big fullback they called "Hunk", number thirty-three. This was going to be a tough game. He watched as the Suffolk quarterback, Foster Hunt, number one, took the ball from center and faded back to pass. Harry held his position as the end ran by him, knowing Karl would pick him up. The quarterback faked the pass and handed the ball to Duane who ran off tackle straight toward Harry. The center came out of the line and attempted to block Harry. Harry shoved him aside with a powerful thrust of his arms and met Duane head on before he could build up to his full speed. Harry drove Duane backward and bulled him to the ground. The impact of the hit swept through Harry. He ignored the pain and jumped up.

"That one won't work, Duane," said Harry with a scowl.

Duane got up slowly. "Is that all the Headhunter has?" he asked sarcastically.

Duane ran back to the Suffolk huddle. On the next play, Starr swept left end and got outside of Tony. Bob and Terry brought him down after a ten yard gain. First down for Suffolk! The next play was Starr around left end. Bud turned the play into Harry and he brought Starr down with a jarring tackle.

"That won't work either, Duane," muttered Harry as they lay briefly on the ground. "I'm gonna bust you every time!"

"Shut up, Quester, you arrogant bore," muttered Duane. "We're moving the ball on you... in case you haven't noticed."

"Try that left end again," said Harry invitingly, "and hold on to your jock!"

They both got up and went to their respective sides. On the next play, the big Suffolk fullback ran off their right tackle and gained eight yards before Terry and Big Jim brought him down. Suddenly, Suffolk was at midfield.

"We gotta stop 'em right here, gang," said Allman running around and smacking everybody on the butt. "Right here!"

The ball was snapped. Foster Hunt faded back and threw a pass to their left end who ran to the Churchland forty yard line. Allman and Karl brought him down hard.

"Time out!" called Allman excitedly. He ran to the sidelines and talked to Coach Braun.

"I'm going to score on you, Quester!" shouted Starr.

Harry looked at Starr, grinned and made a "come-on" motion with his hands at the halfback. Allman came back in. The team gathered around him.

"Okay, Harry," said Allman, "Shift to a fifty three defense... you take middle linebacker. Play Headhunter and go for the quarterback and that halfback!"

"I got it," said Harry wiping the perspiration from his face.

"Now you guys get tough!" said Allman in a whispered shout. "Play

Trucker ball! These guys are big but they're all peanut pussies! We need to knock 'em silly!"

"Yeah," said Harry. "But they're not dumb... so we gotta play smart and be mean both. Watch out for fake plays! They want to score on us right away... and they're gonna try anything to do it!"

"Bubba," said Allman, "watch your ass, 'cause they know Bart's not here... and they're gonna throw some stuff at ya!"

"I'm ready," said Bubba stretching his arms in front of him and snapping the knuckles on his big hands.

"Okay!" exclaimed Allman. "Let's do it!"

The Truckers took their defensive positions. The Red Raiders ran up to the line of scrimmage. The Truckers shifted to a fifty-three defense. The ball was snapped. Hunk Swanson took the ball and charged at Bubba's position. Harry shifted in that direction. Bubba fought off the block and got his arm around the fullback's waist. Harry launched his body and hit the Red Raider from the side. The player in red and white went down with a crash of bodies against the turf. There was a gain of three yards to the Churchland thirty-seven.

"Come on back, Hunk," muttered Bubba as they got to their feet. "That felt real good!"

"Screw you, Hawkins!" muttered Hunk as he crawled painfully to his feet. "I'm gonna run right over your ass!"

"What kinda hunk are ya, Hunk?" asked Bubba, wiping dirt from his face. "Felt like a hunk a' lard!"

Hunk gave Bubba a finger salute and walked back to his huddle.

The Red Raiders huddled and jogged back to the line of scrimmage. Foster Hunt, the Suffolk quarterback looked far downfield as he came to the line. Was it a fake or was he really going to try a pass? Harry's mind saw the whole field... the whole game... it was time for them to try the pass. He had to get to the quarterback!

"I'm coming through, Bucky," whispered Harry.

Bucky patted his left buttock. The ball was snapped. Bucky charged ahead and moved the center to his right. Harry charged through the line taking an elbow in the ribs from a Suffolk guard. The Red Raider quarterback faked to Starr and faded back. Starr broke through the line and raced downfield. Harry hit the Suffolk quarterback as he raised his arm to pass. He picked Foster Hunt up by the waist, drove him back ten yards and slammed him into the ground. Miraculously, the Red Raider didn't fumble.

"Don't you try to pass, Foster!" muttered the Headhunter as he pushed off of the Suffolk quarterback and got up. "I'm gonna drill ya until ya go sit on the bench!"

"You ain't long for this game, Headhunter," said Foster with a sneer. "We're gonna take ya out!"

"Headhunter! Headhunter!" chanted the Churchland fans.

The Suffolk quarterback got up painfully and pointed at Harry. Harry saw the yellow flag fly out of the corner of his eye.

"Unnecessary roughness!" shouted Wimpy Sawyer.

Harry heard the roar from the sideline. "Naaawww! It ain't none of that!" shouted Coach Braun. The Coach was leaning out onto the field like a bird dog poised to run and retrieve. His face was red, his tattered hat beating against his leg.

"Unnecessary roughness!" shouted Wimpy Sawyer again. "Fifteen yards!" The Referee picked up the ball and paced it off to the Churchland twenty-two yard line.

Coach Braun charged onto the field waving his arms. "Wimpy! You know that was a good tackle!" shouted Coach Braun, waving his hat wildly in the air.

Coach Hathaway rumbled onto the field like a pregnant bowling ball. "Get that damn Shotgun off the field," he shouted, "and let's play ball!"

"Shut up, Fatso," shouted Braun. "And get your lard butt off the field!"

"Shotgun," said Wimpy pleadingly. "Now you and Fatso get off the field... or I'll have to penalize both of you!"

"You blind or just... just wimpy, Wimpy?" sputtered Shotgun angrily. He turned his back on them and stalked off the field, jamming his hat down over his ears and pulling the brims down. Fatso waddled back to his sideline.

"Shotgun!" exclaimed Slate in an agitated voice. "Get off the field! You're playing right into Fatso's hands! You're gonna get us penalized right down to our goal... if you keep that up!"

"What do ya mean... playing into his hands?" asked Coach Braun as he reached the sideline.

"I can see it," said Coach Fearless with concern. "Fatso wants to get ya thrown outa the game!"

"Yeah, and Buddinger and Quester, too," said Phelps. "I think Fatso has Wimpy pumped up about the headhunter defense!"

"What the hell!" exclaimed Coach Braun. "What if I do get thrown out?"

"Coach," said Coach Fearless, "This team won't play the same... if you're not here!"

"He's right, Shotgun," said Slate. "So keep it down!"

Churchland lined up in the fifty-three defense again as the Red Raiders came to the line of scrimmage. Instinctively, Harry knew that

Duane would demand the ball this close to the goal line. He hadn't said "we're going to score on you." He had said "I'm going to score on you." Starr's ego was giving it away. He also knew that Duane wanted to run at him. So, he'd be running somewhere near the middle. Harry watched Duane's eyes as they came to the line of scrimmage. Duane avoided Harry's eyes.

"Bucky... Starr's coming up the middle," whispered Harry. Take the right side... I got left... and plug it up!"

Bucky nodded. The ball was snapped to the quarterback. Harry watched a fake to the fullback going off their left tackle. The quarterback spun and handed the ball to Starr headed for the Trucker left guard position. Harry charged into the hole and met the Red Raider right guard head on. He pushed the player back and was surprised to feel the blow of a fist in his gut. He slid off the block and into Duane Starr. Harry hit Duane with a forearm shiver directly against the halfback's arm that was holding the ball. The ball squirted up into the air and off to Harry's right, directly into the outstretched hands of Bubba Hawkins. Bubba looked at it with surprise and started to run. He was immediately flattened by a Red Raider tackle. He fell to the ground and got up holding the ball in the air, his face beaming. Churchland ball!

"Headhunter! Headhunter!" The chant echoed around the stadium.

"Way to go, Bubba!" shouted Allman running up and wrapping his arms around Bubba.

Fatso Hathaway was bouncing up and down the Suffolk sideline screaming at Wimpy Sawyer.

"Unnecessary roughness!" shouted Fatso. "That Headhunter guy! Unnecessary roughness! Can't ya see that, Wimpy? Can't ya see that?"

Coach Braun responded, pacing up and down the sidelines, beating his hat against his thigh and glaring across the field at Fatso. Slate walked beside him, talking to him earnestly.

"Leave it be, Shotgun," exclaimed Slate. "We got the ball!"

Churchland huddled.

"That guard punched me in the gut," said Harry angrily.

Allman looked at Harry with concern. "Hold your temper, Harry," he said. "They been punchin' me too. They're trying to get us outa the game... don't fall for it!"

"I'll be okay," said Harry, containing his anger.

"An' don't bullshit with 'em," said Allman. "That's just what they want! The play is thirty-three on one."

Porter left the huddle.

"Thirty-three on one," whispered Allman. "Break!"

The ball was snapped. Allman handed off to Harry. Harry felt the ball thump into his belly. He wrapped his arms tightly around it and charged at the hole between right guard and right tackle. He popped through the hole and was met by a linebacker. He kept his legs driving and managed to gain three yards. The linebacker fell on him and punched him in the face. Pain shot through his nose.

"That's the way you damn guys want to play it?" asked Harry, blood coming to his nose.

"We got your number, Headhunter!" whispered the linebacker.

"I'll see you on the next play, you bastard!" said Harry through the blood on his lips. Anger rose up in him like a dark shadow!

Harry got up. Duane stood beside him. "You're not going anywhere, Quester," he sneered. "We know everything you're going to try!"

"Yeah?" asked Harry, taking a step toward Duane, his fists clenched. "We know all about that, Duane!"

Big Jim pulled Harry away from Starr.

"Allman said no bullshitting," said Big Jim in his usual unemotional voice.

Harry wiped away the blood and ran back to the huddle. On the next play, Karl ran to the left end. Tony threw a block that got him by the end. He ran for ten yards before he was tackled. That put the ball on the Churchland thirty five with a first down. Harry got the ball on the next play and gained another three yards. Terry Moddy ran it for three more yards and left the field limping.

Hero ran on to the field, pumping his arms, ready to rescue the faltering Truckers. On third down, Hero was stopped for no gain. Bud punted a high ball to the Suffolk twenty five. The Red Raiders returned it to their thirty. They ran it to the thirty-eight and punted. Hero took the punt. Harry threw a block on a racing Red Raider and took him down with a crunch. Hero ran the ball back to the Churchland thirty five.

"We got good field position now!" bragged Hero, getting up from the tackle. "It's time to get going!"

"Good run, Hero," said Allman. "We're gonna get it going!"

The first quarter ended with no score. Coach Phelps and Coach Fearless paced the sideline with Coach Braun as the teams exchanged positions on the field, defending the opposite goals.

"We've gotta find a way to spring Quester," said Slate to Cliff on the sidelines. "They're stopping him at the line.... and Karl and Hero too."

"We need to try the pass, Coach," said Coach Fearless.

"Try it," said Braun. "If it don't work, I have another plan."

****

Allman Buddinger knelt in the huddle behind the Churchland thirty-five yard line. "Okay guys," whispered Allman. "We're gonna start using the new plays. "We'll start with a pass play… they don't expect that. This will be a one thirty pass right twenty. It's the twenty yard pass Harry and I have been working on. Remember, it's supposed to look like a run. I'll fake to Hero and Harry will sneak out to the right flat. You guys in the line… make it look like a run, but don't get off sides! One thirty pass right twenty… on set."

Porter broke away.

"One thirty pass right twenty… on set…. break!"

The Truckers ran to the line of scrimmage.

"Get down!… Get set!"

The ball was snapped. Harry ran as though he were going to block for Hero through right tackle. Allman faked a hand off to Hero, put the ball beside his leg and walked back as though he had done his job and was through with the play. Hero folded his arms tightly and crashed into the line with all the determination of a player possessing the ball. Harry ran through the line and faded out to the right flat just over the midfield stripe. He was surprised that none of the Red Raiders covered him. He faked to the inside and then ran outside to a point near the sideline just beyond midfield.

Harry looked up just as the ball sailed toward the sidelines in a wobbly spiral. It was slightly high. He leaped and caught the ball and came down inside the sidelines. He caught his momentum and balanced precariously. He stayed in bounds and turned up field. He saw the linebacker trying to catch up to him. Duane Starr and another halfback were running at full speed from midfield with an angle to cut him off. Harry reached down and found all the speed he could bring. His legs churned, kicking up turf as he raced along the sidelines. A great roar arose from the crowd in the stands.

The first halfback was closing in on him. Harry chose the right second to cut inside and the Red Raider's momentum carried him out of bounds, missing Harry. He saw Duane closing rapidly. He widened his stance as he ran as Jack had shown him to do and lowered his shoulder. Duane hit him and tried to wrap his arms around Harry's shoulders. Harry's lowered shoulder hit Duane in the midsection and threw him backward. Duane fell to the turf in front of Harry. Harry stumbled over Duane, regained his balance and ran on with the Red Raider safety in hot pursuit. He crossed the goal line as the Red Raider tackled him and slid into the end zone. Harry's face scraped along the turf, reactivating his bloody nose. Another Red Raider fell on top of them and Harry felt a punch to his right kidney that sent waves of pain up his side and into his shoulder. He clawed his way free and jumped up just as Bubba ran up.

"I saw that rabbit punch, you guys!" shouted Bubba angrily.

"Cool it, Bubba," said Harry, wiping away the blood and dirt on his face.

Coach Braun was running along the sideline screaming at the Referee. "Wimpy! Wimpy! Did ya see that?" shouted the Coach in a rage.

The Referee didn't answer. Wimpy Sawyer threw up his arms, signaling touchdown. Coach Braun took off his pork pie hat, threw it on the ground and stomped on it with extra ferocity.

Slate put a restraining arm on Coach Braun's shoulder. "Come on, Shotgun... back off! We scored!"

"Those bastards are rabbit punching in the pile!" shouted Coach Braun, his face red.

"You never did that did you, Shotgun?" asked Slate, his eyebrows raised.

Coach Braun picked up his hat and stalked back to the bench.

Allman ran up and hugged Harry. "Nice catch, Harry!"

"Oh Oh! Oh Oh!" chanted the fans mimicking Allman's zero-zero number. "Ball Fox! Ball Fox! Headhunter! Headhunter!"

Fatso Hathaway was yelling at Wimpy Sawyer from the other side of the field. "He was outa bounds, Wimpy. Dammit! He was out of bounds way back there!"

Wimpy made a palms down pacifying gesture toward Fatso. He ran over to the sidelines and spoke to Fatso. "Take it easy, Coach," consoled Wimpy. "He was in bounds... I was right there... he was in bounds... and you got plenty of time!"

Churchland lined up for the extra point. Harry ran the ball between center and left guard with Renny pulling from the opposite side and leading the way though the hole. He was jarred by a tackle just as he crossed the goal line and fell to the turf. Again, he felt a punch against his back, but ignored it. He got up and looked up at the lights towering above him. It was like being in a giant, illuminated fishbowl surrounded by unbelievable noise. He took a deep breath, savoring the moment. Churchland seven, Suffolk nothing.

"You lucked out on that one, Quester, you bastard," said Starr coming up next to Harry.

"I saw you on your back, Starr," said Harry giving Duane a bump with his shoulder. "You're gonna be there all night!"

Harry ran to his kickoff position. The whistle sounded. The ball sailed through the air and Duane Starr took it on the Suffolk twenty-five. Harry charged down the field and cracked open the blockers in front of Duane. Duane faked and avoided Bob but ran straight into Bubba who bounced all two hundred and twenty pounds of his body on top of the halfback at the thirty-five yard line.

"Baaad Bubba! Baaaad Bubba!" shouted A.P. from the stands. The crowd picked it up.

"Baaad Bubba! Baaaad Bubba!" came the roar from the crowd. The loudest shriek came from Catherine Hawkins.

The Truckers lined up in a fifty-three defense.

"Watch out for trick plays and sweeps," cautioned Harry as he paced up and own behind the line. "They know they can't run through the middle!"

The Red Raiders trotted up to the line of scrimmage with a little less confidence than in the first quarter. The ball was snapped. It was an end around. The left end pulled and ran to the right. The quarterback faked to the fullback and handed it to the end who tried to sweep the right end. Harry ran to his left with Bob. Tony avoided a block and contained the runner to the inside. Bob lunged at the runner. Just before Bob brought the end down, the end lateraled back to Duane Starr who was sweeping wider to the outside. Harry glanced back. Hero had been sucked to the inside by the fullback fake. Duane had a clear path in front of him except for Allman who raced toward the sideline from his safety position.

Harry turned on the speed, forcing his big body to run faster than ever intended. He lunged at Duane as the speedy halfback ran by and managed to get a hand on his foot. Duane stumbled forward, partially regained his balance and tried to run on. Allman hit him at midfield and pushed Duane out of bounds. Duane staggered toward where the Churchland Coaches stood. Coach Phelps and Coach Fearless dodged out of the way. Coach Braun raised his arms to his chest, crouched and stood his ground with a determined look on his bulldog face. He absorbed the full momentum of the Suffolk halfback. Starr fell to the ground in a red and white heap. Coach Braun staggered backward but retained his balance. Coach Fearless offered Starr a hand. Starr got up holding his chest painfully, refusing the hand. He paced back and forth, his hands on his hips, breathing heavily. He pointed accusingly at Coach Braun.

"Shotgun knocked me down… out of bounds!" screamed Duane.

"You trying to hurt me, boy?" asked Braun, an innocent look coming over his bulldog face.

"Shotgun! Shotgun!" roared the crowd.

Fatso Hathaway came running across the field, a rolling, wobbling mound of flesh. "Goddamit Wimpy! Didya see that?" shouted Fatso in a shrill voice. "Shotgun knocked the hell out of my player when he was outa bounds!"

"Ya got that wrong, ya fatso slob!" shouted Coach Braun, meeting Fatso at the sideline. "Your player come off the field… and ran right into me… on purpose!" He held up his arm and displayed a bleeding forearm. "See what he done to me? I'm hurt!"

"You're faking it, Shotgun!" shouted Fatso, angrily confronting Braun.

Coach Braun stuck his face into that of Coach Hathaway. "You're a big fat pussy, Fatso!" whispered Braun between his teeth so no one but Hathaway could hear. "And you're playing dirty! Real dirty! I seen those rabbit punches! How long you been training on that?"

"Listen, Shotgun," said Fatso uneasily, "I'm gonna…"

"Come on, Fatso!" exclaimed Braun sticking out his bulldog jaw. "You're gonna what?"

The scrawny form of Wimpy Sawyer, empowered by the striped shirt, arrived at the side of the two coaches. "You guys had better cool it," said Wimpy in a strained voice stepping between the two Coaches.

"Shotgun! Shotgun!" roared the crowd.

"Fatso, please go back to your own sideline," pleaded Wimpy. "I don't want to have to expel either of you from the game."

"Yeah, Fatso," said Braun, his eyes wide with innocence, "please go back to your own sideline… so I can get this here arm where your player attacked me… treated."

Fatso glared at Braun and Sawyer, turned around and stalked back across the field, his belly bouncing in front of him.

"Boo Fatso! Boo Fatso!" screamed the Churchland fans.

The half ended with the score Churchland seven, Suffolk nothing.

****

The Truckers clattered into their dressing room at halftime. The Coaches jogged along behind them.

"How's your arm, Shotgun?" asked Slate with a sly grin.

"Ya liked that, huh?" growled Braun.

"Yeah," said Coach Fearless, "but ya better not plan to hit any more of their players!"

"Who? Me?" asked Braun, eyes wide with innocence, "the sonofabitch ran right into me. I just couldn't get outa the way… and I had to defend myself… and he did bust open my arm!"

"Yeah, yeah, Coach, I know," said Eddie. "Just be careful. You and Fatso have got Wimpy all worked up… and he just might get pissed and throw one of ya out… or both of ya!"

"Don't let him throw Fatso out," muttered Braun. "I want that sonofabitch in there when we beat 'em!"

The team went into the dressing room and found Bart Whitely waiting for them. His left arm was in a sling. He was sitting on a bench talking to Jack Sanders whose arm was also in a sling. Arnie sat at the end of the bench watching Bart with hostile eyes.

"Hey!" exclaimed Allman merrily. "It's the hospital team!"

"What happened, Bart?" asked Tony with concern.

"I had a fight with Calcione," said Bart. "He cut me."

"Johnny found out what Bart told Harry about the playbook," said Jack.

"Is it bad?" asked Harry, his face still covered with dirt and blood.

"Doc thinks so," said Bart. "But I've had worse. They tried to keep me in the damn hospital… but I snuck out!"

"You sure you're okay, Bart?" asked Coach Fearless.

"Yeah, Coach," said Bart standing up. "I'm okay."

Bart gave Bubba a Trucker salute, hitting him with his good fist on the shoulder. "You're doing great, Bubba!" said Bart.

Bubba faked a Trucker salute at Bart. "Thanks Bart!" he said. "I'm having a ball!"

"Listen, guys," said Bart earnestly, "I learned something else from Johnny. He bought a new 1954 Studebaker Commander… a blue one with a big V8 engine… a really neat looking car that he can't afford!"

"He has it now?" asked Harry incredulously.

"Yeah!" exclaimed Bart. "He's getting a lot a' money from somewhere!"

"Where?" asked Harry.

"He works a big construction job," said Arnie bitterly.

"Naw," said Bart, waving a big hand at Arnie, "he sure can't afford a new Studebaker Commander working on no construction job!"

"What about his Old Man?" asked Harry.

"Maybe," said Bart, glancing at Arnie defiantly, "but I don't think so! The red Studebaker belongs to his Ol' Man! He brags all about the blue one being his!"

"Alright, you guys," shouted Coach Fearless. "Stop screwing around and gather 'roun the Coach!"

The Truckers stopped talking and quickly gathered around Coach Braun.

"Nice block, Coach!" exclaimed Allman with glee.

Braun glowered at Allman then broke into a tiny half smile. "Just keep them guys away from me," he said mischievously. "I saw ya push that guy right at me, Buddinger."

"Right, Coach," beamed Allman. "Lemme know if you want another one!"

"No, Allman," said Slate. "Keep everyone away from Coach Braun. Fatso is trying to get him ejected, you know… and we don't want that!"

"Okay, Coach," said Allman, sitting down on a bench near where Braun was.

"Okay guys," said the Coach, "these Suffolk guys are tough… and they're playing dirty. I seen them rabbit punches. Quester and Buddinger have both taken some… some of you other guys, too. Fatso is trying to get me ejected… and he's told his players to get Quester and Buddinger ejected too. So far, you haven't let it get to you… if it happens some more, I want ya to tell the Refs without losing your temper, and just see what happens."

"We'll settle with these guys after the game!" exclaimed Allman rubbing his right fist into his left palm.

"What about you, Coach?" asked Karl diplomatically. "You going to be able to hold your temper?"

"Who me?" grinned Braun. "Why, I'm just a real nice guy trying to do a job!"

The team laughed loudly.

"I'm gonna be mean enough to keep you guys mean enough," said the Coach. "So far, you've been okay mean… but there's room to improve. These guys are big and tough… but look at 'em… they were sucking wind near the end of the half! They ain't near as in shape as you guys! In the second half you gotta crank up your mean face and whack 'em good… clean, but good!"

Big Jim stood up and faced the team. "We're gonna whack 'em good!" he said in his stoic voice with an expressionless face.

The Truckers applauded loudly for Big Jim's speech. Big Jim sat down and actually grinned slightly at the applause.

"Well said, Big Jim!" exclaimed Coach Fearless with a grin.

"Now listen," said Coach Braun. "I don't know what these guys are gonna do in the second half… but they're gonna pull everything they can think of… that's for damn sure. So, when it happens, don't let it rattle ya. You guys are tough… and smart, and I know you can handle it. I'll be sending in things to do to help out. Be smart!"

Coach Braun stood up and paced around. He planted the ragged hat squarely on his head. The bulldog expression came over his face. "Now here's what we're gonna do," he said. "On offense we're gonna run the new plays… specially the ones with pulling guards. I expect Fatso to try the shifting defense stuff that Great Bridge tried. Quester, you be ready to change the blocking assignments. So… listen up to Quester when ya come to the line."

"He'll shout 'em out right after I say 'get down'," said Allman. "After that, it's regular assignments."

"You guys remember the numbers I gave you to call out the shifts," said Harry.

"Now, what we're gonna do on defense," said the Coach. "We're gonna play Headhunter Free… the Headhunter defense with a new twist. The middle linebacker will be free… free to take position wherever he thinks he can stop the play. That means you other guys will all have increased contain and hole coverage responsibility. So… be ready when I call it!"

"Are there any questions about the Headhunter Free defense?" asked Coach Fearless.

Coach Braun looked around at all of the sweaty dirty faces. He saw a Team looking back at him.

"Welcome back, Bart!" said Coach Braun. "Come sit on the bench with the other walking wounded!"

"Thanks, Coach!"

****

Chapter Sixteen
Suffolk, Second Half

Terry Moddy came back and replaced Hero in the second half. Harry watched the Suffolk kickoff sail into the Terry's arms. Terry ran it back to the Churchland forty where he was hit by two Suffolk players. Two more Red Raiders fell on top of him.

"That's piling on, Ref," said Harry running to where Terry lay.

The Referee ignored Harry. Harry offered Terry a hand and pulled him up.

"Nice run, Terry," said Harry.

Terry groaned. "Those guys are heavy!" he complained as they ran back to the huddle.

"How's the leg?" asked Harry.

"It's okay," said Terry with a dramatic grimace. "But I don't need those big fat guys jumping on it!"

"I told the Ref they were piling on," said Harry. "But he didn't do anything."

"The bastards are blind," said Terry shaking his head.

In the huddle, Allman called the play. "Forty four pull on one," he said. "That's your lead, Harry… your pull, Bucky."

Bob left the huddle and ran to the line of scrimmage.

"Forty four pull on one… break!"

The Truckers ran to the line of scrimmage. Allman began the snap count.

"Get down…"

The Red Raiders shifted into a fifty four defense with four linebackers. Harry quickly assessed the defense. "Three-thirty, twenty-forty," he shouted, changing the blocking assignments to cover the extra linebacker.

"Get ready!…. Hut one!"

The ball was snapped. Bucky pulled out behind the center and ran to the opposite side and through the three hole. Harry followed close behind. Karl took the ball from Allman, paused briefly to allow the blocking to develop and ran to the three hole. Bucky pushed the outside linebacker to the outside and crashed down on top of him. Harry charged at Hunk, the inside linebacker, head on. He got under Hunk and pushed him straight up and back. Karl came through the hole at breakneck speed and flashed into the backfield. Duane Starr ran at him. Karl gave him a fake, but Duane didn't take it. He brought Karl down after a fifteen yard gain. Churchland had the ball at the Red Raider forty-five yard line.

In the huddle, Allman called the play. "If I see them in that fifty-four defense this time, I'm gonna call 'shift' and some number. Ignore the number. It means we'll pass… one sixty pass ten center… that's for Tony to get behind the linebackers… if I don't call shift, it'll be the same play we ran last time… forty-four pull…. all on two. Any questions?"

There were none. Bob left the huddle and ran to the line.

"Forty-four pull…. or shift one sixty pass ten center… on two…. break!"

The team ran to the line of scrimmage. Allman looked up and down the line. The Red Raiders were in a sixty-two defense.

"Get down!…"

Suffolk shifted to a fifty four defense.

"Shift… eight four!"

"Hut one… hut two!" shouted Allman.

The ball was snapped. Harry charged straight ahead breaking through the line on the right. Tony went down field, faked to the outside and ran to the center of the field just behind the linebackers. Allman sent a decent spiral over center. Tony stretched to find the ball, caught it in mid air and started to run, Harry in front of him. They left the linebackers behind. Duane Starr closed on Tony quickly. Harry ran to block Duane. Duane faked Harry and he missed the block. In the process of faking, Duane allowed Tony to gain ground. Duane chased Tony until he was brought down by the Red Raider safety on the Suffolk twenty yard line.

"Drop your jock, Quester?" shouted Duane as he got up.

"Yeah… yeah!" said Harry. "Sure did… nice fake, Duane! I'll take the yardage!"

Duane stared at the ball on the Suffolk twenty yard line and frowned as he walked to his halfback position. Harry ran back to the huddle at full speed.

"Let's shove it down their throats," said Allman in the huddle. "They're expecting us to pass, now. Can we tough out this score the old fashioned way?"

"Tough it out," said Big Jim. "Come my way."

"Lets' do it," said Bubba. "These guys are tired. I can move this guy in front of me!"

"Okay, said Allman. "Twenty four … shift one seventy ten center… that's you Bud … if we shift…. on two."

"I got it," said Bud.

Allman surveyed the line of scrimmage. Suffolk was back in a sixty-two defense.

"Get down!… Get set!… Hut one!… Hut two!"

The ball was snapped. Allman handed directly off to Terry who followed Big Jim through the two hole for a seven yard gain. On the next play, Karl followed Bubba through the three hole for a five yard gain. First and goal for the Truckers at the Suffolk eight yard line!

The Churchland crowd was roaring the loudest of the night. Black and orange pom-poms waved and peanut shells flew in clouds into the air.

"Time out!" shouted Duane Starr.

"Time!" called out the referee.

Harry knelt with the other players behind the line of scrimmage while Allman ran to the sideline to talk to the Coach. He came back with a big grin on his face.

"Okay, guys, here it is," grinned Allman, speaking loudly above the noise of the crowd. "One six option two… shift one two… that's the option to Terry through your hole Big Jim. The shift is the quarterback sneak over you, Bucky. Got it? On one."

They ran back to the line of scrimmage. The ball was snapped. Harry ran to the left in front of Terry, followed by Allman with the ball. Big Jim crushed two players in front of him. Harry followed and got the linebacker. Allman faked turning into the hole and lateraled to Terry. Terry ran across the goal untouched.

"Tough, Tough… Tough-Tough Ter-ry!" chanted the Cheerleaders and Churchland fans as Terry ran to the huddle with a heady gait.

"How's the leg?" asked Harry.

"Feels great!" smiled Terry.

"Nice run," Terry," said Karl.

Harry bulled the ball off tackle for the extra point. Hunk Swanson fell on top of him and punched him in the belly. Harry shoved Hunk away.

"After the game, Hunk," grimaced Harry. "If ya wanna fight, save it for after the game!"

"You're a pussy, Headhunter," muttered Hunk as he got up.

Harry rolled over, got to his feet and said nothing. Churchland fourteen, Suffolk zero! Suffolk returned the kickoff to their own thirty-two yard line. Duane got the ball on the first play. Harry was surprised when Hunk Swanson came out of the backfield and blocked him. He wasn't ready for that and Hunk knocked him down and fell on top of him. Another player fell on top of them and Hunk gouged Harry in the eye. Duane ran on for a gain of eight yards.

"Ow! Goddamit!" shouted Harry struggling to get up, holding his left eye.

Hunk held him down until the last possible minute. Harry felt a rabbit punch in his back. Harry got up holding his eye and went to Wimpy Sawyer. "Ref! Those guys are gouging eyes in the pile," said

Harry.

Wimpy looked at Harry closely. "You alright, Boy?" asked Wimpy.

"I'm okay," said Harry. "But watch 'em! They're gouging in the pileup!"

"You okay, Harry?" asked Allman.

"Yeah… I guess so," said Harry holding his eye. "This guy Hunk… he's keying on me and coming after me each play."

"Yeah?" asked Allman. "Let's go to Headhunter Free!"

Big Jim was standing near. "Set him up, Harry," he said. "I'll take him out!"

"You take him low, Jim… I'll take him high," said Allman rubbing his fist in his palm.

"Okay Jim, I'm gonna shift out over left end and make him come after me."

"Okay," said Big Jim stoically.

Foster Hunt came to the line of scrimmage, a look of smug satisfaction on his face. He started the snap count. Harry shifted out over left end. Bob shifted more to the middle. Allman moved up from his safety position near the linebackers. The Suffolk quarterback looked at them in confusion. The ball was snapped. Foster handed off to Duane Starr who ran toward the right. Harry watched Hunk come out of the backfield toward him. He gauged his block carefully and stood Hunk up at the line of scrimmage with a forearm shiver. He slid off of Hunk and tackled Duane. Big Jim blindsided Hunk with a ferocious hit in the torso. There was the sound of snapping bone. Allman leaped high and hit Hunk in the face with a shattering forearm. Hunk dropped to the turf where he writhed in pain holding his left arm, his face bleeding. Big Jim stood over him like a tiger over his kill, then turned and walked away.

"Time out!" shouted the Referee.

Fatso came running onto the field with his first aid kit and an Assistant Coach. They knelt over Hunk. Then Fatso got up and yelled angrily at Wimpy.

"That was… something…. unsportsmanlike conduct, or something," yelled Fatso. "That big Churchland guy… Jensen… and Buddinger… hit my player from the side after the runner was already past him!"

"I didn't see it, Coach," said Wimpy slowly.

Fatso bumped the small man with his enormous belly. "You must be blind, Wimpy!" shouted Fatso in a rage.

Coach Braun was on the field as soon as he saw Fatso belly bump Wimpy. He ran out, Slate Phelps chasing him.

"What's he trying to sell ya now, Wimpy?" screamed Coach Braun.

"You're setting up to hurt my players, Shotgun," screamed Fatso.

"This boy's arm is broken!"

"You're piling on and gouging in the pile, Fatso, ya slob," screamed Coach Braun. "These blind zebras can't see it… but I can!"

Fatso stepped closer to Braun. "You accusing me of dirty football?" he asked his breath steaming the night air, smelling of garlic. "You're so dirty ya break the noses of your goddam players… just like ya did when they threw ya outa college!"

"What ya know 'bout that, Fatso?" shouted Braun, suddenly aware. "What the hell ya know 'bout that!" His chin jutted forward angrily.

Wimpy pulled them apart. "Last warning for you guys," said the little man in his shrill voice. "Break it up right now… or you're both gone!"

Coach Phelps tugged at Braun's sleeve. Braun turned around and walked calmly off the field as though nothing had happened. Fatso turned red in the face, staggered and knelt on one knee. The Suffolk first aid man put smelling salts under his nose. Fatso got up slowly and walked heavily off the field. The Suffolk men helped Hunk off the field with a sling around his broken arm.

The third quarter ended with the score Churchland fourteen, Suffolk zero.

****

Suffolk punted and Churchland took over the ball at their own forty yard line. Harry looked across the line of scrimmage at the Suffolk players. Some waited on one knee, breathing heavily. Others stood with their backs bent over, their hands on their hips.

"These guys are tired," said Harry. "Maybe we won't have any more of that rabbit punching stuff… after Big Jim and Allman held school!"

"No more rabbit punching!" said Big Jim, nodding his head.

"You're right, they are tired," observed Allman. "Coach wants to run it down the field and run out the clock."

"Let's do it," said Harry.

"Okay," said Allman, "thirty-three on one… shift eighty nine end around if I call it… on one."

Harry took the hand off from Allman and ran right behind Bubba. Bubba stood the Suffolk tackle up and shoved him backward. Harry ran by him and stiff armed the linebacker that had replaced Hunk. He rumbled forward for nine yards before the safety took him down. On the next two plays, Karl and Terry gained sixteen yards. The Truckers had the ball at the Red Raider thirty-five with a first down.

"Twenty-two on four… shift one eight pass center ten… on four," said Allman. "I'm gonna stagger the call… so don't get offside."

The huddle broke.

"Get down…"

The Red Raiders shifted to a fifty-four defense.

"Twenty Thirty, Ten sixty!" shouted Harry.

"Get set… Hut one!… Hut Hut two!… "

A Red Raider charged across the line. A yellow flag flew. "Off sides… defense!" shouted Wimpy.

The Referee picked up the ball and marched off five yards toward the Suffolk goal.

"That quarterback!" shouted Fatso, cupping his hands to form a loud hailer. "He's calling… funny signals! He can't do that!"

Coach Braun took off his hat in exasperation and started to yell back.

"Cool it, Coach," said Slate standing next to him. "Just let Fatso yell all he wants!"

"But… but…"

"I know you like yelling at him, Shotgun," said Slate. "But just can it for awhile and see what happens!"

"Okay, Slate," said Cliff. "But just for awhile!"

In the huddle, Allman called the same play. "On one!"

Allman handed the ball to Terry, but the exchange was muffed and the ball fell to the ground. It bounced crazily and Red Raiders converged on it. Harry fell on top of the ball and grabbed helplessly as it squirted out from under his weight. Big Jim grabbed it, but it was knocked free by a Red Raider. Duane Starr ran in from the backfield and chased the bouncing, rolling ball. He picked it up and was immediately hit hard by Harry. The ball squirted free and rolled toward Allman. Allman picked up the ball in an athletic movement that only he could have done and ran toward the Suffolk goal line, dodging tacklers in the open field. Big Jim and Bubba ran in front of him.

"Get that one on the right, Bubba!" shouted Allman, pointing.

Bubba ran at a red and white uniform to his right and smacked the player with a powerful forearm.

"One more to go, Big Jim!" shouted Allman pausing to allow the big tackle time to position himself.

The safety tried to dodge Big Jim, but saw Renny running at him. He hesitated for a moment and Big Jim collided with him, hitting him with a mighty forearm shiver. There was an involuntary gasp of awe from the crowd that echoed around the stadium. The safety fell and Allman pranced into the end zone. He held the ball high in the air and pranced around the end zone like some elf on Saint Patrick's Day.

"Oh Oh!… Ball Fox!" cheered the crowd. "Biiiig Jim!… Baaaad Bubba!"

"I almost had that ball!" exclaimed Duane shaking his head as he got up.

"You almost had a lotta things, Duane," said Harry. "Almost doesn't count!"

The teams lined up for the extra point. Allman tried to quarterback sneak it over for the point, but it was half a yard short. Churchland twenty, Suffolk nothing. Harry looked up at the game clock on the scoreboard. Eight minutes remained in the game!

Harry ran with Allman to take position for the kickoff. "That was some fancy running, Allman," he said. "You ought to run it more!"

"Are you kidding?" laughed Allman. "And mess up this pretty face like yours and Jack's. Not a chance!"

The Churchland kickoff was low and short. It came down to a Red Raider at their own thirty-five yard line. The Red Raider fielded the ball, turned and lateraled back to Duane Starr at the thirty. Harry crashed though one blocker and launched himself at Duane. Duane dodged Harry and ran toward the right sideline. The Suffolk crowd roared as there was suddenly only one man between Duane and the Churchland goal… Allman Buddinger. Harry picked himself up and ran full speed after Duane, running a good six yards behind him.

"I gotcha now, Duane!" shouted Harry at the top of his lungs. "Look out!"

Duane flinched, jogged to the side and looked back. At that moment, Allman saw his chance. He ran at Duane and took him down at the Churchland thirty yard line.

"Quester, you ass-hole!" shouted Duane angrily as he got up. "You're going to pay for that!"

Allman got up and patted Duane on the head with a big silly grin on his face. "Nice run, Peanut Boy," he said.

Duane brushed away Allman's hand. "Stay away from me, Buddinger, you clown!"

"Aw, you hurt me to the bone, Peanut Boy," said Allman in a mock whine.

"Come on, Allman," said Harry, pulling him away. "That was too damn close!"

Allman and Harry ran back to their defensive positions.

"Score! Score! Score! Score!" chanted the Suffolk fans.

"Defense! Defense!" chanted the Trucker fans. The stadium was in an uproar.

"The Red Raiders have the ball on the Churchland thirty yard line!" said the announcer excitedly over the stadium loudspeaker. It sounded strange to Harry as the sound echoed into the forest around the Stadium.

"Okay guys," said Allman, "line up in sixty-two and shift to Headhunter Free."

"Go get 'em, Headhunter!" said Big Jim slapping Harry on the buttocks.

Harry lined up at right linebacker. The Red Raiders came to the line of scrimmage. The noise in the stadium was deafening, the sound beating into Harry's head as he tried to think. They had plenty of time. They would try to get the ball into Duane's hands somehow... but how? Duane would probably run... but they might throw to him. No... they'd try the run first. It would be some kind of trick run.

"Shift!" shouted Harry. "The team shifted to a fifty-three Headhunter defense. Harry lined up just outside of left tackle behind Big Jim.

"Post!" shouted the Suffolk quarterback.

What did that mean, thought Harry. He watched the quarterback's eyes. He watched Duane's eyes. Nothing. The snap count began. The ball was snapped. The Red Raider quarterback faded back to pass. Harry started to crash through the line after him, but something... some instinct held him and he watched Duane. Duane started toward the line and then turned and ran behind the quarterback. He took the ball from the quarterback's upraised hand and turned on the speed toward his left end. Harry ran down the line, following Duane, hoping that Bud could contain him inside. He glanced toward his goal. The fake pass had sucked Karl, Terry and Allman way back trying to cover the Suffolk ends. Bubba lumbered along in front of Harry. A Suffolk guard pulled and was running interference for Duane. Bud turned the play in. The guard blocked Bubba. Duane ran to the side away from the block and found Harry waiting for him. Duane put a fake on Harry, but Harry held his ground and brought the Suffolk halfback down with a tackle that rattled his teeth. Duane lay on the ground on his back, not moving as Harry got up. There was a gasp from the Suffolk crowd.

"Come on, Duane," said Harry offering his hand. "Get up! I got more of that for you!"

Duane stared at Harry and sat slowly up. He brushed away the hand. "I'm going to score on you, Quester," he gasped. "And, in case you didn't know it, Paige has come back to me."

"You're lying, Starr," said Harry suddenly feeling a deep hurt in his heart.

"You'll see," said Duane in pain. "She knows what's good for her... and it's not you!"

"Time out!" shouted the Referee.

Fatso rumbled onto the field along with his first aid man and water boy. Slate Phelps came out onto the field while Coach Braun watched intently from the sidelines.

"That Headhunter guy!" shouted Fatso pointing a shaking finger at Harry. "He's done it again. Wimpy… he's not playing ball! He's trying to kill these boys!"

"Looked like a good tackle to me, Fatso," said Slate calmly.

Fatso looked at Slate in surprise. "What're you doing out here, Slate? Can't Shotgun handle it any more?"

"He's figuring out our next strategy, Fatso," said Slate with a friendly smile.

"You guys out here to chit chat or tend your players?" asked Wimpy.

Fatso turned back to Duane who was getting shakily to his feet. Slate turned back to Allman and motioned the rest of the team around him. He motioned to Braun who ran onto the field, his flat hat jammed firmly on his head, his face calm. He ran into the huddle.

"Shotgun! Shotgun!" chanted the Churchland fans.

"Okay, guys," said the Coach looking around at each grimy face. "Hit 'em hard and hit 'em clean. Use your heads. No penalties. Play Headhunter Free. With Starr out, I doubt that they can move it. Their kicker would have to be at our twenty-five to make a field goal… so hold 'em where they are."

"What if Starr comes back in, Coach?" asked Allman.

"Go to a sixty one Headhunter Free," said the Coach. "They found out again that they can't run. So, they'll pass to Starr. Quester will be the only linebacker and he'll bird dog Starr. Any questions?"

"Naw, Coach," grinned Allman. "We got it!"

"They ain't gonna score!' said Big Jim in a voice that almost betrayed emotion.

"They ain't gonna score!" shouted the team in unison, mimicking Big Jim. It was barely heard against the noise of the crowd.

Suffolk came back to the line of scrimmage without Duane Starr. Harry wondered what they'd try. Foster Hunt faded back to pass. Harry saw his chance and slipped through a hole in the line. He grabbed Foster Hunt by the waist and spun him around, taking a swipe at the ball. The quarterback pulled the ball in and Harry lifted him from the ground and lowered him gently and dramatically to the turf.

"There you go, Peanut Boy," said Harry with a sweaty grin. "Nice and gentle… just for you!"

"Headhunter! Headhunter!"

"That's illegal!" shouted Fatso, sweat pouring down his flabby face. "He can't do that!"

Coach Braun stood on the sidelines watching Fatso without a motion or a word, his arms folded across his chest, his hat pulled down over his squinty eyes. The Referee spotted the ball at the thirty-eight yard line, a loss of eight yards. Suddenly the Suffolk crowd cheered as Duane Starr ran back onto the field.

"Score! Score!"

Harry took his center linebacker position. The other two linebackers were left and right of him. The Suffolk team came to the line of scrimmage. The snap count started. The other two Trucker linebackers fell back into pass defense positions. Harry roamed up and down the line as the single linebacker, watching Duane like a hawk. Like Coach said, it was bound to be a pass to Duane. Harry would stick to him like glue!

The ball was snapped. Duane moved to Harry's right as the Red Raider quarterback faded back to pass. Duane ran around the Red Raider left end. The pass went to the Suffolk left end. A big tackle came out of the Suffolk line and fell in front of Harry, tripping him up. Harry stumbled forward and saw the Suffolk end turn and look back. Harry saw it coming. The end lateraled to Duane. Harry lunged in front of Duane and caught the lateral. He hit the ground, bounced on the ball and felt all the air rush from his lungs, then a piercing pain. But he hung on to the ball! A great roar rose from the Churchland crowd.

"First down, Truckers!" shouted the Referee pointing toward the Suffolk goal.

Allman ran to where Harry lay hugging the ball in pain. He lifted him by the belt in his trousers and pulled him to his feet.

"Nice play, Harry Ol' Buddy," grinned Allman.

"How much?" gasped Harry. "How much… more time?"

Allman looked up at the clock. "A little over four minutes. Ya need to go out?"

"Naw," said Harry taking a deep breath. "I'll be okay in a few seconds."

In the huddle, Allman took a deep breath. "We don't want those guys to get the ball again."

"So… let's run it down their throats," said Tony wiping the grime from his face.

"Okay," said Allman. "Forty nine… on two."

The ball was snapped and Karl took the hand off from Allman. Harry led the blocking around right end. Bubba and Bud made their blocks and Harry took down the line backer. Karl ran for twenty yards and a first down at the Trucker forty-three yard line. The clock was running under three minutes. Allman took his time in the huddle.

"Good run, Karl," he said. "It's your turn Terry!"

Terry ran the ball to the Suffolk thirty-nine. First down, Truckers. The clock ticked down to three minutes.

"Quarterback sneak," said Allman. "I'm coming to your side Renny."

"There'll be a hole," said Renny.

The quarterback sneak took the Red Raiders by surprise. Allman popped through the line and got loose in the backfield. He ran, zigged and zagged to the Suffolk twenty-five before he was tackled. The clock read under two minutes as they ran back to the huddle.

"Ball Fox! Ball Fox!" chanted the crowd.

"I told you that you should run more, Allman," said Harry.

"I heard ya, Harry, Ol' Buddy," said Allman. "Ya ready now for your turn?"

"Sure," said Harry. He wasn't sure, as his belly still hurt from falling on the ball.

"Okay, thirty-four on one."

Harry took the handoff from Allman and followed Big Jim through a gaping hole in the line. A roar rose from the crowd. Big Jim flattened the man in front of him and kept on going. Harry jumped over the downed Red Raider and ran into the backfield. His belly hurt and he shifted the ball to his other hand. Just as he shifted the ball, the Red Raider safety hit him. The ball squirted out of his arms and fell to the turf. A groan arose from the crowd as the ball bounced to the Suffolk ten yard line. Duane fell on the ball and pulled it protectively to him. Harry put his hands on his knees and cursed himself.

"Thanks for that, Quester," said Duane as he got up, holding the ball aloft. "I'm going to score on you now, for sure!"

Harry didn't say anything. He ran back to the Churchland side of the line. "Sorry, guys," he mumbled. He glanced up at the clock. There was a little over a minute remaining in the game.

"Don't sweat it, Harry Ol' Buddy," said Allman smacking him on the rear. "We got 'em pinned down at their ten!"

"Time out! Time out!" shouted Fatso from the sidelines.

"Time out, Suffolk!" shouted the Referee.

Harry motioned to the team to come around him. They did. "This is going to be a pass to Starr," said Harry. "He told me he was going to score on us… and they don't have time to run."

"Okay, said Allman, "do the sixty-one Headhunter Free again… and don't let Starr catch the ball!"

The first play from Suffolk was a run… Duane Starr around end. He broke loose for fifteen yards before Terry brought him down. First down Suffolk on their own twenty-five. The clock ticked to twenty seconds. The Suffolk team ran immediately to the line. Here it comes, thought Harry. The ball was snapped quickly . Duane took off like a rocket down the right sidelines.

Harry ran with Duane for ten yards or so, but the speedy halfback was faster. He pulled away from Harry and was picked up by Terry. Terry hung with him as the ball sailed high in the air. Harry looked back and saw it coming like a missile of fate toward the speeding Starr. Duane reached out for the ball, his fingers touching it. Terry leaped forward and batted the ball high into the air, falling to the ground. Harry watched the ball sail up and seem to hang above him. He glanced around him. Only he and Duane were anywhere near the hanging ball.

Suddenly the ball descended, dropping like a rock, a hysterical, screaming crowd its backdrop. Duane leaped into the air as the clock ticked toward zero. Harry leaped. He swatted at the ball and knocked it like a speeding volleyball into the Suffolk bench. It hit Fatso square in his ponderous belly, which seemed to absorb it like a giant amoeba and spit it out. Fatso staggered back and sat unceremoniously on his ample rump. The ball bounced in front of the Red Raider bench. Harry and Duane came down in a jumble of arms and legs. The gun went off to signal the end of the game.

Harry got up painfully and pulled off his helmet. "Nice try, Peanut Head," said Harry with a grimace.

Duane got to his feet slowly. "You got the game, Quester," he said savagely. "You can have Paige too. She was a good lay for awhile... that's all!"

Harry looked at Duane in shock. "What did you say?"

"You heard me," said Duane, removing his helmet and displaying an arrogant smile.

Harry hit Duane square in the nose with all the force he could find, splattering blood over both of them. Duane fell back and raised his fists in defense. But there was no defense against Harry's rage. His fists flew in a flurry that blurred in their motion, landing blow after blow on the Red Raider halfback. Duane fell to the ground, his face covered with blood.

Suddenly, both teams were on the field, fists flying. The fans started to come out of the stands. Fatso staggered to where Duane had fallen. He pushed Harry away. Harry saw Allman riding the back of Foster Hunt, hitting him on the head and yelling like a banshee. A big Red Raider hit Harry in the face. Big Jim appeared out of nowhere and punched the Suffolk player on the side of the head. The player fell like a rock. Another Suffolk player jumped on Harry's back. Bubba pulled him off and held him up straight. Big Jim smacked him in the face with a hairy fist. Bubba let go and the player collapsed to the ground holding his face in pain. Tony charged around in the crowd punching at anyone wearing red. A Red Raider decked him, but Tony jumped up and ran on, punching left and right.

Fatso pushed Harry backward with a hammy fist. "Who the hell ya think ya are?" shouted Fatso, great beads of perspiration standing out on his flabby face. "You spiked that ball at me… you're trying to hurt us all!"

Coach Braun showed up at Harry's side. He faked a punch at Fatso, who flinched. "What ya think you're doing, Fatso?" screamed Shotgun, his face and jug ears red as a beet.

Shotgun pushed Fatso backward. Fatso took a wild swing at Shotgun and fell to the ground in front of the bench gasping for breath. Shotgun stepped back in surprise. He took off his pork pie hat and waved it at the fighting players. "Hey! Hey! You guys stop the damn fighting!" he shouted hoarsely.

"Fatso needs some help!" exclaimed Harry, pointing to the Suffolk Coach who lay gasping on the ground like a beached whale.

Cliff saw Big Grady Spearman on the field with his officers trying to break up the fights that had erupted everywhere.

"Grady!" shouted Shotgun, waving his hat. "Over here!"

Officer Spearman came running over.

"Fatso!" exclaimed Shotgun, pointing at the Coach on the ground.

Grady waved his arms in the air and blew his whistle at two officers nearby. "Get a stretcher!"

After five minutes of swinging fists that seemed like ten times that long, the players and fans retreated to their sidelines, herded by the officers. The officers pushed the fans back into the stands. The roar of the crowd continued as the officers tried to create an orderly departure from the stadium. They carried Fatso off the field on a stretcher. It took two officers and two Suffolk players to lift the stretcher.

Harry turned to see Paige running toward him, a black and orange scarf swinging about her as she ran. She ran up to him and he hugged her. A great wave of emotion rushed over him.

"Harry!" exclaimed Paige, her voice near hysteria. "Are you alright?"

"Paige!" exclaimed Harry, wrapping his sweaty and bloody arms around her. "I'm so glad you're here!"

****

Harry and Paige went to the Dixie Drive-in for hamburgers in the Cheese-wagon. The Dixie was just down the street from the Circle, and had become a favorite of the Truckers. Harry drove with his arm around Paige, feeling comfortable but conspicuous. The joint was jumping, the loudspeaker over the front door vibrating to the pulsing beat of *Bo*

Diddley;
> *Bo Diddley buy a nanny goat,*
> *Make his pretty baby a Sunday coat,*
> *Bo Diddley buy a bearcat,*
> *Make his pretty baby a Sunday hat.*

"That song doesn't make much sense," said Paige snuggling up against Harry.

"Yeah," said Harry, "but it's sure got a good beat!"

Harry pulled the green Chevy convertible into the front row. Allman rolled in with Georgia in the Red Rooster. Arnie came in driving his chopped Chevy. Clara was conspicuously absent. Tony drove his Father's fifty two DeSoto with Sherry Montgomery beside him. Johnny Calcione drove in, his horn blaring, in a new blue Studebaker Commander.

"Wow!" exclaimed Paige. "Where did Johnny get that?"

"Good question," muttered Harry.

Bob and Janet came in the Yellow Peril. Allman pulled in next to Harry and Paige in the Red Rooster. He jumped up onto the hood of the jeep and began to shout.

"Truckers twenty, Peanut Heads nothing... not a single point!"

The parking lot erupted in cheers as Bo Diddley came to a rhythmic end. Linwood Honor and Catherine Lawson pulled into the Dixie in his white Ford sedan with the red streak down the side. He pulled up on the other side of Harry's Chevy.

"Hey Linwood!" shouted Harry. "How'd you do?"

"Thirty two to nothing... we beat the crap outa Granby!" shouted Linwood happily.

"Hey that's great!" shouted Harry.

Harry got out of the car and opened the door to Linwood's car.

"What's a Wilson guy doing at The Dixie?"

"Aww, it was Cathy's idea," said Linwood reluctantly.

"Come on, get out!" said Harry.

"What's going on?" asked Linwood suspiciously.

"Come on!"

Linwood got out and followed Harry. Harry climbed on top of the hood of the Red Rooster with Allman and pulled Linwood up.

"What the heck ya doing, Ol' Buddy?" asked Allman in surprise.

"Wilson thirty-two, Granby nothing," shouted Harry poking his fist into the air. "Churchland twenty, Suffolk nothing!"

Allman and Linwood joined him and they shouted it again. "Wilson thirty-two, Granby nothing. Churchland twenty, Suffolk nothing! Portsmouth! City of Champions!"

The parking lot erupted in more cheers as they climbed down from the Red Rooster.

"Thanks, Harry," said Linwood, sounding embarrassed. "That was okay!"

"We're for you guys," said Harry clapping Linwood on the back. "That is… until you play us!"

Linwood grinned. "We'll beat you guys, Harry. I look forward to that!"

"Beat Roanoke first, Linwood," smiled Harry. "Then we'll see!"

Harry got in the Chevy next to Paige.

"You want a hamburger?" he asked.

"Sure," said Paige. "If you do."

****

Harry drove out of the parking lot and north on High Street, his arm around Paige. He flipped on the radio. The Ames Brothers were singing;

You, you, you,
I'm in love with you, you, you,
I could be so true, true, true,
To someone like you, you, you.

"You know why I hit Duane?" asked Harry.

"Why?"

"He… well, he said some pretty bad things about you."

"What?" asked Paige sitting up straight.

"Well… you know," said Harry.

"He said that?" asked Paige indignantly.

"Yeah!" said Harry uncomfortably.

Paige laughed. "In his wildest dreams," she said. "I'm not known as the iceberg for nothing!"

Harry tightened his arm around her. They drove to the front of her house. He stopped the car under a tall pine tree.

"Harry," said Paige, "I think… I think that I… "

"What?"

"I really like you… a lot!"

Harry was embarrassed. What did you say to that? He leaned over and kissed her. She kissed him back. They held the kiss for a long time.

"I really like you, too, Paige," said Harry tasting the sweetness of her lips.

"Good," said Paige. "I'm glad you do."

Harry got out of the car and went to the other side. He opened the door for Paige. She got out and they walked slowly, hand in hand to her front door.

"Good night, Harry," said Paige putting her arm around his waist.

"Good night" said Harry, kissing her on her lips and holding her closely.

She moved closer to him and fireworks went off in Harry's tired body.

"You don't act like an iceberg, now," said Harry breathlessly.

"You just seem to warm up this little iceberg, Harry," said Paige in a sultry voice.

Suddenly, she moved away, smiled at him and disappeared inside the front door.

****

CHURCHLAND BEATS SUFFOLK
TRUCKERS REMAIN UNDEFEATED, UNTIED AND UNSCORED ON SHOTGUN FLOORS FATSO!
By
Al Gollen

The battle on the field was almost as dramatic as the battle on the sidelines in this intense rivalry as the Truckers and the Red Raiders slugged it out! Shotgun Braun and Fatso Hathaway traded insults and matched strategies in a game that was closer than the score indicates. The first quarter was played evenly with no score. In the second quarter, Headhunter Harry Quester scored on a pass. Yes, a pass by the Truckers! The Ball Fox, Allman Buddinger threw a pass to the sidelines. Quester ran under it and had a clear path to the Red Raider goal. In the third quarter, Tough Terry Moddy scored on an option play toss from Buddinger. Then in the fourth quarter, Churchland was driving toward a score when Buddinger fumbled.

There was a mad scramble for the ball, possession changing several times. Buddinger ended up with the ball and scampered in for a score. The extra point failed and Churchland was ahead, twenty to nothing, still unscored on. Churchland was driving again when Quester fumbled at the Suffolk ten yard line. In the dramatic last play of the game, Suffolk's Duane Starr had a long pass in his hands when Moddy knocked it high into the air. Starr and Quester went up for the ball and Quester spiked it into the Suffolk bench! A brawl ensued after the whistle sounded. Both teams were on the field, including the Coaches. In the melee, Fatso Hathaway was injured and taken from the field on a stretcher. In another bizarre occurrence in the second quarter, Starr ran at full steam off the field and collided with Shotgun Braun. Braun came off the victor in that encounter as well as in the rough and tumble game!

Shotgun, currently on suspension based on allegations regarding his credentials to coach and accusations on abusing his players, faces another hearing this week. The

Truckers next go to Richmond to play the Prince George Royals. Their last game is against the Matthew Whaley Colonials, a game delayed by Hurricane Hazel. Neither team presents much of a challenge to the mighty Truckers. With wins over these teams, Churchland will claim the State Group II championship. But, can the Truckers prevent a score? Will they let up after the dramatic game with Suffolk? Suffolk is scheduled to play the Wilson Presidents on Thanksgiving Day. The Presidents, who beat Granby to remain unbeaten, need only a win over tough Roanoke next week to claim the State Group I championship. When asked if the champion Truckers would like to play the champion Presidents, Coach Fearless said that they were focused on the next games and would take whatever comes. Shotgun said he's "ready to play anybody".

****

It was ten o'clock on a bright Saturday morning after the Suffolk game. The whole team was in the stadium in practice uniforms.

"Okay," drawled Coach Fearless, standing next to Coach Braun. "Twenty laps, you guys… for starting that fight after the game."

"Okay, Coach," said Allman with a laugh. "That's twenty for Harry and ten for the rest of us! Right?"

"You know what I mean!" said Fearless forcing a stern look onto his usually happy face. "Take twenty!"

The team took to the track in good humor.

"That was a great game!" exclaimed Tony as he ran.

"Yeah!" said Bubba. "And the fight wasn't bad either!"

"Baaaad Bubba!" grinned Tony.

"Hell of a game, Harry Ol' Buddy!" exclaimed Allman.

"Yeah… you too, Allman," said Harry. "The pass worked."

"Yeah," said Allman, "maybe the Tar Heels will let me pass next year!"

The Team made one lap and watched in amazement as Shotgun joined them running. He wore his white shorts, orange tee shirt with black lettering "CHS" and his uncomplaining, often abused hat jammed down over his thick eyebrows.

"What're ya doing, Coach?" asked Karl.

"Whatta ya think?" growled the Coach.

"Running laps?" asked Allman.

"Doncha think I get to run 'em for starting the fight, too?" asked Shotgun with a scowl that hid a smile.

"Yeah, Coach!" said Harry with a lopsided grin, "I think ya earned the laps, too!"

"Yeah, Quester," said Shotgun lifting an eyebrow over an intense eye aimed at Harry. "You'd like to see me run more of 'em, wouldn't ya?"

"Hey Coach," said Harry, wide eyed. "Run as many as you'd like!"

"I'd run fifty laps for another crack at Fatso!"

****

Harry sat in Mr. Beckler's office with Allman, Karl, Coach Braun, Coach Fearless and Coach Phelps after the brief Saturday morning practice. He hurt all over, particularly his nose. It hadn't bothered him at practice, but sitting still in a chair brought out all the bruises from the previous night.

"It was a great game," said Fred Beckler smoothing back his hair nervously. "All, that is, except for the fight."

"We had the team run laps for that, just this morning," said Coach Fearless, "including Coach Braun!"

Fred looked at Braun curiously. "You ran laps?" he asked.

"Yeah… Al Gollen says I flattened Fatso, so I guess I earned 'em."

"Did you flatten Fatso?" asked Fred.

"Naw," said Shotgun, "Ol' Fatso was trying to push Quester aroun'… so I gave him a little shove to back him off… and he keeled over."

"That's what happened, Sir," said Harry. "I saw it."

"Okay, okay," said Fred. "I'm just worried about this second hearing by the Superintendent. He's going to ask things like that."

"Professor Franklin telephoned me and said he'll be there," said Slate.

"Well, good," said Beckler. "We'll need that. It was my error to not review Cliff's record completely."

"It's my fault that I persuaded you to hire him without doing that," said Slate. "But we lucked out and got a really fine Coach, anyway."

"I suppose so," said Fred somewhat reluctantly.

"Hey, Mr. Beckler," said Cliff wrinkling his brow, "ya want me to resign… I will!"

"No.. no!" exclaimed Fred quickly. "I don't want that. If I did the fans would have my scalp!"

"We'll persuade Superintendent Hobbs," said Slate. "The Suffolk game will help."

"If it weren't for the fight!" said Fred. "What started it anyway, Harry?"

"It was my fault," said Harry. "That guy, Duane Starr, he said something about a young lady I'm dating. He insulted her, and I hit him."

"Hit him?" asked Karl with wide eyes. "You clobbered him!"

Fred let a slight smile come over his round face. "You didn't just hit him, Harry... you broke his jaw!"

"Yes Sir. It seemed the right thing to do!"

There was a knock on the door. Grady Spearman opened the door and came in.

"If it's okay, Mr. Beckler," said Slate, "I asked Grady to come by." We've been looking into a few things you ought to know about."

"We have some more information about the playbook theft and the documents," said Grady.

"Let's hear it," said Fred.

"We know that Benny Norwood took the documents and gave them to Johnny Calcione," said Grady. "We know that someone tried to blame it all on Harry Quester."

"Benny has been kicked off the team" said Coach Fearless.

"We have reason to believe that Calcione either paid Benny or coerced him to take the playbook," said Grady. "Bart Whitely found out about all this and told Harry Quester. Then, just before the Suffolk game, Calcione found out Bart had told Harry and attacked him with a knife... and you know about that."

"Yes, I do," said Fred angrily. "We've got to find a way to stop these older boys from interfering with our students!"

"We also know," continued Grady, "That suddenly, Calcione has a lot of money. He just bought a new Studebaker Commander!"

"Wow!" exclaimed Fred. "Those cars cost almost two thousand dollars!"

"Something like that," said Slate. "Calcione gave the playbook to Suffolk's football manager... a boy named Horace Holly. Quester and Hawkins went to see Holly... he told them he gave the playbook to the Suffolk halfback... Duane Starr."

"There appears to be a link, then, between the playbook theft and whoever sent these... so called anonymous documents to me, Gollen and the Superintendent," mused the Principal.

"That's what I think," said Slate.

"But who?" asked Beckler.

"Someone with enough money to give Calcione what he needed to buy a new Studebaker," said Grady.

Fred Beckler pushed a pencil around his desk while he thought. "Someone wants really bad to discredit Shotgun."

"The same someone wants to get Harry kicked off the team," said Coach Fearless.

Fred pushed the pencil around with more vigor. "I'm glad you're working on this, Grady," he said.

"Thank you, Sir," said Grady. "We're looking at bank records to see who might have paid off Calcione… but nothing yet."

"Try to find something we can use with the Superintendent," said Fred. "I'll see you fellows at the Victory Sock Hop tonight!"

****

Grady Spearman came to the Coach's office that afternoon. He walked in and found Coach Braun and Coach Phelps talking about playing Wilson.

"I think ya oughta play 'em," said Grady. "You'd be the underdog and have nothin' to lose."

"That's what we think, Grady," said Slate.

"Listen," said Grady, "I been snoopin' aroun'… like I said I would. The big question is where did Johnny Calcione get the money he used for the new Studebaker? If we can find that out, we probably got the person who sent those documents to the Superintendent. Because this person, whoever he is, apparently paid off Johnny. We can get him for conspiracy to defraud… and probably some other things."

"Whatcha found out?" asked Braun.

"I've talked to Mr. Norwood and had a look at his bank accounts," said Grady. "Nothing there. Same with Calcione's Father. He knew Fatso when they both worked at the docks in Long Island… but his bank accounts are clean. I talked to Commander Quester… he didn't like it much, but he cooperated. Nothing there. Same with Mr. Stanley, Buster's father. I had a look at Fatso's accounts… even the accounts of his father. Nothing there. Ya got any ideas?"

"Anything on Quester being shot?" asked Slate. "He says they saw Calcione's car there that day."

"Calcione says he don't know nothing about Quester being shot," said Spearman. "And I haven't found nothing to prove he did it."

"Do you really think Fatso is involved?" asked Slate. "It seems strange that he'd risk everything just to discredit Shotgun."

"I don't know for sure," said Grady, "But maybe."

"Then let's go to Prentiss Park and visit Big Ennis at his store," said Slate thoughtfully.

"Why?" asked Grady.

"Just a hunch," said Slate.

"Okay," said Grady, "but it might take awhile to get a search warrant for that!"

****

Chapter Seventeen
The Last Games

Harry and Paige did the jitterbug to *In the Mood* as Rocky Rawls' band played the smooth, rhythmic tune at the Victory Sock Hop. Allman sat with Georgia in chairs at the side of the black and orange decorated gymnasium watching the dancers. Harry saw that he kept glancing at the doors as though looking for someone. *In the Mood* ended.

"Now here's your favorite lady, Patty Parsons, with a Doris Day tune that'll make the gals wanna hug ya real tight!"

Patty Parsons sang in a soft and sultry voice
Once I had a secret love,
That lived within the heart of me,
All too soon my secret love,
Became impatient to be free.

Harry took Paige in his arms and they began to dance.

"You were my secret love, Harry," whispered Paige in his ear. "Ever since that day I saw you on the river!"

"Really?" asked Harry in a surprised whisper. "I thought I'd never get you away from Duane."

"I never really liked Duane that much," said Paige. "He's arrogant and self centered… but my parents think he's great, and his family is real rich. They want me to date him… so I did."

"Well, my family isn't that rich," said Harry.

"I'm glad," said Paige happily.

Harry saw Allman get up and walk quickly toward the door. He glanced over and saw Arnie standing near the door with Johnny Calcione, Carson Quinn and Bryan Muller.

"Excuse me, Paige," said Harry hurriedly.

"Harry!" exclaimed Paige. "Don't go get tangled up with those guys!"

"I got to," said Harry in a tense voice. "Just wait over there… please!"

Harry walked hurriedly to catch up with Allman. They confronted Arnie, Johnny, Carson and Bryan.

"Johnny," said Allman vehemently. "You're a low life sonofabitch! We know all about Benny and the playbook."

"Go to hell, ya clown!" said Johnny bitingly.

"You're gonna pay for cutting Bart!" said Harry angrily.

"Yeah?" said Johnny with a sneer. "Well, you're next, Pretty Boy!"

Johnny advanced on Harry. Bart came up behind Harry and Allman, still wearing his arm in a sling. Arnie put a hand on Calcione's arm.

"Later, Johnny... not now! Where ya been Bart, ya bastard?" asked Arnie caustically.

"Jus' waiting for Johnny to show his mug," said Bart angrily. "So I can work it over some!"

"With one arm?" sneered Calcione.

"That's all I need, ass-hole!" snarled Bart.

"Eat me, ya sonofabitch!" snarled Johnny.

"Back off, Johnny," said Bryan, a worried look on his face.

Bubba ran over and joined Bart.

"Johnny... we know you sent those documents about Coach Braun to the Superintendent," said Bubba threateningly.

"Bullshit, Bubba!" exclaimed Johnny. "I ain't sent nuthin'!"

"You guys are fulla shit!" exclaimed Arnie, looking concerned.

"Were you in on it, too, Arnie?" asked Tony walking up beside Bubba. "You and your Hoods?"

"I don't know what you're talking about, Zee, ya little prick!" said Arnie with a sneer.

"When ya get outa your bandage," said Tony quietly, "look me up and say that, you Hood bastard!"

Big Jim walked silently up behind Allman and stared at the Hoods, his arms hanging loosely by his sides. Arnie flinched and looked at the six boys confronting him. He wasn't used to being faced down and his expression changed to one of anger.

"Get outa our way!" said Carson, puffing up his chest and putting a cigarette behind his ear.

"Come on, Johnny," said Allman, his jaw set. "It was you, wasn't it? And Carson? And Arnie? What about Bryan?"

"What're they talking about, Johnny?" asked Arnie with a frown.

"Yeah!" exclaimed Bryan worriedly. "What the hell are they talking about?"

"Nothing... nothing," muttered Johnny irritably. "They're all fulla shit!"

Johnny tried to push his way through to the dance floor. Big Jim stepped in front of him.

"You with these pussies, Big Jim?" asked Johnny in a voice fringed with fear.

"Answer the question, Johnny," said Big Jim in a low voice.

Johnny backed away. "You guys wanna fight?" he asked. "Come on outside!"

"Let's go!" exclaimed Allman. He walked hurriedly toward the door, his fists clenched.

"Wait a minute!" cautioned Bryan. "I ain't part of nothing done to hurt the Coach!"

"I ain't fighting you guys with these broken ribs," whined Arnie.

"We won't hit your ribs, Arnie," laughed Allman. "We'll just kick in your face!"

"You sonofabitch, Allman!" exclaimed Arnie. He started toward the door. "I thought you was a friend a' mine."

"I am, Arnie," said Allman. "If ya don't mess with the Coach and the team!"

Johnny put his hand into his pants pocket and pulled out a switchblade knife. The music stopped and there was a hushed silence.

"Put away the damn knife, Johnny," said Bryan grabbing his hand. "Ya done too much with it already!"

"Screw you, Bryan!" said Johnny, pushing Bryan's hand away.

Harry jumped on Calcione and grabbed the hand holding the knife. Allman wrestled the knife away from Johnny and threw it into the corner of the gym with a clatter. Harry and Allman pushed Johnny out the door. The rest of them crowded after them, except for Bryan who hung back.

Johnny swung at Allman. Allman grinned and ducked agilely. He danced away from Johnny, then darted in and smacked him on the face with an open hand. Johnny swung again. Allman dodged.

"Whatsamatta, Johnny?" taunted Allman. "I thought you was a big, tough guy!

"You dumb fuckah," muttered Johnny, swinging wildly.

Allman darted in and hit Johnny on the forehead with a powerful blow. Johnny staggered backward into the arms of Officer Grady Spearman.

"You boys having a problem?" asked Grady calmly.

****

Superintendent Hudson Hobbs paced about in his office as Cliff Braun, Eddie Fearless, Fred Beckler and Grady Spearman came in.

"Is Doctor Franklin here?" asked Doctor Hobbs.

"He'll be here shortly, Sir," said Fred. "Slate has gone to pick him up at the hotel."

"Well, have a seat," said the Superintendent.

They all sat down. There was a nervous pause.

"Congratulations on winning the Suffolk game, Fred," said Hobbs.

"Thank you, Sir," said Beckler. "I'm sorry about the fight."

"Yes... yes," said the Superintendent. "We'll have to talk about that."

The door opened and Slate came in with Professor Franklin. Marion Franklin had aged considerably since Cliff had last seen him in the hospital in Memphis. He was a man now in his sixties. His once thick gray hair had thinned, but he still wore a short, well trimmed beard. There was the same twinkle in his eye, as though he were remotely viewing the world and its human comedies through a private telescope. Cliff was glad to see him. Marion Franklin glanced at Cliff and winked. Cliff nodded and smiled.

"Doctor Hobbs," said Slate, "this is Doctor Marion Franklin, retired Dean of the School of Arts and Sciences at Memphis State University."

"I'm very pleased to meet you, Doctor Franklin," said Hobbs shaking Franklin's hand. "Please sit down."

Doctor Hobbs sat behind his desk. Slate and Marion sat in chairs in front of the desk. The skies outside the window were dark, threatening rain, or maybe snow. Cliff sat in his chair uneasily.

"I understand you are a historian, Doctor Franklin," said Hobbs. "That is a field that has always interested me."

"Oh yes," said Marion with a slow drawl. "It is a fascinating and intoxicating study… filled with triumph, tragedy and humor. I have had many occasions to admire the folks in the field of education… your field, Doctor Hobbs… and the many ways you use to bring knowledge to our young people… teaching them to live and love in this crazy, crazy world... and make history!"

"Hrrmph!" said Hobbs, clearing his throat. "Yes, well thank you, Doctor Franklin."

"Please call me Marion."

"Yes, of course… Marion."

"Thank you."

"Well, Coach Braun," said Doctor Hobbs, "As we were discussing before Doctor Franklin arrived, I congratulate you on your victory in the Suffolk game… except of course for the fight that followed."

"It wasn't my victory," said the Coach in a hoarse voice. "It was a team victory… and they won it under a lotta pressure, while a lotta screwy things were happening to us."

"What do you mean?" asked Hobbs.

Cliff twisted in his chair. "Well, this hearing was sorta lurking around the corner… and the injuries to Jack Sanders and Bart Whitely… and the sonof… the guy who stole our playbook and gave it to Fatso… that kinda thing!"

"Yes… yes, all unfortunate occurrences," said Doctor Hobbs, stroking his chin.

"But," said Slate, "a win over Prince George this Friday… and the Truckers are State Group II champs!"

"Yes, I know," said Doctor Hobbs. "It will be an interesting game…

particularly if Prince George manages to score."

"Yes, it will be a great game," said Marion. "I plan to be there if I can!"

"Now, with regard to this hearing," said the Superintendent. "The question seems to be… but first, tell me why the Suffolk game had to end in a brawl, Coach Braun."

"Fatso and I go way back… and we ain't never liked each other," said the Coach. "I guess Fatso and I were brawling all the way through the game. We been brawling for years."

"Fatso was doing everything he could to get Cliff thrown out of the game," said Eddie Fearless. "Anyone could see that! Coach Braun was playing it cool… at least cool for Shotgun!"

"After the game, Quester told me that a Suffolk player said bad things about his girl friend," said Coach Braun indignantly, "and that's why he punched him out."

"And that's a good reason!" exclaimed Slate.

"And that started it all," said Eddie.

"What about that Suffolk player they say you hit on the sideline, Coach Braun?" asked Doctor Hobbs.

"Hell! I mean… excuse me, Sir," stuttered Cliff trying to contain his anger, "but that sonof… I mean, that player ran off the field straight into me… I didn't do nothing but stand there!"

"Slate and I dodged him," said Eddie, "but there was nowhere for the Coach to go."

"The player seemed to get the worst of it, Coach," said Hobbs, squinting at Braun.

"I don't know 'bout that!" said Coach Braun, wide-eyed. He rolled up the sleeve of the shirt on his right arm displaying a big band-aid. "He hit me and busted open my arm!"

"Did you hit Fatso?" asked Doctor Hobbs.

"No Sir, I didn't," said the Coach. "But my knuckles were itching for him! I know that!"

"What do you mean by that?" asked Hobbs

"He came up to me after the game shouting and cussin' and… and just being Fatso. I was really pissed… I mean, mad at him… Sir. But I just shoved him away. He fell down by himself!"

"They say he had some kind of a heart attack," said Fred Beckler.

"It seems violence follows you wherever you go, Coach Braun," said Doctor Hobbs. "Why is that?"

"I dunno, Superintendent," said Cliff, lifting his eyebrows innocently. "I jus' try to be the best Coach I can be… and not let other people get on me! I don't like it when other people try to get on me… ya know?"

Superintendent Hobbs shook his head knowingly and drummed his fingers in a staccato beat on his desk. "The question the School Board raises is... why was Coach Braun hired when he had this expulsion for violence at ECTC... and can he continue as Coach with that incident now well known?"

"I take the blame for that," said Slate quickly. "I persuaded Mr. Beckler to hire him... and I was there at ECTC, so I know what happened."

"Just what did happen at ECTC, Doctor Franklin... Marion?" asked the Superintendent.

"It was a matter of a conflict of personalities, I believe," said Marion. "This Army Major, the one who ran the veteran's programs, was a General Patton type... if you know what I mean..."

"Yes," said Doctor Hobbs, nodding with understanding, "a self appointed tough guy, I assume... slapping soldiers and all that!"

"Yes... exactly," said Marion. "I'm sure you've met the type."

"Yes... yes," said Hobbs. "I have had that unfortunate experience."

"And, for whatever reason, the Major didn't like Shotgun from the day he came to ECTC... and was always giving Shotgun a hard time about something. Shotgun was in my history class and did well there. He told me about the Major from time to time. As for me, I was... and am, a big football fan. I really enjoyed watching Shotgun play. His enthusiasm for the game was so different from the norm, he was exciting to watch! So I took the pains to meet the Major and see what kind of person he was. He was very arrogant... particularly toward the enlisted soldiers."

"I see," said Hobbs, nodding his head in understanding.

"And... Shotgun had been an enlisted soldier," said Marion. "He landed at Normandy and served with honor in Europe for over a year."

The Superintendent looked surprised and snuck a quick glance at Shotgun. "What happened with the Major?" he asked.

"It finally came to a head when there was an unpleasant incident in the cafeteria and the Major got Shotgun so angry that he called the Major... a few choice names," said Marion

"Yes... yes... I've heard a few of those!" observed the Superintendent.

"The next day," continued Marion, "Shotgun went to the President to complain abut the Major. President Holland..."

"Robert Holland?" asked Doctor Hobbs.

"Yes... he was at William and Mary before he became President at ECTC."

"Yes, I know him," said the Superintendent. "I had classes under him there."

"Then you know the kind of quick tempered fellow he is," said Marion watching Doctor Hobbs closely.

"Yes, I do," said Hobbs emotionally. "Yes, I certainly do!"

"Well, the Major won out and Shotgun was expelled," said Marion. "I later learned that the Major had blackballed Shotgun with all the schools that had football teams in North Carolina and Virginia. That's when I called some friends at Memphis State… in Tennessee. I knew I was headed there to be Dean. I wanted to help Shotgun… and the team."

"I see," said Doctor Hobbs.

"Though Shotgun was expelled," said Marion, "I consider the expulsion to have been unwarranted. Doctor Holland did not consider all the things he should have."

"It does sound that way," said Doctor Hobbs. "Holland was always quick to judge!"

"Shotgun did well in football at Memphis State," said Marion, "that is, until he was injured. And, he performed acceptably in academics… even went on and got a graduate degree."

"Very commendable," said the Superintendent. "Any fights?"

"No… no… at least none that I know of," said Marion.

"Did you have any fights there, Coach Braun?" asked Doctor Hobbs.

Cliff squirmed in his chair. "Well, no big ones, ya know… Sir," he said uncomfortably. "But a few… ya know… mostly about gals!"

"I see," said Doctor Hobbs. "And how were your grades?"

"Shotgun is certainly no scholar," said Marion, "But he passed and did well, as usual, in athletics… and history."

"We know now," said Slate, changing the subject, "that someone paid Johnny Calcione a lot of money to steal the Trucker Playbook and give it to a Suffolk player. Calcione just bought a new Studebaker Commander… so he's getting money from somewhere! Officer Spearman is looking into all of this."

"Really" exclaimed Hobbs. "Those cars are expensive!"

"Calcione gave the playbook to Suffolk's football manager," said Grady, "a boy named Horace Holly. Horace gave the playbook to the Suffolk halfback… Duane Starr."

"There appears to be a link, then, between the playbook theft and whoever sent these documents," said Fred Beckler.

"Who would do that?" asked Hobbs scratching his head.

"Someone with a lotta money," drawled Eddie Fearless.

"I asked Officer Spearman to look into this," said Beckler firmly.

"Yes, I suppose you should, Fred," said Hobbs. "With regard to the question of Coach Braun… I must consult with the School Board."

"Thank you, Doctor Hobbs," said Slate diplomatically.

"Coach Braun," said Doctor Hobbs, "You will continue your coaching... and please be careful! No more... incidents! I will take your further employment up with the School Board."

"Okay," said Coach Braun, thankful he still had the job, even for a few more weeks. "And... thanks."

They all got up and walked out the door, except for Slate who remained in the Superintendent's office. Outside the office, Marion Franklin pulled Grady Spearman aside.

"Young man," said Doctor Franklin, "you should go to ECTC and find out who got Shotgun's records away from the records department down there... I'll help you."

****

"Can I have a private word with you, Superintendent?" asked Slate as he closed the door behind the others.

"Certainly, Slate," said Doctor Hobbs cordially.

"I want you to understand Coach Braun, Sir, because he's an unusual person. You see, there are men such as myself who enjoy football and who coach to make a living. Then, every now and then... not very often... a man such as Cliff Braun comes along. Shotgun doesn't just enjoy football... he loves it! He lives for it! He's wed to it! It's his life! He instinctively understands the game... and the boys who play it... far better than most! I mean not just the rules... but the way to play the game and win!"

Superintendent Hobbs watched Slate as he started to become emotional. "Yes... go ahead."

"Well, guys like Cliff... and there aren't many of them... have a capability to go to the next level above coaching... to the level of not only teaching, but inspiring... of taking ordinary players and making them consistent winners. He teaches them to be men! He teaches them how tough they have to be when they go on beyond high School. Guys like that are to be treasured... and they stand out from other coaches the way a great scientist stands above all other scientists. The way a great educator stands out above the folks who are just teachers! They're different, many times eccentric! They are envied... and misunderstood."

"You make an eloquent case, Slate," said Hobbs admiringly.

"This kind of coach is a treasure," said Slate, pacing back and forth. "When you have one of them, it pays to tolerate their eccentricities when you need to, Sir."

"I understand," said Hobbs patiently. "But remember, Slate, I have to abide by the rules... and be fair to all."

****

Bob Porter's harmonica wailed on the long trip to Prince George's County near Richmond. Bob liked romantic melodies. He was playing *No Other Love,* a haunting love song taken from a Richard Rogers melody in *Victory at Sea.* Harry remembered the tune from a record his father loved. The words came to Harry's mind as the harmonica played.

Hurry home, come home to me,
Set me free,
Free from doubt and free from longing…
Into your arms I'll fly,
Locked in your arms I'll stay,
Waiting to hear you say,
No other love have I,
No other love.

Paige was driving to the game with Georgia. That should be an interesting trip! He wondered what the conversation would be. Georgia was constantly teasing him about his relationship with Paige, the "little iceberg". Some of her questions were downright embarrassing. He ignored her. He wondered if Paige was his "no other love".

The Yellow School Bus rumbled past trees along the road whose leaves were yellow, orange and red. They were also dripping wet as a light rain fell coldly on the Virginia forests. Harry watched them dreamily. No one gave this Prince George team much chance against the Truckers. But, every game was a test. Anyone could beat another team on any day if the stars were right. Harry wondered how much it meant to Shotgun to go unscored upon. Probably more than he would admit. He wondered how the hearing with the Superintendent went. Coach hadn't said anything about it.

The bus arrived at the home of the Prince George Royals. It was seven o'clock and dark. The light rain continued to fall as the lights of the stadium flashed on. The players disembarked from the bus and went into the gymnasium dressing room.

****

The Truckers went wild in the first half in the dripping rain and mud. Harry ran at will and scored two touchdowns. Karl and Terry were having an equally easy time of it. Hero had a long run for a touchdown. The score at the half was Churchland forty-nine, Prince George zero.

Bud Darby kicked off to the Royals to begin the second half. Harry was in on the tackle at the Royal twenty-two yard line, his face plowing into the mud. He got up wiping the mud from his face. A Prince George player with an equally muddy face pulled himself up next to Harry.

"Who are you guys, anyway?" asked the Royals player, looking at Harry with confused eyes.

"Just a team from down the road near Portsmouth," said Harry with a grin through his mud smeared face.

"You guys are a nightmare," said the Royals player with a half frown, half grin, "a real nightmare!"

The second team offense played most of the last quarter. Prince George couldn't move the ball at all. They got the ball on their own twenty-five yard line near the end of the game. Harry crouched in his linebacker position behind Buster, who had come in for Big Jim at tackle. A big boy in a uniform covered with mud was lined up in front of Buster.

"Why don't ya jus' lay down now?" asked Buster with a staged growl. "Then it won't hurt so much!"

The big tackle adjusted his position and backed up a bit. The ball was snapped and Buster hit the Royal player with a hard rush. The Royal fell over backward into a mud hole. Buster made the tackle on the quarterback before he could hand off the ball.

"Way to hit, Buster!" said Harry, smacking the squarely built boy on the butt.

"I'm getting the hang of what Shotgun's been yelling at me about," said Buster triumphantly. "It feels good!"

Hero and Matt both scored touchdowns. Hero had a punt runback for a touchdown. Matt scored on a pass from Rob Sonda.

"Hey!" shouted Matt exuberantly. "It feels really good to score!"

"You ran like the wind," said Hero theatrically, patting Matt on the back.

The first team defense came in whenever Prince George had the ball... just to be sure! The Truckers ran off the muddy field at the end of the game with the score Churchland sixty-nine, Prince George zero.

"Well," said Eddie Fearless as the Coaches jogged toward the dressing room in the rain. "That's it! State Champs!"

"You did it, Shotgun!" exclaimed Slate.

"We got one more game," growled the Coach. "We won't really have the championship 'til we win that one!

****

BOTH PORTSMOUTH TEAMS UNBEATEN!
By
Abe Gollen

The Wilson Presidents played a tough Roanoke team to a 20-20 tie last night in the rain to remain unbeaten and claim the State Group I Championship. The Churchland Truckers played a hapless Prince George's County team and won 69-0 in a muddy battle to remain unbeaten, untied and unscored upon and claim the State Group II championship. Portsmouth is proud of its champions!

Each team has one more game. Wilson plays the Suffolk Red Raiders on Thanksgiving Day. Churchland plays Matthew Whaley on Saturday afternoon following Thanksgiving in a game rescheduled by Hurricane Hazel. The Presidents want badly to defeat Suffolk by more than the twenty to nothing score that Churchland ran up on the Red Raiders to show that they are the champion among champions. The Truckers want to close their season without marring their undefeated, untied and unscored upon record. Can Matthew Whaley win? Score?

When asked about the status of Coach Shotgun Braun at Churchland, Superintendent Hobbs stated that the matter is "still under review", and that in the meantime, Shotgun is the Trucker's Coach.

Should Wilson play Churchland? Coach Pistol Pete Sacker says he's ready! Coach Shotgun Braun says he's ready! Superintendent Hobbs says he cannot by the rules sanction a post season High School game and has turned the idea down. A.P. Johns, the unofficial "Mayor" of Churchland Village has proposed that a game be played with the profits going to charity. Superintendent Hobbs has commended A.P.'s idea but said that "it is not possible". Too bad! It would be one heck of a game!

****

Shotgun, Slate, Eddie, Harry, Allman and most of the Churchland Truckers were in the stands to see Wilson play Suffolk on Thanksgiving Day afternoon. It was a blustery day with intermittent sunshine.

"Look at that sonofabitch... that Fatso!" exclaimed Shotgun. "He's sittin' down there in a' easy chair!"

Harry looked down and saw the Red Raiders standing around Fatso, who was sitting in a big cane chair with a cushion. He was talking to them with wild gestures. They ran out onto the field looking uninspired. Duane had a plastic strip on his helmet to protect his broken jaw.

Duane took the kickoff and ran it back to the Suffolk thirty yard line where he was tackled hard by Linwood Honor. He lay on the field as the players broke away from the pile. There was a time out as the first aid man ran to his aid. Fatso stayed in his chair. After a few minutes, Duane got up and limped off the field. He didn't return to the game. Dennis Aimsley scored four touchdowns. Wilson twenty-seven, Suffolk nothing.

****

It was a very gray Saturday afternoon in Churchland Stadium. There was a light drizzle and gusts of wind. The stands were full and people were standing around the track six deep. The Matthew Whaley Colonials in their blue trousers and white jerseys with blue numbers were already on the field when the Truckers ran on. A.P. Johns stood and cheered at the top of his voice. But, the magic of a Friday night was somehow missing. There was no glare from the lights. The mystery of the night forest around them wasn't there. It seemed almost like a necessary chore… to beat Matthew Whaley… not an important game. Yet the crowd was there and the cheers were loud. A.P. could see Linwood Honor and other Wilson players in the stands. They cheered for Churchland, but A.P. knew they'd like to see the Colonials score. He had to talk to Hudson Hobbs again. Maybe if Churchland won this game… and remained unscored on, the Superintendent would see a Wilson-Churchland game differently and find a way to make it happen!

Harry ran onto the field feeling the weight of responsibility on his head. Jack was the big star, and he would be again next year. But the fans had come to expect Harry to dominate on defense… Headhunter Harry and all that! He was having a hard time finding his game face on this gray Saturday afternoon.

Allman and Karl went to the field for the coin toss. Allman came back with the usual grin on his face. "We receive!"

"Okay, Team! Huddle 'roun the Coach!" shouted Eddie Fearless.

The team gathered around Shotgun who was on one knee, the pork pie hat in his hand. He looked around the huddle, meeting the eyes of every player. "It's kinda strange to be here on a Saturday afternoon… feels funny," said the Coach in a low voice. Then he roared at them, "But them lights are still up there! They just ain't on. And the fans are still up there! So get it outa your heads that this game is any different than the other ones. We need this game!"

Then the Coach lowered his voice once more in a theatrical way and became emotional. "You guys are the best team I ever had… including the ones I played on. You guys have been tough and mean!" Then he roared at them again. "If ya think you're tired… in your body, or your cotton picking head… forget it! Any team can score on ya if you're tired… if ya jus' don't care. And it only takes one guy like that to mess up a team. So if any of ya think this game is a pain in the tail… if you're tired of being mean and taking the hits… if ya ain't willing to be as mean as ya have been all year… and meaner!… then go sit on the bench! I really mean that! I'd rather play a third string mean guy than a first string guy who's relaxed and started his darn vacation! Now I don't know what this Willy Burg team is gonna try... so play smart. And be loose!"

Allman started shaking and shimmying. "I'm loose as a goose, Coach!" he said, his voice shaking as he shimmied.

Coach Braun started shaking, and so did the whole team. The skies clouded over and a light, dismal rain began to fall.

"Good!" shouted the Coach with a growl and a fierce look on his bulldog face. "Now let's hear how mean ya are!"

A giant growl rose from the Trucker huddle.

"Now get out there! Get out there!" shouted Shotgun Braun in a hoarse voice that cascaded up into the stands.

The team broke the huddle with a roar that startled a flock of sea gulls at the end of the field. They flapped away with a rustling flutter of squawks and feathers. Harry ran onto the field, his heart thumping, but the adrenalin he was used to feeling wasn't there. Suddenly, the stadium lights came on, changing the afternoon gloom into bright illumination. Harry looked up at the lights and felt energy surge into his body. He reached down and pulled up his game face and began to feel the adrenalin rush into him.

On the sidelines, Coach Braun looked up at the stadium lights, smiled and nodded his head. Frank Beckler had not let him down... and the timing was perfect!

The Matthew Whaley kickoff fluttered through the rain and down into the arms of Karl Darby on the Churchland twenty-five yard line. Karl caught it and sped down the right sideline with Harry and Bubba in front of him. Harry knocked a Colonial off balance and Karl sped by him. He ran it to midfield before he was tripped up.

"Huddle up!" shouted Bob Porter.

In the huddle, Allman was calm, with a dead serious face. "Coach wants to run it down their throat until we see what they got," he said. "Ya ready, Harry... Karl... Terry?"

"Yeah," said Harry. "I wanna see some big holes up there, Jim, Bucky, Renny... Bubba!"

"Big holes!" said Big Jim under his breath.

"Now remember," said Allman, "these guys are all assholes ya hate! So take 'em down! Thirty-one on two."

Porter left the huddle.

"Thirty-one on two," said Allman. "Stick it to 'em! Break!"

The huddle broke and the black and orange clad Churchland Truckers ran to the line of scrimmage.

"Get down!... Get ready!... Hut One!... Hut Two!"

Bob Porter popped the ball into Allman's hands with a smack Harry could hear from his fullback position. Allman turned and handed the ball to Harry who aimed himself directly at the hole between Bob and Bucky. It was there! The hole opened magically in front of him and he saw Big Jim drive the linebacker to the outside. Harry burst through the hole, stiff armed another linebacker and ran strongly into the backfield. A halfback lunged at him, draping himself around Harry's waist. Harry dragged him for ten yards. The crowd roared as the Colonial was dragged up the field. The safety came up and knocked them both down. Harry jumped to his feet and ran back to the huddle. The ball was at the forty five yard line.

"Lemme try that hole!" exclaimed Terry, always the opportunist.

They ran the left halfback through the thirty two hole with Harry and Karl leading Terry into the line. Again, the hole was there, the linebackers blocked. Harry plowed through the line and ran down the field to block the halfback. Karl got the other halfback. Terry ran directly at the safety, gave him a fake and sprinted by him.

"Goooo Terry!" shouted Karl running after him.

Terry ran across the goal line as Churchland Stadium rocked with noise. The band struck up the Trucker Fight Song. Churchland seven, Matthew Whaley, zero.

****

The Truckers went into the dressing room at the half ahead twenty-eight to nothing. The Coaches came in behind them with A.P. Johns.

"What's A.P. doing here?" whispered Tony.

"Who knows?" said Bubba. "A.P. turns up everywhere."

The players clumped to the benches and sat down.

"You guys got two quarters of football to go," said Coach Fearless. "We thought you'd like to hear from your best fan. So here's A.P."

A.P.'s leathery face broke into a grin from ear to ear and he stepped forward. "I've watched the Truckers for years and years. This year you Truckers are making history," he said in his personal way that made people feel special. "You guys hang around my store and break things and scare little ol' ladies away… but I love ya! I know you hear the fans cheering… but do you know what really goes on in the stands?"

A.P. paused and looked around the room, the question on his lips.

"Some of you have never been in the stands… maybe never will be… but those people up there know every one of you by name… yep! Every one… some better than others… but all of you! And they love you! They feel like they know every one of you! They know who the guys are this year… they know who'll be there next year! They watch every play knowing you're gonna break it for a touchdown... or cream some guy on the other team with a big block. They live for it! You have guys that carry the load this year... but they aren't stars... they're team players like all of you. You and the Coaches have made it that way! That's why you're something special... you're the Truckers! The Truckers! That's something real special!"

A.P. paused to catch his breath and contain his building emotions. He looked around at the dirty faces that watched him closely. All eyes were on him... all faces showing the emotion he felt.

"The fans want you to go unscored on... that's history! The fans want you to play Wilson... that's history! That will be your crowning triumph... your chance to make this team more than just special! So, I'll tell you... this isn't your last game! One way or the other, you're going to play Wilson!"

A cheer erupted from the players. They stood up and pumped their helmets in the air.

"Bring 'em on!" shouted Allman happily.

"Thanks, A.P." said Coach Braun as A.P. stepped back. He glared at the players. "So, you're ahead, twenty-eight to nothing. Feeling pretty good, are ya?"

The Coach paused and stared at each player with intense eyes. Then he shouted at them, his eyes bulging from his bulldog face.

"Don't ya dare feel good about that first half! These Willy Burg guys haven't even given us a game! We oughta be ahead a zillion to nothing! But they can wake up! And they can score on ya! And they can even beat ya if ya go to sleep on us! I don't see any mean faces in here. I wanna see some really pissed off faces! I want you guys to go back out there and smear these Co-lo-ni-al guys! That rain is gettin' worse... so here's your chance to get really dirty and muddy and gritty... and tough, and mean! I mean real mean! I want these Co-lo-ni-als to eat mud, bleed and crawl back on their bus to nurse their bruises. Don't you let the fans down! Don't you let A.P. down! It's two more quarters of hard nosed football!"

"Hard nose! Hard nose!" shouted Allman stamping his feet.

The team joined in and the clatter of cleats and young voices rocked the dressing room. Allman and Karl led them to the door and they charged back onto the field.

"Is it time to go back on the field?" asked Slate, looking at his watch.

"Naw," drawled Eddie. "But they're ready!"

****

In the second half it was more of the same. Harry ran over the

Colonials. Karl and Terry ran over the Colonials. They all got wonderfully muddy. Then the football decided to have its own way. Late in the fourth quarter, the Colonials punted in the rain. The ball wobbled through the air to Karl Darby at his own thirty yard line. A freak gust of wind caught the ball as it descended. It came down short and bounced off of Karl's foot. It rolled crazily toward the Churchland goal.

A great moan from the sold out crowd arose as a Colonial chased it and fell on the ball at the Churchland twenty-four yard line. It was the first time Matthew Whaley had the ball in Churchland territory.

"Okay guys," shouted Allman. "Now's the time to suck it up and get really tough!"

"No one scores on us!" shouted Big Jim, wiping the rain from his muddy face.

Harry lined up in the Headhunter Free defense. He sensed that the Colonials would try a run… and then a pass. He lined up behind Renny Dickson. Matthew Whaley tried a run. It was aimed at their right tackle. Harry ran down the line and aimed himself at the runner. Big Jim Jensen met the runner head on and threw him down into the mud.

"Way to go, Big Jim!" said Harry, slapping the big man on the butt.

Big Jim nodded stoically. "No one scores!"

On the next play the Colonial quarterback faded back and tried a pass. Karl Darby easily batted it away from the intended receiver.

"Here comes another pass," whispered Harry. "I'm coming through hard, Bucky."

Bucky patted his left buttock. The ball was snapped and Harry crashed through the line. He grabbed the quarterback's jersey and whirled him around, flinging him down into the mud at the Churchland thirty yard line.

"Headhunter! Headhunter!"

The tension in the air was unbearable as the Colonials lined up for a long field goal try in the rain. Coach Braun paced the sidelines.

"You get that kicker, Headhunter!" shouted Braun loudly. "You put his face in the mud and stomp him!"

The Colonials came to the line. Harry moved to position near left tackle. He watched as a big Colonial back shifted with him. At the last minute, Harry moved into the line near the center. Bucky looked at him, a question in his eyes.

"Change it up Bucky," whispered Harry. "I got the center… you get the kicker."

Bucky nodded. The ball was snapped, wobbling back to the holder. Harry rushed the center with uncontrolled fury, knocking him flat on his back, opening the way for Bucky. The Colonial holder fumbled with the wobbly pass from center. Bucky crashed over the fallen center, rushed hard and jumped into the air, his arms raised high. At the same time, Bubba slanted in from tackle. The kicker found the ball with his foot… it bounced off of Bucky's helmet and spun crazily into the air. Tony caught it, bobbled it, caught it again and began to run. Bubba got in front of him, and together they ran the length of the field. Tony was untouched for the final Trucker touchdown. Harry ran easily for the extra point. Churchland forty-nine, Matthew Whaley zero! The stadium erupted in cheers. The stadium lights flashed out… and then on again! And then off and on again! They kept flashing.

Harry ran with Allman and Bubba to where Coach Braun stood. They were joined by Karl and Big Jim. Together they lifted the Coach above their heads and sat him on Big Jim's shoulders. The Truckers gathered around him, shouting.

"Shotgun! Shotgun!"

The fans flooded onto the field shouting and cheering. Black and orange pennants waved wildly. The fight song echoed around the stadium.

"Truckers! Truckers!"

****

On a drizzly Sunday afternoon, Coaches Braun and Fearless sat in their office at Churchland High School. Outside, the rain continued to fall and the wind whistled around the gymnasium.

"Well, you did it, Shotgun," said Eddie Fearless holding up the sports page. "The perfect season!"

"Yeah," growled Coach Braun. "But I almost had me a heart attack on that field goal try."

Heck," drawled Eddie, "I knew they wouldn't make it!" He patted the sports page on the table.

CHURCHLAND COMPLETES THE PERFECT SEASON
UNDEFEATED, UNTIED AND UNSCORED UPON
By
Al Gollen

Matthew Whaley came to Churchland expecting to lose. And they did. Churchland forty-nine, Matthew Whaley zero. The Truckers bulldozed the Colonials in the first half with scores from Harry Quester, Karl Darby, Terry Moddy and Johnny Current. Twenty eight to nothing was the score at the half. In the second half it was more of the same until the football decided to have its own way. Late in the fourth quarter, the Colonials punted in the rain. The ball came down to Karl Darby at his own thirty yard line. A freak gust of wind caught the ball as it descended. The ball *came down short and bounced off of Darby's foot. It rolled crazily toward the Churchland goal as the crowd held its breath! A Colonial chased it and fell on the ball at the Churchland twenty-four yard line. It was the first time Matthew Whaley had the ball in Churchland territory. Matthew Whaley lost yardage back to the Churchland thirty. The Colonials lined up for a long field goal try in the rain. Would the Truckers be scored on? The ball was snapped. Bucky Allison crashed over center. Bubba Hawkins slanted in from tackle. The ball bounced off of Allison's helmet and went into the air. Tony Zee caught it and ran untouched for the final Trucker score, escorted by Bad Bubba. Churchland forty-nine, Matthew Whaley zero! Shotgun was carried off the field on the shoulders of his team and mobbed by fans coming out of the stands. Give the man his due. He has proven he's a great coach!*

A.P. Johns, the unofficial "Mayor" of Churchland Village says that he has asked Superintendent Hobbs to allow the President's-Truckers game to be played in Wilson's downtown Frank D. Lawrence stadium with the profits to benefit charity. Hobbs has had nothing to say. A.P., one of the feistiest of Churchland's great fans says that, one way or the other, the game will take place. We shall see!

"I'm glad they didn't make it," said Shotgun emotionally. "I could never say it, but not being scored on… well, it means this team is… really somethin' special! Somethin' that don't happen very often!"

Slate Phelps came into the office with A.P. Johns.

"A.P. says that the Superintendent turned down any post season games and has forbidden the teams to play in Portsmouth," said Slate.

"Well, that's a heck of a note!" exclaimed Eddie.

"I've talked to Pete Sacker," said A.P. "He says he'll scrimmage Churchland… on your practice field."

"A scrimmage?" asked Eddie in disbelief.

"And your practice field is in Norfolk County," grinned A.P., "not in Portsmouth!"

"How can we control a scrimmage?" asked Shotgun.

"Funny," said A.P., "that's the first thing Pete asked."

"Well, how do ya?" drawled Eddie.

"I've volunteered to set it all up and referee," grinned A.P. "And Pete will get Wimpy Sawyer to referee with me… in an unofficial capacity of course… and Grady Spearman will be there!"

"Beckler will never let it happen," said Shotgun with disgust.

"Why tell him about it?" asked Slate. "We won't be in the stadium… and after all, it's just a post season scrimmage."

"I don't even know if I'll be around next year!" said Cliff despondently.

****

Chapter Eighteen
The Scrimmage

It was a bright, sunny Saturday in late November. Birds chirped in the trees of the forest around the practice field next to Churchland High School. The bus from Wilson High School was parked at the curb sporting blue and orange streamers. It was one thirty in the afternoon and already, there were at least five hundred fans standing around the practice field. Some brought folding chairs. Some sat on the ground. Others milled about as students circulated selling drinks and chips. More cars arrived in the nearby parking lot and more people trekked toward the practice field carrying blankets and folding chairs. Lieutenant Eddie Spearman and his men were busy directing traffic and keeping people off the area selected as the playing field. The playing field was unmarked, except for stakes on the sides that marked off a hundred yards and the two goal lines.

Churchland Cheerleaders in their white skirts and jerseys with the big orange "C" were joined by Wilson Cheerleaders wearing blue outfits with a big orange "W". They circulated among the crowd accepting gifts for charity. Rocky Rawls and his band set up on the sideline and tuned up. Suddenly, the whole area was alive with *Rock Around the Clock*.

Put your glad rags on, join me, Hon,
We'll have some fun when the clock strikes one,
We're gonna rock around the clock tonight,
We're gonna rock, rock, rock, 'til broad daylight,
Gonna rock, gonna rock around the clock tonight!

At one forty-five, the State Champion Wilson Presidents ran onto the field wearing white trousers with an orange stripe framed in blue down each leg. Their jerseys were white with orange numbers shaded in blue. The fans from downtown clapped and cheered.

At one fifty, the State Champion Churchland Truckers ran on to the field in their menacing all black uniforms. The Churchland fans went wild. The trousers were midnight black with an orange stripe. The jerseys were black with orange numbers. Shotgun led the pack followed by Allman and Karl. They ran to their designated side of the practice field.

"Where's the field?" asked Tony.

"There ain't no field," answered Bubba. "Just a lotta grass and dirt… and them stakes over there."

A.P. Johns and Wimpy Sawyer took the field waving their hands, signaling quiet. Wimpy blew his whistle and A.P. lifted a Churchland cheerleader's megaphone. The crowd quieted.

"This is not an official game," shouted A.P. into the microphone. "Everybody here is here 'cause they want to be. Any contributions will go to the children's fund at Portsmouth General and Maryview Hospitals. So will all profits from drinks and chips. This is a friendly cross town scrimmage between two great championship teams. We'll play two twelve minute quarters. Teams will kick off at the beginning of each quarter. Wimpy and I will keep time on the field. There'll be touchdowns but no extra points... 'cause there aren't any goal posts! All the normal rules of football as played by these teams apply."

Wimpy came over to A.P. and poked him in the ribs. He and A.P. talked for a few seconds. A.P. raised the megaphone again.

"I want to emphasize that this is a friendly scrimmage," shouted A.P. "Anyone fighting will be asked to leave the game. Anyone fighting on the sidelines will be asked to leave the vicinity... immediately!"

There was a roar and laughter from the crowd. A.P. made dampening motions with his hands. "Please keep the noise to a reasonable level," he shouted, "and keep at least ten yards back from the stakes... and don't go into the forest over there! No drinking beer, wine, whiskey or moonshine... and keep the cigarette butts off the practice field! Use the trash cans over there. Officer Spearman and his men will assist us in enforcing these rules!" A.P. paused and grinned. "And if anyone thinks up a way to make trouble, I'll think up another rule!"

There was more laughter from the crowd. Wimpy blew his whistle. "Play ball!" he shouted.

Allman, Karl, Linwood and Dennis ran onto the field for the coin toss. Coaches Shotgun Braun and Pistol Pete Sacker followed them and met at midfield.

"This time, I'm not blocking with you, Shotgun," said Pete with a grin.

"Aw... ya never could block 'less I was helping ya, Pete!" said Shotgun with a forced grin on his bulldog face.

"Whatever you say, Shotgun," smiled Pete.

They shook hands warmly.

"Good luck, Shotgun," said Pete, breaking away.

"Don't need no luck, Pete," said Shotgun, crushing the porkpie hat onto his head. "You keep it... 'cause you're gonna need it!"

Pete grinned good naturedly and ran back to his sideline on the side away from the forest. Shotgun ran back toward the forest. In the midfield huddle, A.P. addressed the team Captains.

"I expect you guys to help us out here," said A.P. "I don't want any disputed calls, even if we screw it up. I don't want anything but friendly sportsmanship. I don't want Shotgun and Pistol Pete yelling at each other… at least not too much!"

"I'll throw anyone out of the game immediately if anything starts to look ugly!" exclaimed Wimpy.

"Hey!" exclaimed Allman with a smile. "We love each other… don't we Linwood?"

Linwood grunted. "We'll obey the rules," he said stiffly. "You guys do the same!"

"Okay, said A.P. "You're the visitor, Linwood… call the toss."

"Heads," said Linwood,

The coin sailed into the air, fell and rolled briefly in the grass before it settled on a side.

"Heads it is," said A.P.

"We'll receive," said Linwood.

"We'll take the goal away from the school," said Karl.

"Hold on to your jock Linwood!" said Allman, pointing to Linwood with a cocked pistol finger and winking his eye.

Dennis grinned in his usual friendly way. "We're gonna fix this scoring thing, Allman… right away!"

The three boys turned and ran back to their sides.

"Gather 'roun the Coach," shouted Eddie Fearless.

The Truckers gathered around Coach Braun as Rocky Rawls and his band hammered out *Shake, Rattle and Roll*.

I said Shake rattle and roll,
I said Shake rattle and roll,
You never do nothin',
To save your doggone soul.

Jack Sanders, Bart Whitely and Arnie Eberly were all on the sidelines with the Truckers in street clothes. Jack and Bart still wore slings. Arnie stood stiffly at a distance from the others.

"You guys have all the skills to beat this team," said Shotgun with intensity. "I don't care if they're Group One champions or Group Zero champions… ya can beat 'em if you play smart, play mean and hit 'em hard! They'll be the best team you play this year… but nothing more than that! Coach Phelps and I both played for Wilson… ya all know that. We were just kids like they have over there now! You guys are kids… but this season ya grown up to be men! Men! And I mean that! There's not a player over there that you guys can't beat up and take down… but you're gonna have to be extra mean and take a few licks!"

"We're tougher!" observed Big Jim.

"Right you are! Now watch out for Aimsley," continued the Coach. "He can run… and ya gotta get him before he gets loose. Scooter likes to throw the ball to Honor… so I want you, Karl, to stay with him wherever he goes. Harry, we're gonna start with Headhunter Free… I want you to knock Scooter down before he does anything if ya can… and stay with Aimsley. On offense, we're gonna start running 'til we see what they have… but we'll do it with the pulling plays. Any questions?"

"No questions, Coach," said Allman.

"Then get mean…real mean… and get out there! Get out there!" shouted Shotgun leaping to his feet and waving his dilapidated hat over his head in tight circles.

The Truckers broke from their huddle and charged out onto the field. Harry caught a glimpse of Paige standing with his Mother and Father. He put tender thoughts aside and looked up at the sun. It shone brightly on them. He reached down to find his game face. It was there, waiting for him. Today, he didn't need the lights. He pulled the game face on and breathed deeply. He felt a surge of energy as adrenalin pumped into him.

Bud Darby kicked the ball high. It fluttered down into the waiting arms of Dennis Aimsley. Dennis took it, faked right and ran left. Harry saw Linwood coming at him at full speed. He tried to fake him off, but Linwood didn't bite and hit him hard. Harry staggered back, regained his balance and fought Linwood off. Dennis followed Linwood and tried to run away from Linwood's block of Harry. Harry slid off Linwood's block and made a diving tackle, pulling Dennis' legs out from under him. They crashed to the ground at the Wilson thirty-five yard line.

Harry rolled over to find Linwood staring down at him. "Just like old times, Linwood!" said Harry.

Linwood offered him a hand. Harry took it. Linwood pulled him up. "Yeah," said Linwood with a condescending wink of his eye. "Just like old times when I shoved ya all around the field!"

Harry gave Linwood a tight smile and ran back to take up his Headhunter defensive position. The Presidents huddled briefly and ran confidently to the line. Harry watched them closely. Aimsley looked at Harry and winked. Yeah… it made sense. Give it to Aimsley and watch him run through the poor Group II country cousins. Harry winked back. He patted Bucky on the right hip. Bucky patted his left hip. The ball was snapped. Willy Scooter took the ball straight back and handed off to Dennis. Dennis slanted to his left toward Linwood's end. Bucky stood the center up straight and Harry charged through the line as Willy handed off to Dennis. Harry hit Dennis before he could build up steam and brought him down hard for a two yard loss.

The Churchland fans started the chant. "Headhunter! Headhunter!"

"Nice tackle, Harry," said Dennis politely, pulling himself to his feet.

"Maybe we underestimated you guys!"

"Thanks, Dennis," said Harry as he got up. "Maybe you did!!"

"That was a lucky one, Harry," said Linwood from behind him.

"That's the way it's gonna be, Linwood," said Harry

On the next play, Wilson faked to Dennis and handed off to Bobby Sheets, the other halfback. Harry bit on the fake and Bubba brought Bobby down after a three yard gain. Third and nine for the Presidents. Billy Scooter tried a pass to Linwood. Karl Darby knocked it down. The crowd went wild with cheers. The Presidents lined up to punt. The punt was low and went directly into the arms of Terry Moddy. He ran straight ahead at full speed and took the ball to the Churchland forty yard line before he was tackled.

In the huddle, Allman was excited. "They thought they could score on us right away," he said. "We showed 'em… and now we gotta score on them… right away. Thirty five pull on two. That's Harry through Bubba's hole with Bucky pulling and leading. Open it up, guys!"

Porter left the huddle.

"Thirty five pull on two," said Allman. "Break!"

The Truckers ran to the line of scrimmage and confronted a line bigger than they had ever encountered. Wilson played a five man front with three linebackers, two halfbacks and a safety.

"Get down!… Get ready!… Hut one!… Hut Two!"

The ball popped into Allman's hands. He dropped back as Bucky pulled from left guard and ran behind center to the right tackle hole. Allman pushed the ball into Harry's belly and he clasped it with both hands. He followed Bucky into the hole between right tackle and right end, directly toward Linwood Honor. He saw Linwood dodge inside Bubba's block and step into the hole. Bucky crashed into Linwood and Harry cut to the outside. Linwood slid off Bucky's block and tried to regain the outside position. Harry ran past him and into a tackle by Dennis. He was disgusted with himself as he fell to the turf.

"Good run, Harry," said Dennis, slapping Harry on the rump as he got up. "How's the grass taste?"

"Only five yards, Dennis," said Harry, wiping grass and turf from the side of his helmet. "Not good enough."

Karl and Terry both ran and were stopped short of a first down. Bud punted to Dennis, and the fast Wilson halfback returned the ball to the Wilson forty-five. Harry watched as the Presidents came to the line of scrimmage. He was surprised to see another face at Linwood's left end position. Linwood lined up as a blocking back just behind the line of scrimmage in front of Harry. Only Dennis and the fullback were in the backfield.

Willy Scooter started to bark signals. Harry watched Willy's eyes and shifted his linebacker position to the right. Linwood went in motion and followed Harry along the line as he sought a weakness. The ball was snapped. Willy handed off to Dennis. Dennis ran to the side of the line where Harry wasn't. Linwood came crashing through the line and caught Harry off balance as he tried to shift to the left. The blow Linwood delivered hurt and Harry crashed to the ground. Dennis rounded Tony's end and was brought down by Allman who rushed up from his safety position. It was a ten yard gain for the Presidents. First down at the Churchland forty-five yard line.

"Time out!" shouted Coach Fearless from the sidelines.

A.P. blew the whistle and signaled time out.

Coach Braun ran onto the field and into the Trucker huddle.

"They're blocking me, Coach," panted Harry.

"I saw it," said Braun, rubbing his nose thoughtfully. "They've got Honor being the Headhunter Hunter."

"How do we counter that, Coach?" asked Allman.

"You guys on the line," said Braun. "When you see Honor in front of you, drop your man and take him down! Harry is our best tackler… I want him as unblocked as possible!"

"Take Honor down!" muttered Big Jim.

"Harry, you stay in front of where ya think Aimsley is gonna run," said the Coach.

"Yes sir, Coach," said Harry, nodding. "I will… but I think they told him to run where I'm not!"

"You'll have to adjust, Quester! Now these guys are hitting hard," said the Coach. "I know you can hit harder! Do it! And watch the pass to Honor in the flats. They'll go to it if you stuff the run!"

"We got it, Coach," said Allman confidently. "Let's stuff 'em!"

Coach Braun ran off the field. The team took up defensive positions. Harry took a linebacker position directly behind Tony on the left end. The Presidents ran up to the line of scrimmage. Linwood grinned at Harry and took up a blocking back position directly in front of him. Harry shifted toward center. Linwood went in motion. Harry stopped and shifted back to the left. Linwood shifted left, but the ball was snapped before Linwood could fully adjust. Harry knew exactly where Dennis was going to run… to the right, away from Harry. Linwood came crashing through the line only to meet Big Jim who took him down like a tree struck by lightning. Harry shifted quickly to the right and ran down the line with Dennis. Bud tried to turn the Wilson halfback in, but Dennis was just hitting full stride. Harry called on his top speed and tackled Dennis before he could turn up field and light his rockets. He got the halfback by the waist and drove him hard out of bounds near the edge of the forest.

"Out of bounds!" shouted Wimpy blowing the whistle.

Dennis got up holding his arm. "Where's out of bounds?" he asked painfully.

"Somewhere along here," said Harry, "where the grass stops, I guess… you okay?"

"I'm okay, Harry," said Dennis with a grimace. "Give me all ya got!"

The two teams traded the ball for the remaining time in the first quarter with neither side gaining the advantage. The first quarter ended in a zero to zero tie. A.P. blew his whistle. "End of the first quarter!" he shouted. "Ten minute time out for both sides!"

The crowd roared its approval as both teams ran to their sidelines.

****

Slate stood on the sideline with Coach Braun as the Truckers ran off the field for the time out. They watched a long black Packard sedan with the Superintendent and Fred Beckler inside pull in to the parking lot next to the practice field.

"Uh oh… here it comes," said Coach Braun worriedly.

"They won't be able to stop it," said Slate. "The fans would chase 'em off the field… and they know it!"

"Okay, guys," shouted Eddie Fearless, "huddle up here!"

The Truckers took a knee around Coach Braun, who squatted in the dirt.

"Whatta ya think, Coach Fearless?" asked Coach Braun.

Eddie looked at Shotgun in surprise. "We can hold these guys," drawled Eddie. "We gotta figure out a way to score… and I think we're gonna have to pass. What was that pass that worked in the Suffolk game, Buddinger?"

"One thirty pass right twenty," responded Allman immediately. "I pass to a spot on the sidelines twenty yards away… Harry runs a post pattern and then somehow ends up under the ball."

Coach Braun lifted an eyebrow. "I think Pete is waiting for us to try that," he said. "And they've got much better halfbacks than Suffolk."

"Well… let Harry throw it… and I'll catch it!" said Allman, his face lighting up.

"Come on, Allman," said Braun. "We want to score… but we're not that desperate."

"I think it'll work," said Allman. "We never done it before… so they won't expect it."

"Can you throw the ball, Quester?" asked Coach Braun.

"Yes Sir," said Harry. "I can throw it twenty yards… not much more with any accuracy."

"He can throw it, Coach," said Eddie Fearless. "I seen him throw it!"

"That's a thirty-one pass right… or left, twenty," said the Coach.

"Right is better," said Harry.

"Alright… alright… thirty one pass right twenty," said the Coach. "Buddinger, I want ya to fake it to Darby into the line, handoff to Quester and sneak out to the flat. Moddy, you come over and get in front of Quester like you're blocking for the run. Dickson, Hawkins, Bud… you guys will have to make it look like a run and block like… heck."

Harry looked at Coach Braun with new respect. The Coach could see the whole field even better than Harry could. And he was willing to take a risk when he had to.

"We can do it, Coach," said Bubba eagerly.

"We'll start off the next quarter running like we did. When I think we're ready, Buddinger, I'll give ya the nod and ya can try it."

"I'll be watching, Coach," said Allman. "I think I can hit Tony or Bud long, too. I've been practicing with them… and throwing long."

"We'll see," said the Coach. "I would really like to run over these guys. If ya been mean enough, they should be slowing down some this next quarter. I want you guys to go back in there mad as hell, knowing that they're slower than they were at first. You guys are in better shape… ya gotta exploit that by knocking 'em down every play… every play! I wanna see some gritty football out there… real gritty!"

"What about the defense, Coach," asked Harry.

"The Headhunter Free is working," said the Coach, "but if I know Pete Sacker, he's gonna come up with something."

"They got Honor shadowing me while I'm shadowing Aimsley," said Harry.

"I've been thinking about trying Headhunter Center," mused Coach Braun.

"You mean that four man line thing we ran a few times at practice?" asked Coach Fearless.

"Yeah," said Braun. Four men on the line… two guards and two tackles, with Quester as a nose guard… except he can either rush or fall back into Linebacker. That leaves us three guys playing deep linebacker, two halfbacks and a safety. The key to it is the decision by the deep linebackers to stay put or rush the line… if it's a run."

"We can mix it up a little," said Bob Porter. "The outside guys can stay put until we see what's happening and I can rush."

"That'll work," said Harry. "And Bob and I can agree which side to take so we got a linebacker crashing on each side."

"Alright," said Coach Braun, drawing exes and ohs in the dirt with his finger, "we'll try Headhunter Center. We'll start off with a standard six-two-two-one. Then we'll shift to Headhunter Free. When the time is right, I'll call in Headhunter Center. Any questions?"

"We're ready, Coach," said Allman. "and they kick to us this time!"

"Then get out there… and get real mean! Get out there!" shouted Coach Braun hoarsely.

The Truckers ran out onto the field and began hopping up and down in place as Rocky Rawls' band hit it with *Shboom*.

Now every time I look at you,
Something is on my mind, dat-dat-dat-dat-dat-duh,
If you do what I want you to,
Baby, we'd be so fine.

"I hope they do what I want 'em to," muttered Coach Braun twisting his hat in his hands.

Slate watched as Superintendent Hudson Hobbs and Principal Frank Beckler, both dressed in coat and tie, walked to the sidelines. Georgia immediately ran up to them with a giggle and a wiggle and sold them an RC Cola and a bag of chips. They stood together munching the chips and watching the Presidents run on to the field. A.P. blew his whistle loudly and the fans cheered wildly. Wilson lined up to kick off.

****

Churchland defended the goal near the school. Linwood pointed down the field toward Harry, saying silently "I'm coming to get you!"

Harry nodded and pointed at Linwood, making "come on" motions with his hands. The ball was kicked and it sailed back to Terry Moddy, who caught it and began running hard up the middle. Harry ran full speed toward Linwood, his face set in a Headhunter scowl. Linwood charged along as fast as he could run, his arms pumping furiously. Neither player made any attempt to avoid the other. The two collided at the Churchland forty yard line with a crash that drew a moan from the crowd. Both players fell to the grass as Terry was tackled at the Churchland forty-two.

"Helluva hit, Linwood," groaned Harry as he crawled to his feet, his body aching from the impact, his head ringing with multiple bells.

Linwood lay on the ground and didn't move.

"Linwood?" asked Harry bending over him. "Linwood… you okay?"

"Time out!" shouted Wimpy, blowing his whistle.

Harry knelt beside Linwood, his face a mask of concern. Wilson's trainers ran up to where he knelt.

"I think he's out," said Harry.

"We got it," said Coach Sacker, waving Harry away.

Harry got up and backed away. The crowd was hushed. Harry watched as the trainer waved smelling salts under Linwood's nose. Then Coach Sacker held up three fingers in front of his face. Linwood sat up and a sigh of relief came from the crowd. The trainers pulled Linwood to his feet and helped him off the field. Harry ran back to the huddle.

"Super hit, Harry!" exclaimed Bucky slapping Harry on the rump.

"Yeah… yeah," mumbled Harry. "I'm just glad he's okay!"

"Okay, said Allman, "here we go. It'll be a forty three pull on two."

Porter left and ran to the line of scrimmage.

"Forty-three pull on two… break!"

The Truckers broke out of the huddle and ran eagerly to take their positions.

"Get down!... Get set!... Hut one!... Hut two!"

The ball was snapped and quickly handed to Karl Darby. Bucky pulled behind center and ran to the three hole. Bubba and Bud opened the hole and Bucky met the linebacker head on and struggled to push him back. Harry followed Karl, swinging to the outside. Karl hit the hole, his legs churning. The hole was blocked by the struggle between Bucky and the Wilson linebacker. Karl turned his back to Bucky and shoved with his legs trying to force as much as he could.

"Harry!" shouted Karl.

Harry looked up and Karl lateraled the ball back to him. The ball bounced off his hands. He bobbled it for a moment and then gained control. He put his head down and charged at the Wilson end who had come in to replace Linwood. He lowered his shoulder and butted the player, knocking him down. He stumbled forward, regained his balance and started to run. He ran as hard as he could and saw Dennis closing on him. Dennis hit him at the Wilson forty yard line. Harry staggered forward with Dennis hanging on to one leg. He came down at the Wilson thirty five.

"Nice tackle, Dennis," muttered Harry as he jumped up.

Dennis looked at Harry with narrowed eyes and shook his head.

"Is Linwood okay!" asked Harry.

"He'll be back!" exclaimed Dennis and ran back to take his defensive position.

Harry ran toward the huddle. He saw Linwood standing on the sideline watching him. He gave Linwood a thumbs up and nodded. Linwood nodded back grimly. First down Churchland on the Wilson thirty-five! Harry ran back to the huddle.

"Okay guys… real quick… thirty one pass right twenty, on set," said Allman in an excited voice. "Warm up your arm, Harry!"

"It's warm!"

Bob Porter left the huddle.

"Thirty one pass right twenty, on set! Break!"

The huddle broke and the Truckers ran to the line. The Presidents were just getting back into position as Harry took his stance.

"Get down!… Get set!"

The ball smacked into Allman's hands. He whirled and faked a handoff to Karl who went crashing into the line. Harry paused a split second and took the hand off from Allman. He headed for the hole behind Karl as he watched Allman slip out to the right flat. Harry put on the brakes just before he got to the hole, dropped back a step and ran along the line to the right. He lobbed a pass downfield toward Allman. It wasn't a perfect spiral, but it would do. It seemed to be just beyond Allman's grasp. He tipped the ball into the air with the kind of athletic move only Allman could make and caught it on the run. He pranced down the sideline like a big elf in shoulder pads and ran unmolested past the stake that marked the goal. A.P. raised his arms signaling touchdown.

The Churchland fans went wild. Rocky struck up a rock n' roll version of the Churchland Fight Song.

Oh when those Churchland Truckers fall in line,
They're gonna win this game another time…

The Churchland Cheerleaders yelled and jumped, their skirts swirling about them. Churchland six, Wilson nothing!

"Oh Oh! Oh Oh!" shouted the crowd. "Ball Fox! Ball Fox!"

Harry ran to where Allman still pranced around holding the ball aloft. He smacked him on the butt. "Good catch Ol' Buddy," he said.

"Thanks, Ol' Buddy," said Allman with an excited, toothy grin.

"Let's don't rub it in, Ball Fox!" said Harry with a grin.

"Yeah… yeah, okay!" said Allman tucking the ball under his arm and running back to the Churchland bench.

"Way to go, Allman!" exclaimed Coach Fearless.

"Thanks, Coach!" said Allman wiping the sweat from his face. "Will ya save this ball for me?"

"Okay, Buddinger," said Fearless. "I will."

"Stop grandstanding, Buddinger," shouted Shotgun waving his pork pie hat at the quarterback. "Get your butt back on the field!"

"Okay, Coach," exclaimed Allman and ran back to line up for the kickoff.

Harry looked downfield and saw Linwood lining up to receive the ball. He pointed to Linwood and then himself and smacked his right fist into his left palm. Linwood replied with a forced grin and pointed his finger at Harry. Bud kicked the ball and it went to Bobby Sheets. Bobby ran down the center of the field and then changed direction to the sideline away from Harry. Harry adjusted and ran after him. Linwood closed in and gave Harry a hard bump that knocked him off balance. Big Jim made the tackle at the Wilson thirty-eight yard line.

"Welcome back, Linwood," said Harry.

"Thanks," muttered Linwood. "We're gonna get you now, Harry!"

Churchland lined up in a six-two-two-one defense, with Harry at right linebacker. Linwood lined up as a blocking back in front of Harry.

"Shift!" called Harry.

The Truckers shifted into the Headhunter Free defense. Harry ran back and forth along the line trying to confuse Linwood. For some reason, Linwood wasn't all that interested in keeping up with him. Harry turned his head back toward Karl.

"Karl! Linwood's going long, I think!" whispered Harry, pointing to Linwood and shielding the gesture with his body.

Karl gave him a thumbs up, turned and whispered something to Allman. The ball was snapped. Harry crashed through the line and chased Willy Scooter back and to his left. Scooter ran at full tilt to avoid Harry. Harry lunged at Willy, but the quarterback got the ball away. It was a long, floating pass toward the Churchland goal. Linwood was streaking down the sideline to get under it. Karl was beside him matching him pace for pace. Allman was between Linwood and the goal, back pedaling and watching both of them. Linwood jumped for the ball and had it in his hands. Allman timed it perfectly and arrived airborne just as Linwood was starting to haul in the pass. He swatted the ball and it flew out of Linwood's hands. They all came down in a tumble of bodies.

"Ya almost screwed us up, Linwood!" said Allman hauling Linwood up. "It looks like your bell ain't ringing no more."

"I'm okay, Buddinger," muttered Linwood in frustration. "And I'll be back!"

"Ya'll come on!" exclaimed Allman. "We's awaitin' for ya!"

They all ran back to take position. Wilson ran Dennis Aimsley twice and gained only six yards. The Presidents punted to the Truckers. Terry returned the punt to the Churchland thirty-two yard line.

"Okay, one sixty post, on three," said Allman. "That's you to the post, Tony. Are ya ready?"

"Sure Allman," said Tony. "I'll be there!"

"We oughta run it," said Bob. "Long passes are dangerous!"

"They're not expecting it!" said Allman.

Porter left the huddle.

"One sixty post, on three… break!"

Harry prepared himself to block for Allman on a long pass. The ball was snapped. Allman faded back and watched Tony running full speed toward the Wilson goal. He pumped his arm in Bud's direction. Harry blocked a guard that had broken through the line. Allman took his time, gripped the ball carefully and threw a long spiral toward the racing Tony Zee at the Wilson twenty yard line. Dennis Aimsley was a blur as he flew through the air and intercepted the ball. He hit the ground running and headed for the left sideline. Harry threw his legs into high gear and took off to intercept Dennis. Linwood threw a hard block at Harry that knocked him down. Dennis sprinted by Harry and was tackled by Allman at the Churchland thirty-five yard line.

"You got me that time, Linwood," said Harry, shaking his head.

Linwood got up smiling and offered Harry a hand. "It's time to get this thing on the right track, Harry, me boy!"

Harry took the hand and was pulled roughly to his feet. They both ran back to their positions. Harry looked to the sidelines and saw the Coach motioning at him. He held his head and then made centering motions with his hands. Harry nodded back.

"Okay, guys… Headhunter Center… line it up!"

Harry took his position as nose guard over the center. He turned and looked at Bob, then patted his butt. Bob nodded. Harry watched the big Wilson center come to the line of scrimmage. Harry had signaled Bob that he was going to rush the quarterback. Now he had to do it! He watched as Linwood came to the blocking back position on the left side and looked at Harry with a confused stare. The ball was snapped. Harry hit the center with a forearm shiver that staggered the big man backward. He charged around the center on the side where Linwood wasn't and grabbed at Willy Scooter's arm as he tried to hand off to Dennis. The ball fell to the ground and Willy fell on top of it.

"Where the hell did you come from, Harry?" grunted Willy as he got up clutching the ball.

"From a magic place, Willy," grinned Harry. "And I'll be here again!"

On the next play, Harry watched where Linwood lined up. He lined up to left of center this time. Harry patted his left leg indicating he was going to drop back and fade left.

"Got it!" said Bob in a low voice behind him.

Dennis took the ball and ran to his left. Bob faded right and plugged the hole where Dennis tried to run. Bubba made the tackle and drove Dennis backward. The next play sent the Wilson fullback up the middle.

Harry had dropped back, but quickly returned to plug the middle between Bucky and Renny. Wilson gained only three yards and had to punt. Karl Darby returned it to the fifty yard line.

"Okay, Harry," said Allman in the huddle. "These guys won't expect a fullback to go long. So I'm gonna fake a run to ya, Harry. After ya hit the line, run the post and I'm gonna heave it to ya! Bud, you and Tony go out and do sideline patterns at about twenty yards. Try to pull the halfbacks with ya. Karl, stay in to block. Terry... go short over the middle and try to pull in the safety. On Two. Any questions?"

"We'll try it," said Harry.

Porter left the huddle.

"Sandlot play on two... Break!"

Harry ran to his fullback position. The ball was snapped. Allman faked the ball to Harry. Harry hit the line at full speed, bounced off a tackle and ran into Linwood Honor.

"'Scuse me, Linwood," muttered Harry, freeing himself of Linwood and turning on the speed for a down field sprint.

Harry ran as fast as he could go to the ten yard line and looked back. The ball was in the air in a wobbly spiral headed for him. Out of the corner of his eye, he saw Dennis sprinting toward him. Except for Dennis, he was all alone. He watched the ball. It was going to be short. He tried to slow as the ball came down behind him. He twisted to grab at it. It hit him on the right shoulder pads just as Dennis smashed into him. Harry, Dennis and the ball all hit the ground.

"Damn, Harry," exclaimed Dennis as they lay on the ground together. "That almost worked! I'll have to keep a better eye on you!"

"I screwed that one up, dammit," muttered Harry as he got up.

The game see-sawed back and forth with neither team getting inside the other team's twenty yard line. Wilson had the ball on Churchland's forty yard line.

"Two minutes left, Coach," said Slate.

"The Headhunter Center is working," said Coach Braun. "Ol' Pete hasn't figured it out, yet!"

Wilson completed a short pass to Linwood in the center of the field that moved the ball to the Churchland thirty. The clock ticked down to ninety seconds. The crowd produced a constant crescendo of noise that made it hard to hear anything on the field. Dennis ran the ball straight ahead and gained four tough yards. The ball was on the Churchland twenty-six.

"Sixty seconds remaining!" shouted A.P.

Harry patted his butt. He had to get in there and disrupt the play. It was going to be an Aimsley run or a pass to Honor... he knew it! The ball was snapped and Harry crashed by the Wilson center, who by this time wanted little to do with the Headhunter. Harry hit Willy as he made a long lateral to Dennis. It was an end sweep! Harry bounced off of Willy and chased Dennis toward the end near the Churchland side. He had to catch him before Dennis turned up field and was able to summon his full speed. Harry felt his lungs burning and his muscles crying out for oxygen as he sprinted after Dennis. No matter… his lungs and muscles had learned in the summer what was expected of them and they responded. Harry saw Tony blocked by a Wilson player and Bob running to contain the sweep. Dennis kept on running and it looked like Bob was going to turn him in. Dennis faked Bob and turned to the outside, summoning his extra speed.

Dennis ran behind a tree on the sideline and Harry had to dodge the tree to keep up. The fleet halfback weaved in and out of the trees at the edge of the field as Churchland players tried to catch him. He ran past the stake that marked the Churchland goal line amid great cheers from the Wilson fans on the sideline. Wimpy Sawyer signaled touchdown and blew the end of game whistle. A.P. ran to Wimpy and started to argue.

Shotgun threw his dog-eared hat to the ground and stomped on it with fury. "That… that sonofa…gun! He ran through the woods! Outa bonds! Outa bounds!"

Coach Braun ran down the sidelines toward where Wimpy and A.P. were in a heated argument. Coach Fearless and Coach Phelps ran after him.

"What in the name a' hell kinda call was that, Wimpy?" shouted Shotgun, his face red, his pork pie hat jammed down over his jug ears, his face a mask of anger.

Pete Sacker ran to where the referees stood, followed closely by Fred Beckler and Superintendent Hobbs, running awkwardly in their suits and ties.

"Back it off, Shotgun!" shouted Wimpy. "Or I'll throw ya outa the game!"

"Ya can't see them damn trees, Wimpy?" shouted Shotgun.

Slate put his arms around Shotgun and pulled him back.

"The stakes line up on the other side of the trees, Shotgun," said Pistol Pete squatting, squinting and lining up the stakes.

"Awww… bullshit Pete!" shouted Shotgun waving his hands in frustration.

Superintendent Hobbs reached for the whistle around Wimpy Sawyer's neck. He put it in his mouth and gave it a long blast.

"Time out!" shouted the Superintendent above the noise of the crowd. "Time out!"

The crowd quieted. The Coaches turned and stared at the Superintendent, surprised by a side of the man they had never seen.

"I officially declare this... this unofficial contest a tie... a tie between two great Portsmouth teams!"

"But..." began Shotgun.

"Quiet, Shotgun," said Slate forcefully. "Listen to the man!"

Shotgun mumbled and snorted, his face and ears still red.

"This has been an unsanctioned, friendly scrimmage," continued Hudson Hobbs. "I have enjoyed it. We have all enjoyed it. I want to thank Frank Beckler for hosting us and A.P. Johns for setting it all up, and all you great fans for coming out to honor our two champion teams!"

There was a cheer from the crowd and a drum roll from Rocky Rawls.

"I also want to thank our two great teams and their coaches for a wonderful season. Now let's finish off the drinks and chips and go home happy about it all!"

There was a loud, long cheer from the crowd. Pete Sacker held out his hand to Shotgun. Shotgun eyed the hand as though it had poison smeared on it, but took it anyway.

"Good game, Shotgun," said Pistol Pete. "You have a great team!"

"Thanks, Pete," said Slate. "Shotgun agrees. You have a great team too... right Shotgun?"

"Yeah... yeah," said Shotgun, his brow furrowed, his eyes intense.

Marion Franklin walked up beside them. "Come on, Shotgun," said Marion, grabbing him by the arm. "Let's hear it for Pete's great team!"

Shotgun paused and looked at Marion in a strange way. A look of revelation came over him. He turned and looked Pete in the eye.

"Pete," said Coach Braun, "ya really got a great team!"

"Thanks, Shotgun," said Pete, smiling. "The scrimmage will go in the books as a six-six tie!"

"Okay, Pete," said Shotgun," but we'll always know about them damn trees!"

****

Harry walked toward the Wilson bench while the crowd milled around on the field. He saw Linwood and Dennis together and walked toward them, his helmet in his hand. He held out his hand to Linwood.

"Great game, Linwood," said Harry happily. "Just like old times in Park View... but better!"

Linwood shook the hand. "You played a great game, Harry," said

Linwood with a nod. "You've gotten a little tougher since Park View!"

"Well, maybe," said Harry. He held out his hand to Dennis. "Nice run, Dennis… those trees threw some good blocks on me!"

Dennis laughed good naturedly and shook Harry' hand. "All I could see was that goal line stake," he said. "And I just kept running!"

Paige, Cathy and Barbara ran to where the boys stood. They threw their arms around them and hugged them, sweat, dirt and all.

"What a game!" exclaimed Barbara.

"I was really mad at you, Harry," said Cathy. "You knocked out my man!"

"No he didn't," said Linwood defensively, "he just rung my bell a little."

"He got even and rung my bell more than a few times," said Harry, putting his arm around Paige.

"I wasn't worried about Harry," said Paige looking up at him with soft brown eyes. "Somehow, he always finds a way!"

The Superintendent blew Wimpy's whistle again. The crowd quieted and turned to hear him. He had Pete and Cliff beside him. "Now listen, folks," said the Superintendent in a loud voice. "I want to tell you that I'm looking forward to a fine football season next year… and I know you join me in welcoming Pistol Pete… and Shotgun… back to coach their teams!"

There was a moment of silence as the impact of the statement sunk into the crowd. Then there were wild cheers. Rocky Rawls' band burst into another chorus of *Rock Around the Clock*. Hudson Hobbs lifted Pete and Cliff's arms into the air triumphantly. Cliff looked embarrassed and broke the Superintendent's grip on his arm.

"Welcome back, Shotgun!" exclaimed Eddie Fearless above the noise, holding out his hand.

Shotgun looked confused, but he held out his hand and shook hands with Eddie, Slate and Marion.

"I'll be back next year," said Shotgun, his bulldog face breaking into a wide grin. "And I'm gonna have them damn trees cut down!"

****

Harry and Paige walked off the field together, and were joined by Allman and Georgia.

"Well, Harry Ol' Buddy," said Allman, grabbing Harry by the shoulder. "That was a helluva lotta fun… all of it!"

"Yeah, Allman it was," said Harry. They stopped and Harry gave Allman the Trucker salute with a thunderous blow to the chest. "Good luck at Carolina next year, Allman."

Allman returned the blow. "And the same to you next year as a Trucker... and at Navy... but you'd be better off down at Carolina with me."

Harry smiled. "Maybe, Allman," he said. "But wherever we go, we'll always be buddies!"

"You got that right, Ol' Buddy!" said Allman.

"You two are making me cry with all this buddy stuff," said Georgia wiping away an imaginary tear.

"Yeah?" asked Allman with an impish grin. "Wait'll ya see what I do to ya tonight!"

Georgia hit Allman on the chest, imitating the Trucker salute. "Ha!" she exclaimed. "You ain't got enough stuff to do me in!"

Allman laughed and Paige blushed.

"I wonder what the Superintendent found out," said Harry. "I mean, about the playbook and the documents... and all that!"

"I reckon we'll find out," said Allman.

****

Coaches Braun, Fearless and Phelps and Principal Fred Beckler sat in the Superintendent's office after the scrimmage. Grady Spearman came in and sat down with them.

"Now what we found out was that Fatso was behind all this stuff that's been going on," said the Superintendent. "He's been arrested and won't be back coaching next year."

Coach Braun muttered something under his breath that no one could understand.

"What was that Coach?" asked the Superintendent.

"Nothing, Sir," said Slate. "Nothing at all."

"Anyway, Lieutenant Spearman," said Doctor Hobbs, "please tell these folks what you discovered."

"Yes Sir," drawled Grady Spearman. "Bubba told me after the Princess Anne game what Horace Holly had told him... that Calcione had bullied Benny Norwood into stealing the playbook and giving it to him. Horace said he gave it to Duane Starr. That's when I started looking into things. So, when Mr. Beckler here turned the case over to the police after the Suffolk game, we knew Calcione was involved... and we knew that Norwood had taken the playbook. We knew that somehow Calcione had gotten enough money to buy a new Studebaker Commander... a car that costs over two thousand dollars... the kind money Calcione don't have."

Grady paused and looked around. He continued, "We interrogated Arnie Eberly... it don't seem that he was involved or knew about it... he might be involved, but there isn't any proof of it. We questioned Bart Whitely.... 'specially after Calcione cut him up. He wouldn't press charges on Calcione... but it don't seem that Bart was involved either, except to tip you guys off about Norwood and Calcione. Calcione bullied Norwood to take the playbook... didn't even pay him off. So, I'm not putting charges against Benny Norwood... unless you folks want to."

"No," said Fred, "not for now... but let's hear all of it."

"Calcione never admitted taking money from anyone... or having anything to do with the documents that came to the Superintendent."

"But he admitted stealing the playbook?" asked Cliff.

"Yep," said Grady. "We had him on that... what with young Horace Holly, Benny Norwood and all."

"He couldn't wiggle out of that!" said Slate with satisfaction.

"We figured the money that Benny got could have come from several places... from people that had that kind of money. There was Benny's father at the Pontiac Place... there was Duane Starr's rich ol' man at the Peanut Factory... there was Calcione's father who has made some money, though it's not clear how... taking book, maybe. He's been investigated several times... but nothing turns up. Calcione does live in a fancy house out there near the Norwoods... so he's getting' money from somewhere. We found out he knew Fatso when they both worked up in New York at the docks during the war. So, maybe there was a connection. Then, since they tried to pin it all on Harry Quester, we talked to Commander Quester. We talked to Mr. Stanley. We got subpoenas on all those bank records... but found nothing."

"What was it that proved that Fatso... Coach Hathaway did it?" asked Fred Beckler

"We talked to Slate some more and he remembered that Fatso's father still owns that grocery store over in Prentiss Park. I remembered that Ennis Hathaway Senior once took book and made some money from betting... and that we could never nail him with it. We subpoenaed Fatso's accounts and old Mr. Hathaway's accounts and found nothing. We were stymied. There just wasn't any record of big money being withdrawn or passed. Then Slate came up with this idea, and we got a warrant to search Ol' Mr. Hathaway's store. Maybe Fatso got some money in cash from his old man...cash we couldn't trace. Question was...did Big Ennis keep that much cash around... more than two thousand dollars! Slate said he's always kept a lotta money there in a room in the back of the store... didn't trust banks."

"What did ya find in Big Ennis' store?" asked Fred,

"We found a lotta cash in the back room in several cigar boxes locked in an old combination safe. Old Mr. Hathaway didn't wanna open that safe real bad… but we said he'd hafta go to jail if he didn't."

"How much was there?" asked Cliff.

"A little over five thousand dollars," said Grady. "But we also found a note that said 'loaned Ennis Jr. twenty five hundred dollars, to pay back later'… that was the clincher."

"You see," said Slate, "it was Fatso all along. He paid Calcione twenty five hundred dollars to have the playbook stolen… and blame it on Harry… and to get the documents and send them anonymously to the Principal, the Superintendent and the newspaper."

"Calcione went down to ECTC in Greenville and bribed a student who worked in the records section down there… for a hundred dollars… to make copies of Shotgun's records for him," said Grady. "Doctor Franklin suggested we go down there to see how the records were obtained… and we did. And he helped us."

"So, Fatso went to jail yesterday," said the Superintendent, "but his father bailed him out."

"He'll go to trial next month on charges of conspiracy to defraud, among other things," said Grady.

"Does he admit it all?" asked Slate.

Grady grinned. "No Sir, Slate," he said. "He don't admit nothing!"

"It's hard to imagine why a man would hate so much," said Eddie Fearless, "that he'd do all those things… just to get revenge on Coach Braun."

"It ain't hard to imagine," said Shotgun.

****

Slate, Eddie and Shotgun walked together to the football stadium. The sun still shown brightly. The air was brisk and smoke from burning leaves in the nearby village filled a soft breeze with autumn fragrance. Shotgun took off his weathered hat and took a deep breath.

"Great football weather," said Eddie, sniffing the air.

"Yeah, Coach" said Shotgun emotionally. "I wish we had another game!"

"It was a great team," said Eddie. "Tough… and smart!"

They walked together onto the field and stopped at the twenty yard line. Slate looked up into the stands at the press box, at the lights standing as silent sentinels over the field. He looked at the benches paraded along the sidelines and heard the roar of the fans in his mind.

"You know, Shotgun, being called 'Coach' is a special thing," said

Slate emotionally.

"Yeah… I know it, Coach," said Shotgun twisting his treasured hat in his big hands.

"It means a lot to be Coach!" drawled Eddie. "It means a lot to call a man 'Coach'… 'cause ya know what it means!"

"Yeah," said Shotgun staring out at the football field in a trance. "I kinda like it!"

"You put extra meaning into the word 'Coach', Shotgun," said Slate admiringly, "and you do it in spite of yourself!"

"With your help, Slate… and yours, Eddie," said Shotgun in a hoarse and emotional voice. "I learned a lot this year… a lot!"

"We all did," said Eddie.

"But… we got next season to get ready for!" said Shotgun.

"We'll be ready, Coach" said Eddie confidently.

"Yeah, Coach… next season will come," said Slate, a far way look in his eyes, "but we'll always remember the Perfect Season!"

****
The End
****

Powerful Publisher LLC
Virginia Beach, Virginia

www.powerfulpublisher.com